THE
WIFE'S
DILEMMA

Part 2
of
The Windsor Street Family Saga

By

VL McBeath

The Wife's Dilemma
By VL McBeath

Copyright © 2021 by VL McBeath.
Published by Valyn Publishing.

For more about this author please visit
https://valmcbeath.com

For permission requests, write to the author at:
https://vlmcbeath.com/contact/

Editing services provided by Susan Cunningham at Perfect Prose Services
Cover design by Books Covered

ISBNs: 978-1-913838-16-4 (Ebook Edition)
978-1-913838-17-1 (Paperback)

Main category - FICTION / Historical
Other category - FICTION / Sagas

Legal Notices

This story was inspired by real-life events but as it took place over one hundred years ago, parts of the storyline and all characterisation are fictitious. Names have been changed and any resemblance to real persons, living or dead, is purely coincidental.

Explanatory Notes

Meal Times

In the United Kingdom, meal times are referred to by a variety of names. Based on traditional working-class practices in northern England in the nineteenth century, the following terms have been used:

Dinner: The meal eaten around midday. This may be a hot or cold meal depending on the day of the week and a person's occupation.

Tea: Not to be confused with the high tea of the aristocracy or the beverage of the same name, tea was the meal eaten at the end of the working day, typically around five or six o'clock. This could either be a hot or cold meal.

Money

In the nineteenth century, the currency in the United Kingdom was Pounds, Shillings and Pence.

- There were twenty shillings to each pound and twelve pence to a shilling.
- A crown and half crown were five shillings and two shillings and sixpence, respectively.

For further information on Victorian-era England visit:
https://vlmcbeath.com/victorian-era

Previously in
The Windsor Street Family Saga

The Sailor's Promise
An introductory novella to the series

Set in Liverpool (UK), *The Sailor's Promise* begins in 1871, nine years before the events of *The Wife's Dilemma*.

This is a serialised saga, inspired by a true story and it is **recommended that the books are read in order.**

For further information and to get your copy of *The Sailor's Promise*, visit my website at:

https://valmcbeath.com/windsor-street/

Please note: This series is written in UK English

CHAPTER ONE

Liverpool, February 1881

An icy blast swept through the bedroom before the front door slammed shut. Nell jumped to her feet, pushing the letter she'd been reading into her apron pocket and yanking the drapes across the gap that had given her some daylight. She rubbed her hands over her face and gazed at the double bed to her right where her young daughter Elenor was taking her afternoon nap, her mousy hair fanning out on the pillow. She was going to miss her. And Leah. Her smile faded as she moved to the cot at the foot of the bed and ran a hand across the dark hair of her baby. At least she would be oblivious to her absence. *One day they'll understand.*

She crept from the room and pulled the door closed behind her.

"Are they asleep?" Her sister Maria glanced up the stairs as she hung her coat on a hook in the hall.

"They are."

Maria was stoking the fire in the living room when Nell joined her.

"Let me bring the water back to the boil and we can sit down. It won't take a minute." She picked up the battered copper kettle and stepped into the kitchen that was off the back corner of the room. "Do you want a scone?"

"I'll get it." Maria disappeared into the pantry, returning a moment later with a cake tin. "What have you got to look so pleased about?"

Nell busied herself with the teapot. "Is it obvious?"

Maria rolled her eyes. "I've not been gone more than half an hour and your face has gone from one of misery to having a grin from ear to ear."

Nell chuckled. "I've had some news, but promise you won't put a dampener on things."

"Why would I...?" A frown clouded Maria's face. "Is this anything to do with Jack?"

"It might be." Nell cut two home-made scones in half and carried them through to the living room. "He'll be home on Monday."

"How do you know that?" The lines in Maria's forehead creased. "And why would it make you so happy? It's hardly an unusual occurrence."

"A letter came while you were out." She disappeared back into the kitchen. "He posted it when he arrived in Boston and said the mail ship was leaving port three days before he sailed. That means I can expect him three days after it arrived, which is Monday."

"That still doesn't explain why you're so happy."

Nell's smile faltered and she took a deep breath. "He's going to captain his own ship for the next voyage."

"About time too." Maria's face was straight as she took a seat by the fire.

"Don't be like that. You know how hard he's worked these last nine years to pass his exams, but getting a master mariner certificate doesn't automatically mean he can take charge of a ship. Anyway, there's more to it than that..." Nell's heart raced as she took the seat opposite Maria, spread a thick layer of butter onto the scones and handed one to her sister. "He's taking me with him on his first voyage. To *America*. Can you believe it?"

Maria's mouth fell open. "You're going to sea?"

"Yes!" Nell clapped her hands under her chin. "Isn't it wonderful?"

"No, it's not. You can't go on a cargo ship full of men."

"It won't be a cargo ship. He wouldn't offer to take me unless it was a passenger ship."

"I wouldn't trust anything he promises. Read it to me where it says you're going on a passenger liner."

Nell stood up, tears in her eyes. "I knew you'd spoil it. For once in your life, why can't you be happy for me?"

"Because if I know Jack, this will all be a figment of his imagination, something to gloss over the fact that he should never have gone back to sea in the first place."

"That's unfair. We both made the decision for him to work towards being a master mariner so that I could travel with him. That was always the plan."

"But when you came up with such a hare-brained scheme, you didn't have two little ones to take care of." Maria pointed to the room directly above them. "You can't take them with you."

Nell wiped her eyes with the back of her hand. "That's

why I'm only going on the first voyage. To start with at least."

"And no doubt you'll expect me to look after them. Don't you think I'll have enough to do if I'm left here on my own?"

Nell stamped her foot. "You're not on your own, but if you'd rather not do it, Rebecca will have them."

At the mention of their younger sister's name, Maria put down her plate. "You've spoken to her about it?"

Nell's cheeks flushed. "Not since I got the letter, but she knows I always planned to go with him. It's not unusual for the wives of captains to accompany their husbands."

"Maybe not if they've stayed childless, but that young poppet upstairs hasn't had her first birthday yet; you can't consider leaving her."

Nell sighed. "I won't be away for long. Jack said he'll be captaining a transatlantic steamer and that we'll be back within the month. She's so young, I doubt she'll miss me."

"Don't you fool yourself, and what about Elenor? Have you told yourself she won't miss you either?"

Nell shuddered at the scowl on Maria's face. "Well, she won't. She doesn't miss Jack when he's on the short voyages, so why should she miss me?"

"Because you're her mam, and a pretty poor one at that if she doesn't notice you've gone. She wouldn't see Jack on a regular basis, even if he worked around here, but she expects you to be here. Your role in life is to look after those kiddies, not go swanning off around the world."

"I won't be swanning anywhere; I'm taking a trip I was promised nine years ago. It's not my fault it took Jack so long to be offered the captain's position."

"It was Jack's fault he went off on an eighteen-month trip after he'd promised to give up the sea. That held him back for years."

"He didn't do it straight away ... and anyway, it wasn't eighteen months. It was only sixteen."

Maria snorted. "Oh, I beg your pardon; I'm sure that made a difference."

Nell strutted back to the table. "Now look, this tea's stewed. I need to add more water to it." She disappeared into the kitchen, but Maria's voice followed her.

"How will you feel when he starts making these long voyages again? As a new captain, they won't keep giving him the trips to New York he's got used to."

Nell hesitated. "I'll have to go with him more often then."

"That's the most irresponsible thing I've heard."

Nell jumped as Maria peered through the kitchen door.

"You know how hard it is being a sailor's widow. They go off all around the world, leaving us for months on end without any thought to how we'll pay the bills or feed the children. You've had no money for the last week as it is. If you remember, Jack once promised he'd give up the sea; now might be the time to make good on that promise."

"If you don't like it so much, why don't you stop your George going away? He could easily get a carpenter's job around here."

"It's not that easy, as you well know." Maria's lips tightened. "He'd never earn the same money here as he does at sea."

Nell poured the boiling water into the teapot and pushed past Maria into the living room. "The money shouldn't matter so much now the boys are working. They were still at school when he first went away."

"We can't assume they'll live here forever…"

Nell held up a hand to quieten Maria as she walked to the bottom of the stairs. "That's Leah crying. I'd better go and bring her down before she wakes Elenor. You get that tea poured."

Nell reached for the letter as she climbed the stairs, but the sight of Leah pulling herself up on the side of her cot caused her to push it back into her pocket.

"There's a clever girl." She closed the door and picked up her youngest daughter. "Who's going to see Dada?"

"Dada?" Her elder daughter, Elenor, sat up and rubbed her eyes.

"He's coming home. Very soon." Nell perched on the edge of the bed, sitting Leah on her lap as Elenor pushed a stray piece of hair from her face.

"Dada's coming home?" Her pale blue eyes sparkled.

"Do you remember him?" Nell's heart fluttered as her daughter nodded. "He remembers you, too; you're his special girl. Now, let's get you dressed and we can go downstairs."

Elenor clapped her hands together. "Is Alice home?"

At mention of her niece's name, Nell stood up. "Why don't we go and see?"

Tea was almost ready when another blast of frozen air blew into the back room causing Elenor to leave her doll and hurry into the hall.

"I'll be glad to see the end of this weather; it's freezing

out there." A young man with a mop of ginger hair and bushy moustache rubbed his hands together as he walked to the fire. "Evening, Aunty Nell."

Nell looked up at her eldest nephew. "Evening, James. Are you on your own? Where are your brothers?"

"And Alice?" Elenor's bottom lip pouted.

James ran a hand over Elenor's head. "Alice will be here in a minute; she's popped to see Aunty Rebecca. I've no idea where Billy and Vernon are. Neither of them came into the alehouse."

"It's a shame Vernon can't find work closer to home." Nell pulled out a dining chair and placed it in front of the fire.

"He wants to work on the bigger ships and the docks aren't deep enough this far up the river." James blew out his cheeks. "Thank goodness I got out of doing that."

"It's not too late for you to go back." Maria's face didn't crack a smile.

"Oh, leave him alone." Nell tutted and turned back to James. "Are you all set for tomorrow?"

"I think so, but you'd better ask Mam. I know she's done the washing, but I'm not sure about the packing."

"Yes, it's all done."

"I wish you could stay for another couple of days. Uncle Jack's due back on Monday, and you'll never guess what." Nell bounced on the balls of her feet.

"You've got some good news judging by the look on your face. Has he been made captain of his own ship?"

"He has. Although your mam's not very pleased." Nell scowled as Maria stood up to go to the kitchen.

"Why?"

"Because he's taking me with him on his first voyage." Nell put a hand over her mouth to suppress her squeal. "Isn't that wonderful!"

"Oh, Aunty Nell, it is. After all these years."

"I know. I still can't believe it…" Nell's cheeks ached with smiling, but she stood with her back to Maria as she returned with a pan of scouse.

"Don't you go encouraging her. If it wasn't for you, she wouldn't have these fanciful ideas in the first place."

"She wanted to go to sea long before I went."

"She'd have forgotten about it by now if it hadn't been for you; now come and sit at the table. The others should be home soon."

James hadn't stood up when the front door opened again and Alice let herself in.

"Sorry I'm late. I bought some thread for Aunty Rebecca, so I popped in to deliver it."

"My missed you." Elenor wrapped her arms around Alice's skirt.

"And I've missed you too. Shall we sit down?"

Elenor scurried to her seat in the corner of the room as Maria began spooning out plates of the stew.

"I don't know where the other two have got to."

"Their tea will keep." Nell looked at James as they took their seats. "Is it another trip to New York tomorrow?"

"It is. I should be back by the end of the month."

"It all sounds so exciting." Nell sat back as Maria handed her a plate. "Will you be waiting on the first-class passengers again?"

"I imagine so. They try to have the same crew on each

voyage so we all know our places. It means they only have to hire a crew once a year."

Nell's brows drew together. "I don't think they do that on the cargo ships your Uncle Jack works on."

James laughed. "That's because half the crews refuse to go back once they've had a taste of the high seas in midwinter. It's brutal sailing around those southern oceans; only the real men can take it."

A flush of pride brought another smile to Nell's face. Jack was certainly a real man. How she missed him when he was away, even if it was only for a few weeks at a time.

"Hopefully his cargo days are over. I can't wait to see all those glamorous rooms and cabins on the ocean liners, not to mention America!" She grinned at Alice. "Uncle Jack's been made captain, and he's taking me with him on his next trip."

Alice whooped with delight.

"Will you stop it?" Maria took her seat at the table. "What's got into you all?"

"Aren't you even slightly curious?" James asked.

"No, I'm not. Now get your tea eaten."

Ignoring his mother, James turned back to Nell. "I hope they let me ashore this time. The Americans are so frightened of anyone from Europe arriving with cholera, they force all the steerage passengers into huge huts and leave them there for days."

"That doesn't sound much fun." Nell shuddered. "What happens to the first-class passengers?"

"Oh, they get the nod through. If you're rich enough to travel first class, you're not expected to have any infections.

Sadly, they treat most of the crew worse than the steerage. They only allowed the officers off the ship last time."

"That's a shame. It might be all right for me, though." Nell grinned. "If I'm the captain's wife, they'll have to let me in."

James grimaced. "Knowing you, they will. I'll have been working for years and never set foot on shore, and you'll turn up and they'll wave you through on your first visit."

"I hope she does. Why should men get preferential treatment?" Alice ran a hand down Elenor's back. "I'll take care of the girls for you while you're gone. I love looking after them and it'll be good practice for when I'm older."

"They'll love that." Nell watched as Alice gave Elenor a crust of bread. "James, would you mind if I walk to the docks with you in the morning to check Uncle Jack's ship is running to time? I don't know how I'm going to wait until Monday."

CHAPTER TWO

James closed the front door behind him and offered
Nell his arm as they set off down Merlin Street.

"Shall we go and find out where Uncle Jack's
up to?"

"Yes, please." A shiver ran down her spine. "I won't be
able to bear it if he's been delayed."

The wind had dropped since the previous day, but a
heavy frost had made the ground slippery and slowed their
progress.

"Roll on summer." James manoeuvred his sea bag over
his shoulder and pulled up the collar of his coat as they
reached Windsor Street.

"It'll be worse once you're at sea."

"Not for a steward." He winked at his aunt. "The
passengers won't go on deck in this weather and so we'll be
doing our bowing and scraping in comfort."

"Doesn't it make it difficult when the seas are rough?"

"Only the seasickness. Most of the passengers have
never been on a ship, and they're not used to it. It shouldn't

be too bad today, though. It should be calm enough, and while we sail between Ireland and the mainland, it gives everyone chance to get their sea legs. It's only once we reach the open ocean that things change."

Nell grimaced. "I hope I don't suffer when I finally go aboard. Is there any way to prepare for it?"

James laughed. "Short of crossing the Mersey to New Brighton and back non-stop for five days running, probably not. But don't worry. Uncle Jack will be there, and the ship's doctor will take care of you. He'll want to keep his boss happy by making sure you're comfortable."

"I can see it all now." Nell paused as they reached the end of Windsor Street and the river came into view as they rounded the corner. "I'm calling at your Uncle Tom's on the way home to borrow a travelling case." She thought of the small brown case her brother had kept in the outhouse since his one and only trip to sea. "I'm going to practise packing it this afternoon."

James laughed. "Patience, Aunty Nell. I'm sure Uncle Jack will have some shore leave first. You've plenty of time."

"Not too much, I hope."

Nell's nose was numb by the time they reached the dock road, and she glared up at the myriad of red-bricked warehouses that cast shadows over them as the weak winter sun failed to climb high enough in the sky. The only things to shimmer were the masts of the many sailing ships moored to the quayside on the opposite side of the road. She guided James towards them.

"Shall we cross over here? It may be warmer on the other side."

He shivered. "I doubt it, but we can try."

He led her across the road, dodging the horses as they headed straight at them. Once they reached the other footpath, they hurried towards the landing stage, arriving ten minutes early.

"I'll say goodbye then." James unhooked his arm from his aunt's. "Remember me to Uncle Jack and enjoy your trip. I imagine you'll be in America when I get back."

"Oh, I hope so. You have a safe trip and I'll see you when we're both home."

She watched as the slim figure of her nephew walked up the gangplank, and with a final wave, he disappeared into the bow of the ship. She sighed at the sight of steam bellowing from its funnel. *What a wonderful life.*

She made her way towards a smart red-brick building on the opposite side of the road. The Steamship Bohemian Company. The sign was discreet, but she'd been here often enough over the years, whenever she'd had word that Jack was on his way home. She hovered near the door, reading the timetables of ships that were expected over the next few days. Yes, there it was. The SS *Bohemian*. Jack had been right; it was due in on Monday. Only two days to wait.

Nell had a skip in her step as she walked home, but as she passed the customs house and took a shortcut back to Parliament Street, the ice on the footpath returned. Not for the first time, she was thankful she'd had her boots resoled. Maybe if Jack had had a good trip, he'd buy her some new ones before they left for America.

She struggled up the hill, her feet slipping as she walked, until she turned right into Windsor Street and headed towards her brother's house. As soon as she arrived, she rapped on the front door and let herself in.

"It's only me. May I come in?"

"Gracious, you're early." The buxom figure of her sister-in-law, Sarah, appeared in the hall.

"I'm sorry, I've been down to the landing stage with James and thought I'd call in on the way back to save me a trip later."

"You'd better come in then. You'll have to excuse the mess; I've not had chance to tidy up yet."

"I'm sorry to come so early." Nell tried not to stare at the mound of breakfast plates on the table as one of her young nieces sat on the floor by the fire. "I thought you'd have Ada doing that."

Sarah fluffed up the cushions on the armchairs. "There's laundry to do so she's out the back."

"Of course; I can't imagine what it must be like washing for ten."

Sarah grunted. "You should be glad Jack's away as often as he is. At least it will save you having so many children. Now, what can I do for you?"

"Oh, yes." Nell's cheeks flushed. "I was hoping to borrow a travelling case."

"What on earth do you want one of them for?"

Nell grinned. "Jack's coming home on Monday and he's been promoted to captain. He's taking me with him on his next voyage."

"No!" Sarah gasped. "I'll wager Maria's not best pleased."

Nell grimaced. "Is she ever? She'll get used to it."

"Are you sure?" Sarah's eyebrow lifted. "When did you tell her?"

"Yesterday afternoon. Why?"

Sarah laughed. "Because it means I need to get this place tidied up. She'll be around here as quick as you like after dinner today."

Nell had no doubt her sister-in-law was right. "I'd better leave you to it then. If I can take the case, I'll be off."

Elenor was at the dining table when Nell arrived home, fingers of bread spread thickly with butter on a plate in front of her. Alice had Leah perched on her knee, and her eyes widened as they settled on the travelling case.

"Where did you get that from?"

Nell had no time to reply before Maria wandered in from the kitchen. "You took your time... What on earth are you doing with that?"

Nell composed herself. "If I'm going away with Jack, I thought I'd practise packing my bag."

"You won't get much in there. One dress and it will be full."

Nell stared down at it. "It's not that small, but now Jack's a captain I imagine he'll buy a trunk for my dresses, so I can use this for smaller things. Anyway, I won't let you spoil this." Nell marched out into the hall. "I'm taking it upstairs."

Half an hour later, Nell placed her brush and comb set on the top of the clothes she'd squeezed into the case. That would do it, assuming Jack got her a trunk. She chuckled to herself. *Of course he will. As the captain's wife, I'll need to be well dressed. He'll probably buy me a selection of new clothes.*

"There's a cup of tea down here." Maria's voice drifted up the stairs. "Are you coming?"

"Yes, I won't be a minute." Nell lifted her blouses from the case and pushed it under the bed. *Not long now.* She was unable to keep the smile from her face as she headed back downstairs, but it slipped as she saw the glare on Maria's face.

"The house won't clean itself, you know. What have you been doing?"

"Nothing, just sorting a few things out."

"Well, get a move on. I want to call on Sarah this afternoon and I don't want to be late."

"All right, let me drink me tea, and I'll be right with you."

Nell stood in the window of the front room, watching Maria disappear down the road. She should be gone for a good couple of hours. She wandered back to the living room, where Alice was showing Elenor some stitching.

"Will you be all right looking after Elenor, or shall I take her with me?"

Alice glanced up from her work. "Where are you going?"

"Only over the road to Aunty Rebecca's. I'll take Leah with me if you like."

"Yes, please. Elenor's fine on her own, but I struggle with the two of them when I'm supposed to be working."

"I'm not surprised, but if Elenor gets too much, bring her over the road. I don't want to slow you down."

With Leah resting on her hip, Nell hurried across the road and let herself into her sister's house without bothering to knock.

"It's only me." She popped her head into the back room. "May I take Leah upstairs?"

"I'll come with you." Rebecca stood up. "I've already put Florrie down. I was beginning to think you weren't coming."

"I'm sorry, I thought Maria would never leave."

Rebecca led the way upstairs and held back the covers at the bottom end of her daughter's cot. "Didn't you tell her you were coming over?"

Nell laid Leah in the cot where her niece lay at the other end. "No, it would only have given her something else to moan about. I don't know what's got into her."

Nell waited for Leah to close her eyes and followed Rebecca back down the stairs.

"She doesn't want you going away, that's what it is."

"But why should she be so concerned? It won't be for long and hopefully it will get the idea of travelling out of my system." Nell accepted the cup Rebecca handed to her. "Would you go, if you were me?"

Rebecca sighed. "The way things are at the moment with Hugh, I'd come with you next week."

Nell grimaced. "Why? What's Mr Grayson done now?"

"Oh, nothing you've not already heard. The constant criticism, never giving me enough housekeeping, the complete disregard for the girls, the sulking. Honestly, I can't remember what I ever saw in him."

"I'm sorry."

"It's not your fault.

"Maybe not, but I shouldn't go on about Jack with you being so unhappy."

Rebecca rested her head against the back of the chair. "I don't blame you. I remember when Hugh and I were like that. The trouble is, he's got worse over the years. Enjoy being happy while it lasts."

"It has lasted. It was our ninth wedding anniversary last month. I hope he's remembered."

A wry smile crossed Rebecca's lips. "I've only been married for six months longer than you and things haven't been right for years. Probably since we all moved up here, now I think about it."

Nell cocked her head to one side. "Do you still think he wants to keep us away from you? I thought he'd got over that."

"Who knows? I'm just thankful I persuaded him to move here at the same time as you. I'd have been so miserable on my own in the old place."

"And I don't know what I'd do if you weren't over the road. It's all well and good having the neighbours, but I wouldn't tell them anything of importance. The whole neighbourhood would know about it within the hour." Nell grinned but Rebecca remained pensive.

"Perhaps you're still happy because Jack goes away every month. He's not around for long enough to annoy you."

"Maybe." Nell shrugged. "I can't deny it's easier now he does the transatlantic trips. That last long voyage he did, sixteen months, was too much."

"It may be for you; I'm not so sure about me. I keep reminding Hugh that George became a ship's carpenter because he could earn more money at sea than he ever could at home. Unfortunately, he never takes the hint."

Nell raised an eyebrow. "Be careful what you wish for. Maria and George are apart for more than they're together, but they still bicker the whole time he's home. It would be hard for you with the girls and no man about the house. At least we have Billy and Vernon at home all the time."

Rebecca grinned as she stood up. "I'm sure they'd help me too if the need arose. Would you like more tea before I collect Isobel from school? When Jack's home, I won't see as much of you as usual. I need to make the most of it."

CHAPTER THREE

Nell bustled into the living room and studied the clock on the mantelpiece. Ten past eleven. If Jack's ship had docked early this morning, as it usually did, he'd be here any minute now. She peered at herself in the mirror over the fireplace and pinched her cheeks. *That will have to do.*

The house was unusually quiet, and she peered out of the back window to see Maria and Alice finishing off the washing. *I really should go and help them, but...* She shook her head. *Let me go and check.* She hurried to the front door and peered down the road that was lined on either side with rows of small terraced houses. *No. Not yet.* Her heart fluttered. *Come on, Jack. Where are you?* She stared again at the end of the road. *Maybe if I put the kettle on...*

As the water boiled, she wandered into the front room and gazed through the window. The clock ticking on the mantelpiece counted the seconds, but irritated that it was too slow, she wandered into the back yard.

"Are you being a good girl?" She ran a hand over Elenor's head as she helped Alice turn the mangle.

Elenor grunted. "It's hard work."

"I know it is." She crossed the small paved yard to the only spot with any sunlight and took Leah's hand as she sat in the pram. "She'll be able to help you soon."

Elenor laughed. "She's too little."

"She won't be for long." Nell watched Maria pull the wet clothes from the washing tub. "I've boiled the water, but Jack's not arrived. Shall I make the tea anyway?"

Maria rubbed an arm across her face. "You could give us a hand here first. Take the washing that's been squeezed and get it hung up over the rack."

"Now?"

"Yes, now. What's the matter with you?"

Nell hesitated. "But ... it makes the room look untidy. Can't we at least wait until he's home?"

"Don't be ridiculous; he's seen washing hanging up. Here, get a move on. Besides..." Maria gave her a sideways glance "...if he's missed you, he won't even notice."

Nell flushed as she took the clothes from Maria. "I suppose so, but I'll make the tea anyway. You look as if you're nearly done here."

The tea had brewed by the time Maria carried Leah back into the living room. "Still no sign of him?"

"No." Nell's hands were clammy, and she wiped them on her skirt.

"I'm sure he won't be long. The weather wasn't good last night, so maybe they've been delayed."

"I hope you're right." Nell took a sip of her tea. "If he's not here after dinner, I'll walk down to the office and check the timetable."

"Are you sure? It's freezing out there. Why not wait

until our Billy comes home and ask him to call this afternoon?"

"I don't want to wait that long."

Maria tutted. "Come on, you've waited for Jack enough times now to know they're rarely on time. If the tide was low last night, they probably pulled further out to sea."

Nell's shoulders slumped. "You're right, but I was so excited..."

"Him being delayed won't make any difference to when you go on your adventures. The new ship will leave at the same time."

A fresh pot of tea sat on the table, but as Nell prepared to serve the dinner, a knock on the front door stopped her.

"This must be him." She wiped her hands on the front of her apron and hurried into the hall. "Why's he knocking though? It's never locked." She flung open the door, but her smile dropped when the postman thrust an envelope at her.

"Telegram for you, Mrs Riley. Good day."

"A telegram?" Nell's brow creased as she tore open the envelope.

Mrs Riley STOP Visit Bohemian shipping office soonest STOP News regarding MM Riley STOP

News? *What does that mean?* Her fingers trembled as she stared at the paper.

"What is it?" Maria appeared at the door.

"I don't know." She wandered back to the living room and sank into a chair. "It's a telegram telling me to go to the Bohemian office; they have some news about Jack." Her stomach churned. "Something's wrong, isn't it?"

Maria sat in the chair opposite. "What does it say?"

Nell read it out.

"It doesn't say much; it could be anything. He may have been delayed in Boston or taken a different ship..."

Nell's eyes welled with tears as she gazed at Maria. "Do you think so?"

"I'm sure there's a perfectly reasonable explanation, so sit down and I'll pour the tea. Billy will be home for dinner shortly, so he'll walk you to the office as soon as he's finished. I don't think you should go on your own."

Nell wiped her eyes with the back of her hand. "Yes, he'll know what to do."

Nell left the dinner dishes on the table and fastened her cloak while she waited for Billy to come in from the yard. He rubbed his hands together when he finally joined her.

"Come along, Aunty Nell. Let's get you down there so you can stop worrying."

She studied her nephew. With his dark hair, he was different to his brothers and obviously his mother's son. "How can I not worry when I get a telegram like that? They wouldn't have sent it if there was only a minor delay."

"Maybe not, but as Mam said, he could have been delayed in Boston ... or been given his ship to captain before he had time to come home. There'll be a perfectly good explanation."

"I hope you're right."

Once they were outside, Nell took the arm Billy offered her and they set off towards Windsor Street. The frost had melted, but with her short legs, Nell struggled to keep up.

By the time they reached Parliament Street, she was out of breath.

"Can we slow down? I need to be able to talk once we get there."

Billy squeezed her hand. "Don't worry, I'll come in with you. I don't have to be back at work until two o'clock, so I have time."

Nell put a hand to her chest. "Thank you. What would I do without you?"

"You'll never be without us. One of us will always be there for you, but we'd better get a move on. We're only halfway there."

Fifteen minutes later, the red-brick facade of the Steamship Bohemian Company offices came into view, but Nell's face sagged as they approached.

"Do they close for dinner?"

Billy said nothing but continued walking until he reached the door.

"It looks like it." He rattled the handle as he peered through the glass, but the door didn't budge. "Oh, wait. Here's someone now."

A young clerk opened the door and looked down his nose at them. "May I help you?"

Billy took off his cap and clutched it in his hands. "This is Mrs Elenor Riley; she's had a telegram from you about her husband, Master Mariner Jack Riley. Can you tell us anything about it?"

"Mrs Riley?" The colour that had been in the man's face faded. "Ah ... yes, please come in and take a seat. I'll get Mr Palmer to see you."

The clerk disappeared, leaving them standing in the entrance hall.

"That didn't sound very encouraging." Nell twisted the rings on her third finger.

"He probably doesn't know why you're here." Billy ushered her to a seat. "I reckon he's one of those superior types who's really quite junior but doesn't want anyone to realise he knows nothing."

Nell took a deep breath, but her heart was racing; the grandeur of the chandelier hanging in the centre of the room didn't help. She studied the elaborate glass beads. *Imagine having to clean them.* She put a hand to her chest. *I'd rather not.*

Billy rested a hand on hers. "Don't look so worried." When she didn't respond, his eyes followed her gaze. "Do you like chandeliers? I imagine it's similar to the ones you get on the passenger ships ... in the first-class areas at any rate."

"Do you think so? I can't imagine a ship with such luxury. Have you noticed the wallpaper, too?" She gazed around the reception area. "It's incredible."

"It will have cost them a bob or two, that's for sure. Not that it's necessary when there are people starving outside."

"I suppose they need to keep up appearances." Nell jumped at the sound of her name but shrank back in her chair as a tall, thin man with a pencil moustache approached.

"Mrs Riley, I'm Mr Palmer, the office manager."

Nell took his outstretched hand. "Good afternoon, Mr Palmer. This is my nephew, Mr Billy Atkin."

The two men shook hands before Mr Palmer led them down a long corridor and into a small but comfortable office. A large rectangular table, sitting under a smaller chandelier, filled the middle of the room, but Nell's attention was drawn to the numerous paintings of ships that covered the walls.

"Shall we sit down?" Mr Palmer gestured to two chairs on the opposite side of the table to where several sheets of paper were laid out.

Nell waited for Billy to hold out a chair for her and held her breath as Mr Palmer cleared his throat.

"Thank you for calling. I'm sorry it was necessary to send you a telegram, but we wanted to get this over with."

"Get what over with?" Nell reached for Billy's hand as Mr Palmer flicked through his papers.

"Let me see. Yes, Captain Riley. He was due home earlier today on the SS *Bohemian*. I was preparing to offer him command of his own ship when the news came in. A likeable chap, as I remember."

"What news?" The sting of bile rose from Nell's stomach.

"Ah, yes, well..." Mr Palmer leaned forward and clasped his hands on the desk. "It's with regret I must inform you that there's been an accident..."

The pit of Nell's stomach churned, and she put a hand to her mouth. "What sort of accident? Is he all right?"

"I'm afraid not. The SS *Bohemian* was sailing around Mizen Head on the south-western corner of Ireland yesterday evening as the weather conditions deteriorated. They hit some rocks, and the ship ran aground. Based on the information we have so far, over thirty men lost their lives, including the master and three of the mates. One of them being First Mate Riley."

"No..." Nell stared at the man across the desk, but she couldn't focus. All she could see was Jack. Tall, strong, handsome Jack. The image in her head was almost a year old, and he was smiling down at her as she lay in bed cradling their new daughter. He'd smiled, his eyes sparkling when he told her there was plenty of time for them to have a son. But he'd lied. There was no more time...

"Mrs Riley?"

Nell flinched as Mr Palmer raised his voice.

"I'm sorry. I didn't mean to make you jump. As things stand, we believe it was an accident, but there'll be a formal inquest in the next few weeks, once we have more information." He stood up and moved towards the door. "Please accept the condolences of the company."

Nell wiped a tear that was running down her cheek. "That can't be it. You need to find him... It's too soon..."

"I'm afraid there's no doubt, Mrs Riley." He held the door open, but Nell's feet refused to move as she focussed on Billy. "I need some money."

"Money?" Mr Palmer straightened his back and closed the door again.

"Jack's wages. I can't go home without them. I've two daughters..." Nell's voice cracked.

"She has a point." Billy stepped forward to face Mr Palmer. "My uncle would have collected his wages as he disembarked and taken them straight home. At the very least, my aunt should get them."

"That would be most irregular. We can't give so much money to a woman."

"I understand that, but if my uncle was here…"

"He'd hand his wages to me." Nell forced herself to stand up. "How do you think the wives of sailors manage while their husbands are away…?"

"Please, Mrs Riley." Mr Palmer held up his hands.

"No, I won't be quiet. Have you any idea how we cope when we're left to run our own homes for weeks or months at a time, while the man of the house is away at sea? We don't have the luxury of being looked after … I'm responsible for the housekeeping money and you need to let me have what's rightfully mine."

Billy took her arm and led her back to her chair. "Aunty Nell, please. Let me deal with this."

"Well, tell him." Nell's hands trembled as Billy sat her down.

"Mr Palmer, I'm sure you understand what my aunt's saying. I know what it's like. Me own mam runs our house while Dad's away."

"But Officer Riley was due a month's wages. We can't hand that amount over…"

"All right." Billy stepped towards Mr Palmer. "You can't deny that the money should go to my aunt, but if you won't give it her all now, could she have some housekeeping to tide her over?"

"I deserve more than that …"

"Please, Aunty." Billy smoothed down his moustache. "I'll tell you what, perhaps I can act as her guardian. If you give me the balance of the money, I'll deposit it in an account for her and make withdrawals as and when she needs it."

Mr Palmer bristled.

"I'm entitled to it." Nell once again forced herself from her chair, but caught Billy's arm as her legs buckled. "You can't deprive me of my husband *and* his wages."

"Very well." Mr Palmer opened the door for a second time. "I've no cash here, but let me escort you to the cashier; I'm sure he can sort something out for you."

Billy helped Nell to her feet and held her as they walked back to the entrance hall.

"You take a seat here and I'll sort everything out."

Nell stared out of the window as the sun disappeared into the sea, leaving a trail of red and purple clouds in the sky. *Such pretty colours. Jack loved the sky like that. He always said it meant tomorrow would be a good day.* She shook her head. *He was wrong.*

"Are you all right, Aunty Nell?"

Nell jumped at Billy's voice. "Oh ... I was thinking..."

"There's no need to apologise. Look, they gave me everything Uncle Jack was owed." He showed her a selection of notes and coins before putting them in his inside pocket. "Let's get you home and we can count it later." He stood up and led Nell from the office before hailing a carriage. It came to a halt a little ahead of them, and Nell stumbled as she climbed inside, thankful Billy was there to catch her and settle her into the seat.

"Come on, Aunty Nell. Take some deep breaths for me." He squeezed her hands. "I'm sorry I can't come with you, but I'll pay the driver in advance and ask him to take you straight home. He'll look after you."

She said nothing as the dock road faded in and out of view. Nothing made sense any more.

"I'll see you tonight." Billy once again patted her hand, but Nell sat motionless until he moved away and the carriage jerked her backwards as it pulled away from the side of the road.

It had taken the best part of an hour to walk from their house on Merlin Street to the office, but it only felt like seconds later when the carriage came to a stop outside the house. Nell's vacant eyes gazed through the windows, but the driver had no sooner jumped from his seat than Maria was in the street.

"What on earth are you doing in a carriage?" She stood with her hands on her hips. "You've not got money to waste."

"She's had rather a shock." The driver opened the door and rolled down the steps. "The young man who was with her asked me to bring her home and hand her over to a Mrs Atkin."

"That'll be me." The lines on Maria's forehead deepened as she stood up straight and put an arm around Nell. "What sort of shock?"

"He didn't say, but if you can take her from here, I'll be on me way."

Nell stared after the carriage as it disappeared down the road, but Maria placed her hands on her shoulders and forced her into the house.

"Come on, let's get you in and you can tell me all about it."

Nell heard the front door click shut behind her but stopped to look around as it immediately opened again and

Rebecca pushed her way in, her young daughter in her arms.

"What's the matter? I saw the carriage."

"So did half the street, I imagine. You'd better lock the door or they'll all be here." Maria helped Nell to the living room. "She's not spoken since she arrived." She pulled out a chair at the dining table and settled Nell down while Rebecca put her daughter on the rug and poured three cups of tea. She pushed one to Nell, stirring three heaped teaspoons of sugar into it.

"Get that down you; you're as white as a sheet. What on earth's the matter?"

Nell said nothing, but picked up her cup and wrapped her hands around it.

"Is it Jack?"

Nell nodded but paused to take a sip of her tea. "He's not coming back."

"What do you mean, not coming back? Of course he will." Maria stirred her own tea but suddenly hesitated. "Nell, talk to us."

"There's been an accident." Nell clanged down her cup unable to stop the tears falling onto the table. "Over thirty dead, including three officers ... and one of them was Jack." She let out a heartbreaking sob.

"Oh, my dear girl, I'm so sorry." Maria stood up and wrapped her arms around Nell's shoulders.

"I knew it was too good to be true ... I was too happy." Her voice squeaked as she spoke. "We had too many plans ... We were going to *America*..." She wiped her eyes with the back of a hand. "How stupid was I to think someone like me could do that?"

"There, there. Let it all out." Maria rested her head on Nell's.

"I'm so sorry, Nell. Really, I am." Rebecca squeezed her hand. "Would you like me to tell Mrs Blackmore from church? She'll let everyone else know."

Nell nodded as Maria's grip tightened.

"I've spent half my life looking after you; I'm not going to stop now."

"But I wanted Jack to do that." Nell's sobs grew louder as she leaned against Maria. "Why did he have to die?"

CHAPTER FOUR

Nell wandered into the back bedroom and stared at the double bed she shared with Elenor. It was wash day and Alice had left her some clean sheets, but they could wait. She perched on the edge of the mattress and put her head in her hands. Was it really only a week since she'd received Jack's letter telling her he was coming home? It felt like an eternity.

Tears streamed down her face. *The Lord must surely hate me ... but why? What have I done to deserve this?* She took a handkerchief from her sleeve and wiped her face, but flinched when an arm settled across her shoulders.

"Come on now, wipe those eyes." Maria sat beside her.

"I won't have any tears left soon." Nell leaned into her sister's shoulder. "Why do the people I love the most always leave me?"

"We won't all leave you ... you'll always have me and Rebecca."

"But you both have your own families to take care of. I'll be nothing but a burden."

"We'll have none of that. I've been like a mam to you since you were five years old. Do you think I'll abandon you now?"

"But George won't want to support me and the girls..."

"Don't talk nonsense, of course he will. He thinks of you as another daughter."

"But Jack was the one who paid the rent. Who'll pay it now?" Nell sobbed as she spoke.

"Stop worrying." Maria wiped a tear from her cheek. "We've enough men in this family earning a wage, and Alice is working, too. Besides, George has a softer heart than you realise."

"He won't be happy, though."

"Stop this. I came up to tell you Rebecca's here and she's putting the kettle on. She's brought a cake, too. Come downstairs and we'll make the bed later."

Rebecca wrapped her arms around Nell as she walked into the living room. "Please don't cry."

"I can't help it. All I can think of is how happy I was this time last week. And now it's gone."

"I know, and we're all so sorry. Everyone sends their condolences."

"Don't be sad, Mama." Elenor knelt on a chair beside Alice on the far side of the table. "We don't like you being sad."

"I'm sorry. I'm being silly. Give me a minute and I'll pull myself together." She took a deep breath and rubbed the back of a hand across her eyes.

"There's nothing silly about it." Rebecca pulled out a chair for her. "Now, come and sit down while Maria makes the tea."

Nell did as she was told as Rebecca slid into the seat beside her.

"It's funny, but with the three of us here, it's almost the same as when Dad died. Do you remember? You and me together, with Maria being Mam and Tom pretending he was Dad even though George was at home in those days."

A weak smile crossed Nell's lips. "And Jane."

"Shh." Rebecca sighed as she glanced towards the kitchen. "The less said about her, the better, but we've got each other, and that's all that matters."

"But you have Mr Grayson and the girls ... and George will be home again soon."

"That doesn't matter. Even before Jack's accident, I saw more of you than I did of Hugh; he spends too much time in the alehouse nowadays."

"I suppose so." She squeezed Rebecca's hand. "Did I hear you'd brought some cake?"

"You did. A Victoria sponge. Maria's putting it out."

As she spoke, Maria appeared from the kitchen carrying the cake on top of a stack of plates. "And very nice it looks, too."

Maria placed the knife back on the plate as the front door opened and a tall man with a balding head and dark beard peered around the living room door.

"Am I in time?"

"Uncle Tom!" Elenor giggled as the man reached across the table and ruffled her hair.

"Trust you to arrive when we've emptied the teapot." Maria stood up and scowled at her brother.

"Don't look at me like that; I've come to see how Nell's getting on." He put a hand on her shoulder and took the empty chair at the table. "How are you doing?"

"I've been better, but I'll survive." Nell reached for her handkerchief. "What have you been up to?"

"Nothing much, other than working."

"Have you only just finished?" Maria picked up the teapot but stopped when he nodded. "Until this time on a Saturday? That's not like you."

"Don't start. This was supposed to be a friendly visit."

"I bet you've not been home yet." Maria disappeared into the kitchen and put the kettle back on the stove with a clang.

"Not yet. I'm on my way." Tom rolled his eyes at Nell. "And she wonders why I never call."

"She worries about Sarah and the children, that's all." Nell stood up from the table. "Will you excuse me a moment? I need to get something from upstairs. You won't go anywhere until I'm back, will you?"

"Not if you don't want me to." He winked at her as she left the room.

Once she reached the bedroom, Nell shut the door behind her and leaned against it, taking a deep breath to steady herself. *I need to do it now.* She knelt beside the bed and pulled out the travelling case. The small brown box was all that remained of her dreams. She flicked open the catches and gazed into the empty interior. There'd be no new trunk or fancy dresses now. No standing on the deck watching the waves lapping at the edge of the ship or seeing the shoreline of America as they pulled into port. She choked back tears as she closed the lid and pushed herself to her feet. There'd be no anything.

She took hold of the cracked leather handle and lifted it from the bed. It felt heavy despite being empty and with a sigh she made her way back downstairs. She forced a smile as she walked into the living room. "Here we are."

Tom's brow creased. "What are you doing with that?"

"Sarah lent it to me. Didn't she tell you?"

"How can she, when she never sees him?" Maria folded her arms across her chest.

"Will you give it a rest?" Tom banged his hand on the table and turned back to Nell. "Why did she lend it to you?"

"Jack had promised to take me on his next voyage, and I wanted to be packed and ready to go."

Tom's forehead creased. "He hadn't got a job on a passenger liner, had he? I thought he was going to captain a cargo ship to start with?"

"Oh, no ... I think it was a passenger ship." Nell licked her dry lips. "He promised I could go with him. He wouldn't have taken me on a cargo ship. Would he?"

"No, he wouldn't." Maria slapped Tom across the shoulder on her way back to the kitchen. "Will you stop upsetting her?"

"I was only asking." He rubbed the spot Maria had struck but kept his focus on Nell. "I'm sorry you won't be going. Maybe one day, hey?"

Nell scoffed as she stood the travelling case by the wall. "How will I meet another ship's captain around here?"

"You never know, an attractive young woman like you. I'm sure there'll be lots of men interested when you're ready."

Maria placed the fresh pot of tea on the table. "Whether there are or not, they're unlikely to come round these parts, and I, for one, am glad. The last thing we want is Nell going off to sea."

"The last thing you want, you mean. I'm sure Nell would be perfectly happy if she found the right man."

"Please. Don't argue." Nell held up her hands. "Can we be civil for once?"

Maria took her seat. "Don't blame me."

"I'm not blaming you, but it's becoming a habit." Nell looked at Tom. "Didn't you see Billy on the way here?"

"I did, but he wanted to stay in the alehouse. He was with our Sam, and Vernon had arrived, and so I left them to it."

"Ah, so you've not come straight from work." Maria's voice was triumphant. "I thought it was too good to be true. I hope you've not been spending the housekeeping money."

"I'm sorry, Nell, but I get enough of this at home. I'm not staying here to listen to it, too." Tom pushed himself up from the table. "I'll see you soon."

Rebecca picked up her cup as the front door slammed. "Do you have to have a go at him every time you see him?"

Maria straightened the tablecloth. "He deserves it. He's not the one who sees Sarah in tears when the money runs out. He never gives her a second thought."

"Two of the boys are working now. That should make things easier for them."

"I don't think Len will be earning enough to make a difference; he's not long since started his apprenticeship." Maria's voice rose as she headed back to the kitchen. "Anyway, Tom should be setting them a good example, not taking days off as and when he feels like it. How would you like it if Mr Grayson did that?"

Rebecca said nothing as Maria continued to shout from the kitchen, "You mark my words, he's up to no good."

"What do you mean?" A scowl crossed Nell's face.

"How often do you see him on his own? Wherever he goes, he's got his head together with somebody or other. Plotting and scheming, if you want my opinion."

"What, like we've got our heads together now?" Nell's frown deepened. "What's wrong with him talking to people?"

"It's not the fact that he talks to them; it's the way he does it." Maria stirred a spoonful of sugar into her tea. "I've seen him several times, and whoever he's with, they always have their heads together, looking over their shoulders to check there's no one listening in. If anyone approaches, they jump away like naughty kids."

"Someone like you, you mean."

"Well, yes … but not only me. Sarah's seen it too."

Nell finally laughed. "That makes it very suspicious then; of course he doesn't want Sarah knowing what he's up to. What man ever tells his wife what he's doing?"

CHAPTER FIVE

T he air was cold as Nell put an arm out of the bed on Monday morning and she quickly pulled it back under the blankets. The boys were moving about downstairs, but the delicate frame of Elenor as it nestled into her side made her reluctant to move. Nell ran a hand over her daughter's hair as tears welled again in her eyes. She didn't understand her dada wouldn't be coming home, but it would only be a matter of time before she started asking questions. Questions that, in all probability, she wouldn't be able to answer.

The sound of Leah crying in her cot broke the silence, and Nell slipped her arm from beneath Elenor and climbed out of bed.

"There, there. Don't cry. Mam's here." She reached into the cot and picked her up.

"She always wakes me up." Elenor's hair was ruffled as she peered out from under the blankets.

"That's because it's time to get up." Nell wandered to

the bed against the other wall. "Alice has already gone, and Billy and Vernon will be going to work soon."

"My don't want to get up." Elenor snuggled back beneath the bedcovers.

"Don't you want some breakfast? If we don't go now, it will be all gone."

"It's cold."

"Let's be quick then. Straight out of bed and into your dress."

It took less than five minutes to get both girls dressed, and Nell sat Leah on the bed while she picked up the black mourning dress she'd borrowed from Sarah. *What a dreadful thing to have to wear.* She'd worn it for the first time yesterday, when they'd been to church, and it had made her already pale complexion appear ghostly. She groaned as she gave it a shake and climbed into it. Only another one year, eleven months.

Nell's hands were numb as she splashed a handful of water over her cheeks from the washstand in the corner of the room. She shuddered as the water hit her face. If she hadn't been awake already, she certainly was now.

"Come on, your turn."

Elenor wriggled as she attempted to wipe a flannel over her face.

"All right, that will do. Come along." She balanced Leah on her hip as she took Elenor's hand and led her down the stairs, her tiny feet stopping on each step before she moved to the next.

"Here you are." Maria disappeared into the kitchen as soon as she saw them. "The boys have already gone."

Nell sat Leah on a chair near the fire while Elenor took

the seat at the table next to Alice. "It was too cold to get out of bed. I'll have to start lighting the fire up there again."

"I don't know why you stopped."

Nell closed her eyes and took a breath. "Yes you do."

"And I told you, you were being daft. We can afford enough coal for you to get a fire going."

"Maybe we can, but I can't rely on the boys for everything."

"You can and you will. You do enough for them; it's about time they repaid the favour. Now, sit down and drink this tea."

Nell wrapped her hands around the cup and looked across to Alice. "You're late this morning. I thought you'd have gone with the boys."

"I don't need to go out any more." A grin lit up her face. "I got a certificate of competence on Saturday and now I'm a qualified waistcoat maker I can work here."

"That's wonderful ... but why didn't you tell me?"

Alice's cheeks coloured and she looked to Maria.

"Because you were rather upset if you remember and then Uncle Tom arrived; it felt rather insignificant with everything you were dealing with."

"But it's not insignificant; it's a wonderful achievement." She smiled at Alice. "I wish I'd done something like that when I was your age; if I had, I'd be able to help with the bills now."

Alice cocked her head to one side. "Why didn't you? Aunty Rebecca does her sewing."

Nell shrugged. "I was never very good with a needle and thread, so it didn't seem worth the effort."

"Couldn't you have done something else instead?"

"I suppose I could, but I didn't need to. When I was your age, your dad still lived at home and I was happy to let him and your mam take care of me." She sighed. "I suppose I was lazy. I thought I'd get a husband one day and not need any money of my own. That's why I'm pleased for you. You make the most of this opportunity while you can. At least that way, you'll be able to stand on your own two feet if you ever need to. Not like me, dependent on everyone."

Maria had clearly been listening from the kitchen. "If that's the way you feel, it's not too late. You can always learn to make waistcoats yourself."

Nell nearly choked on her tea. "I'm still no better at sewing than I used to be."

"There must be something you could do though, if you wanted to." Alice spoke with a confidence Nell never remembered having at her age.

"You're probably right. I just need to work out what it is." She helped herself to a couple of slices of bread and buttered one for Leah. "Was that the postman?"

"It was." Maria hurried out into the hall and returned seconds later. "It's for you."

"Me?" Nell's brow furrowed. "Who on earth from?" Her heart raced as Maria handed her an official-looking envelope and reached over to the mantelpiece for the letter opener.

"Open it and find out."

Maria and Alice watched as she sliced open the top and with trembling hands pulled out a thick sheet of cream writing paper. She scanned the elegant cursive script and looked up.

"It's from the Steamship Bohemian Company. They've

set the date for the inquest; the first and second of March at the Assizes Court in St George's Hall."

Maria's face paled. "I hope they don't want you to go."

Nell read the letter again. "It doesn't say I have to, but they'll arrange a chaperone if I'd like to sit in the public gallery."

"How ridiculous. A woman in your situation shouldn't be going out, let alone attending something like that."

Alice's forehead creased. "What situation?"

Nell flicked a crumb from her dress. "I think she means because I'm in mourning."

"You know that's what I mean. How can you be grieving for Jack if you're gallivanting around town?"

Nell folded the letter and put it back in the envelope. "I'd hardly call it gallivanting, and it would be nice to find out what happened."

"I'm sure you'll be able to read about it in the newspaper."

Nell's head jerked up. "That's no way to find out."

"What else can you do? I don't like the idea of you going with a stranger, and everyone else will be at work."

"Uncle Tom might go with her." Alice's face was a picture of innocence, but Maria glared at her. "Don't you start. He doesn't need any encouragement to miss work."

Nell picked up her cup. *I'll have a word with Billy and see what he thinks. If we can get five minutes on our own.*

The fire was burning low in the grate as Billy picked up the packet of playing cards and dealt them out. He sat between

Maria and Alice while Nell sat opposite. He turned up the last card. The six of clubs.

"This is the last game for us, young lady." Maria picked up her hand as she spoke to Alice.

"Aw, I wanted to win."

Billy laughed. "Maybe tomorrow. Me and Aunty Nell will win tonight whatever happens in this game. Besides, Mam's right. As soon as we finish here, I'm going to the alehouse for a quick one before they close."

Nell's heart quickened as she played a card. "Would you mind getting some coal for me first?"

"You've decided to heat the bedroom, have you?" Maria collected the first trick.

"Only tonight. I'd like to take the chill off the room."

"I can manage that." Billy collected a trick of his own. "We'll be finished here soon enough."

Nell played a card. "I hope so, if you want to get to the alehouse."

With the remaining tricks shared between them, Billy pushed himself up from the table. "Right, a bit of coal for you, Aunty Nell, and then I'll be off." He headed out of the back door to the coal bunker while Nell gathered up the cups and saucers.

"You two go on up. I'll wash these."

"Ah, thank you." Maria yawned. "I'll see you in the morning."

Nell watched them disappear up the stairs, then stood up to close the living room door. She leaned her back against it as she waited for Billy to reappear.

"Here we are. This should be enough. I'll take it upstairs for you."

"Actually…" Nell hesitated. "May I ask you a question?"

Billy glanced at the clock on the mantelpiece. "Er … yes, of course."

"I'm sorry, it won't take long, but I wanted to speak to you without your mam being around." She pulled the envelope from the pocket of her apron and handed it to him. "I got this earlier. It's about the inquest into your Uncle Jack's accident. Do you think I should go?"

Billy opened the letter, his lips moving as he read it. "Do you want to?"

"I do, but your mam doesn't think I should. Not while I'm in mourning."

Billy looked back to the letter. "They can hardly delay the inquest for two years."

"Would you come with me?" Nell's eyes pleaded with him. "That would make it better, wouldn't it?"

"I'd love to, but it's a Tuesday and Wednesday." His face fell. "I won't be able to get out of work."

"Oh." Nell's head dropped.

"I'll tell you what, Uncle Tom will be in the alehouse. If I get there in the next ten minutes, I'll have a word with him for you."

"Your mam said I shouldn't encourage him. She says he misses more days at work than he goes in."

Billy grinned. "Mam doesn't know the half of what he's up to. Leave it with me. I'm sure he'll be only too happy to accompany you."

CHAPTER SIX

Despite the mornings getting lighter, it was still dark as Nell crept out of bed and reached for her robe. Without a backwards glance, she slipped it over her shoulders and headed out onto the landing, a candle in her hand. It was unusual for her to find the house quiet, and she tiptoed down the stairs, doing her best to avoid the creaks she knew would have Maria onto the landing before she could reach the bottom.

A wave of relief ran through her as a dull orange glow greeted her from the grate in the living room. Placing the candle on the mantelpiece, she rubbed her hands together as she crouched down to add more coal from the dented black scuttle. She shivered as the flames grew, and after feeling their warmth, she headed to the kitchen to boil the kettle. She hadn't finished filling it with water when she jumped at a noise behind her.

"You're up early." Maria walked straight to the pantry.

"I was awake half the night, so I thought I might as well come down."

"I don't know why you're putting yourself through this. There's no need for you to go."

Nell sighed as she watched Maria shape the dough she'd made the previous evening. "I have to. I need to know what happened, and reading it in the newspaper isn't enough."

"I'm sure Tom could go on his own and tell you tonight. He's obviously not planning on doing any work today."

Nell shook her head. "Can't you let me do something for myself? I lost more than my husband last month and I want to know why."

Maria bent down to put the bread in the stove. "Well, if you come home upset, don't say I didn't warn you. The inquest will go into far more detail than you'll want to hear."

"I'll be fine." Nell shivered as she headed into the living room. "I need to warm up first, though. It's freezing in here."

By the time the boys had eaten breakfast and left for work, Nell's stomach was churning. She glanced at the clock. Almost eight.

"Tom will be here in a minute. I'd better get my hat on."

Maria stood up to clear the table. "Why so early?"

"It will take us over half an hour to walk up there, and I want to get a good seat. It starts at nine..." Nell stopped at the sound of a knock on the front door and smiled as Tom let himself in.

"Morning. Are you ready?"

Nell took a deep breath. "Almost. Let me get my cloak."

"I still think this is a daft idea." Maria collected up the plates. "Why did you have to encourage her?"

"She's every right to go." Tom put a hand on Nell's

shoulder. "I'd want to know what happened if the roles were reversed."

"That's because you're a man and everyone would expect you to be there. It's no place for a woman, especially not one in mourning." Maria indicated towards Nell's dress.

"Why do you always have to be so bossy?" Tom glared down at Maria. "Let her make up her own mind, for once."

Nell slung her cloak over her shoulders. "Shall we go? It'll take us long enough to walk up there and we don't want to arrive at the last minute."

Tom hurried to open the front door with Maria close behind.

"You take good care of her. Do you hear me?"

Tom groaned. "Loud and clear."

They set off at a brisk pace, ignoring the eyes of the neighbours as they peered through their windows.

"Thank you for doing this." She pulled her cloak more tightly around her as gulls circled overhead. "I know Maria means well, but ... well, I suppose she's been a bit overpowering lately."

"You need to take a stand with her. Jack wouldn't be happy to see her bossing you about like that."

"You're right, but I have to live with her. I don't want us to fall out."

"If you ask me, the best thing you could do is find yourself another husband, one that works around here, and make a home for yourself."

Nell shook her head. "I can't do that; not yet. Jack's not been dead a month and I'm in full mourning. Maria's right, and I shouldn't be going to the inquest."

Tom scowled. "It's hardly socialising! Besides, I can't see

anyone keeping you locked up at home for the next two years, not even Maria."

Nell grimaced. "Maybe not."

"Well, count to ten and forget about her for now. You're legitimately allowed out of the house for the inquest, so make the most of it. It will probably do you both good."

Nell sighed. "I hope so."

Tom patted her hand. "Come on, let's get a move on or we'll be late."

As they approached the imposing shape of St George's Hall, with its Roman columns towering over the square in front of it, Nell was surprised to see a small crowd had already gathered outside the entrance to the court.

"I didn't expect so many to be here."

Tom checked his pocket watch. "They mustn't be letting anyone in yet. It's quarter to nine, so we won't have long to wait."

As they joined the queue, a man in uniform opened the heavy wooden door to reveal a series of steps going down to the basement, and a corridor to the right.

"One at a time. Along the corridor, up the stairs and through the door to the left."

Tom put an arm around Nell's shoulders as she followed the crowd up the stairs.

"There aren't many other women here." She studied the faces in front of her. "And none in mourning clothes."

"Stop worrying."

Nell's heart was pounding as they reached the door to

the courtroom, and she paused as she scanned the dark mahogany walls.

"Keep moving. Visitors in the back two rows only." Another man in uniform ushered her into the room but blocked the stairs that led to the front. "Assessors and witnesses only, down here."

Nell gazed at the four rows of semicircular benches that faced the front of the room, as Tom nudged her towards the back bench.

"Keep moving until we reach the middle."

Nell shuffled along until she arrived at the centre of the bench and looked directly down onto an elaborate chair that faced the rest of the room. *At least we have a good view.*

"Is that where the judge sits?"

"I imagine so." Tom put his head down. "I don't make a habit of coming here myself."

"That's a relief. It's very grand, isn't it?" She pointed to an area beyond the metal railings around the front of the balcony. "I wouldn't like to be a criminal standing there. It must be terrifying. Where do those steps lead to?"

Tom stood up and peered at the steep staircase that disappeared behind the panelling. "Down to the cells, I would say."

Nell shuddered. "That makes it worse. Remind me never to do anything I shouldn't."

"You'd better not upset Maria then." Tom squeezed her hand, but Nell scowled.

"That's not even funny." She leaned forward and watched as the rows in front of them filled up. By nine o'clock, with most seats taken, an oversized door at the front of the room opened and the usher called for them to stand.

Seconds later, a judge in a black silk robe and grey bobwig strode onto the platform and took his seat.

Nell held her breath as he arranged a series of papers on the desk. Once they were all in position, he peered out at those in the gallery and instructed them to be seated.

"Captain White?" he said a moment later.

"Here, milord." A tall man in full naval uniform stood up and gave a slight bow.

"Captains Wilson and French?"

The two men who sat beside Captain White also stood up and bowed. "Yes, milord."

"Excellent." The judge addressed the rest of the court. "Along with these appointed assessors, over the next two days I'll determine the circumstances leading up to the sinking of the SS *Bohemian* on the night of Sunday the sixth of February and the subsequent deaths, which have now been confirmed as thirty-five, including the master, three officers and all the engineers."

Tuts sounded around the room.

"Thankfully, twenty-two of the crewmen survived, and those who are able, will take the stand to explain what happened in the last few hours of the ship's voyage."

Nell closed her eyes. *Why was Jack one of those taken?*

Tom leaned towards her. "He was the first mate and a captain in training. He had to stay with the ship."

Nell took a handkerchief from her sleeve and dabbed her tears. *He still should have survived. Why didn't they make it to the lifeboats?*

She gulped back a sob as Mr McIsaac, the second mate and only officer to survive, took the stand.

"Officer Riley was at the wheel as we approached land at Mizen Head…"

Nell took a sharp intake of breath. *He can't blame Jack!*

"…but shortly before the fog dropped, he handed the wheel to the third mate, Officer Saunders. He was new to the ship and was taking instructions from the captain."

A novice? Nell gaped at Tom. "He shouldn't have been in charge if it was foggy."

Tom's face was stern, but he didn't respond as Mr McIsaac continued.

"We proceeded at full speed, but shortly after half past nine, the captain appeared from the chart room. That was when I heard…"

"Yes?" The judge peered at the officer, who took a deep breath.

"That was when the captain shouted, 'Good God, man, what have you been doing? Hard a-port, hard a-port…'"

Nell gasped. "He knew they were going to hit the rocks."

"I'm not surprised the captain panicked. He shouldn't have trusted such a dangerous situation to a third mate."

Nell put a hand to her mouth. "And by the time he realised, it was too late…"

The muttering in the room caused the judge to bang his gavel on the desk.

"If you wish to stay in this court, you will sit in silence." He peered up to the gallery.

"I presume, Mr McIsaac, that you hit the rocks shortly afterwards."

"Yes, milord. Within the minute."

"Thank you." The judge made a note on his pad. "Talk us through the sequence of events after the boat had struck the rocks at Mizen Head. Why weren't the lifeboats deployed?"

A good question.

The officer's hands trembled as he spoke. "The first two lifeboats off the starboard side were lowered, but the waves were too high for them and they filled with water as soon as they hit the sea..."

"What about those on the port side?"

"We managed to get one off, but the other was destroyed when the main mast fell on it."

"And you were in the one usable craft?"

"Yes, sir."

Nell wiped her eyes. *Aren't lifeboats built to survive rough seas?* Unable to hold her tongue, she looked at Tom. "That's why the second mate survived, because he was in the only lifeboat fit for the water. Why couldn't it have been Jack?"

The judge seemed unmoved by the details. "Once you reached shore, did you return to look for anyone else who may have stayed with the ship?"

The second mate stared at his feet as he shook his head. "Once we left the boat, we checked the waters around the wreck and were able to pick up a further six men. The sea was fierce though, and it was only with a great struggle that we reached the shore the next morning. At around the same time, the boatswain was washed up close by. He'd grabbed a bale of cotton as the ship broke up and it had acted as a raft. He was only half conscious when we found him, but he claimed he hadn't seen anyone."

"And there were no men after that?"

The officer hesitated. "As the fog lifted, we used the binoculars to do a final search of the area and saw two men clinging to a rock about a mile and a half offshore." He struggled to speak. "The sea was still too rough to go out to them and they'd slipped into the sea before we could reach them."

"And reading your written testimony, it appears you have reason to believe these men were the master and first mate?"

The second mate raised his head. "We can't be certain, but yes, that's what we believe."

"Thank you, Mr McIsaac. We'll now adjourn for dinner. Please be back for two o'clock."

As the court stood, Nell squeezed her eyes tight, tears streaming down her cheeks. The image of Jack clinging to a rock in the middle of the storm was etched in her mind. How had he felt in those last minutes? *Did he think of me and the girls?* She shook her head as Tom put an arm around her shoulders.

"Come this way. You need something warm inside you."

They followed the crowd to the nearby market. It was bursting with people, and as they walked in, the stench of the meat and fish that had been laid out since early morning caused Nell to put a hand over her nose.

"You should be used to the smell." Tom laughed as he rubbed his hands together. "At least it's warmer in here than outside."

Nell shivered. "Not much, and I don't come here very often. Thank goodness we have our own shops."

Tom found a stall selling ready-cooked food, and with a tepid cup of vegetable soup in one hand, and a less than fresh crust of bread in the other, Nell found a seat on one of the benches that dotted the market.

"I wish they could have got on with it, rather than putting us through this." She dipped her bread into the soup.

"It's all right for them. I imagine they're having a full dinner up there."

"What a time to stop, though. Do you think the third mate will get the blame for steering in the wrong direction?" Nell asked.

Tom shrugged. "The captain's got to take ultimate responsibility. More lives were lost than necessary because most of the lifeboats were useless. There may be a case for compensation if that's found to be the main cause of the deaths."

"Compensation?"

"Yes, why not? If Jack was working under conditions that ultimately led to his death, you should be entitled to something."

Nell's eyes narrowed. "That would be nice. Not that it will bring him back." She breathed in deeply. "All I can see is him clinging to a rock. It must have been horrible."

"And these companies should be made to pay. For all they know, you and the other wives and children could end up in the workhouse through no fault of your own. Haven't you wondered why a lot of the shipping lines have representatives here? They're frightened about how much this will cost them."

.   .   .

They arrived in the courthouse for the afternoon session ten minutes ahead of the restart. Tom escorted Nell back into their seats, and she rearranged her skirt so it provided a degree of padding on the hard wooden benches.

"I hope we're not here long. These seats aren't half uncomfortable."

"It depends on how many more witnesses they have. I imagine they'll have a few if the hearing is going on until tomorrow."

Nell's brow creased. "But we've already heard what happened."

"From one man. Who's to say he saw everything relevant, or hasn't made it all up to get himself off the hook? They'll need to listen to everyone else before they come to a decision on whose fault it was."

Nell's eyes widened. "We have to listen to it all over again?"

"They have to make sure everyone else's versions agree with the one we've heard."

A shiver ran down Nell's back. Perhaps Maria had been right. "That could take hours."

As soon as they were outside St George's Hall, Tom hailed a carriage to take them home and as they arrived in Merlin Street, Nell groaned. Maria was waiting for them with several neighbours. *I won't even get a minute to myself.*

Maria was at the bottom of the steps as Nell climbed down. "What are you doing in a carriage for the second time in as many weeks? Jack's wages won't last forever."

Tom held up a hand as he ushered Nell to a seat by the fire. "Leave her alone. I paid for it."

"I knew she shouldn't have gone…"

"Maria! Stop." Tom's voice stopped Maria dead, but his tone softened as he walked into the living room. "Is there any tea in that pot? Nell could do with one if you can stop talking for long enough. And put an extra spoonful of sugar in it."

Maria grumbled as she grabbed the pot and hurried to the kitchen.

"Will you be all right?" Tom stooped down at the side of Nell's chair.

"I think so, thank you."

"I'll go back tomorrow to hear the summing-up and tell you what they decide."

Nell rested her head on the back of the chair and stared at the laundry rack hanging over the fire. "Thank you."

He patted her hand then straightened up and poked his head into the kitchen. "I'm off, but I'll call tomorrow. Go easy on her. She doesn't need you criticising her."

Maria was unusually quiet as she handed Nell a cup of tea and sat in the chair opposite. "Was it a difficult day?"

Nell continued to stare at the rack. "I've had better."

"Alice has taken the girls for a walk to the park."

"They'll like that. I should take them more often … once the weather warms up."

"Yes." Maria hesitated. "I'd better get the tea made. The boys will be home soon."

Unbidden, two streams of tears trickled down the sides of her face. *Will I ever close my eyes again without seeing Jack clinging to that rock?* She didn't want to even try.

Her untouched drink had long since gone cold when the sound of the front door forced her to sit up and wipe her face. She busied herself stirring the cold liquid as Billy joined her.

"Evening, Aunty Nell. How did you get on today?"

"Today? Oh, yes, it was fine. They haven't reached a verdict yet. They'll do that tomorrow."

Billy took the seat opposite her and flicked open the newspaper. "Will you go and listen?"

"No, she won't." Maria carried a loaf of bread to the table. "Uncle Tom's going on his own and will report back."

Billy frowned at his mother. "He's going again? Good for him."

"What do you mean, good for him? He's probably on the sick. You shouldn't encourage him."

"He's not necessarily skiving. He's got his reasons for following the trial but needs to be careful who sees him in court."

"Why's he so interested, all of a sudden?" Maria scowled at her son. "I thought he'd only gone to escort your Aunty Nell."

"He did, but the verdict's of interest to all the shipowners in Liverpool, and indirectly the workers, too, so he wants to know what's going on."

"I'm sure it's of no concern to him. Now, go and wash your hands. Tea won't be long."

CHAPTER SEVEN

At three o'clock the following afternoon, Tom strode into the back room, his flat cap tucked beneath his arm. "On your own?"

Nell looked up and smiled. "For now. Maria and Alice have gone to see Sarah. Did they reach a verdict?"

"Eventually. They ran through all the questions again, looking for reasons to explain what happened."

"And did they decide whose fault it was?"

Tom stepped over to the fire. "The captain was found to be at fault, but it ended up being recorded as accidental death."

"Accidental! How did they arrive at that?"

"The captain had instructed the third mate to do one thing, but he'd misinterpreted the order and steered too close to the shore. Due to the speed they were travelling it was too late to do anything once they realised the mistake."

"But what about the lifeboats? It wasn't an accident they weren't seaworthy. Wasn't the company found responsible for that?"

Tom shook his head. "The judge concluded they probably would have been seaworthy if the ship hadn't been travelling at such a speed."

"But that was the captain's fault."

"It was, but they couldn't find him guilty when he's not here to defend himself."

Nell flopped into the armchair by the fire. "So no one will be charged for causing the death of thirty-five men?"

"I'm afraid not." Tom clenched his fists. "Which annoyingly means there's no need for the company to pay compensation."

"Nothing?"

"Not a penny." He sat down opposite her. "I don't doubt the captain would have faced trial if he'd survived, but they decided the third mate had acted appropriately, even though he'd misunderstood the captain's instructions. To be honest, I don't think they wanted to lay the blame on men who had lost their lives, but once again it means a company has got away with murder."

"Once again?" Nell's brow furrowed.

"Oh, it's not the first time. Every shipping disaster you hear about can usually be traced back to companies cutting costs, but they always manage to influence the inquest to make it look like they're the innocent party." Tom cracked his knuckles. "I even saw the owner of the *Bohemian* shaking hands and smiling with the assessors when he knew he was off the hook."

"But that's terrible."

Tom grimaced. "It is, but they won't get away with it for much longer. We'll make sure of that."

"What will you do?" Nell sat up straight as Tom tapped the side of his nose.

"I can't say too much, but we're working on something."

"And might that mean I'll get some compensation?"

Tom raised his eyebrows. "I can't promise, but let's see how we get on."

Nell walked him to the door and was about to close it after him when the postman arrived with a late letter for Maria. Nell frowned as she studied it. It looked like George's writing, but they'd had a letter from him only last week. She wandered into the living room and placed it on the mantelpiece. *Strange.*

Maria and Alice arrived home with the girls ten minutes later. As soon as Maria walked into the living room, Nell handed her the letter.

"This has come for you. It looks like George's handwriting."

Maria's eyes narrowed as she picked it up. "I didn't expect anything so soon. Will you read it to me?"

Nell slipped the paper from the envelope and scanned the page. "Oh, it's nothing to worry about. It says he'll be home next week."

Maria stared up at Nell. "That's unusual. He's not due until the end of the month. Does he say why?"

"No. Just that we should be expecting him."

Maria scratched her head. "Well I never, in over twenty years at sea, I've never known him be over a week early."

"I suppose we'd better get a move on with the spring cleaning then. We won't have long."

. . .

After days of scrubbing and polishing, washing and ironing, the muscles in Nell's arms and legs ached. It had been a busy few days, but with the house now looking as good as it had for months, she stood at the living room window watching the rain roll down the glass. It had been like this for most of the week, and judging by the colour of the sky, there would be no let-up today. She sighed as she watched Maria and Alice once again sitting at the table with some material in front of them.

"Will you be doing that all afternoon?"

Maria shrugged as she handed her daughter the cloth that was taking the shape of a waistcoat.

"What else is there to do? I only need to flick a duster around the place tomorrow morning."

"We could play cards ... or dominos?"

Maria tutted. "Then what would we do tonight? Come and sit down. You must have some mending to do ... or finish that bonnet you're knitting for Leah."

Nell's shoulders slumped as she flopped down in a chair beside the fire. "I finished it last night and there's nothing I want to start now." She suddenly brightened. "I know, I could do some baking. Make a cake for Leah's birthday."

"What difference does it make? She's only one; she won't know anything about it. Besides, I already have a couple of cakes in the pantry; any more and they'll go stale before we get round to eating them."

Nell sank back into the chair. "We can't sit around all afternoon."

"In case you haven't noticed, Alice and I are perfectly well occupied. What's got into you?" Maria's tongue stuck out from between her lips as she threaded a needle. "You need to buck your ideas up. Moping about won't do you any good."

"I'm sorry, but I can't carry on as if nothing's happened." She glanced at the clock on the mantelpiece. "It's time the girls were awake. I'll go and see to them."

Through the darkness of the bedroom, two eyes sparkled at her as she peered over the cot. She leaned over and lifted Leah out, holding her tightly and burying her face into the child's neck. It might be her first birthday tomorrow, but what had she got to look forward to? A life without a father, and a mam with no money. *She deserves better than that.*

Nell's tightening grip caused Leah to struggle. "All right, all right. Let me get you changed." She put the child on the floor and washed her down before slipping a clean dress over her head. She was about ready when the front door opened and a man's voice carried up the stairs.

"I'm home!"

George. What's he doing here already?

She left Leah where she was and moved to the landing, but with the living room door closed, she crept down the stairs, praying that the creaky steps wouldn't give her away. When she reached the hall, she put an ear to the door to hear George talking.

"There were a few problems around Suez, so the captain decided not to stop at the last port."

"Well, it makes a change for you to be early. Come and sit down. I was about to put the kettle on."

"Where's Nell?"

"You got my letter? She's upstairs with the girls."

"How is she?" George's voice was sympathetic.

"She's managing but it was a huge shock, as you can imagine."

"It was to me, too. I was glad to be lying on the bunk when I read the letter. Do we know what happened?"

"After a fashion. Tom went to the inquest, so he'll be able to give you all the details. Not that he was happy with the outcome."

George grumbled. "A cover-up was there? I bet that's fired him up."

"What do you mean?"

There was a long pause before George spoke again. "Alice, go and see if that water's boiled. I'm gasping here."

"What do you mean about Tom?"

Nell pressed her ear closer to the door as Maria's voice dropped to a mumble.

"He's missing work more than he's there, and poor Sarah's beside herself with worry."

"That's for him to tell you. Why do you always have to poke your nose in?"

"Because..." Maria lowered her voice further "...with Jack gone, we've lost an income. We won't be able to help them out if he loses his job."

"We wouldn't be helping them out even if Jack was still around. Stop worrying about Tom. He knows what he's doing."

"But I worry about us, too. Jack always paid the rent..."

"I'm aware of that. We'll have to start charging the boys more keep. For now, at least."

"What do you mean?"

"I presume Nell will remarry at some point, so she'll either move out, meaning you won't need to spend so much on food, or her new husband can carry on where Jack left off."

Nell noticed the hesitation in Maria's voice. "I-I don't know about that. She's still in mourning."

"Obviously not straight away, but I imagine she will, soon enough."

"Perhaps. It won't help us this year, though. Have you brought me a decent amount of housekeeping?"

"I can pay the rent for the next six months, if that's what you mean. The boys will have to buy the food."

"Is that how long you'll be away on the next voyage? Six months."

"It's likely to be longer than that, but I can't give you any more money. You'll need to take a lodger if our Billy and Vernon don't earn enough ... or hope that *his nibs* comes home while I'm gone. Have you heard anything from him?"

"Yes." Maria's voice brightened and Nell imagined her hurrying to the mantelpiece to retrieve James' latest letter.

"Here, read it. He's doing very well..."

"I don't need to read it. He made a right fool of me when he took that job. I only want to know whether he'll be home to give you some keep..."

"I'm sure he will."

"Well, as long as he doesn't arrive while I'm here, we'll all get along fine."

"Here we are, the tea's ready..." Alice's voice brought cheer back to the room, but Nell's stomach churned as she crept back up the stairs.

We'll need to take in a lodger? There's not enough room as it is.

Elenor was lying on the floor next to Leah when Nell returned and closed the door, resting her back on it while she caught her breath.

"Mama."

She flinched as Elenor tugged on her skirt.

"Yes, I'm here." She bent down and wrapped her arms around her daughter. "Come on, let's get you dressed and we'll go in the front parlour to play some games."

Elenor's forehead furrowed. "Aunty Ria says no."

Nell bit down on her lip. "This is our house as well as hers, and you're allowed in there if I'm with you. In fact, I'll make some sandwiches and we'll have a picnic."

Elenor went to clap her hands, but the confusion returned to her face. "In the house?"

"Yes." Nell's smile became genuine. "Uncle George is home and it's Leah's birthday, but it's too rainy outside, so we'll have a picnic in the front room."

"A birthday tea?" Elenor's eyes were wide as she finally brought her hands together. "I like them."

"Come along then. Let's be quick."

George was in the back yard when they arrived downstairs, and Nell sat Leah on the floor while Elenor scrambled onto a chair beside Alice at the table.

"That's a good girl. You sit there while I make the picnic."

"Picnic?" The lines across Maria's forehead were deep.

"For Leah's birthday."

"May Alice come?" Elenor hugged her cousin.

"If she wants to." Nell stepped into the kitchen, but Maria was right behind her.

"What are you doing? It's not Leah's birthday until tomorrow."

"I know, but as you said, she'll be none the wiser ... and it can be a celebration for George coming home if you'd like to join us."

"George won't want to go out. Besides, it's pouring with rain."

"That's all right, we're only going to the front parlour."

"The front room?" Maria took a step closer to her sister. "You can't eat in there. It's for special occasions only."

"This *is* a special occasion. A birthday and a homecoming."

"I suppose, but what's brought this on?"

Nell reached for a jar of damson jam. "I should be celebrating Leah's birthday with Jack tomorrow, but as that won't be happening, this is the next best thing." She spread the jam onto four pieces of bread and added a top to each piece, cutting them into small triangles and arranging them on a plate. Next, she helped herself to several fairy cakes, which she placed around the edge.

"I'll be back to pour the tea. If you and George would like to join us, you're more than welcome."

"Thank you, but if you insist on going into the front room, it will give me a chance to speak to George."

"Very well. Send the boys in when they get home, if you like." Nell wandered back to the living room. "Come along, we're ready. Alice, will you bring Leah?"

. . .

They'd eaten the food and emptied the glasses when the front door slammed. *George hasn't forgotten his habit of going to the alehouse every night then.* Nell bent down beside Leah.

"I think it's time you two were in bed. I'll tidy this lot up later." She bent down to pick Leah up. "Elenor, say night night to Alice. We'll see her in the morning."

"What about me? Don't I get a goodnight kiss?" Tears were in Maria's eyes as she appeared at the door.

"I was about to bring them in." Nell watched her sister kiss the top of Elenor's head.

"Night night, lovely. And you." She ran a finger down Leah's cheek. "You get them settled and I'll tidy up in here."

Nell smiled. "Thank you. I won't be long."

Neither of the girls was remotely tired as Nell tucked them into bed, and she sat with them for longer than usual, waiting for them to doze off, before she crept from the room. Maria was by the fire waiting for her when she returned downstairs.

"Have they gone off?"

"Just about, but they weren't keen." She sat opposite Maria and picked up her cup and saucer. "I didn't even welcome George home. When's his next voyage?"

"Not for a couple of weeks."

Nell bit on her lip. "You do realise what that means, don't you?"

"What?"

"He'll be here when James gets home at the end of the week."

Maria's face paled. "Oh goodness, how had I forgotten? We don't want a repeat of what happened the other year."

"No, we don't, although I suppose it was inevitable they'd meet again sooner or later." Nell shuddered. "We've been fortunate that this will only be the second time in eight years."

"George won't have given it a thought either. Perhaps we should keep it like that … for a few days at least."

Nell straightened her back. "What do you mean?"

"Don't tell him about James. We want to keep him in a good mood for as long as we can."

Nell paused. "Is he happy about me being here?"

"Yes. Why wouldn't he be?"

"Because I can't pay my way."

"As if that matters. We've lived together for most of our lives. Why should anything change now?"

Nell groaned. "Because it's not just me any more. I've the girls to support as well."

"Don't be silly. We've always taken care of you, and he knows we need each other for support while he's away."

"You don't need me…"

Maria stared at her. "Haven't you realised that I need you as much as you need me?"

"No." Nell studied her sister. "You're always the one in charge, telling us what to do."

"Only because I'm the eldest, and when we were younger, I had no choice. Do you remember when you first married Jack and you moved into his room on Windsor Street?"

Nell nodded. "How could I forget?"

"I missed you dreadfully. That was why I was so keen for us to move in together. It worked well enough while Jack had the office job, but I thought it was better once he went back to sea."

Nell's brow creased. "You were furious with him."

"I know, but only because he'd broken his promise to stay with you. Once he'd gone, I was happy because I realised I had you to myself again. Is that selfish?"

The side of Nell's cheek creased. "It would have been nice if you'd said something."

Maria sighed. "I'm sorry. I didn't want to have to admit it."

"Well, if it's any consolation, he only went back because I encouraged him."

"You wanted him to go back to sea? Why? You always said you wanted him to stay at home."

"Because he told me I could travel the world with him if he became a master mariner. He wouldn't let me tell you in case you tried to stop me. That was why I was so excited about him coming home this time and being in charge of his own ship. We'd talked about me going away with him for nearly ten years."

"But you had the girls."

Nell held Maria's gaze. "It didn't matter. I was so desperate to go that, had I enjoyed the first voyage, I'd have done anything to stay with him, even if it meant taking them with us."

"But you couldn't do that."

"It's not usual, I'll admit, but someone has to be the first. Why not me?"

"Because it's too much of a risk. What if anything happened to the ship?"

Nell shrugged. "If we'd all been together, it wouldn't

have mattered so much, would it? They wouldn't have been left as orphans."

"Nell! That's a terrible thing to say. What about me … and Rebecca? Our hearts would have been broken."

"I'm sorry." Nell fidgeted with her teaspoon. "At least you don't need to worry about it now. We won't be going anywhere."

CHAPTER EIGHT

George was still at the breakfast table when Nell arrived downstairs the following morning. He nodded at her as she sat Leah on the floor and helped Elenor onto a chair.

"I was sorry to hear about Jack. I spoke to Tom last night and it sounds like it should never have happened."

Nell sat down and poured a cup of tea. "No, it shouldn't, but there's no point crying. It won't change anything."

"That's not what Tom thinks."

Nell's eyes narrowed. "Why, what's he been saying?"

"Nothing, but he's not happy about workers being treated so badly while company owners get away with murder. Literally, in some instances."

"But that's the way things are. What can he do about it?"

"We'll see." George pushed himself up from the table and reached into his jacket pocket to pull out an envelope.

"I need to go, but Tom asked me to give you this." He glanced over his shoulder as Maria burst through the back door into the kitchen. "I don't know what it's about, but he told me not to mention it in front of her."

Nell pushed the letter into her apron pocket as Maria joined them.

"Ah, you're here. I was beginning to wonder where you'd got to."

"I didn't think there was any rush. Is it still raining?"

"No, it's stopped. I've pegged out some washing. It would be nice if it dried before it starts again."

"Where's Ally?" Elenor pushed her plate away as she climbed down from her chair.

"She'll be here in a minute. You sit back down." Maria lifted Elenor back onto her seat as she sat beside her. "Would you like her to take you out later?"

Elenor nodded, but Nell interrupted. "Actually, if it's not raining, I've arranged to take them to the park with Rebecca. We're meeting Mrs Blackmore, and I thought you and Alice would be sewing."

"We will. It was only an idea." Maria looked over to George. "What will you do today?"

"I'm meeting some of the lads in town to see what's going on." He studied the clock. "In fact, I need to be going. I'll see you later."

Nell helped herself to a piece of bread as Maria fussed about the table. "You carry on, I'll catch up with you."

"There's no rush. I could do with another cup of tea."

Nell fingered the envelope in her pocket. "What about Alice? Doesn't she need any help?"

"My'll help her." Elenor jumped down from her seat, but Nell caught her arm.

"Come and sit down. You need a coat on to go outside."

"No." Elenor struggled. "I want to go."

"Here, let me take her." Maria stood up and took Elenor's hand. "Let's get you wrapped up."

Nell's heart pounded as she waited for Maria to go outside, and as soon as the door shut, she retrieved the envelope. Her brow creased as she read the envelope. *It's addressed to Sarah.* Her fingers trembled as she pulled out the letter, but no sooner had she straightened out the paper, than the back door opened and Maria returned.

"They'll be back shortly. Alice is nearly done."

"That's good." Nell pushed the letter under the table. "I suppose we'd better tidy up if Alice wants to do her sewing."

"There's no rush. She can have a minute to sit down before she starts."

Nell stared at her sister. "You're in a good mood this morning."

The corners of Maria's lips curled upwards. "No more than usual."

Nell snorted. "You could have fooled me. Is it anything to do with George being home?"

"He's in such a good mood. Don't you think it's nice? I hope we can keep it like that."

Nell raised an eyebrow. "Have you decided when you'll tell him about James?"

"No." Maria fidgeted with the teaspoon on her saucer. "I wondered if it might be better to keep them apart. Do you think Rebecca will let James stay over there so they needn't see each other?"

"I'm not sure that's a good idea. What will James think if you tell him he can't come home … especially if you want some money off him for his keep?"

Maria groaned. "I hadn't thought of that, although he may be pleased. He won't want to be under the same roof as his dad, but if he knows it's only once, he should understand."

"Perhaps." Nell patted her sister on the hand. "I'll tell you what, I'll speak to Rebecca later. She'll have to ask Mr Grayson anyway. You know what he's like."

Maria finally smiled. "Would you mind? I can't bear the thought of the two of them being here together."

Rebecca was sitting by the fire knitting when Nell arrived, and once the children were playing with a rag doll in front of the fire, she took the seat opposite her.

"You're tidied up quickly."

"Hugh didn't come home for dinner, so I only had me and Florrie to take care of. What's up with you? You don't look very pleased. Is it because George is home?"

"Oh, you know."

"I saw him going out last night. I didn't think he was due back yet."

"He wasn't. For the first time I can remember, he was early, but…" Nell took a deep breath "…it's going to coincide with James being home."

"Oh goodness." Rebecca let her knitting fall onto her lap. "Have you told George?"

"Not yet and Maria wants to keep it that way. Not that I blame her."

"Don't you think George will have calmed down by now?"

Nell shrugged. "He may have done. The problem is, after what happened last time they met, Maria's not keen to risk it."

"What will you do?"

Nell studied her sister. "Do you think Mr Grayson would let James stay here?"

"Here?" Rebecca's voice squeaked. "Well, I'm not sure..."

"He'll only be home for three or four days ... and he's very tidy. It must come with the job."

"Still ... you know what he's like. He likes his privacy."

"He knows James well enough, though. Will you at least ask him?"

Rebecca folded up her knitting and put it back in her bag. "I suppose so, but I can't promise."

"No, I understand. The thing is, Maria and George have both been in a good mood since he got back, but it won't last if James is with us."

"Very well." Rebecca pushed herself up from the chair. "Let me put the kettle on before we go out."

Nell stayed where she was and took the letter out of her pocket while she waited for Rebecca to return. "I got this letter this morning."

"Who's it from?"

Nell smoothed it out on her knee. "You might want to

sit down. George gave it to me after Sarah had passed it to Tom."

"That sounds intriguing."

"It is."

Rebecca took the seat opposite.

"It's from Jane."

"Jane!" Rebecca's hands flew to her cheeks. "What on earth...? Why did he give it to you?"

"Because it was written for me although it was addressed to Sarah. Do you think Sarah could have been in touch with her all these years?"

Rebecca blew out through her lips. "They were always close. What does she want?"

"She says it's to send her condolences. Sarah must have told her about Jack and she felt she had to say something."

"Sarah's a dark horse. What did Maria say?"

Nell grimaced. "George told me not to tell her. It took me about two hours to get around to reading it this morning, because she wouldn't leave me alone."

"I can't believe you've heard from her after all this time." Rebecca shook her head. "Will you reply?"

"Do you think I should? Maria will be furious if she finds out."

"I don't know. What would you say?"

Nell fidgeted with the corner of the paper. "I'd probably ask what she's been doing since she left Toxteth. It must have taken a lot for her to write."

"I suppose so." Rebecca bit her lip. "Did she say anything to suggest she's still married? Or that she's been widowed? Maybe things will be different if she's on her own..."

"She doesn't say, which makes me think he's still alive. I'm sure she'd have mentioned it if he wasn't."

"You're right. What about children? How many does she have?"

Nell frowned. "She only mentions the daughter she had when she still lived around here."

"I bet she knows everything about us if Sarah's been writing for all these years. She'll have told her everything. We're at a huge disadvantage. We've no idea what happened to her after she left."

"No, but Sarah will. I also get the feeling Jane would like to come back."

"Why? What's she said?"

Nell handed Rebecca the letter. "Read the last line."

"Let me see. '*Longing to see you all again. Your loving sister, Jane.*'" Rebecca's head jerked up. "She can't turn up unannounced."

"It wouldn't be unannounced though, would it? She'd arrange it with Sarah. In fact, she'd probably stay with them when she arrived."

"Surely Tom wouldn't let her ... or do you think he's known all along?"

"I'm guessing he must have. He also must be happy about it, given he passed the letter to George."

Rebecca put her hands to her face. "If she comes back, it will make the disagreement between George and James seem petty."

"I know." Nell stared at the rug. "I need to pay Sarah a visit and find out where Jane is, and why she's suddenly written."

"That won't be an easy conversation, given how friendly Sarah is with Maria."

"Maybe not, but I need to find out what she's up to. Despite Jack's accident, I don't believe this letter was purely to send condolences."

"Don't you?" Rebecca twisted her wedding ring. "Whatever it is, let's hope she doesn't want to come home."

CHAPTER NINE

Alice was tidying her threads on the living room table when Nell returned home. She wasn't sure if Elenor was helping or hindering, but she looked happy as she collected up the bobbins.

"You look busy."

"We have been." Alice took the cotton from Elenor. "Mam's gone out the back. She won't be a minute."

Nell looked at the garment on the table. "How are you getting on? Is it nearly finished?"

"I hope so. I've promised to deliver it on Friday and don't want to be late. I'm expecting a few more orders if they like what I've done." Alice held up the waistcoat. "What do you think?"

"I'm sure they'll be thrilled. You'll be able to look after yourself if you carry on like that." Nell paused as the back door opened and Maria joined them.

"Don't go giving her ideas. She'll be looking after us, not herself."

Nell rolled her eyes at her niece. "There's still no harm

in her putting a few shillings away when she can. If she ends up like me, she'll be glad of it."

Alice chuckled. "I can always go back to making waistcoats again if I need to ... if I even stop making them at all."

Nell put a hand on her shoulder. "Trust me, once you have a few kiddies it becomes a lot more difficult, especially if you need to provide for yourself. Having a little something tucked away won't do you any harm."

"I suppose so. I'll try."

"Good girl." Nell was about to follow Maria to the kitchen when Billy arrived home.

"My, is it that time already? Are you on your own?"

"I saw Dad and Vernon going to the alehouse, but I wanted to check on James' ship. He's due home on Friday."

"Friday!" Nell hesitated as Maria's mouth dropped open.

"What's wrong with that?" Billy asked. "We knew he was due back."

"We didn't think it would be until the beginning of next week." Maria picked up the cushions on the chairs and shook them. "Let me get the tea on."

"What's the matter?" Billy's brow furrowed. "I thought you'd be pleased."

"I am pleased, but..." Maria sighed. "You didn't say anything to your dad, did you?"

"No, why?"

"Because he needn't know." She headed to the kitchen but returned to set the table.

"What do you mean? Of course he does."

"Not yet, he doesn't. Now, let me get this food on the table."

Nell raised an eyebrow at her sister. "What's the hurry? You only need to carry the bread and a pan through."

"I want it to be ready for when they get home ... but yes, you're right, I'll wait. I know, I'll bring the bread and keep the scouse on the heat." She bustled back to the kitchen. "I'm not thinking straight."

"Because James is coming home?" Nell placed the butter and a jar of jam on the table.

"No, not at all. Besides, we don't know for sure that he will be here on Friday. He may be delayed."

"He won't be delayed until George goes back, if that's what you're thinking..." Nell raised an eyebrow at her sister.

"I know that, but if they are delayed, he may not bother coming home if he has to turn around and go straight back out again."

"Don't be silly. When did that ever happen...?" Nell shook her head but paused when the front door opened and George appeared in the living room with Vernon.

"That was well timed." Nell smiled. "Have you had a good day?"

"Not bad." George strode across the room and sat in his usual chair at the head of the table; Vernon took the seat to his right-hand side. "Come on, Billy, get a move on."

"I'm coming." Billy took his place beside Vernon and looked across to George. "Have you done much today?"

"I've been job-hunting."

"Job-hunting!" Maria looked as if she was about to drop the pan and hurried to place it on the table. "What do you mean? Aren't you going back to sea?"

"I've not decided yet. I've heard that some of the blokes I used to work with have had a pay rise, and they're earning almost as much as me now. It hardly seems worth going away any more."

"But you can't do that."

George glared at her. "Why not?"

"Well, because ... I'm sure the company will be expecting you back for the next voyage. You can't let them down."

"Someone may have been spinning a yarn." Billy helped himself to a piece of bread. "There've been no pay rises at our place."

"Not that you know about, but I'll wager there are for someone like me." George stared at Vernon. "Are there any jobs going at the shipyard?"

Vernon shrugged. "Not that I've heard."

"Hmm, I'll walk up there with you in the morning and see what I can find out."

Vernon grinned. "If you get a better-paid job, will you get me one, too?"

"You wait your turn." George turned his attention to the food Maria had placed in front of him. "You've not finished your apprenticeship yet."

Billy looked up from his plate. "I have and they still won't pay me any more money. Four barrels I made today, too."

"Perhaps you should go to sea then." George reached over for a slice of bread. "There's always work for a cooper on the long voyages."

"No!" Maria's face was scarlet, and she placed a hand to her chest. "I-I'm sorry, I-I don't think that's a good idea."

"I don't see why not. I've earned a good living over the years, so why can't Billy?" George didn't smile as he stabbed a piece of meat.

"No, I'm sorry. Let me add some more water to the teapot." Maria scrambled to her feet as George spoke to Billy.

"I saw you at the shipping office after you left us. Were you looking at the timetable?"

"Erm ... yes."

"Your brother's due home, then, is he?"

"How did you know?" Billy glanced towards the kitchen, but there was no sign of Maria.

"Why else would you be looking?"

"No reason." Billy coughed to clear his throat. "He's due back at the end of the week. Friday, they reckon."

"That trip went quickly." Vernon reached for the last piece of bread.

George snorted. "He's only been to New York and back. It's hardly worth the effort."

"He's doing all right out of it, though. He earns more money than me." Billy's cheeks flushed as George glared at him.

"Don't even think it's an option for you. It's bad enough having one son doing a job like that, let alone two."

Maria returned to the table with the teapot and a plate of sweet buns. "Are you talking about James?" Her voice squeaked.

"Who else?"

"I'm sure he works hard. It's just not a job you'd ever do."

"Damn right I wouldn't, and neither would he if I had

anything to do with it." George banged a hand on the table. "He should get a proper job like the rest of us."

Nell waited until everyone had helped themselves to a bun and reached over for the last one. "I always enjoy hearing James' tales of the first-class passengers. It's like being transported to another world."

"And that's where they should stay. There's no place for them in these parts, and I won't have them being discussed around this table."

"Oh, I'm sorry." Nell's cheeks burned as she focussed on her plate.

"He's nothing but a storyteller. You can't believe a word he says." Vernon smirked at his dad. "Dad goes to a lot of places and you don't hear *him* telling tales."

"I'm sure James doesn't make it up, though. Jack used to tell me similar stories."

"That was different. He had a respectable job." George pushed himself up from the table. "If you'll excuse me, I'll see you ladies in the morning." He motioned to Billy and Vernon. "Are you coming?"

"I'm ready." Vernon finished the last of his tea and jumped up, but Billy stayed where he was.

"Not tonight, if you don't mind. I'll see you later."

Nell waited until the front door closed. "Alice, would you mind taking Elenor and Leah up to bed for me? I'd like a quick word with your mam."

Elenor clapped her hands. "Can we have a story?"

"If you're quick. I'll be up shortly."

Maria stood up to clear the table as Nell kissed her daughters goodnight. "What do you want to speak to me about that won't wait?"

"You don't seem your usual self. Is everything all right?"

"It's nothing, but I don't want George suggesting Billy go to sea."

Billy moved from the table and took a seat by the fireplace. "You've no need to worry about me. I'm not going anywhere ... especially not on a ship."

"Maybe not, but I don't want him giving you ideas. I don't think any of you realise how much I worry when your dad and James are away at sea, especially after what happened to Jack."

"You must be pleased about George looking for a new job then." Nell raised an eyebrow at Maria.

"I should be, but I don't know. He mentioned yesterday that he'd like to stay at home, but I'd no idea he meant immediately."

Billy shrugged. "I suppose he's not as young as he was, so life at sea may be getting too much for him."

"You may be right, but it will bring him and James into more regular contact, which scares the life out of me."

"I wouldn't be worrying about that. They're old enough to sort themselves out." Billy stared at his mother. "Is that why you didn't want me to mention that he'll be home this week?"

Maria sighed. "I was hoping James would have been and gone before your dad got home, but with him being early..."

Nell sat back in her chair. "I mentioned it to Rebecca earlier, but the way Mr Grayson is, she wasn't keen on James staying over there. She said she'd ask, though."

"You want to throw James out?" Billy's eyes were wide.

"I don't want to throw him anywhere, but I thought it would be for the best if he stayed over the road this once."

Billy blew out his cheeks. "I can't see James agreeing to that. If you ask me, you need the two of them to sit down and talk to each other."

The colour left Maria's cheeks. "Don't you remember the last time they were both home together?"

"Not really, although I do remember being sent to my room a lot."

"There was good reason for that. It was the first time they'd met since James had left his apprenticeship and disappeared. We hadn't told your dad at the time, but when we did, he was furious."

Billy grimaced. "I can imagine. It was a few years ago though, and he seems to be in a good enough mood this week. Even when I mentioned that James would be home on Friday, he didn't seem too concerned."

Maria sat down with them. "That's because he's not seen him. Give them five minutes together in the same room and I fear they'll be at each other's throats."

CHAPTER TEN

The sound of the clock ticking on the mantelpiece was usually something Nell paid no attention to, but today was different. James should have been home hours ago, but there was still no sign of him.

Maria bustled into the living room from her place by the front window. "What's happened to him? If he was on the ship, he really should be here by now."

"He can't be far away." Nell straightened the cushions on the chairs by the fire. "We'd have heard by now if there'd been an..." She paused as she remembered the day she'd received the telegram. "I'm sure he'll be fine; he must have been delayed."

"But what if something's happened? This isn't like him."

"There must be a perfectly simple explanation." Nell patted the back of a chair. "Come and sit down."

Maria had no sooner taken a seat than the click of the front door had her on her feet again. She hurried to the hall, but within seconds, her shoulders slumped. "Oh, it's you."

"That's nice." Alice joined them with Elenor and Leah. "Are you still waiting for James?"

"Yes, I thought you were him."

"That's strange. He's usually here by now."

"We know that, thank you." Maria disappeared into the front room. "I've a mind to go down to the dock and see what's going on. This waiting's no good for my nerves."

Nell followed her sister to the front parlour. "Why don't I put the kettle on and calm us all down? It might bring James home too." When she got no reply, Nell wandered to the kitchen. Once the kettle was on the stove, she took her time arranging the milk jug and sugar bowl on a tray with the cups and saucers. *Surely there's not been an accident. We'd have heard...* Her stomach churned. *Please, God, don't do this to us again.*

She carried the tray to the table, where Maria had taken a seat with Alice and Elenor.

"Here we are. Let's get a cup of this down us." She stirred an extra spoon of sugar into everyone's tea, but hadn't sat down before the front door opened. Maria almost dropped her cup in her hurry to put it back on the table, but she hadn't got to the door when James walked in, closely followed by Tom.

"Where on earth have you been?" Maria stood with her hands on her hips. "I've been worried sick!"

"I'm sorry. We had a passenger who delayed us for a couple of hours and then Uncle Tom took me for a pint, which turned into two."

"You!" Maria glared at her brother. "Have you any idea how worried I've been?"

"Calm down, woman." Tom's voice was measured but his eyes were cold. "I had to tell him about Jack."

Maria's hand flew to her mouth. "I'd forgotten you wouldn't have heard, but it was because of Jack I was so worried."

"And I'm so sorry, Aunty Nell. Really, I am." James put an arm around Nell's shoulders and rested his head on hers. "You know how much we got along."

"You and everyone else." She leaned into his chest as Maria continued to badger Tom.

"Shouldn't you be at work?"

"I wanted to speak to him about some business, too, and so this morning seemed as good a time as any."

"What do you mean?"

"Never you mind." Tom tapped the side of his nose. "Now, is there a cup of tea going?"

"Not for you." Maria made a point of putting milk into one extra cup, but Nell wandered to the kitchen for another.

"Yes, there is. I'll put the kettle on again. Come and sit down." Nell took hold of James' arm. "Did you have a good trip?"

James stared down at her. "I did. I'll tell you all about it later."

Nell's chin trembled. "Hopefully, it will cheer me up."

Maria pushed her tea towards her son. "You have this. How long are you home for this time?"

"Only two full days. I need to be back on board by ten o'clock on Tuesday morning."

Maria turned to Tom. "Did you tell him about George?"

"I thought I'd leave that to you. I take it he isn't here."

James's pale features became ashen. "What's going on?"

"Dad's home." Maria's voice was a pitch higher than normal. "Thankfully, he's been in a good mood since he arrived, and he knows you're due back today, but ... we wondered if it would be better if you didn't stay here."

"Where do you want me to go?" James swivelled to face Nell. "Am I being kicked out?"

"No, not at all, but we thought it may be better if you stayed with Aunty Rebecca... Not that you have to if you don't want to."

"What about Mr Grayson?"

Nell struggled to control her voice. "She's going to ask him."

"So you don't even know if I can stay there? What if he says no?" He scowled at Maria. "You don't want me here, do you? I'll tell you what, if you do my washing this afternoon, I'll go straight back to the ship. It will clearly be for the best."

"Don't talk nonsense." Maria was on her feet. "Nell, tell him."

"Me!"

James walked to the door. "Don't bring Aunty Nell into it. This was your idea, wasn't it?"

"Don't be like that." Maria stepped around the table and held the chair for James. "Come and sit down."

His eyes narrowed as he retook his seat.

"The thing is, your dad's talking about getting a land-based job."

"What!" James gasped. "He's not going away again?"

"He's not decided, but there's a good chance he won't." Nell rested a hand on his. "If that's the case, it may be as well to try and put your differences behind you. Staying with Aunty Rebecca may help while you talk."

"I don't have any differences; he's the one with the problem."

"Maybe, but you can't blame him for being upset when you took the job without a word to anyone, especially your old master."

"That was only because he'd have tried to stop me. All I wanted was to do something of my choosing."

"All right, calm down." Tom put a hand on his nephew's shoulder to keep him in his seat. "He'll almost certainly go away again next month. He's only making enquiries at the moment."

"You seem to know a lot about it." Maria's tone was brusque, but Tom shrugged.

"We spoke about it in the alehouse the other night, and I gave him the names of a few men to talk to. I'm not convinced he's serious about staying, though."

"How can you be so sure?"

Tom once again tapped the side of his nose. "You'll have to trust me."

Tom slammed the front door behind him as Maria picked up James' sea bag and headed to the wash house.

"I'll go and get this started. Alice, you can come and help."

Alice groaned and reached for Elenor's hand. "Let's go and play catch."

Nell watched them leave. "Poor Alice, we shouldn't

have conversations like that in front of her. We were just so relieved to see you…"

"She's a right to know what Dad's like."

"But I worry she's too young. I'll tell you what, why don't we visit Aunty Rebecca and make sure she's got a bed ready for you?"

James stared at the table. "I don't think so. Mam and Uncle Tom are right. I need to speak to Dad, especially if he's going to be here every time I come home. I can't avoid him forever."

"All right, I'll go on my own then." Nell stood up, but she hadn't reached the living room door when she stopped and turned back. "Dad's here." Her voice was no more than a whisper, but George still heard her.

"Yes, I'm here."

James jumped to his feet. "Dad!"

"James." George scowled as Nell hovered between the two of them.

"Let me top up this teapot." She scurried to the kitchen but stopped as soon as she was through the door, her heart pounding.

"I didn't think you were due back until next week." James kept his voice level.

"Until after you'd gone, you mean. Unfortunately for you, we didn't stop at Suez and it took a week off the voyage."

"I see."

There was a long pause that jolted Nell into filling the kettle, but James kept his eyes fixed on the table.

"Mam tells me you're thinking of getting a new job."

"Not yet. I'd been told I could make as much money on land as at sea, but whoever'd heard that, was wrong."

"That's a shame ... if that's what you want to do."

"And do you still want to do this damn stupid job of yours?"

James finally straightened his back and raised his head. "Yes, I do. I enjoy it."

"Good money, is it?"

"I can't complain."

"In that case, you can damn well pay me back the money it cost for the apprenticeship you didn't finish." George's voice bellowed around the room. "And apologise to your old master for walking out on him. I saw him this morning and I didn't know where to put myself."

"Pay you back?" James' voice squeaked. "I can't afford that."

"You should have thought of that before you sloped off to sea."

"But I never wanted to be a carpenter in the first place. You forced me into it."

"I was trying to do the best for you. I even got the master to agree to you living here rather than with him."

"That was to save you money."

"And it's as well it did. The whole performance still cost me a fortune."

James perched on the edge of a chair. "I don't earn that much."

"Well, you can give me ten shillings a month, on top of your normal rent, until the end of next year and we'll call it quits. The extra money can go towards your mam's housekeeping. If she wants us to be civil to each other, then this is a good start ... and I don't want to hear a word about the job."

The sound of the lid rattling on the kettle brought Nell back to her senses. *Tea. Yes.* She hurried to pour the water over the tea leaves already in the pot, but hesitated as she started back towards the living room. It was all unusually quiet. She took a deep breath and kept walking.

"Here we are. I'll bring some cakes in as well. Or do you want something else? I don't suppose you've eaten since you got off the ship."

James' cheeks coloured. "Cake will be fine. I had a pie in the alehouse. Thank you."

"Right, good. Let me get it then. George, would you like anything else?"

"Some peace and quiet would be nice."

Nell hesitated. "Right-o. Let me see to James and I'll go and help Maria."

CHAPTER ELEVEN

Tea was over, but Nell waited for the front door to close behind George before standing up to clear the table. "Are you all staying in tonight?" She looked at each of her nephews.

Vernon shook his head. "We'll follow Dad to the alehouse later, or at least I will."

"I will as well, but we wanted to talk to James while Dad's not here." Billy smiled at his brother. "Why can't he even listen to talk of the passenger ships?"

"Don't start that." Maria reached for the cake stand. "You should be glad he can sit at the same table as James; don't get ahead of yourself. Go and sit by the fire while we finish off here."

Nell hurried back from the kitchen. "Don't start your tales yet. It won't take us long to get this lot tidied up."

"I won't, but I still don't know why he's so angry about me being a steward, other than the fact that I gave up my apprenticeship. It's a perfectly respectable job and the shipping companies would be in a right mess if everyone had his attitude."

Billy's brow furrowed. "Are many of the lads on the ship local?"

James frowned. "Not that many, now I think about it."

"I wonder if it's a Liverpool thing then. Perhaps we're brought up to do the heavy lifting and stewards are men from further afield who may otherwise be butlers. You know, those who might work in a stately home."

"It could be, although…" James waited as Nell walked back into the room. "You'll never guess what. On the last voyage, we had a woman working as a stewardess."

"A woman?" Billy and Vernon spoke together as they stared at their brother.

James nodded. "I've come across them working on ships when we've been to Australia, but never on the transatlantic routes. Mrs Birch her name is."

"That's shocking." Maria joined Nell by the fire. "A ship's no place for a woman."

"It's not as bad as it seems. I spoke to her, and the company are making quite a thing of it, because it means the passengers won't have to take a maid with them."

Maria rolled her shoulders. "I can't see Lord and Lady Muck wanting to swap a ladies' maid for a stewardess, especially not if there's only one of them."

"Well, no, the real toffs won't, but there are a lot who pretend they have more money than they do, and it's to encourage them to travel first class. Quite a good ruse really."

"It might be for the company, but what about the poor

women who have to work? For a kick-off, where did this Mrs Birch sleep with all those men?"

"She had her own room near the first-class cabins with the other ladies' maids. She was well away from the stewards."

"It's still not right, if you ask me."

"Mam, she was fine." James rolled his eyes at Nell, but Maria kept talking.

"It doesn't sound fine. Who did she talk to?"

"The passengers, for one, and the ladies' maids when they weren't attending to their mistresses. She spoke to a few of the stewards, too. That's how I heard the company plan to take more of them on. They want to put some into steerage class as well, to protect any single women travelling."

Maria shook her head. "I don't know what the world's coming to."

"It's nothing to worry about. Companies have realised that ladies would prefer a stewardess rather than a steward, and so they think hiring more will encourage them to travel on our ships."

"At least they'll be able to keep each other company." Nell gazed into the fire. "It might be quite nice."

"Nice! What are you talking about?" Maria glared at Nell, causing her to look up.

"Think about it. If I was crossing the Atlantic, I'd like to have a maid."

"I'd like to have a maid around here, never mind on a ship." Maria stood up to throw more coal onto the fire. "Besides, if the stewardesses are looking after the women passengers, who's looking after them?"

"Mam, calm down. At the moment, she reports to the ship's doctor, but when there are more, they'll report to one of the officers. In time, they may report to one of the stewards."

"I don't think it's right," Vernon said. "Women should be at home. She can't be married."

James shrugged. "I didn't ask."

"Well, if she is, she shouldn't be working on a ship, and if she isn't, then I agree with Mam: she'll be no use as a chaperone. They should hire an old maid for that."

Nell raised her face from the fire. "That's not a nice thing to say."

"But it's true. If a stewardess needs protecting from the male passengers and crew, she needs to be someone nobody would bother with."

"Vernon! We won't have any talk like that." Maria scowled as she retook her seat. "Quite frankly, if women must go on these ships, they should be with their husbands or fathers. They should be the ones responsible for them. As it is, they're putting another woman at risk because of their selfishness."

James shook his head. "You've got a lot to learn, Mam. Times are changing. They're so keen to keep women safe, they're segregating most ships so that even husbands and wives don't see each other for most of the voyage, unless they're in first class, obviously. Single women are being encouraged to travel."

"That's even more ridiculous."

"Why are you so against it?" Nell's brow creased. "You look after yourself while George is away, and I'll be looking after myself from now on. We don't always need a man to watch over us."

"So you'll be happy for your daughters to travel on their own one day, will you? I can tell you now, Alice will be doing no such thing."

Alice sat with them at the table, but she slumped back in her chair. "Why not? I'd like to see the world, too."

"Then you'd better find a husband with enough money to take you."

Billy squeezed her hand. "And if not, we'll go together one day. I'll take care of you."

Maria's mouth fell open. "Am I the only one who has no intention of going on one of these ships? Dad would be furious if he could hear you all."

"I don't." Vernon pushed himself up from the chair. "I'm off to the alehouse. Anyone coming?"

James got to his feet. "I think I will. I reckon I've caused enough excitement around here for one evening."

James was already at the table when Nell arrived for breakfast the following morning.

"You're down early. Couldn't you sleep?"

James shook his head. "Billy and Vernon make such a noise getting out of bed, I thought I may as well join them down here. You've only just missed them."

Nell chuckled. "Yes, I heard them go. As I do most mornings." She poured herself a cup of tea.

"Ah, here you are." Maria carried in some fresh bread. "I was about to come looking for you. We need to get this laundry started."

"It's not seven o'clock yet."

Maria shook her head. "Don't you know me by now? I want to get it all pegged out this morning so I can go out later."

Nell took a bite of bread. "Where are you going?"

"Only to see Sarah."

"Oh."

Maria stopped tidying the table. "What's the matter? Don't you want me to go?"

"It's not that. I thought you'd be helping Alice with that new order she got."

"She needs to learn to start doing it herself. I haven't time to sit around here every afternoon."

"Can't you help her, Aunty Nell?"

Nell couldn't miss the twinkle in James' eyes and tapped him on the arm. "Less of your cheek. You know what I think of sewing."

He laughed. "Perhaps you'd come for a walk with me then? I can tell you some tales from the last trip."

A smile crept across Nell's lips. "Yes, I'd like that."

Nell pushed the pram as she walked beside James towards the dock road. The mild weather had brought out the crowds, and as they reached the customs house, they had to weave between the horse-drawn carriages to cross the road. Once they reached the far side, they headed towards the landing stage where James found a seat overlooking the river.

"It's nice to see a bit of blue sky for a change." She manoeuvred the pram to shield Leah from the sun's rays then lifted Elenor from the seat positioned over the baby's feet and sat her on the bench. "What's the weather like in New York?"

"It depends on the time of year. It can be lovely in the summer, but there's a reason we don't sail in December. In my opinion, we shouldn't go in January either. It's much colder then. Not that we have to go outside much. The staterooms run the length of the ship, so we only need to venture out if one of the passengers wants to take the air. Which they rarely do in January."

Nell rested her hands on her lap as she gazed across the river. "It sounds wonderful. Do you think they'd ever let visitors on the ship to have a look round? I'd love to see them."

James laughed. "I doubt it, not for the general public anyway. I could ask if they'd let me show you around though, if you like?"

"Could you do that?" Nell beamed at him.

"I don't see why not. The worst they can say is no."

"When would you ask?" Her eyes ran along the rows of ships berthed in the docks. "Is the ship nearby?"

He laughed. "I can't do it today. I'll need to find the captain in a good mood. Leave it with me and I'll see if I can speak to him on the next voyage."

"Ooh, that would be smashing." She linked her arm through his and rested her head on his shoulder. "Please find him when he's in a good mood."

They sat for longer than Nell realised, and as some nearby church bells struck three o'clock, she jumped to her feet. "We'd better go. I wanted to call on your Aunty Sarah on the way home, and I'll have to help make tea." She called to Elenor, who was running along a small stretch of footpath, and lifted her onto the pram.

"What do you want to see Aunty Sarah for?"

"Oh, no reason, other than I've not seen her for a while."

James gave her a sideways glance. "Why the urgency for today?"

Nell let out a deep sigh. "If you must know, I want to have a word with her about your Uncle Tom."

"Not you as well. I thought Mam did enough of that."

"She does, but your mam's been known to exaggerate, so I want to check if he is skipping work as much as she says. That's why I'd rather speak to Aunty Sarah on her own."

"I don't think he does miss work, certainly not as much as Mam would have you believe, but even if he does, why should you and Mam get involved? It's up to him what he does."

"Maybe, but I'd like to check, and to make sure Aunty Sarah's all right." Nell bit down on her lip as James stayed silent. "At least this way, I'll be able to call without your mam noticing."

"Aunty Sarah will probably tell her."

I doubt it. "That's all right, I'll have spoken to her by then."

The sun disappeared behind the houses as they turned into Windsor Street, and Nell adjusted the collar of her cloak against the breeze.

"It's going to be cold tonight."

"We've not far to go. I'll walk you to the house and then

go to the alehouse." James grinned down at her. "That way Mam won't wonder what I've done with you."

"You're good to me."

They stopped when they reached Sarah's front door.

"Shall I come back for you?"

"No, there's no need, but don't get home ahead of me. An hour should be plenty." As he disappeared around the corner, Nell knocked on the front door and let herself in. "It's only me. May I come in?"

Sarah appeared in the hall as Nell lifted the girls from the pram.

"I had a feeling you'd call. Come in."

Sarah's daughters were all in the living room when Nell ushered Elenor inside and sat Leah on the floor. The younger two took no time welcoming their cousins, but the eldest, Ada, stayed at the table with her sewing.

Satisfied they were settled, Nell gestured towards the front room. "Do you mind if we go next door?"

"If we must. Ada, keep your eye on everyone." Sarah strolled to the hall and pushed open the door to the front room. The sun had long since disappeared from the room, and with no fire, Nell shivered as she took a seat by the empty hearth. "I'll keep this brief."

"I presume you've come about the letter."

Nell nodded. "I've so many questions, I thought it was best to speak to you. Have you been in touch with her all these years?"

Sarah took the seat opposite. "What do you expect? She was my best friend. I couldn't turn my back on her. You may not remember, but she was the reason I met Tom."

"Then why didn't you defend her when Maria found out about her marrying Mr Read?"

Sarah sank back in the chair. "Don't think I didn't want to, but we hoped Maria would mellow."

"Really?"

Sarah snorted. "It seems naïve now, but yes, we thought that once she got to know him better, she'd understand. He really is a nice man."

Nell's brow creased. "Did Maria ever meet him?"

"Oh, yes, in those early days when he and Jane were walking out together. I think she liked him too until she found out about the marriage."

"Can you blame her when Jane hadn't told anyone? How did you expect Maria to feel, turning up at the church to find her sister married? She hadn't even had any banns read." Nell sat up straight in her chair as Sarah studied her.

"I don't suppose you remember much about it. How old would you have been? Ten? Twelve?"

"Twelve. I may not have been old enough to understand all the ins and outs, but I *was* old enough to know how angry Maria was. How could Jane have done that to her?"

"Because she had no choice." Sarah raised her hands and let them fall back onto her lap. "She knew Maria would raise an objection to the marriage if they'd had the banns read."

"Of course she would. She was marrying a Catholic!"

"But that doesn't make him a bad man. He allowed Betty to be baptised into the Church of England, hoping it would redeem him. He even thought of turning himself shortly after, but with everything else that was happening, he changed his mind."

Nell's shoulders slumped. "Does Maria know that?"

Sarah shook her head. "I doubt it. She blamed Jane for what happened and there was no talking to her. That was when they decided it would be better if they moved away."

"Why didn't you speak up once everything had died down?"

Sarah's expression glazed over. "That's something I ask myself every time I get a letter from her. Maybe she wouldn't have gone if I had, but the truth was that once Patrick made up his mind to go, there didn't seem any point. I wanted to stay in Maria's good books."

Nell remained silent while Sarah wiped her eyes with her handkerchief. "Where's she been all these years?"

"In Ireland. Belfast to be precise."

"And is Mr Read still with her?"

Sarah nodded. "He is, and they have two sons now as well. Matthew and John."

"So we've two nephews who are Catholic?" Nell put her head in her hands. "It gets worse."

"No, they're not. Jane didn't want them brought up as Catholics, but the family wouldn't have them baptised into the Church of Ireland, and so they've not been baptised at all."

Nell's head shot up. "And that's supposed to make it better?"

"What else could she do?" Sarah paused. "The thing is, they're at an age where they really should be baptised. Before they're ready for confirmation."

"How old are they?"

"Eight and six at the moment."

Nell's forehead creased. "But Betty must be about seventeen."

"Jane had a lot of *problems* when they first moved, and she didn't think she'd have another child. When Matthew was born, it was like a miracle. That's why she wants to come back…"

Nell stared at Sarah, her brow creasing as she struggled to understand. "But she can't come back just for a baptism… She'd need to live here."

"They want to come home."

"Oh, my word." Nell's stomach somersaulted. "They can't do that. Maria will never allow it."

"That's why she wrote to you, to test the waters to see if everyone's still angry with her. Jack's passing gave her the excuse."

Nell held Sarah's gaze. "It doesn't matter what I think, does it? It's Maria she needs to ask."

Sarah let out a false laugh. "Don't think she hasn't wanted to, but I thought you'd be more understanding, especially when you heard about the boys."

"So you're using me?"

"No, not at all, but we want Maria to understand why Jane did what she did, and she'll listen to you."

"She might listen to you if you had the courage to talk to her. I thought the two of you were close."

"We are, which makes it more difficult. How would she feel if she knew we'd been in touch all these years? It would end our friendship."

"But you think it's all right for me to upset her?" Nell stood up. "I'm sorry, but I won't do it, not after everything she's done for me. Rebecca won't either."

"You've spoken to Rebecca?"

"I had to speak to someone."

Sarah sank back into her chair. "Very well, but please, promise me you'll think about it. Talk to Rebecca again and tell her about Matthew and John. If you remember, we were all happy once, and we'd like to be together again."

Nell reached for the door handle. "We weren't the ones who married a Catholic."

"Maybe not, but it didn't change who Jane is. She's still your sister ... and my friend."

"I'll speak to Rebecca, but I'm not promising anything." Nell stepped into the hall, but immediately turned back. "By the way, does Tom miss work as often as Maria seems to think he does?"

Sarah followed her to the door. "Who knows? You'll have to ask him that yourself."

CHAPTER TWELVE

James was late for breakfast the following morning and he smiled at Nell as he took his seat at the table.

"All on your own?"

"I am. Your mam's gone to the shop with Alice and the girls. I was about to tidy up."

"Give me a minute and I'll be out of your way."

"There's no rush; you take your time. It's your last day on dry land for another month. You may as well make the most of it. Are you all packed?"

"I think so. Mam left a pile of clothes on the bed and it looked as if everything was there." He took a bite of his bread. "How did you get on with Aunty Sarah yesterday? Is she worried about Uncle Tom?"

Nell paused as she stared at her nephew. "Oh, yes, Sarah. No, she didn't seem too concerned, although she gave the impression she didn't know what he was up to either."

James laughed. "I doubt she does. In fact, I'm not sure anyone does. Listening to him in the alehouse, he seems to be a law unto himself. Credit to him though, he never seems to get in any trouble for it."

"I suppose that's something. I've decided to stop worrying about him. He's old enough to look after himself."

"There is one thing to worry about, though. I heard him talking to Dad last night about finding him a job."

Nell's brow creased. "I thought he'd changed his mind because he wouldn't be able to earn enough money."

"That's what I thought, but it seems Dad was talking to the wrong people. There are better-paid jobs if he goes further up the river, closer to where Vernon works."

"Don't you think he'll go away next week then?"

James shrugged. "I can't say for sure, but I think he will. It could be his last trip, though."

A shiver ran down Nell's spine. "What do you think of that?"

"Not a lot, although things have been better this week than they have for years. I suppose if things get worse again, I can always transfer to the Australian liners. I wouldn't need to come home as often then."

"Don't say that." Nell put a hand on his arm. "I'd miss you."

He laughed. "And I'd miss you too. It's a shame you don't have your own house; if you did, I'd stay with you when I was home."

Nell sighed. "In case you'd forgotten, this is my house. My name's on the rent book at any rate, not that you'd know ... and not that I'd kick anyone out. I need your mam and dad now more than ever."

. . .

Nell was still folding the tablecloth when Maria arrived home with the girls.

"You're late tidying up."

"I kept James company while he had breakfast. You've just missed him. He's popped into Liverpool."

"Did he say why?"

"No, but I got the impression he was meeting a friend. He didn't think he'd be back for dinner." Nell huffed. "Three days really isn't long enough for him to be home and see everyone he wants to."

"We should be thankful that's all he's here for. It's been quite a squeeze with him and George at home, and when George is here all the time, we'll have the same problem every month."

"Is he still thinking of giving up the sea?"

Maria carried some of the shopping through to the kitchen. "More than thinking. He's gone to see someone about a job this morning. Tom put a good word in for him, apparently."

"That's good. I think."

"What do you mean, you think? It'll be marvellous to have him back."

"You've changed your tune. You were panicking when it was first mentioned."

Maria smiled. "I was being silly. Now him and James can be in the same room as each other, I can relax, especially if it means there's one less of them to worry about."

"Maybe you will, but I'm bothered the house won't be big enough for all of us, especially as the girls grow."

"Oh, we'll manage." Maria reached for her sweeping brush. "Can you make a start on the dinner while I tidy upstairs? That meat will need a couple of hours to cook."

"Will do, but I don't want to be late eating. I'm going over to see Rebecca this afternoon, and I want to be home in good time to see James. We won't see much of him in the morning."

"He's leaving here about six o'clock."

Nell grimaced. "Then I need to say my farewells tonight."

Rebecca was tidying up after dinner when Nell arrived.

"Gosh, you're early. I still need to get Florrie into bed for her nap."

"I'm sorry." Nell took the cloth from her sister. "You go and see to her and I'll finish these."

"Are you sure?" A look of concern crossed Rebecca's face. "You don't look happy. Is everything all right?"

"I don't know. You take Florrie up and I'll put the kettle on."

Rebecca raised an eyebrow as she picked up her daughter and hurried up the stairs. She was only gone for a minute before she rejoined Nell in the kitchen. "You've got me worried now. What's the matter?"

"I'm probably being silly, but I'm concerned about George giving up his job and staying at home." She carried the freshly made pot of tea to the living room table. "There won't be enough room for us all. Especially when James is home."

"I didn't think he was serious about staying."

"Neither did I, but Maria said he's gone for a job interview today. I've a feeling Tom put him up to it."

Rebecca's brow creased as she poured the milk into the cups. "He's due back on the ship next week. Surely he couldn't pull out at such short notice. Remember Jack all those years ago, when he couldn't get out of his last voyage?"

How can I forget? "That's true, but Tom seems to have more influence than Jack ever had. It wouldn't surprise me if he pulled some strings."

"Even if he does stay at home, it's not the end of the world. You've managed this week."

"Managed being the operative word. It was only bearable because we knew James would be going tomorrow. If the two of them are at home every month, it won't be ideal. Besides…"

"Besides what?" Rebecca handed Nell her tea as they took their seats on opposite sides of the fireplace.

"I've not lived with George since I was about seventeen. The whole reason for sharing a house with Maria was so we could keep each other company while the men were away. With George living with us again, well, I don't know. It will change things."

"He doesn't get in the way much though, does he? From what I can see, he's in the alehouse more than he's at home. And he'll be at work all day."

Nell fidgeted with the teaspoon on her saucer. "I can't explain it, but Maria's different when he's around. I don't blame her, I suppose I would be if Jack was here, but she's not her usual self."

Rebecca chuckled. "I'm sure that's only because George

is home so infrequently. If he's around all the time, she'll soon go back to being her usual self."

"I hope so. I'll find out soon enough."

"Here, have one of these to cheer you up." Rebecca stood up to fetch the plate of cakes. "It's not like you to be so down."

Nell helped herself to a slice of ginger cake. "I'll be all right. The idea that George may be here for good has come as a bit of a shock."

"How's Maria taken it?"

"Oh, she's thrilled. She said it's one less for her to worry about. Not that I've ever noticed her worrying about him."

"I wonder if Jack's accident changed that."

"It might have. Talking of which, I went to visit Sarah yesterday."

Rebecca's eyes widened. "About the letter? What did she have to say?"

"It's as we thought. Jane wanted to make contact again and thought I was the best hope of persuading Maria to take pity on her."

"She said that?"

Nell nodded. "Pretty well. She doesn't want to upset Maria by talking to her about Jane, but thought she'd listen to me."

"Good grief." Rebecca gasped. "What did you say?"

"What could I say? I told her that I wouldn't do her dirty work ... and neither would you."

"No, I will not! How could she even think we would?"

"Because she had some news she thought would change our minds."

"What could possibly do that?"

"The fact that Jane's been in Ireland since she left here and has now got two sons. Matthew and John."

"And they're being brought up as Catholics?" Rebecca's eyes were wide again.

"No. That's the thing. She said Jane wants them baptised into the Church of England, but obviously can't while they're over there. That's why she wants to come home."

"And Mr Read doesn't mind?"

"Apparently not. According to Sarah, he was going to turn, until Maria argued with them."

Rebecca ran a hand over her head. "Perhaps we should say something. We can't be responsible for them not being baptised."

"But why involve us? Sarah should be the one to mention it."

"But she doesn't see that?"

"No, she thinks Maria will be so cross she won't be able to explain what happened. The thing is, even if I tell her, I'll have to admit it was Sarah who gave Jane our address, so she's going to be involved whatever happens."

Rebecca paused. "What about George? Do you think he could talk to her? He passed you the letter after all."

"George. That's an idea." Nell's forehead creased. "He told me not to mention it to Maria, so I wonder if he knows." She paused. "How do I find out without telling him what's going on?"

Rebecca brightened. "I could ask Hugh if he's ever heard anyone in the alehouse talking about Ireland, or anyone called Patrick Read. He won't know who he is; I've never told him about Jane."

"Why don't we try that? We'll have to be quick, though. George may still go away again next week."

"Don't worry. I'll speak to Hugh tonight."

CHAPTER THIRTEEN

At quarter past seven the following Thursday morning, Nell hurried down the stairs to find Rebecca standing by the front door.

"Am I late?"

"No, I'm waiting while George sorts himself out. Maria looks quite upset, so I didn't want to disturb them."

Nell sighed. "She'd built herself up to thinking he'd be staying, so it came as quite a shock when he changed his mind."

"I imagine you're pleased though; at least you can carry on as you were."

"I am for now, but I still worry about what will happen when he's home again. At least I've a good six months to think about it."

Rebecca looked over to her own house. "I thought Hugh was going to join us. I don't know where he is."

"Has he still not heard them talking about Ireland?"

"No. He said they're always on about work and never

mention the families. Perhaps you should ask George yourself before he leaves."

"Is there any point? Unless..." Nell stared at her sister. "He could tell me whether Tom knows. If he does, we could get him to ask Maria. She's always cross with him anyway."

"Of course." Rebecca rolled her eyes. "Why didn't we think of that earlier?"

"Because we're daft, but move over, he's here now." Nell walked around Rebecca as she stepped onto the footpath to make room for George.

"Is this a leaving party?" He wore a bemused expression as Mr Grayson joined Rebecca and Nell. "I don't usually get such a send-off. Are you trying to get rid of me?"

"Not at all." Nell took his arm as a cold wind swirled around her ankles. "I was hoping to have a word with you while you're alone. Would you mind?"

She ushered him several yards down the road. "Do you remember giving me a letter not long after you arrived? A letter Tom had passed to you." She paused when a frown settled on his face. "You told me not to mention it to Maria."

"Ah, that, yes. What about it?"

"Did Tom tell you who it was from?"

"I don't remember." George scratched his head. "I think he said it was from a mutual friend who wanted to see you and Sarah again. Is she coming to visit?"

"No, not at the moment." Nell gestured back to the house. "We'd better go. Maria and the boys are here."

Maria's eyes were noticeably red as Nell returned to Rebecca's side and took hold of her arm. "Why do these men do this to us all the time?"

"Do what?" Rebecca's forehead creased.

"Come home and make us miserable."

"Jack didn't make you sad, did he?"

"Not deliberately, but every time he left, he'd take a piece of me with him, even though I'd vow to be strong." Nell wrapped her arms around herself and nodded towards Maria. "How often do you see her cry?"

"Not very, I must admit. I suppose I should be thankful Hugh's land-based."

"Yes, you should ... and that he's home every night, even if he does spend most evenings in the alehouse."

George threw his sea bag over his shoulder as Billy and Vernon joined him.

"It's been good to see everyone again. With any luck, I'll be home for Christmas." He turned to wave, then he set off down the road with a son on either side of him.

"I'll be off too. See you tonight." Without another word, Mr Grayson followed them, and a minute later, without a backward glance, they all disappeared into Windsor Street.

"There he goes. We can get in out of the cold now." Nell watched Maria as she silently slipped back into the house. "Perhaps I'll give her a few minutes. I hope you don't mind a visitor so early in the morning. At least I can tell you what George said."

The rims of Maria's eyes were still red as Nell returned half an hour later, but she was kneeling on the living room floor, a scrubbing brush in her hand.

"I'm sure you didn't have to do that now."

"Why not? It takes my mind off other things. I'm nearly done, if you'd like to put the kettle on."

Nell tiptoed across the wet floor to the kitchen. "At least this might be the last time he leaves."

Maria caught hold of one of the armchairs to pull herself up. "I hope so. I'm tired of being on my own."

"At least you can make that decision…"

"Oh, Nell, I'm sorry. That was thoughtless of me. I'm sure you'll find someone else one day."

Nell twisted her mouth. "I'm not sure I want anyone else at the moment. I'm more worried about what will happen if George comes home for good."

"What do you mean?"

She shrugged as she reached for the tap. "When we moved in here, it suited us to live together because we were both on our own, but now … well, you won't be."

"That doesn't matter."

"It does to me. I'll feel like a little girl starting out all over again."

"Well, what else can you do if you don't want to remarry? You'll need money to do anything else."

"Don't think I don't know." Nell's shoulders slumped. "Perhaps I should take a job."

"A job?" Maria shook her head. "What on earth would you do? And what about the girls? They need you here."

"I've no idea, but there's no reason I can't think about it. We can talk about it later."

Once dinner was over and the table cleared, Maria and Alice stayed where they were with their sewing while Nell took a seat by the fire, watching Alice's needle thread in and out of the cloth.

"Would I make enough money to live if I became a seamstress?"

Maria snorted. "I doubt it based on the bit of money Alice earns. It's not enough to live on. Not unless you have half a dozen seamstresses living in one house, all contributing to the rent."

"That many?"

"Probably. Don't forget, you need to buy the material for the garments out of the money they pay you, so you only make a couple of shillings per item."

Nell studied Alice. "How many waistcoats do you make a week?"

"One or two."

"So you only make about four shillings a week?" Nell's brow creased. "What about doing repairs? You wouldn't need to buy any material then."

Maria rested her hands on the table and stared at her sister. "Nell, you don't even like doing your own mending, let alone anyone else's."

"I could learn to like it if I was getting paid."

Maria tutted and picked up her work again. "If you're serious about getting a job, you could always do some domestic work around Upper Parliament Street. It would be handy enough."

"More cleaning?" Nell paused. "I suppose I could, and at least I can do that. I wonder how much I'd earn."

"I've no idea, but more than a couple of shillings, I should imagine."

Nell sat back and gazed at the ceiling. "Not much more, though. Still, it would give me some money of my own." A smile crossed Nell's face. *I could save up and take myself to America one day.*

Alice looked up as she fastened off her piece of thread. "Will you be able to do it while you're still in mourning?"

Nell's shoulders slumped as she glanced down at her dress. "This stupid thing. The Queen may want to spend the rest of her life in mourning, but the rest of us need to make a living if we lose our husbands. How are we supposed to do that if we're expected not to leave the house?"

"You rely on family for support." Maria glared at Alice. "You have to show your respects to Jack."

"But it's nonsense. I don't need to wear black to show how much I miss him. I already miss him every hour of every day, and I'd feel exactly the same wearing normal clothes, but at least it would give me the chance to feed his daughters."

Maria's mouth dropped open. "You can't stop wearing it."

"Why not? In fact, I'll change out of it right now." Nell stood up and raced from the room, but Maria followed her to the foot of the stairs.

"Nell, come back. At least wait until George comes home. There's no urgency to find a job, and that way it will be a more respectable length of time since Jack's passing."

Nell's heart was racing as she stopped on the landing. "It still won't be two years."

Maria climbed halfway towards her. "But it will be

longer than two months. You can't come out of mourning so soon."

When Nell failed to reply, Maria reached for her hand. "Come on. Sit back down and we'll sort something out."

CHAPTER FOURTEEN

A shaft of sunlight broke through the clouds and sparkled on the mirror that hung on the wall opposite the window in Rebecca's living room. Nell turned in her chair to study the sky.

"There's more blue up there than I've seen in a while."

Rebecca followed her gaze. "Let's hope it's a sign of things to come. It's nearly May after all."

Nell smiled. "It'll be nice to go to the park without shivering all the way around."

"If you've got time. Are you still serious about getting a job?"

Nell shrugged. "What else can I do?"

"You don't need to do anything if George decides to carry on at sea. Why don't you wait and see what his plans are first?"

"Because I'm sure he'll stay at home after this trip, and when he does I'd like to have something sorted out."

"I don't like the idea of you being a servant, though. You

were the wife of a master mariner. I'm sure you can do better than that."

"Like what?"

"I don't know." Rebecca stared out of the window. "What about being a housekeeper? It's still domestic service, but at least it sounds more respectable ... and you'd earn more money, too."

"I'm not sure I could do that. They won't take just anyone, especially not without references. I might even need to do the bookkeeping."

"But you've got experience of running a house, and you did your own bookkeeping when Jack was at sea. Don't underestimate how qualified you are compared to most women."

"I can hardly write my own recommendation, though."

"I'm sure we could find someone to vouch for you. Give you a character reference or something. I know ... the vicar! He'd do one for you."

Nell's forehead creased. "Isn't he against women working?"

Rebecca tutted. "He is, but that's under normal circumstances. It's different now you're a widow."

"Perhaps ... or maybe he'll offer me a job cleaning the church."

Rebecca grimaced. "You won't earn enough to live on if he does. No, a housekeeper is much more suitable. Why don't you speak to James about it when he gets back? It won't be long now."

"I could do. He's always very supportive."

"There, that's that then. I presume Maria will take care of the girls."

Nell's head jerked up. "I haven't asked her, but I'd be surprised if she wouldn't. Her and Alice pretty much have them most of the day as it is."

Rebecca laughed. "Well, if you have any problems, you can always send them over here."

"I will, thank you." Nell looked at the clock. "I suppose I'd better go. You need to pick Isobel up soon."

"I do, and I need to see to Florrie. Don't let Maria boss you around or have you doing something you'd rather not. Do you hear me?"

Nell grimaced. "I'll try not to." She walked to the front door, but as she closed it behind her, Sarah was on the other side of the road. They waved to each other as Nell made her way over.

"I didn't know you were visiting today."

"I've not been here long. I only popped in for some peace and quiet."

"Ah, well, I hope Maria was in a good mood." Nell laughed, but her face became serious. "While you're here, can I ask if you wrote back to Jane?"

"I did." Sarah pursed her lips. "I told her you were thinking things through."

"But that's a lie. I told you I wouldn't upset Maria."

"But she's obviously still on your mind..." Sarah's eyebrow raised.

"Only because I can't bear to think of those poor boys not being baptised."

"Precisely. If Maria would only accept Jane back, we could do what's right for them."

Nell's mind raced as she paused. "How much does Tom know?"

"Enough."

"Why can't he be the one to talk to Maria? They're always at each other's throats, so one more argument won't hurt. Besides, despite what she says, he's one of the few people she'll listen to."

"No."

"What do you mean, no? You can't dismiss it that easily."

"I want her to welcome Jane back because she wants to, not because Tom has forced her into it."

"But at least he could start the conversation. Please will you ask him?"

"I think it would be better all round if you did it." Sarah placed a hand on Nell's arm. "Please. I don't think you realise how much influence you have on her."

Nell watched Sarah disappear down the road and let herself into the house. Maria was alone at the table.

"Has Alice taken the girls out?"

"She has. She should be back shortly. Elenor had too much energy to be in the house and Alice finished her latest waistcoat not long after you left."

Nell sat by the fire as Maria topped up the teapot. "I'm glad she has a job she can do at home once she's married. It will give her some independence."

Maria's back straightened as she placed the tea on the table. "She won't be working once she has a husband and house of her own to take care of."

"Well, she should. Then she won't end up in the same situation as me. No husband, no income, no skills."

"What's got into you?" Maria took the seat opposite.

"You were all set to be a domestic servant when you left here earlier."

"Rebecca doesn't think I should. She reckons I should be a housekeeper, but I don't know that I'd be good enough."

Maria stiffened. "Rebecca should keep her ideas to herself. You've no experience to be a housekeeper. Besides, they're usually full-time jobs, and live-in positions at that."

Nell groaned. "I hadn't thought of that. Why's everything stacked against us? When did a man ever worry about something like that? They can go away without a care for anyone."

"It's the way of the world, and you should be used to it. I still think you should stop worrying about getting a job and concentrate on the girls." Maria stood up to pour the tea. "No one will think any the worse of you."

The following morning, as Nell was finishing breakfast, the front door opened and Tom barged into the living room. He peered into the kitchen before taking a seat.

"Is Maria here?"

"She's in the yard with Alice. Why?"

"I want to know what she's playing at, forcing you to get a job."

"Who told you that?" Nell placed her cup back on its saucer.

"Sarah told me you plan to take a job. Why would you do that unless Maria's told you to?"

"She's done no such thing."

"So you're not looking for a job?" Tom's eyes narrowed as he peered at her.

"No. Not yet anyway."

"What's that supposed to mean?"

Nell sighed. "I'm waiting to see what happens with George. I only shared a house with Maria because we were on our own when Jack and George were away, but if this is George's last voyage, I'll need to be able to take care of myself."

"No, you won't. Once he's back, George will get a job around here, and with the boys earning as well, there's no reason why they can't take care of you."

"Maybe they will, but it will be like being a child again. I have nothing of my own and I can't live like that. I'm used to having my own money."

"But you're still in mourning…" Tom paused as the kitchen door opened. "Ah, here she is."

"Tom!" Maria flinched when she saw her brother. "What are you doing here at this hour of the day? Why aren't you at work?"

"I've things to do."

"What sort of things?"

"Don't change the subject. Why are you encouraging our Nell to go out to work?"

"I'm not, it was her idea…"

"To work as a domestic?" Tom's glare rested on Nell.

"That was only an idea. Rebecca thought I should aim higher."

"Rebecca's encouraging you, too?"

"She's supporting me. Tom, I need some money of my own. It's not unusual for women to work."

"It is in this family." He stood up and reached for the door handle. "You should have been entitled to compensation for Jack's accident so you don't need to work." His face was red as he pointed at her. "Don't you do anything without asking me first. Do you hear?"

CHAPTER FIFTEEN

The church bells signalled the imminent start of the Sunday service as Nell walked through the churchyard with Maria and the family. She admired the daffodils growing amongst the gravestones.

"Spring's definitely on its way."

"It's certainly warmer ... until we go into church." Maria gave an involuntary shudder as Nell positioned the pram near the door and lifted Elenor down from her seat before picking Leah up.

"I hope Tom's here this morning. I want to find out what he meant the other day about getting compensation."

Maria tutted. "Take no notice of him. The enquiry found the shipwreck was an accident, so nobody's going to pay compensation. It's him trying to sound important."

"Maybe, but I need to know if he's serious. I'll see if I can talk to him after the service."

"Don't expect me to join you. I've no desire for an argument straight after church."

Nell gritted her teeth. "I'm sure I can find my own way home."

Tom and Sarah sat two rows in front of them, and not for the first time, Nell marvelled at how they managed to fit so many children into one pew. The older boys, Sam and Len, sat at the far end, while their older sisters alternated with Sarah as to which of the four younger children they had on their knees. They were going to struggle when that was no longer an option. At least Tom looked to be in a good mood as he sat unflustered on the aisle end of the pew. She knew the first hymn was one of his favourites and she watched him sing it with great gusto. *A promising start.*

At the end of the service, Nell passed Leah to Maria and bided her time while Tom let the family file out past him. He was about to follow them when she caught hold of his arm.

"May I have a word?"

"In here?" His face was stern.

"No, of course not. Outside. Just the two of us."

"Very well." He held out an arm to guide her to the door, where he turned right, away from the gate, and headed towards the back of the church. "We shouldn't be disturbed here. What can I do for you?"

Nell hesitated. "Two things, actually. First, what did you mean when you mentioned compensation last week? I didn't think I was entitled to anything because it was an accident."

"It was no accident." There was a snarl in Tom's voice. "The enquiry was made to look as if it was. There's a growing number of us who are fed up with the workers being treated badly, and we want to do something about it.

Bohemian are on our list of those who need teaching a lesson."

Nell's eyes widened. "What will you do?"

Tom looked over both shoulders. "We want as many men as we can muster to strike down their tools until the owners treat them fairly."

"And do you think they will?"

"If we can get enough of them to stop work, the companies will have no choice. The hard part is persuading men to give up a day's wages … or more. Especially when there are others who'll gladly take over from them. We're still working out how to do it."

"So you think getting men to stop work will force Bohemian to pay me compensation?"

"Not only you. There are the other widows or mothers who got nothing after the shipwreck, not to mention other cases where men have been killed or injured. You all deserve something," Tom snarled. "The thing is, it's easier said than done, but as you're family, I'll make them a priority."

"That's nice. How long do you think it will take?"

"That's anyone's guess. It depends when we can get the men out."

"I see." Nell's shoulders dropped.

"Not a word to Maria, though. She won't understand. Now, what was the other thing?"

Nell took a deep breath as she stared up at her brother. "Jane."

Tom's face reddened. "I told Sarah not to tell you."

"I'm afraid she didn't listen. She said Jane wants to come home."

"What!"

"That's what I thought. Apparently, she's got two sons, but because they're in Ireland, she's not had them baptised."

Tom clenched his fist and thumped it into his other hand. "I take it Maria doesn't know."

"No, she doesn't."

"That's a relief. There'd be a right to-do if she did."

Nell nodded. "So I believe, but from what I can gather, Jane's quite determined. She wrote and asked me to talk to Maria about her coming back, but I don't want to."

"I don't blame you."

"I wondered though if you'd speak to her instead. You know, explain about the boys and everything. I'm sure Maria wouldn't want to see them unbaptised when there's an alternative."

"Has Sarah put you up to this?"

"No! If I'm honest, she won't be best pleased that I've told you, but I think you'd be the ideal person. I don't want to fall out with Maria ... but you..."

Tom smoothed a hand over his moustache. "No, I don't think so. In fact, I don't want anyone mentioning this to Maria." He put an arm around Nell's shoulders to usher her back to the front of the church. "Let me speak to Sarah instead and tell her to stop this nonsense."

They turned down the path, but as they rounded the corner, Sarah was waiting for them.

"Where've you been? The dinner will be ruined at this rate."

Nell's cheeks flushed. "I'm sorry, I wanted a word with Tom ... about the compensation..."

Sarah's eyes darted to Tom. "What's going on?"

"Nothing for you to worry about." Tom strode past her. "You'd better hurry up if you don't want the meat burnt. I need to walk Nell home first."

Tom refused to go into the house and Maria looked up from setting the table as Nell walked into the living room.

"You took your time."

Nell diverted her gaze. "We were talking. He didn't have much to say about the compensation, other than there may be some pressure put on the company to support families of sailors who are lost at sea. Not that he said how they'll do it. It's wishful thinking, if you ask me. What do you want me to do?"

"We're nearly ready to serve. You can carve the meat if you like."

Nell wandered to the kitchen. She hated lying to Maria, but it was her own fault. If she didn't get so cross about everything...

"We'll need a bigger piece again next week." Maria studied the bacon joint as Nell took it from the stove. "I hope there are no delays for James this time."

"It will be nice to have him back. I do miss him while he's away."

"Well, you've nobody to blame but yourself." Maria's glare was brief, but it was there.

"What do you mean?"

"You were the one who encouraged him to go."

Nell put down the knife. "Only because it was what he wanted to do, and I didn't want him miserable for the rest of his life."

"He'd have settled into being a carpenter once he'd finished his indenture."

"Even if he had, he'd have gone to sea like George. He wasn't going to be stopped."

Maria busied herself draining the water from some carrots. "That's as maybe, but you can't complain that he's never here."

"I wasn't complaining. Why do you have to twist everything?"

"I'm trying to make everyone see sense, that's all. And that includes you."

CHAPTER SIXTEEN

Two days later, three weeks and five days after he'd left for sea, James walked back into the living room with the same smile as when he'd left. With a feeling of déjà vu, Nell could have sworn she and Maria were sitting in the same seats, and at least he was on time and there was no sign of Tom.

Maria took the sea bag from him and carried it to the back yard as James slumped into the seat opposite Nell.

"You're nice and early. Did you have a good trip?"

"It was fairly straightforward, there and back again with no awkward passengers." His face lit up. "I'm home for a week this time, too."

Nell beamed at him. "Did you ask if I could go and visit the ship while you're here?"

James stared into the fire as he ran a hand over his head. "I did, but I'm afraid the answer was no."

"Oh, what a shame. I..." Nell stammered as the back door closed and Maria reappeared. "I'm looking forward to hearing all about your trip. Did you get the chance to go ashore in New York?"

He shook his head. "I wish. No, they put names in a hat and drew three out, but mine wasn't one of them."

Nell sensed his disappointment. "Did they tell you all about it though? What New York was like?"

James laughed. "Did they ever. They didn't shut up about it!"

Nell paused as Maria placed a new loaf on the table. "You can tell me later, when you've had something to eat."

James gave her a wink. "I will, once Alice gets home. I saw her popping into the shop with the girls."

"She'll be back shortly. She likes to hear about your trips."

"How are things here? Did Dad get a job, or has he gone on another voyage?"

"He's gone again, although we all expect this to be his last trip."

James' shoulders relaxed. "That's something then. How long have we got?"

Maria glared at him as she placed a fresh pot of tea on the table. "He'll be home by the end of the year, and you should be pleased. Now, come and have something to eat. We can't sit around all morning."

"No, we can't." Nell pushed herself up from the chair. "You two sit and have a chat. I'll go and start the washing."

Nell wiped an arm across her forehead as she fed the clothes through the mangle for the second time. *One more go should do it.* She paused and straightened up as the back door opened and closed and James joined her.

"Are you nearly done?"

"I am for now. At least you can't bring much home when it all has to fit into that small bag."

"It doesn't feel like such a blessing on the ship, I can tell you." He smiled down at her. "I'm sorry I couldn't arrange a visit for you. I tried my best."

Nell sighed. "I'm sure you did. It was only an idea. I should know my place by now."

"Maybe one day." He strolled to the back wall. "How was Dad after I went back? I never get the truth from Mam."

"He was all right. We thought he was going to stay, but two days before the ship sailed, he changed his mind. We never got a good explanation why, although I wonder if he was testing the water. I've a feeling this will be his last trip, though."

James creased the side of his lip. "It sounds like he couldn't get a job. From what I heard last time I was here, that was the only thing that would force him to go away again. Perhaps Uncle Tom's not as well connected as we think."

Nell wandered to the clothes line with a shirt and two pegs. "I hope you're wrong."

"Why? What's the matter?"

"Oh, nothing really. It's just that with your dad coming back for good, I thought I'd find myself a job, but Uncle Tom wasn't happy about the idea."

James' forehead furrowed. "Why would you want to do that?"

Nell shrugged. "It's hard to explain, but if he's here all the time, it'll be like turning the clock back ten years. I've the children now and I feel I should have a little money of my own ... and some independence."

"We can look after you."

"But I'm used to taking care of myself. The only alternative is if your Uncle Tom can get compensation for Uncle Jack's accident."

"He's still talking about that?"

Nell studied him. "What do you mean, still?"

"I heard him mention it last time I was home, but nobody thought he stood a chance of getting anywhere with it given the verdict from the inquest." James paused. "If he's not successful, what sort of work are you thinking of?"

"Probably domestic service. Your mam suggested a cleaning job, but Aunty Rebecca thought a housekeeper would be better. What do you think?"

James paced between the door and back wall of the yard until he stopped and leaned on the wall of the outhouse. "Would you still like to visit America?"

Nell sniggered. "I'd love to. You know that. That's another reason for getting a job. One day I may have saved up enough money to take myself."

James held her gaze. "What if you could get paid for visiting?"

"Paid? What do you mean?" Nell put down the shirt she was about to hang.

"Do you remember last time I was home, I mentioned we had a stewardess on board the ship? A Mrs Birch."

Nell put a hand to her chest. "You're not suggesting I do the same?"

"Why not? Many of the duties are similar to those of a domestic maid, but it sounds grander ... and you'd get a lot more money."

"But ... what about the girls?"

"What about them? They'd stay here with Mam and Alice."

Nell took a deep breath and reached for the wall as a shiver ran down her spine. "Do you think I could?"

"I don't see why not. I was talking to Mrs Birch while we were away, and she said other companies are already thinking of taking on stewardesses. The thing is, there's already a lot of demand for the positions, and rumour has it that they'll take widows or other family members of ex-sailors in preference to anyone else."

"Why would they do that?"

"To make up for the fact that they lost their men at sea." He pushed his hands in his pockets as he stared towards the wall at the end of the yard.

"A sort of guilt offering, you mean?"

"No, I don't think so. They want to support families who've lost their breadwinner. I suppose it's a form of compensation but they'd rather people work for the money than get it for nothing."

"It's hardly for nothing..." She strolled back to the pile of shirts.

"Maybe not, but I thought that seeing how much you've wanted to go to sea over the years, you might like the chance."

"But I wouldn't know where to start." Nell's hands shook as she fumbled for a peg.

"They'd give you some training. I spoke to Mrs Birch

about it, and her job's very similar to mine, although she obviously only works for the ladies on board."

Nell shook her head. "I really don't know. Not if it means leaving the girls..."

James walked to the washing line and passed her a couple of pegs. "You don't need to decide now, but don't forget that if you get a housekeeper's job, it's likely to be a live-in position. There's probably not much difference."

"But it would be around here."

"The girls won't know if you're in Upper Parliament Street or New York if you're away all week."

"Maybe they won't, but I would."

"Well, that's for you to decide. Why don't you think about it?"

Nell watched James as he disappeared back into the house. *I'm unlikely to think of anything else.* She picked up the last shirt but stopped as she reached for the pegs. *Imagine not having to do this for a few weeks. And being able to visit New York.* She shook the smile from her face. *How can I? What if anything happened to me?* With a deep sigh, she hung up the final shirt. *No. Go back inside and forget this conversation ever happened.*

CHAPTER SEVENTEEN

Nell had no idea what time it was, but given it was still dark outside, she knew she should be asleep rather than tossing and turning, dreaming about sailing into New York harbour. *Confound James.* He'd described it in such detail she couldn't get it out of her head. *But what about the girls?* She rolled onto her side and rested an arm round Elenor. *They'll be perfectly safe here with Maria. And Alice. They love her.*

With a sigh, she squeezed her eyes tight, praying it would be enough to force her to sleep, but minutes later, she swung her legs over the side of the bed and reached for her robe. The house was silent as she picked up the candle and slipped from the bedroom and down the stairs. Half past four. *It's no wonder it's still dark. Perhaps five minutes by the fire and then I'll go back to bed.*

The sound of footsteps on the stairs startled her from a dreamless sleep.

"What on earth are you doing there?" Maria's voice was

brusque, and Nell rubbed her eyes against the brightness of the room.

"I came down because I couldn't sleep, but then I must have dozed off." She pushed herself out of the chair. "I'll go and get dressed. Give me ten minutes and I'll be back to help you with the breakfast."

She crept back into the bedroom, not wanting to wake the girls, but Elenor sat up as she walked in. "Where've you been?"

"Only downstairs. I'm back now." Nell sat on the edge of the bed and wrapped her arms around her daughter's delicate frame. "Shall we get dressed and then we can go for breakfast?"

James was at the table when she returned, and she frowned at him as she placed Leah on a chair.

"You're early this morning."

He smirked at her. "Not as early as you, by all accounts. Couldn't you sleep?"

Nell peered into the kitchen to check Maria was busy then sat down. "No. Thanks to you. I've not stopped thinking about sailing to New York."

"That's not a bad thing, is it?"

"Yes, it is when I have them to think about." Nell nodded towards Elenor, who was feeding Leah a piece of bread. "I can't just do what I want."

"It's about time you did. If you wait for permission, you'll never do it. If it's something you want to do, you should at least go and find out about it."

"It's not that..." Nell paused as Maria joined them. "Did

you say you were going into Liverpool later. Would you mind if I walk with you?"

Maria took the seat at the head of the table. "You can't go into Liverpool, you're still in mourning. What do you want anyway?"

Nell grabbed the bodice of her dress. "Something new to wear, for one thing. I'm sick of this."

Maria stared at her. "We've already had that conversation. You can't stop wearing it so soon, but even when you do, your old dresses are in the wardrobe. Besides, you've no money and I'm not wasting any on a dress."

"What am I supposed to do when I need new clothes then? Are you going to make me beg?"

"Don't be silly, but you don't need a new dress at the moment. When you do, I'll give you the money."

No! Nell glared at Maria. "You can't treat me like a child. Even Alice has more money than I do. Perhaps if I had an allowance, I could save up and decide when things need replacing?"

"I hardly think that's necessary." Maria poured three cups of tea.

"But it is." Nell stood up from the table. "If you'll excuse me, I've remembered I've something else for the washing."

Nell held her head high as she left the room, but as soon as she was upstairs, she slammed the bedroom door behind her. A second later, there was a knock.

"Are you all right, Aunty Nell?"

She opened it to find Billy on the landing. "Yes, I'm fine. I spilt some tea on my dress and decided it could be washed. You go down, I won't be a minute." Satisfied that Vernon had joined his brother on the stairs, Nell closed the door again and walked to the wardrobe. She didn't have a lot of choice, but at least the pale blue dress was nice enough. She took it from the wardrobe, admiring its sleek lines, but hung it up again. *I can't wear it yet; I need something to do the laundry in first.* She pulled out her grey day dress and lay it on the bed while she unfastened her buttons. *This is the last time I'm wearing this.*

Five minutes later, she returned to the living room with her mourning dress over her arm. Maria stared at her as she walked to the kitchen.

"What are you doing?"

"I'm not wearing this dress for a moment longer. I'll put it through the wash this morning and give it back to Sarah."

"But you can't..."

"Will you stop saying that?" Nell plonked her hands on her hips. "It's obvious I need money of my own, which means I need a job, and I won't get one wearing this. If you'll excuse me, I'd better get a move on. I don't want James going into Liverpool without me."

Nell linked her arm through James' as he pulled the front door closed behind them.

"Do you really want to go to Liverpool, or will anywhere do?"

Nell grimaced. "Anywhere will do. I wanted to talk to you and there's no chance of that while we're at home."

"That's what I thought. Come on, let's walk down to the river." They strolled in silence until they reached Windsor

Street. "You're determined to get a job then?" James gave her a sideways glance.

"What choice do I have? You heard your mam. I can't even buy new clothes unless she says so, and I've the girls to think about."

"Shall we go to the Bohemian office then?"

Nell's face paled. "Oh, I don't think so. I need more time to think about it ... and for you to give me more details. Do you really think I'd be suitable?"

"I don't see why not. When I spoke to Mrs Birch, she said she hadn't done anything similar."

"Why did she take the job? Has she been widowed, too?"

"She didn't say, but her father had worked on the ships, which was how she got the job."

"And you think Bohemian will give me a job because of Jack?"

"I'd say there's a good chance. We can always make an appointment and ask."

Nell hesitated. "I don't know. Would I have to go by myself?"

James patted her hand. "Not if you don't want to. I'm not back on the ship until next Tuesday, so we can either go now or you can wait another month."

"Hmm." A knot formed in her stomach as they turned the corner onto the dock road. "If they give me a job now, when do you think I'd start?"

"I doubt it would be before next year."

"Next year! It's only May."

"I know, but they usually employ people for a season rather than one trip."

Nell's brow creased. "A season? How long would that be?"

"From January or February until November. Most lines don't operate in December and early January because of the weather."

"So I'd need to do a full year?"

The disappointment must have shown on her face.

"That's what they prefer, but sometimes they make exceptions. Given you're in such a strong position, you could ask them for a trial voyage. I've not known them do that for stewards, but they may be more flexible for women, with you being more delicate."

Nell thought her heart would stop. "Do you think they would? If I'm honest, going to New York once would probably be enough to get this travel thing out of my system."

James laughed. "I'm not sure that's what they want, but there's no harm in asking. I could have a word with Mrs Birch, too, and find out if it was an option for her."

"Has she signed up for the season?"

"I think so. She's been with us on all the trips so far this year and she'll be on the next one. Her circumstances are different, though. She has no husband or children, and so it probably suits her."

Nell clung to James' arm as they walked along the increasingly busy footpath that ran adjacent to the river. "If they'd give me a trial, they may let me go this year. What do you think?"

"I'll tell you what, why don't we call in now and make an appointment? Then we can find out and put you out of your misery."

"All right then." Nell bit her lip as James led her towards the familiar offices of the Steamship Bohemian Company. She doubted much had changed since she'd last been here. Once they'd broken the news of Jack's death, and been vindicated at the inquest, they'd have gone back to normal. They probably had the same person cleaning the chandeliers. *I wonder if they've given that job to a widow, too.*

They were no more than ten yards from the front door when Nell stopped, pulling James to a halt as she did.

"What's the matter?"

"Did you see your Uncle Tom go in?"

Lines creased James' brow as he scanned the crowds. "No, I can't say I did. You must have imagined it."

"I don't think so. Can we find a seat for ten minutes and hope he comes out again? I don't want to go in while he's there."

"Do you think he'll try and stop you?"

Nell's heart was pounding as she nodded. "Very probably. He was angry with me the other week when he heard I wanted a job. Hopefully, he's talking about the compensation and I won't need the job."

"Maybe." James continued a slow walk until they drew close to the door. "I don't see any sign of him in the foyer. Why don't I pop in while you wait here?"

"What if he comes out?" Her eyes were wide.

"Stop worrying. I'm sure you're imagining it, and I'll only be a minute."

"Very well." Nell's stomach churned as she stood by the door, staring at the ships berthed in the docks. The sailing ships that had once graced the shore had largely been replaced by the steamships, but she could only see one passenger liner. The others must be further up the river. She sighed. *If I could just take one trip...*

"There we are. All done."

Nell jumped as James reappeared beside her. "What's done?"

"We have an appointment on Monday afternoon, but the man I spoke to seemed to think you'd be ideal. He said they like to do the right thing for widows of ex-workers. They'd give you training on how to serve, so it doesn't matter that you haven't done anything like it before."

A shiver ran down Nell's spine. "Did you ask about a trial voyage?"

James straightened his back and grinned down at her. "I did. They've never considered it, but having women on board is all rather new to them, so the chap I spoke to thought it was an excellent suggestion."

"Does that mean it could happen?" Nell managed a smile, but it dropped as an image of Maria's face flashed into her mind. "You won't tell your mam, will you? Or Uncle Tom, for that matter. I take it you didn't see him in there."

"No, not a sign, so stop worrying. Your secret's safe with me."

CHAPTER EIGHTEEN

By the time they arrived home from the river, the clouds had dispersed, causing the sun to glisten on the small bay windows that lined the street. Nell studied the house as they approached.

"It's as well I gave them a good polish yesterday. Look at hers next door. Your mam would have my guts for garters if I left them like that."

James laughed. "Trust you to notice. You can't be so picky on the ship. There's no keeping those waves off the portholes."

"I'm sure that's different, and I'm hardly likely to do them myself." Nell unbuttoned the top of her cloak. "I think this can go in the wardrobe for next winter. I need my summer one out."

James raised his face to the sky. "I hope it's like this next week when we leave. It's a lovely sail-away if the weather's good."

"I'd better have my trial voyage in August then." Nell

chuckled, but stopped when Sarah stepped from the house. "I hadn't realised she'd be here."

"Good afternoon, Nell. James. Have you had a pleasant afternoon?"

James raised his hat. "Good afternoon, Aunty Sarah. Yes, very pleasant, thank you. We weren't expecting to see you today."

"It wasn't planned, but I called to see your Aunty Nell."

"Me?" Nell's stomach churned.

"Don't look so surprised. Would you give us a minute, James?"

"Yes, of course." He raised his hat once again. "I'll go and tell Mam to put the kettle on."

Sarah watched James go into the house, but her eyes became cold as she stared at Nell. "Why did you tell Tom about Jane?"

"I thought he already knew." Nell shrank back to the wall as Sarah's glare persisted. "He was the one who gave George the letter and so I assumed..."

"You had no right to. I asked you not to mention it to him."

"No you didn't." Nell's forehead creased. "You didn't say a word about him, That's why I thought he'd be the ideal person to talk to Maria. He's not likely to be worried if he upsets her."

Sarah gave a sarcastic laugh. "You think Tom would be the best person to tell Maria about Jane... What's the matter?" She stopped as Nell's eyes widened and she followed her gaze.

"What's going on?" Maria glared between the two of them. "Why were you talking about Jane?"

"I-it's nothing…" Nell took a step backwards as Maria walked towards her.

"Nothing! You mention the name of that traitorous sister of ours and tell me it's nothing."

"Calm down." Sarah took Maria's arm.

"No, I won't calm down." Maria yanked her arm away. "Is this anything to do with you?"

"No. I promise, it was Tom…"

"No it wasn't." The words were out of Nell's mouth before she could stop them.

"Are you going to tell me what this is about then?" Maria continued pacing towards her.

"No. I don't know … ask Sarah…"

Maria glared at her sister-in-law. "I suggest we go back into the house. We've given the neighbours enough entertainment."

Nell's face coloured as she spotted several heads peering from the front doors of nearby houses. She was about to follow Maria inside when Rebecca hurried across to her.

"What's going on?"

Nell pulled her to one side. "Maria overheard Sarah talking about Jane."

"Good grief. I'm glad I didn't come out earlier. I'd only just got in after picking Isobel up from school. Are they waiting for you to go inside?"

Despite the sun on her back, Nell shuddered. "I hope not."

"Ah, you're here."

Nell turned round as James joined them. "Have you been sent to get me?"

He shook his head. "No, I've been sent out. Alice will be here in a minute with the girls. What's all this about?"

"You'll have to wait." Nell looked at Rebecca. "Would you mind having a few visitors? I'd rather not still be here when Sarah leaves."

"Of course not." Rebecca waited for the girls to join them, then escorted them across the road. "Alice, will you go into the back room with the children while I talk to Aunty Nell and James in the front room?"

"Are Mam and Aunty Sarah having an argument?" Alice's deep brown eyes were wide.

Nell put a hand on her shoulder. "It's only a disagreement, nothing for you to be worried about."

Alice failed to look convinced as she carried Leah into the living room while Rebecca opened the door to the front room.

"I thought it would be an idea for us to sit in here. I'm sure you'd like to know when Sarah leaves."

"As long as she doesn't see us." Nell studied the selection of chairs that surrounded a low-level table in the middle of the room. "You put the kettle on; I'll rearrange the seats."

Sarah hadn't reappeared by the time they'd emptied the teapot and finished the cakes.

"They must be having quite a chat." James stood up to pace the room. "Either that or they've killed each other."

"Don't say that. It's quite possible." Nell grimaced. "It's all my fault, too. If I hadn't said anything to Tom…"

"You can't blame yourself." Rebecca's voice squeaked.

155

"It was Sarah who encouraged Jane to write to you. You had every right to mention it to Tom."

James stopped where he was. "Is this Aunty Jane really so bad? I can't say I remember her very well."

Nell kept her eyes fixed on the window. "You were only little when she left."

"And no, she wasn't that bad. She was lovely. To me at any rate." Rebecca collected up the cups. "I liked Mr Read, too, in those early days."

James shook his head. "We may disagree with the Catholics about many things, but are they really so bad that it stops families being together?"

"It is to your mam ... so it has to be to the rest of us. Oh, look." Nell pushed her chair back towards the fire. "Sarah's leaving."

James stepped to the back corner of the room. "She looks rather flustered."

"I'm not surprised." Rebecca put the cups down and crept to the side of the window. "There's no sign of Maria."

Nell ran her hands over her face. "What do we do now?"

"I'd give her a few minutes and let her calm down. I'll make some more tea."

"But Sarah won't have accepted any responsibility. She'll have blamed me." Perspiration broke out on Nell's forehead. "I feel sick at the thought of going home."

James retook his seat. "Don't worry, I'll be with you. I'm used to her having a go at me."

"But I've got to live with her."

James winked. "Maybe you don't."

.   .   .

156

Half an hour later, Nell took a deep breath as she stood at Rebecca's front door readying herself to walk across the road.

"You'll be fine." James draped her cloak over her shoulders. "Billy and Vernon will be home soon, and we have Alice with us. She won't say anything while she's around."

"You're right. But when you all go to the alehouse tonight ... and Alice is in bed..."

"Stop that." Rebecca joined them and handed Leah to her. "Keep the girls close and you'll be fine."

Maria was nowhere to be seen when they walked into the living room and James went into the back yard looking for her.

"She's not there."

Alice's lower lip wobbled. "She may be upstairs. Shall I go and see?"

"Leave it to me." James walked to the bottom of the stairs and shouted up. "Mam, are you up there?" When he got no answer, he opened the door to the front room before he rejoined Nell and Alice. "There's no sign of her. She must have slipped out of the back entry."

"She can't have run away." Alice choked back a sob. "Let me go and check." She raced up the stairs and seconds later called down. "She's up here."

Nell almost dropped Leah onto the floor as she hurried to the stairs and into Maria's bedroom.

"She's just lying here." Alice took out her handkerchief as Nell approached the bed where Maria lay, staring at the ceiling.

"Maria, can you hear me?"

When she didn't move, Nell put a hand on her shoulder and gave it a shake.

"Maria. It's me. Talk to me. Please." Nell glanced at James. "Take Alice downstairs."

Without a word, James put an arm around his sister and led her from the room.

"Maria. Speak to me."

A tear rolled down Maria's temple onto the pillow. "Sarah's gone behind my back for all these years."

Nell sat on the bed beside her. "She's betrayed us all."

"How could she? I thought she was my friend."

"And I'm sure she is..."

"Was."

"I imagine she'd still like to be, in the same way she wanted to be Jane's friend."

"How could she have any more to do with Jane after what she did!" Maria spat out her words. "And she involved you, too."

"I'm sorry. I wanted nothing to do with it ... until she mentioned the boys."

The trickle of fluid increased as Maria closed her eyes. "She won't blackmail me into having her back. She should never have had them."

Nell took Maria's hand as she struggled for something to say. "It was obviously the Lord's will. We don't have control over these things."

Nell held her breath, waiting for a response, but Maria rolled over on the bed, burying her face in the pillow.

"That's where you're wrong. She knew exactly what she was doing."

CHAPTER NINETEEN

The following morning, Nell stood up from the breakfast table, where James and Alice were still eating.

"I don't know what's happened to your mam. I'd better go and check on her."

Tears weren't far from Alice's eyes. "She will be all right, won't she?"

Nell's smile was weak. "She will but she doesn't feel herself at the moment. I'll take her a cup of tea and see if she'll come down later."

"I don't like her being like this."

Nell rested a hand on her niece's. "Don't worry, we'll sort her out. Perhaps you can sit with her later."

Nell crept up the stairs and knocked on the bedroom door before she went in. Maria didn't appear to have moved and was still lying on her back, staring at the ceiling.

"I've brought you this." Nell placed the cup and saucer on the window ledge and sat on the edge of the bed. "How are you feeling this morning?"

Maria didn't move, and Nell flinched seconds later when she spoke. "I suppose you think I'm being unreasonable, too."

"Why would I think that? Is that what Sarah said?"

"That's all she kept saying. 'Be reasonable. Give her another chance. Think of the boys.'" Maria's voice was venomous. "Did she think of my boy?"

Nell's mouth dropped open. "What do you mean?"

"Fred. He'd be alive if it wasn't for her." Tears fell to the pillow as Maria buried her face in it.

"Fred? He died of measles. What's it got to do with Jane?" When she got no reply, Nell shook Maria's shoulder. "Talk to me. Why are you blaming Jane?" She let out a deep sigh. "All right, suit yourself. I'll leave your tea here."

James and Alice were clearing the table when she arrived back downstairs.

"You don't need to do that."

James laughed. "It's my job, remember. That's why Dad hates it."

"Maybe it is, but not while you're here." Nell took a stack of plates off him. "Sit down and Alice and I will do it."

"How's Mam?"

Nell sighed. "She's not talking much. All she said was that Sarah kept telling her to be reasonable." She stepped closer to James as Alice went into the kitchen. "I think I should pay Sarah a visit. I want to find out what else was said."

"Shall I come with you?"

Nell bit her lip. "I'd love you to, but do you think you should? I may as well go when Tom's at home. He needs to know what happened, if he doesn't already."

"I think the four of us should have a talk. This shouldn't only be between you and Aunty Sarah. Let me speak to Uncle Tom in the alehouse tonight and find out when he'll be home. I expect Saturday afternoon will be best, once he's finished work and been for a pint. I'll give you the details in the morning."

"Very well, but not a word to your mam."

As the afternoon drew on, Nell carried another cup of tea upstairs, only to find the previous one still untouched. She leaned over the bed to see Maria open her eyes.

"Aren't you getting up today?"

Maria turned her head towards the cup and saucer and edged up onto her elbows.

"That's better." Nell put the cup down to arrange the pillows. "I imagine you're hungry. You've not eaten anything."

"I don't want anything." Maria took the cup from Nell. "I can't believe Sarah's been going behind my back all these years. How could she?"

"I'm sure it wasn't intentional. She told me that her and Jane were best of friends and they hoped Jane would only be away for a couple of months. They didn't know she'd be gone for so long."

"How could she expect things to be forgotten so soon? It was nearly twenty years ago, and to my shame, I still can't forgive her." Maria wiped the tears from her cheeks. "Sarah was my friend, too. Or I thought she was."

"Of course she was." Nell twisted her fingers together on her lap.

"Then why didn't you put a stop to this nonsense before it started? You should have known…"

"Don't blame me!" Nell jumped to her feet. "I knew nothing about it until a few weeks ago. I knew you'd be upset, but I didn't know what to do. Not when I heard she had two boys who haven't been baptised."

Maria's steely gaze bored into Nell. "She should have thought of that before she got married."

Maria was at the table buttering a piece of bread when Nell arrived downstairs the following morning. She looked up as Nell joined her.

"What time do you call this?"

"I didn't sleep very well last night and must have dozed off once Alice and the girls came downstairs."

"A guilty conscience, I shouldn't wonder."

Nell bit her tongue as she poured herself some tea. "I wasn't sure you'd be down this morning. Where is everyone?"

"Billy and Vernon are at work, and James has walked the girls to the shop. They won't be long."

"Oh, good." She helped herself to some bread. "Do you have any plans for today?"

"None, thanks to that sister of ours."

"What about calling on Rebecca then?" Nell tried to keep her voice steady.

"Did she know about any of this?"

"No." Nell focussed on the table. "Not until she saw us outside the house. I've told her about it since."

"What did you say?" Nell could feel Maria's eyes boring into her, but refused to look up.

"Only that Jane had written and wanted to come home."

"So she had no part in the plan?"

Nell sighed. "There was no plan. Jane sent a letter to Sarah, who passed it to me. She hoped I'd broach the subject with you, but I told her I wouldn't. What more can I say?"

"But you think I'm being unreasonable?"

Nell leaned back in her chair. "I'm concerned for the boys. If Mr Read's happy for them to be baptised into the Church of England, who are we to stand in their way?"

"It's not that simple..." She hesitated as the front door opened and James strolled in.

"We're back."

"Oh, good." Nell jumped up and went to get the girls from the pram while Alice collected the groceries. Once her arms were full, Alice walked into the living room as James came back to hang up his coat. He leaned towards Nell, his voice low. "Half past two this afternoon."

"To visit Sarah?"

He nodded. "Uncle Tom said he'll be back by then."

Nell peered around the door to check Maria had gone to the kitchen. "Can we go for a walk first? I don't want to stay in any longer than necessary."

The walk to Tom's house normally only took two minutes, but their route via the park had taken over an hour. James reached for the door knocker but paused. "Are you ready for this?"

Nell took a deep breath. "I think so."

He hadn't finished knocking when the door opened and Tom stared down at them.

"Who is it?" Sarah shouted from the back room but stopped as she reached the hall. "Oh, it's you. What do you want?"

"We need to talk." Nell stepped into the house and indicated towards the front room. "In here?"

"If we must, although there's not a lot to say."

"I'm afraid I disagree..." Nell pulled herself up to her full five-foot one inch.

"That's enough." Tom ushered them all into the front room and closed the door. "Will someone tell me what's going on?"

"She hasn't told you?" Nell raised an eyebrow at him.

"All I know is what James told me ... and that Sarah's been behaving strangely for the last couple of days."

Sarah took a seat by the fire, not looking at her husband. "And what did he tell you?"

"Only that you and Maria had argued about Jane and that Maria's been hysterical ever since."

Sarah twisted a piece of hair around her fingers. "I'm sure he's exaggerating. It was only a slight disagreement."

"No it wasn't." Nell held Tom's gaze. "I've never seen Maria in such a state. She only came out of the bedroom this morning."

"Is that right?" Tom questioned James.

"I'm afraid so. She was lying on the bed when we got home and wouldn't speak to us."

"What in God's name did you say to her, woman?" Tom glared at his wife as she reached for her handkerchief.

"I didn't say anything; it was her. She heard Jane's name and became hysterical."

"And that was it?"

"Yes."

"That's a lie!" Nell's nostrils flared. "You were in the house for nearly an hour. We watched you leave. You must have said something."

"All I did was defend myself." Sarah buried her face in her handkerchief. "She wouldn't stop telling me I shouldn't have kept in touch with Jane."

"By saying what?" Nell was past being nervous.

"I told her she was being unreasonable, which she was, and that she should let Jane bring the boys home so they can be baptised."

"Did you think for a moment about her feelings?"

"What feelings?" Sarah spat out her words. "She doesn't have any."

Nell's mouth dropped open as she turned to Tom. "Did you hear that?"

"Well, she doesn't." Sarah gaped at them. "All she's bothered about is which church we attend, but there are people involved here. Two little boys we've never even met."

"And what about her son? Did you stop to think of him?"

Everyone in the room stared at Nell.

"Which son, Aunty Nell?"

Nell's eyes flicked between Tom and Sarah. "Fred. You remember?"

Tom ran a hand over his moustache. "Of course we do, but what about him?"

Nell raised her arms from her sides and dropped them again. "I don't know the details, but Maria blames Jane for his death."

Sarah's mouth opened and closed several times, but no words came out. After a moment, Tom spoke. "She said that?"

"Yes. That's why she's so upset."

"But he was ill. There was nothing anyone could do for him." Sarah's voice was weak. "How could Jane be responsible for that?"

"I-I don't know. She won't talk about it."

Sarah shook her head. "But it was nothing to do with Jane. How could it have been?"

Nell suddenly became aware of her heart pounding. "I really can't say, but it appears there's more to this than we thought."

"All right, we need to put an end to this." Tom stood over Sarah. "For a start, any talk of Jane coming home has to stop. For now, at least. I've no idea why she thought Maria would have mellowed, but there's obviously something she's not telling us. You'll have to write and tell Jane that coming home isn't an option."

"But she has her heart set on it..."

Tom snarled. "She'll have to unset it. You can give me the letter to post so I can make sure it reaches her."

Nell rested a hand on her brother's arm. "Thank you. I think that's for the best. I don't think Maria could face seeing her again."

"Jane was so looking forward to it..." Sarah wiped her eyes with a handkerchief.

"I'm sorry, but ... well, we'll let ourselves out." Nell hadn't reached the hall when she turned back to Tom. "One more thing, when we see each other in church tomorrow, not a word about this. I think the less said now, the better."

Sarah gritted her teeth. "She'll have to apologise before I speak to her again."

"Thank goodness for that. At least it means you won't do any more damage."

CHAPTER TWENTY

The washing was nearly finished for another Monday morning when James wandered into the back yard looking for her.

"Ah, here you are. You get left to do the tidying up, do you?"

Nell chuckled. "I don't mind. It gets me out of the house."

"I've had a word with Mam and told her she needs to stop this nonsense. It wasn't your fault Aunty Jane wrote, and she shouldn't take it out on you."

Nell winced. "What did she say?"

"Not much, but hopefully she'll think about it. I told her we're going for a walk this afternoon and when we get back, I want to see a smile on her face."

"You said that and you're still standing?"

James laughed. "She didn't look very pleased, but then she hasn't for the last few days anyway."

"At least it gives us a reason to go out later." Nell

grinned. "The longer this goes on, the fewer doubts I have about getting on a ship and leaving her to it."

"It might not be all bad then." He winked at her. "We need to leave here by about quarter past one, if we're to be at the office for two."

"I'd better get a move on then. I'll be in for dinner shortly."

Seagulls circled overhead as they walked along the dock road, their squawking competing with the hooves of the horses on the cobbles. Normally, Nell would admire them as they flew between the ships' masts as they swayed on the water, but today her stomach churned, and she focussed on the uneven cobbles underfoot.

"What do you think they'll ask me?"

"They'll want to know something about your background and why you want the job."

"But why do I want it?" She bit her lip as she stared up at him. "I can hardly say it's because I want to visit New York."

"Tell them about Uncle Jack and how you've wanted to go to sea for years. You could also say you've only recently found out that shipping lines are hiring stewardesses and you'd like to take the chance now they are."

"That's a good idea." Nell gulped. "Do I ask about a test voyage?"

"I don't see why not. It's a new venture for women, so it seems sensible to check whether you'd like it. Don't be too disappointed though, if they say no."

"Don't worry, I won't. Going for a full season suddenly seems like a good idea."

They reached the offices of the Steamship Bohemian Company with five minutes to spare, and James held the door open for Nell as they went inside. A clerk looked up from a desk near the door, but Nell waited for James to speak to him.

"Mrs Riley's here for an interview with Mr Hobson."

The clerk raised an eyebrow as he ran a finger down a list of appointments in his ledger. "So she is. Take a seat. I'll tell him you're here."

Nell wiped her hands on her skirt as she sat down.

"Are you all right?" James studied her face. "You've gone very pale."

"I think so. It reminds me of when they told me about your Uncle Jack. It feels like no time at all…"

"It's only been three months. Do you want to come back later in the year?"

Nell shook her head. "No. Now we're here, I may as well get it over with. I'm sure that getting away on a ship will do me the world of good."

James patted her hand. "Take a few deep breaths. Hopefully, I can come in with you."

They hadn't sat for more than five minutes when an elderly gentleman walked towards them. "Mrs Riley?"

Nell's stomach churned. "Yes, that's me."

"Splendid. I'm Mr Hobson." He gave a half bow then addressed James. "Walk this way, please. You too, sir, if you wish."

"Yes, thank you." James helped Nell to her feet and

offered her his arm as Mr Hobson led them down a wood-panelled corridor towards the back of the building.

"Come in and take a seat; there's a good thing."

James held a chair out for Nell, then sat down beside her.

"Right, what may I do for you?" Mr Hobson folded his hands together on the desk as he peered across at her.

"Well..." Nell coughed. "I'd been told you may have a job for me. A stewardess ... going to America."

Mr Hobson's eyebrows drew together. "Who told you that?"

"If I may interrupt, sir." James sat forward in his seat. "I called one day last week to enquire on behalf of my aunt. I work as a steward with the Red Cross Line and became aware of the new fashion for hiring stewardesses. Mrs Riley was recently widowed when the SS *Bohemian* sank off the coast of Ireland, taking the life of her husband, Master Mariner Jack Riley. I was led to believe the company like to take care of widows and that she'd make an ideal candidate."

Mr Hobson studied her. "Indeed we do. Can you tell me what experience you have, Mrs Riley?"

"Experience?" The question threw Nell and she put a hand to her chest as she stared at James. "Erm, none as a stewardess, although I have run my own home for over ten years..."

A patronising smile flicked across Mr Hobson's lips. "While I'm sure that's very worthy, might I suggest that running a home and being a stewardess are quite different."

James sat forward once more. "Forgive me for interrupting, but when I was here last week, I was told that previous experience wasn't necessary as the company would provide training."

"We do, but only of a supplementary nature." Mr Hobson's brow creased. "If you're not familiar with this sort of work, then I'm afraid I can't help you."

"But we were told…" Nell's voice squeaked, causing her to cough.

"Who did you speak to?" Mr Hobson raised an eyebrow to James.

"A man called Havers, if I remember rightly."

Mr Hobson shook his head. "Oh, Mr Havers. I'm afraid he's new to the company and had no right to give you that sort of information. I'm so sorry."

Nell's eyes flicked to James as Mr Hobson stood up. "Is that it? You won't consider me?"

"I'm afraid we can't, not without some sort of experience." He held open the door for them.

"What sort of experience?"

A smirk settled on Mr Hobson's face. "You could become a maid or something similar. Spend some time in service."

"Are you sure there's no other way?" James shook Mr Hobson's outstretched hand.

"I'm afraid not. Good day to you."

They walked back down the corridor in silence and James held open the door as they stepped onto the footpath.

"I'm sorry, Aunty Nell. The chap Havers led me to believe it was a foregone conclusion. I don't understand what happened."

Nell sighed. "It's not your fault. They've probably not got themselves sorted out if the roles are new."

"You could be right." He offered her his arm as they started in the direction of home. "What will you do now?"

Nell shrugged. "It looks like I'll have to go into service."

James stopped, his mouth open.

"What are you looking at me like that for? You heard Mr Hobson. If I want to work on the ships, I need experience. I also still need a job, so I may as well kill two birds with one stone."

"So you want to press ahead with being a stewardess?"

"Why wouldn't I? By the sounds of it, they assume all widows go into service when they lose their husbands, which is why they ask for experience."

James carried on walking. "I thought you'd have been put off."

"No." Nell jutted out her chin. "If you ask me, Mr Hobson is nothing but an old man who's not got used to the idea of women working. If I go back with experience..." Nell paused and brought James to a standstill once more. "Do you think all companies would be the same? Wanting experience?"

James puffed out his cheeks. "I can't say for sure, but not necessarily. I thought you'd be better starting with Bohemian though, given they were responsible for Uncle Jack and his accident. The other companies may not have such a reason to employ you."

A knot tightened in Nell's stomach. "You could be right, although I wonder if it's worth trying anyway."

"Possibly, but I'm back on the ship tomorrow. I won't have time to make any enquiries. You could take the next month to think about what you want to do." James indicated for her to carry on walking.

"I don't have much choice, do I? You will help me, whatever I decide, won't you?"

"You know I will. Will you say anything to Mam?"

Nell gave an involuntary shudder. "Not with the mood she's in. Not a word to Uncle Tom either."

"Don't worry, I won't mention it. We'd better get home, though. Mam will be wondering where we are."

CHAPTER TWENTY-ONE

Nell puffed out her cheeks as she sat in a chair by the fire and gazed at Maria and Alice, who sat at the table, focussed on their sewing. She hated it when James was away. The girls were playing nicely enough, but the next argument wouldn't be long in coming. She let out a sigh. *I could call on Mrs Blackmore. I've not seen her since we were in the park the other week.* She got to her feet.

"I'm going to pay Mrs Blackmore a visit. I'll take the girls with me to give you some peace and quiet." She picked Leah up and rested her on her hip as she ushered Elenor into the hall. "Come along, let's get our cloaks on."

Once they were ready, she opened the door and was about to step outside when the postman stopped her.

"A letter for you, madam."

A frown crossed her face. "Thank you." *Who's writing to us?* She watched him leave then stared down at the envelope. *Good grief. Mrs Blackmore will have to wait.* Pulling the door closed behind her, she hurried across the road and straight into Rebecca's living room.

"I hope you don't mind me calling."

"No, not at all." Rebecca stood up from the floor where she'd been arranging wooden blocks into words with Isobel. "What's the matter?"

"This." Nell waved the letter at Rebecca as she sat Leah on the floor alongside Elenor, who had started building a tower. "I was about to visit Mrs Blackmore, to get away from Maria, but as I was leaving, the postman gave it to me."

Rebecca took the envelope from her. "It's addressed to Maria. What about it?"

"Don't you recognise the handwriting?"

Rebecca peered down at it. "It's not from Jane, is it?"

"It looks like it. Sarah was supposed to be writing to tell her that coming home wasn't an option, but it looks like she's taken matters into her own hands."

"Oh my goodness. What are you going to do?" Rebecca wandered to the table and sat down.

"I've no idea."

"Can't you hide it and, if anyone asks, pretend it didn't arrive? Maria wouldn't have been able to read it anyway."

"I could do. It would certainly be the easiest option, but do you think she'll write again if she doesn't get a response?"

Rebecca pursed her lips. "She may ... or she may assume Maria doesn't want to see her if she doesn't reply."

"Should I write and tell her I got the letter but didn't pass it on because it would upset Maria too much?"

"That might stop her writing again ... although it would mean you'd end up being in contact with her yourself. If Maria found out..."

"Hmm." Nell jerked her head up again. "Sarah must have given her our address. She didn't have it last time she wrote. That's why the letter came via Tom. How could she do that when Tom had told her to put an end to all this?"

"Why don't you speak to Tom again?"

Nell took a deep breath. "I'd rather not cause any more trouble."

"There is another option." Rebecca licked her lips. "Why don't we open it and see what she wants?"

"We couldn't. Could we?" Nell leaned forward and ran a hand over the envelope. "I wonder if she'll say anything about Fred."

"Why would she?"

"Because I told Sarah that Maria blames Jane for his death. She may have told her."

"How was Jane responsible?" Rebecca's brow furrowed. "They were already not speaking to each other when he caught measles. Jane couldn't have given it to him."

"That's what Sarah said."

"Perhaps we shouldn't read it then. If it says anything important, we'd have to admit to opening it."

Nell closed her eyes and let out a deep sigh. "I wish I hadn't seen it."

"Don't say that." Rebecca stood up to stop her daughters fighting. "Imagine what would have happened if you hadn't."

Nell picked up Leah and sat her on her knee. "I don't know what to do. I wish James was here."

"He won't be back for a couple of weeks. Can you wait that long?"

"Who knows?" Her forehead creased. "I could ask Billy, although I'd worry he'd mention it to Vernon."

Rebecca grimaced. "You don't want that."

"No, I don't." Nell sighed. "I don't know what to do."

"Why don't I ask Hugh first? He won't tell Maria what's going on."

Nell studied her sister. "That's not a bad idea, although what about Tom? Might Mr Grayson say something to him?"

"Yes, he might if he thought that was the best thing to do."

"That's no good then." Nell checked the clock. "Any chance of a cup of tea while we think about it? I've still time before I need to get back."

Maria had gone to bed, but Nell was still by the fire when Billy arrived home that evening. She smiled as he walked in, thankful he was on his own.

"You're early tonight."

"There wasn't much going on, to be honest." Billy frowned as he took the chair opposite. "Uncle Tom and Sam weren't there, which was strange."

"Were they in last night?"

Billy nodded. "Yes. And Uncle Tom said he'd see us tonight. Have you been to visit lately?"

Nell grimaced. "Not since your mam fell out with Aunty Sarah."

"Ah, yes, I'd forgotten. Do you think that could have anything to do with it? Aunty Sarah may not want Uncle Tom mixing with us."

"I doubt she'd be able to stop him." Nell paused and studied him. "How much do you know about the argument?"

"Nothing. Nobody ever tells me anything."

"And Uncle Tom's not said anything?"

"Why would he?"

"No reason." She pushed herself up from the chair. "I think I'll go up to bed. I'll see you tomorrow."

Despite the weariness in her limbs, sleep evaded her until the first shafts of light peeked through the drapes covering the window. By the time Billy and Vernon raced down the stairs, she felt like she'd been asleep for no more than half an hour. Rubbing her eyes, she forced her legs over the edge of the bed and sat quietly watching Elenor and Leah play with a rag doll through the bars of the cot. *Would they even miss me if I wasn't here?* Her heavy sigh was enough to distract Elenor, who turned and hugged her legs.

"You were sleepy."

"Yes, I was. Shall we get you both dressed?"

Elenor scrambled for her dress. "Alice has gone. She's waiting."

"We'd better be quick then."

Maria and Alice were at the table when they went downstairs, and Maria gave Nell a cursory glance as she sat the girls at the table.

"Couldn't sleep again?"

"No, I couldn't." She waited for Maria to pass the bread. "I've been thinking about finding some work again. I don't want to wait until George comes home. I'll need money before then."

"What about Tom?"

"He doesn't own me. If I want to get a job, surely it's up to me. I can't sit and wait for compensation that may never come. Elenor will need some new clothes soon."

"He won't be happy."

"I won't be telling him." Nell glared at Maria as she stirred some sugar into the tea.

"Don't look at me." Maria shimmied in her seat.

"What will you do, Aunty Nell?" Alice's dark eyes looked across at her.

"I'll see if I can get a job in one of the houses on Upper Parliament Street. I mentioned it to James when he was last home and he said he'd help me to find a position when he's back."

"It sounds like you've got it all worked out." Maria stood up and headed towards the kitchen.

"And why wouldn't I? I told you weeks ago this was likely, so don't sound surprised."

"I suppose you'll expect us to look after the girls."

"I'll look after them." Alice passed Elenor some bread.

"We like Alice." Elenor wrapped her arms around her cousin.

"That's settled then." Nell fought to keep the grin from her face as Maria strutted back into the room. "It makes sense."

"It does no such thing. I'm going to make the beds. This floor needs washing when you've finished here."

Nell waited to hear Maria on the stairs and smiled at Alice. "What will you do today?"

"I've a list of people wanting waistcoats, and so I'll be sewing. I can still look after the girls, though."

"You're a good girl. Are you sure they won't slow you down?"

"They won't." She stroked Elenor's head. "You like to help, don't you?"

Elenor nodded.

"As long as you don't mind."

"It's better with them here anyway." Alice hesitated at the sound of Maria's footsteps coming through the ceiling. "Mam's not very happy when it's just the two of us."

"I don't think she's happy however many of us are here."

"What's wrong with her, Aunty Nell?"

Nell feared Alice would start sobbing. "I'm not sure, but your mam and I have another sister, besides Aunty Rebecca, and she upset Mam a long time ago. Aunty Jane her name is. She married a Catholic, which is why Mam's cross with her, but I get the feeling there's something else she's not happy with."

Alice's eyes widened. "But marrying a Catholic's wrong enough."

"I know, but it seems to have upset your mam much more than it should."

"Is that why I've only got three brothers instead of four, because God was punishing her for being angry?"

Nell did a double take. "Where did you hear that?"

"Mam was talking to herself when she was in the bedroom and I heard her."

Nell put down her bread and leaned back in her chair. "I've never heard her say that. What did she say?"

"She was asking God why He'd taken her son and why He'd punished her." Alice stared at the table. "I shouldn't have listened, should I?"

"I'm sure you didn't do it on purpose. Sometimes we overhear things we're not supposed to, but it doesn't make it wrong." Nell bit her lip as she studied her niece. "Did she say anything else?"

"No ... well ... I really shouldn't say."

"Please, you can tell me. It might help us work out why your mam's so cross. I'm sure you'd like that."

Alice hesitated. "You won't tell her I overheard, will you?"

"Of course not."

"All right." Alice took a deep breath. "She said that Fred would never have died, if it hadn't been for *her*."

"Did she say who *her* was?"

Alice shook her head. "She just kept calling her a traitor."

"And you're sure you didn't hear the name Jane?"

Alice shook her head. "No. I promise."

"Very well, let's say no more about it. I don't think we should tell anyone else. Not at the moment anyway."

"And I don't ... but..."

"But what?"

"Can you tell me anything about Fred? I've never heard of him."

Nell's eyes glazed over as she recalled her young nephew. "He was a lovely little boy. He would have been younger than Billy, but older than Vernon."

"Did I know him?"

Nell shook her head. "No, he was only three when he was taken from us, long before you were born. It took your mam years to get over it." One side of Nell's lip creased. "If she ever did."

"It doesn't sound like she has..."

Nell took a deep breath and patted Alice's hand. "Why don't you take the girls outside for ten minutes and get some colour back in your cheeks? I'd better get this floor washed."

Nell stayed at the table and watched as the girls bounced a ball to each other in the yard. *Oh, to be young.* She pushed herself up and wandered to the kitchen. At least Alice had helped her make up her mind. Nobody was going to see Jane's letter until James got home.

CHAPTER TWENTY-TWO

As Sunday morning breakfast ended, Nell dried the dishes while Maria and Alice readied themselves for church. She'd almost finished when the back door closed, causing her to turn round and glance into the living room. Billy sat alone by the fire.

"Was that Vernon who went outside?"

"It was." He looked up from the newspaper while Nell dried her hands on a cloth and joined him.

"You were back early again last night. I'd not long since gone to bed."

"I wasn't in the mood to stay out. Vernon was with some of the lads from work, so once the dominos ended, I left."

"Wasn't Sam in?"

Billy's brow creased. "No, I've not seen him or Uncle Tom for a few days now. I'm hoping they'll be in church this morning."

"Uncle Tom's not been in again? That's very strange." Nell wiped a cloth over the table.

"I'm sure he'll have a reason; he usually does."

"I don't doubt it." Nell straightened up again. "I forgot to ask yesterday. Did you check when James' ship's due in?"

"Tomorrow."

"Ah, good." Nell grinned. "He's promised to help me find a job."

"I thought you'd gone off that idea."

"It wasn't me; it was your Uncle Tom." She perched on the chair opposite. "He doesn't want me to work and thought he'd get me some compensation instead. The thing is, I can't see it happening and I need the money."

"I can always let you have some if you need anything." Billy reached in his pocket for some change. "How much do you want?"

"You put your money away, I'm fine. I don't need anything at the moment, but at some point Elenor will need some new dresses, not to mention me. I can't have you buying things like that."

"That's a shame." A scowl settled on his face. "Wouldn't it be easier to find another husband?"

Nell shook her head. "I'm not ready yet. Your Uncle Jack was special. I don't know how I'll replace him."

"I understand. What will you do then?"

"I'm hoping to get some work in one of the big houses on Upper Parliament Street. A maid or housekeeper."

"Will you move out?"

Nell shrugged. "I'd rather not, but I may have no choice. I hope James hasn't forgotten."

"He won't have. I think you're his favourite person. It's a shame you and him can't get married."

Nell's cheeks flushed. "I don't think the church would like that! Besides, if I do get married, it will be to someone who has a land-based job. I couldn't go through all the worry of having a husband on a ship again."

"Ah, you'll have to marry me then."

Nell flicked a hand across his shoulder. "Be off with you. That wouldn't be any better."

"All right, maybe we won't get married, but if we're both on our own when we're older, we can share a house." Billy grinned at her. "I'll look after you."

"I may take you up on that, although I'm hoping Elenor or Leah will do that if I can find them respectable husbands."

"That's a long time off yet." He stood up as Vernon rejoined them. "I'd better nip outside myself. We need to be going shortly."

The air was warm as Nell pushed the pram with Billy at her side, while Maria walked ahead with Vernon and Alice. Nell manoeuvred the pram into the churchyard but stopped and nudged Billy as Maria headed towards Sarah, who stood on the path with Tom and their eldest son, Sam.

"This will be interesting." Nell's stomach churned. "They've done a good job of avoiding each other these last few weeks, but there's not much chance of that now."

Billy's hand tensed on her arm. "I'm not sure that's the word I'd use. Let's go and calm things down." He didn't wait for Nell to catch up. "Morning Sam, Uncle Tom."

"Billy ... and Aunty Nell." Sam was the image of Tom as a boy, with his dark combed-back hair and brown eyes.

"Good morning." Nell nodded to her nephew, but Billy interrupted her.

"Where've you been these last few days?"

Sam coughed and looked to his dad but hadn't answered when Maria grabbed Billy's arm.

"We don't have time to talk now." She pulled him towards the church, ignoring Sarah as she passed within inches of her.

"She's not cheered up then?" She scowled after Maria.

"At least she's talking now. Not that she's anything nice to say."

"What do you expect?" Sarah stared after her. "She needs to get in there and ask for forgiveness."

Nell bit her lip. "She's been upset. Perhaps it would help if you could see her point of view."

"She should see mine ... and Jane's. Now if you'll excuse me, I need to take my seat."

Nell watched Sarah guide several of the children into church but was relieved when Tom didn't move.

"Is everything all right?" She looked up to see him staring into the distance. "I believe you've not been in the alehouse much this week."

"I've been busy with work."

She raised an eyebrow. "That's not like you."

"We're working on the strike plans. It's not the sort of thing we can do while the bosses are around."

"No, I don't suppose you can." They started walking to the church. "Has Sam been with you?"

Tom ignored her. "We'd better take our seats. The choir will be here in a minute."

Nell sidled into the pew and smiled at Mrs Blackmore, who turned to greet her.

"I'll speak to you later." She flicked through her hymn

book but watched Tom as he continued towards the front of the church and took his seat without even a sideways glance at Sarah.

What's he hiding? Her eyes narrowed as she stared at the back of his head. *I hope it's to do with work.* The congregation obscured her view as they stood to sing the first hymn, so she sought out Rebecca, who sat on the opposite side of the aisle with Mr Grayson and the girls. In comparison to Tom and Sarah, they looked happy.

At the end of the service, Nell waited for the vicar to walk to the door before she stepped out of the pew and let the others file out after her. Mrs Blackmore was waiting for her as she joined the queue to leave.

"You look as if you have the weight of the world on your shoulders."

Nell grimaced. "It's not that bad, although sometimes it feels like it. I can't really talk now." She indicated to Maria, who stood several feet ahead of them. "Perhaps we can go to the park later and I'll tell you what's going on."

Mrs Blackmore beamed at her. "Yes, I'd like that. We could sit at the bandstand."

"Splendid. I'll call around two o'clock."

Billy was waiting for her as they left the church and she pulled him to one side. "Have you fallen out with Sam and Uncle Tom?"

Billy kicked at a stone on the ground. "Not exactly."

"What's that supposed to mean? Is that why you've been coming home early? To avoid them?"

Billy glanced over his shoulders. "Uncle Tom wants me to protest against the conditions at work and strike down my tools. The thing is, I don't want to. We need the money ... especially with Vernon being involved."

"What's he doing getting involved? He's only an apprentice."

"You know what he's like." Billy ushered Nell further away from the door. "The thing is, he doesn't seem to mind losing a day's wages and won't listen when I tell him it could go on for longer."

"He thinks one day of protest will be enough?"

"That's what Uncle Tom's telling everyone, but I don't believe him."

Nell's stomach churned. "Your Uncle Tom's got a lot to answer for. Is Sam going to protest?"

Billy nodded. "That's why he's mad at me. They say it will only be a success if we all stop work, but at the moment, most of us don't want to."

"I can understand that." Nell looked towards the back of the church where Sarah stood with the vicar. "I'm guessing your Aunty Sarah isn't very pleased about it either."

"I don't know if he's told her."

Nell raised an eyebrow. "Well, somebody should. She might not be able to stop Uncle Tom, but she'd certainly have something to say to Sam."

"It can't be me." Billy's dark eyes were wide.

"No, me neither. Not with the way things are at the moment." Nell sighed. "Perhaps we should mention it to your mam. She might like to have a word with Vernon."

Billy shook his head. "He'd kill me if she found out. He'd know I'd said something. It's supposed to be a secret."

"He couldn't stop *me* telling her though, and I heard from Uncle Tom."

"He wouldn't believe you. He'd get mad with me without asking any questions. He's already cross."

Nell rested a hand on his arm. "Leave it with me, and if Vernon accuses you of anything, point him in my direction. I'll put him right."

CHAPTER TWENTY-THREE

The following morning, it was already light when Nell woke, and as soon as she opened her eyes, she swung her legs over the side of the bed. Monday was always wash day, but with James due home, she wanted to have the clothes on the line by the time he arrived. Alice and the girls were still asleep as she tiptoed from the room; they could follow her down when they were ready.

Maria was setting the table when she arrived. "You're up early for a change."

"I want to get the washing done before James gets home."

"So that you can go for a nice cosy walk this afternoon..."

"What's wrong with that?" Nell followed her sister into the kitchen. "In fact, what's wrong with you? You've not had a civil word to say to anyone for weeks."

Maria glared at her. "What is there to be civil about? My whole family's against me ... after all I've done ... and taken the side of that traitor."

"We've done no such thing. If you weren't so grumpy, people may have a bit more sympathy with you."

"Don't blame me…"

"I'm not blaming you; I'm telling you how it is. Try putting a smile on your face and see what a difference it makes." Nell poured the boiling water into the teapot and carried it to the table. "I'll go and put the heat under the washtub while this brews. Tell Alice she's no need to come outside until she's eaten."

Alice straightened up and put a hand on her back as Nell pulled the last of the shirts from the dolly tub and dumped them into a rinsing bowl. She indicated towards the empty water. "We could do with James bringing his washing home while the water's still nice."

"He'll be here soon enough." Nell used a pair of wooden tongs to transfer the shirts to the mangle. "If we can get these squeezed out, it won't take long once he arrives."

Alice shrieked as Elenor and Leah ran towards her and grabbed her legs.

"Got you." Elenor giggled as Leah fell backwards. "She keeps falling over."

"She's only a baby, you have to look after her, do you hear me?" Nell stood Leah back on her feet and rubbed down the back of her dress. "I don't want her getting all wet in here. Why don't you go and see Aunty Ria?"

Alice peeled Elenor's arms from her legs. "Do as you're told. I'll be in shortly."

Nell continued with the mangle, but she'd no sooner

pulled the last shirt through, when James appeared by the door to the wash house.

"You're here." A smile spread across Nell's lips as Alice hugged her brother's arm.

"We're nearly finished. We'd hoped to have it done. What time is it?" Nell straightened up and tucked several pieces of stray hair back into her bun.

"Nearly ten o'clock. There's no rush. I'm here for four days."

"Is that all?" Nell's shoulders slumped.

"It's longer than I thought. Now we're into the summer months, there are more passengers wanting to make the journey. It'll be busy until September, I should imagine."

"I suppose so, but I've a few things I wanted to talk to you about."

James laughed. "You'd better be quick then." He handed her his bag. "Mam's making a pot of tea, so I'll sit with her for a while."

"Come back outside if she bites your head off."

"She seemed all right when I came in. She even smiled at me."

Nell raised an eyebrow at him. "I'd make the most of it, if I were you. I don't think she's smiled at anyone since you went away."

"She was obviously saving it for me." He turned to go back into the house. "I'll speak to you later."

Maria had abandoned James and was in the kitchen when Nell and Alice went back into the house.

"You took your time." She stirred the pan of scouse. "The tea in the pot will be cold."

"I'm sure I can add some hot water if I need to." Nell closed the back door and followed Alice into the living room where James sat with his legs stretched out in front of the fire. He sat up straight when he saw them.

"Are you all done?"

"We are ... for now. How was your trip?" She felt the side of the teapot and reached for a couple of cups.

"Very good. It was a lovely sail in this morning, too. The air was so clear, you could see the Welsh hills for miles."

"It sounds wonderful." She gazed through the window. "Maybe one day."

"Maybe one day what?"

Nell hadn't heard Maria walk up behind her.

"Maybe one day I'll get a job." Nell couldn't keep the scorn from her voice.

"I thought we'd decided that we'd give you some money as and when you need it." The brusqueness hadn't left Maria's voice.

"You might have thought that, but I didn't agree to it. Besides, you might need the extra money yourself over the next few weeks."

"What do you mean?" Lines formed on Maria's forehead.

Nell strolled to the table. "I've heard there are some on the docks who want the men to strike down their tools until they get better pay and working conditions."

James sat forward in his seat. "Where've you heard that?"

"From a couple of people, as it happens. I've also been told that Vernon's keen to join in."

"Vernon?"

Nell pursed her lips as Maria stared at James.

"Is this where they don't go into work and so they don't get paid?"

"It is. What else can you tell us, Aunty Nell?"

"Not a lot, other than Tom's involved and they're turning on men who won't join in."

"So Billy could be dragged into it as well?" Maria's face paled. "We can't have both of them out of work. How will we manage?"

Nell shrugged. "That's a question for you, but perhaps you should think again about me getting a job."

Nell couldn't keep the grin off her face as she selected a well-worn straw bonnet for her afternoon walk.

"Are you ready?" James stood by the living room door, watching her.

"I am. Shall we go?" She smiled at Alice as she sat at the table with her sewing, but Maria didn't look up.

"Don't be late. I want you to do the tea."

"I won't." She rolled her eyes at James as he held the front door open and closed it behind them. "This is what she's been like all the time you've been away. I'm fortunate Aunty Rebecca's always glad of a visit."

"I'm sure it won't last."

"I hope you're right." Nell glanced over to Rebecca's house. "I feel guilty not inviting her out, but she knows I want to talk to you."

"That sounds intriguing. Is it to do with the job? Have you decided what you want to do?"

Nell cocked her head to one side. "I'd say, yes and no and yes." She laughed as James studied her.

"What are you talking about?"

"I'm answering your questions. Is it to do with the job? Yes and no. Have I decided what to do? Yes."

"Ah. I can see you're in one of those moods. What's yes and no supposed to mean?"

"It means I want to speak to you about the job, but there's something else as well. I didn't know who else to talk to."

They took a right-hand turn at the end of the road and headed towards the park. "That sounds serious."

"It is." She reached into her handbag and produced the letter she presumed was from Jane. "This arrived a couple of days after you left."

"It's addressed to Mam." He took it from her and turned it over in his fingers. "It's not been opened."

"No. I happened to be at the door when the postman brought it and I recognised the writing."

James studied the envelope again. "You think it's from Aunty Jane?"

"I do ... and I panicked. After the way your mam's been, I couldn't let her see it, but then I didn't know what to do with it."

"No. I can see that."

"I wondered about telling Uncle Tom and letting him deal with it, but then Alice said something that gave me second thoughts."

James' eyebrows drew together over the bridge of his

nose. "You've told her?"

"Not about the letter, but when your mam refused to leave the bedroom, Alice confided that she'd overheard her talking to herself. She said something like *Fred would never have died if it wasn't for her*. She didn't know who *her* was, but said your mam called her a traitor. I'd say she's talking about Aunty Jane."

"Why didn't you want to mention this to Uncle Tom?"

Nell sighed. "Because at the time, shortly before Fred passed, Uncle Tom and Aunty Sarah were very friendly with Aunty Jane and her husband. They went everywhere together. If your mam's suggesting Aunty Jane had anything to do with his death, they must know something about it ... even though they've denied it. It could also explain why Jane moved to Ireland shortly afterwards."

"I thought they went because this Mr Read was a Catholic and Mam didn't approve."

"That was how it started, but after what's happened these last few weeks, I'm not convinced that's the only reason."

James groaned. "Do you believe she had something to do with Fred's illness?"

"I've no idea, but it's the best I can come up with. I wish she'd stop writing, but don't want to tell her myself."

"Would you like me to do it?"

Nell's face brightened. "Would you? That would be such a weight off my mind."

He ran his fingers over the letter. "We should probably open it. Mam would have asked one of us to read it to her anyway, so it's not as if it would have been private."

"It still feels wrong..."

"If I'm going to write back, I need to know what it says."

Nell focussed straight ahead at the approaching park gates. "You're right. Shall we find a bench?"

They followed the path leading to the lake in the centre of the park and Nell scanned the track that ran around the lake. "The nice weather's brought everyone out. Most of the seats are taken."

James stood beside her and pointed to his right. "They look like they're going. Let's be quick..." He hurried off, leaving Nell to follow. When she arrived, she was relieved to find the bench was in the shade of a large sycamore tree.

"This is very pleasant." She smiled up at James. "I wish it would stop the butterflies in my stomach, though."

"Stop worrying. She'll never know." He took the letter from his pocket. "It's a shame I don't carry a letter opener." He wriggled a finger into a small hole at the top of the envelope and pulled it up to tear the paper. "There we are. Let's have a look."

Nell watched as he read the letter and handed it to her. "What does it say?"

"Take a look. It appears that Aunty Sarah's told her about the argument and she's not happy."

Nell ran a finger beneath each line of text. *"You've no idea how disappointed I am. You can't stop me from coming home."* She looked up at James. "Good grief."

He pointed towards the end of the letter. "If you read a little further, she says she's coming home whether Mam likes it or not."

Nell sat back and closed her eyes. "We have to stop her."

"Either that, or we tell Mam. We can't let her bump into

her at the shop without warning."

Nell stared out over the lake, watching the children laugh as they played with their toy boats. "It's times like this I wish I could get away. If we can't stop her coming, it'll be intolerable."

James reread the letter. "I'll speak to Uncle Tom and get him to put some pressure on her. He must know what's going on."

"Unless Aunty Sarah's arranged it behind his back, which wouldn't surprise me. Besides, what I said earlier about him wanting all the men to strike down their tools means he's not been in the alehouse much this week. That probably means he's not been at home either."

"What a mess." James shook his head. "Is this why you want a job?"

"Not exactly. I wanted to go into service to get some experience before any of this happened."

"You're still keen to go on the ships then?"

"Oh, yes, but the way things are, I'd consider a live-in position if it got me out of the way."

"Where are you thinking?" His eyes surveyed the mansions that edged the park. "One of them?"

"Possibly. Or on Upper Parliament Street. I'm not too choosy." She laughed as she studied the size of the houses. "Although the owners here would need to have plenty of other maids. Could you imagine cleaning one of them on your own?"

"Shall we start on Upper Parliament Street then? Those houses are small in comparison."

Nell grinned. "I won't argue with that. Can we start looking tomorrow?"

CHAPTER TWENTY-FOUR

J ames was at the table by the time Nell and the girls arrived downstairs the following morning.

She smiled when she saw him. "You're up early."

"I always struggle to sleep when I'm back on land." He laughed. "I must miss the waves rocking me to sleep. Anyway, I've been thinking about you and your job and decided we'd better set off early."

Maria joined them from the kitchen. "Aunty Nell doesn't get up early. You should have warned her."

"Yes, I do. It's still not seven o'clock, and it's taken me half an hour to get downstairs. Haven't you noticed I've brushed my hair out and refixed it? I need to make a good impression."

"And you're in your Sunday best. Very smart you look too." James winked at her and Nell's cheeks flushed as she brushed an imaginary fleck from the pale blue skirt.

"It's about the only decent dress I've got." She took a seat at the table. "And I've beaten Billy and Vernon down, so I can't be that late."

"You're not. Take no notice of Mam. Now, I suggest we leave here by about half past seven if we're heading to Upper Parliament Street. If we need to go to the mansions at the park, we can go there this afternoon."

Nell handed Elenor a piece of bread. "If you say so."

"You're going ahead with it, are you?" Maria tutted as she sat down. "What sort of job are you looking for?"

"I don't know yet. I'll find out what's available and see what I think."

"Don't forget you've still got work to do around here. I'm not doing it all myself."

Nell's eyes flicked to James. "What if they want someone full-time? I can't afford to turn it down."

Maria huffed. "I told you to get a morning job, cleaning out the fires, or something like that. You don't need to work all day for the sort of money you need."

Nell took a deep breath. "Let's see what's on offer, shall we?"

Half an hour later, following a fleeting visit from Billy and Vernon, and with nothing but tea leaves in the bottom of her cup, Nell let James help her on with her cloak.

"Good luck, Aunty Nell." Alice grinned as James held the door open, but Nell clenched her teeth.

"Thank you, I think I'll need it. I'll see you later."

With the front door closed behind them, James offered her his arm. "How are you feeling?"

"My stomach's churning so much, I wasn't sure I could eat that bread, but I wasn't giving your mam the satisfaction of seeing me nervous."

James laughed. "You've nothing to worry about. If they

don't offer you a job, that's their loss. Do you want to ask about a housekeeping job or being a maid?"

Nell linked her arm through his. "Or being a cleaner like your mam wants. What do you think? Being a housekeeper would be nice, but I've no experience."

"I reckon you could do it. You've run your own house for long enough."

"That's what your Aunty Rebecca said. She doesn't want me to be a cleaner, but don't forget, I've always lived with your mam and she does most of it."

"She might keep the money, but she doesn't do the bookkeeping."

"I don't do it so much now that Billy's taken over from me."

"But nobody need tell them that. I'm sure you know a lot more than you give yourself credit for."

"So you think I should aim for a housekeeper's job?"

"You should do whatever makes you happy and stop worrying about the rest of us. It's you who'll be doing the work."

Nell grimaced. "Everyone seems to have forgotten that."

A quarter of an hour later they approached the corner of Windsor Street and Upper Parliament Street and once there, Nell slowed to a stop.

James looked in both directions. "Which way?"

"Right, I would say, away from the docks. The houses are smarter up there."

"As you wish." They turned onto a wide road of fashionable Georgian townhouses, the majority of which were occupied by local merchants. "Where do we start?"

Nell's heart pounded as she studied the three-storey

houses, their basement windows thrown open to reveal the clattering of pots and pans inside. "I don't know. We want somewhere that'll have a housekeeper, but not one that's too formal."

"What about this row? You probably won't get a position at the first house we call at, but there must be fifteen or twenty to choose from in this terrace. You should find something in one of them."

Nell took a deep breath. "All right then. Will you knock?"

They walked up the steps of the first house, and James banged on the door. A moment later, a smartly dressed woman who looked very much like a housekeeper opened it.

"Good morning, madam." James gave a slight bow. "I wonder if you might help. My aunt is looking for employment and we wondered if you had anything that may suit."

The woman looked Nell up and down, causing her to shudder. *Thank goodness I put on my best clothes.*

"What sort of thing does she have in mind? We have an opening for a scullery maid in a week or two."

"Oh ... no." The heat rose in Nell's cheeks. "I don't mean to be ungrateful, but ... do you have anything more ... senior?"

"No, I'm afraid we don't. Good day to you."

They were still on the top step as the door closed in their face.

"Oh." Nell's shoulders dropped and James took her arm and led her back down the steps.

"Don't be too despondent. We didn't expect anything from the first house."

"You're right. I just hoped…"

"Come on, let's try next door."

A middle-aged gentleman in a dark morning suit opened the door to the next house along. James repeated his lines, but the butler interrupted him.

"There are no senior jobs for women here, only scullery maids and cleaning roles, and we have no vacancies for either. Now, if you'll excuse me."

Nell shivered as the door was shut. "I know I need a job, but I should be grateful they have no openings. Imagine working for him."

"He'd probably be fine if you got the position."

"I wouldn't want to take the chance." She studied the rest of the houses in the block. "Do you think it will be like this everywhere?"

James shrugged. "We won't know unless we try."

"I don't know that I can bear being scrutinised by many more self-important servants."

James put an arm around her shoulders as he guided her back down the steps. "Cheer up, it may not be that bad. I'll try another tack with the next house."

A smartly dressed woman of a similar age to Nell opened the door when James knocked.

"Good morning." He tipped his hat to her. "My aunt here is looking for employment and we wondered if you had anything that may suit. She'd be looking for one of your more senior roles."

The woman glanced at Nell. "No, I'm afraid we don't. I'm here on my own, with a general domestic and cook, and have no intention of leaving."

She started to close the door, but James held up a hand to stop her.

"Actually, could I ask one more question? Would you happen to know whether any of the other houses around here are looking for staff? Perhaps a personal maid."

The woman smiled as she studied James and Nell glowed with pride. He did look very smart in his well-pressed suit. "You may wish to try number eighty-seven. I can't promise, but they may be able to help."

James gave a deep bow. "You've been most helpful. Thank you."

Nell linked her arm back into his as they descended the steps. "Personal maid? Where did that come from?"

"From the ship. Often women bring their maids, and once you'd said no to being a scullery maid, I didn't want to ask after a cleaning job. It seemed like a reasonable suggestion. Don't you think so?"

Nell stared up the road as they walked towards number eighty-seven. "I've no idea. I've never fussed after another woman."

"You look after Elenor and Leah, don't you? Attending to these rich women isn't much different. Trust me, they've no idea how to take care of themselves."

Nell laughed. "I'm sure you're exaggerating, but maybe I could try it."

They reached the front of number eighty-seven and paused while Nell adjusted the collar of her coat.

"Ready?"

She nodded. "Ready."

James walked up the steps and knocked on the door,

taking a step back while he waited. Within seconds, a white-haired man in a dark suit opened it.

"May I help you?"

"Good morning." James gave his usual bow and Nell marvelled at how impressive he must look on the cruise liners. "I understand you have a vacancy for a housekeeper. My aunt here is looking for a position and your residence was recommended to us." He extended his hand towards Nell and she joined him on the top step.

"Recommended?" The man's gaze flicked between the two of them. "Not that I'm aware. I'm sorry you've wasted your time."

As the door closed, James stepped forward and stopped it with his foot. "Forgive me; but is the mistress of the house in?"

"The mistress doesn't receive visitors before luncheon. If you have a card, I can leave it for her."

Nell's forehead broke out in a sweat. *A card. What on earth would I be doing with one of them?*

James patted his jacket. "Yes, here you are. Would you explain that I'm representing my aunt and that we'll call again at two o'clock?"

The old man studied it. "Very well, sir."

Nell gripped James' arm a little more tightly as they walked down the steps and continued up the road. He said nothing and she looked up to see his ginger eyebrows drawn together.

"Are we going to carry on knocking at other houses? It's not half past nine yet."

"I suppose we should. Just because we're calling back there, doesn't mean they'll offer you a job."

"Don't you think it strange that the butler didn't know anything about there being a position though?"

"I do, but I wonder if it's because it's his job they're trying to fill and they've not told him. That's why I asked to see the mistress."

Nell stared up at her nephew. "What good will it do me if they need a new butler? I can't do that."

James chuckled. "Don't look so worried. Butlers are going out of fashion nowadays, especially in houses like these. It wouldn't surprise me if they want to replace him with a housekeeper but haven't told him yet. Looking at the age of him, I'd say you could do twice as much work as him."

"I daresay I could, but I don't want him to lose his job on my account." Nell straightened her back. "I think we should call somewhere else, if that's the case."

"I doubt he'd lose his job because of you. If they're looking for a housekeeper, they'll have already made the decision. Would you turn it down if they offered you the position?"

"Probably not."

"Why don't we wait and see what they have to say this afternoon then? We can carry on with the other houses later if we need to. Even if they don't have a suitable position, they may know someone who does."

Nell's brow creased. "I suppose that makes sense. In the meantime, shall we stroll up the road to see how many more houses there are? I'm not ready to go home yet."

CHAPTER TWENTY-FIVE

As two o'clock approached, Nell and James strolled back up the wide footpath of Upper Parliament Street, towards number eighty-seven.

"I do hope they have a position," Nell said as they arrived. "It would save any more looking."

"It would, but we need to make sure it suits you. Have you had any more thoughts about living in?"

Nell studied the neat Georgian windows, framed with their fashionable drapes, and sighed.

"It wouldn't be ideal for the girls, but at least it would get me away from your mam while there's all this talk of Aunty Jane. Besides, it would give me a taste of what it would be like to go to sea. I can't be nipping home every evening if I get on a steamship."

James stopped and cocked his head at her. "You have a point."

"I hope it's not such a disaster that I won't want to leave the house ever again."

James patted her hand. "All right, but let's hope it

doesn't come to that. Come along. We don't want to be late."

Nell wondered if the butler had been waiting for them, such was his speed to open the front door once James had knocked. He welcomed them with a low bow and led them up the stairs to the first-floor sitting room.

"Mr Atkin to see you, madam."

Nell stayed a few paces behind James, but when they walked into the room, she couldn't resist glancing around. She had never seen such splendour in a home and involuntarily ran a hand over the back of a red velvet settee positioned opposite a fire with an ornate wooden surround.

The lady of the house sat on a matching chair in the bay window, alongside an impressive palm plant. Her dark navy dress, with its elaborate collar and cuffs of white lace, strained to cover her large frame.

The woman appeared not to notice her, but a wave of heat travelled up Nell's neck to her face. *I hope she didn't watch us arrive.*

James stepped forward and took the hand she offered. "Good afternoon, madam. May I introduce my aunt, Mrs Riley?"

Nell shuffled to James' side and inclined her head as James continued.

"Due to unfortunate circumstances, she needs employment, and we were led to believe you may have a suitable position."

The woman looked Nell up and down. "What can she do?"

"Her husband was a master mariner, and she's been

running her own home for nearly ten years. She could manage the day-to-day running of this house, too."

"A housekeeper, you mean?"

James nodded. "Indeed."

"Does she have references?"

"Not as such, but I'd be happy to vouch for her, as would the vicar of St Philemon's."

"She's local then?"

"She lives off Windsor Street."

Nell's heart pounded as the woman gave her a second look.

"You're right in thinking I may have something suitable. The butler will be leaving us shortly and I've decided I'd like a female assistant for a change, possibly to act as a companion as well as housekeeper. Is she accomplished in the art of conversation?"

"I would say so. She has good knowledge of the local area and a great interest in foreign lands."

"Why would you be interested in that?" The woman scowled at Nell, causing her cheeks to burn.

"I suppose I'm curious by nature, and my husband used to thrill me with tales from his travels. He made places sound so exciting."

"Is he no longer with us?"

"No. Sadly, he was lost at sea." Nell lowered her head as James stepped forward.

"Hence my aunt's need for a job."

"Can I assume she has no children?" The woman directed the question to James, and Nell held her breath as he answered.

"Actually, she has two daughters, but they live with my

family. My mother and sister would care for them. They wouldn't stop her working."

"Very well." The woman rearranged the skirt of her dress. "Leave her with me for the rest of the afternoon and we'll see how she performs. If you pick her up at four o'clock, that should give us enough time."

Nell's heart skipped a beat at the thought of being left alone. *This is getting serious.*

"Thank you, madam." James gave another bow. "Shall I see myself out?"

"No. Why don't you let your aunt...? What's her name?"

"Mrs Riley."

The woman adjusted her position. "Why doesn't Mrs Riley show you out, and then she can go to the kitchen and bring back a pot of tea for two."

Nell thought her legs would collapse as James gave a final bow and indicated for her to walk with him. Once they were on the landing, she paused and took several deep breaths. "I wasn't expecting that. What do I say?"

James laughed. "Be yourself. Pretend you're talking to Mam and you'll be fine."

"But she's even older than your mam. We'll have nothing in common. I don't even know the woman's name."

James rolled his eyes. "Ask someone in the kitchen."

"And where's that?" Nell's voice squeaked as James led her down the stairs.

"Don't look so worried. We'll find it together. I expect it takes up most of the ground floor, so it shouldn't be hard to find. I can see I need to give you some lessons in how to deal with women like her in case you get the job."

Nell took another breath as they headed for a door at the end of a corridor that ran along the side of the stairs. "Do I ask her about the job, or do I wait for her to tell me?"

"Ask. It will show you have some initiative. She won't want someone who's frightened of her own shadow."

"Right." Nell gulped.

"Remember. Treat her as you'd treat Elenor." James grinned. "Although you'd be as well not to cut her food up."

Nell batted the back of her hand on James' arm, but he ignored her and knocked on the door. He didn't wait to be invited in and within seconds a small round woman wearing a grey dress with an oversized white apron hurried towards them.

"What are you doing in my kitchen?"

James once again gave a small bow. "We're sorry to disturb you, but we're here because my aunt's been asked by the lady of the house to collect a pot of tea for two. May I leave the two of you together?"

"You're here for a job, are you?" The cook watched as James pulled the door closed behind him. "Have you got it?"

"No, not yet. I don't think so, anyway. She wants to talk to me first."

"That's a good sign. She rarely takes to people. I'm always glad to be down here out of the way."

"Do you live in?" Nell's voice was a pitch higher than she'd like.

"We all do. There are two rooms in the attic. Me and Ethel share one, and Mr Jacobs, the butler, has the other." Her face paled. "You won't want a room, will you?"

Nell shuddered. "I hope not, but it'll be up to her, I suppose. By the way, what's her name?"

Cook tutted. "Didn't she tell you? She's a madam for that. Mrs Cuthbert, wife of Mr Cuthbert who works at the customs house."

Nell gazed at the selection of cupboards and worktops that surrounded the large wooden table in the centre of the room. "He must be important."

"I'll say, judging by the amount of money she spends. Have you had a look round upstairs yet?"

"Only the sitting room."

"Well, she's spared no less expense anywhere else, except the attic, of course. You see if I'm right."

Nell's heart had calmed itself by the time she picked up a tray loaded with a teapot, two cups and saucers and a plate of cakes. She took the steps slowly and was glad to see a console table on the landing where she could balance the tray while she knocked on the door.

"Come in."

"Here we are, madam. Cook added some cakes too."

"Splendid. Pop the tray on the table and come and tell me about yourself."

Once the tray was in position, Nell glanced at the chair on the opposite side of the bay. *Do I sit down? No, wait to be asked. If I get the job, there won't be any of that.*

Nell kept her summary short, speaking only of where she lived and the fact she shared a house with Maria and her family. When there was a suitable pause in the conversation, she bent forward to pour the tea.

"Do you take milk and sugar, madam?" *Thank goodness I've seen James do this when he's been teasing Maria.*

"One sugar and plenty of milk. I can't drink it if it's too strong."

Nell added milk to the cup and picked up the tea strainer. It was something they didn't bother with at home, and she prayed it wouldn't cause her to spill tea everywhere. Finally, relieved to put the teapot down, she reached for the sugar tongs and dropped one cube into the light-brown liquid.

"There you are. Shall I stir it for you?"

"There's no need. I'm not incapable."

Thank goodness for that.

"Aren't you pouring one for yourself?" Mrs Cuthbert rested her spoon on the saucer.

"Yes, of course, but I wanted to make sure you were satisfied first." Nell's heart was pounding again. "Shall I sit down?"

Mrs Cuthbert looked first at Nell and then at the chair. "You shouldn't need to be told."

What does that mean? Nell hesitated as she perched on the edge of the chair, her cup and saucer resting on her knee. "You have a lovely house. Have you lived here long?"

"Several years now. My husband was in London before we moved up here."

"So you're not from Liverpool?"

"Good heavens, no." Mrs Cuthbert looked as if a nasty smell had passed under her nose. "We were in Bristol to start with. A very different city."

Nell nodded, although she had no idea whether that was good or bad. "May I ask about the job? What would it involve?"

Mrs Cuthbert studied her. "What do you expect? All the usual things a housekeeper would do. Managing the staff, ordering groceries, submitting the bills to Mr Cuthbert. That sort of thing."

"Yes, of course; I just wondered if you had any particular routines or chores."

"Nothing out of the ordinary, other than acting as my companion, should I require you."

"Very good." Nell bit down on her lip. *Do I ask? What the heck, I might as well.* "Would you expect me to live in, or would it be day work?"

Mrs Cuthbert's eyes bored into Nell. "Of course you'd live in. What good are you in the middle of the night, if you're not here?"

"The middle of the night?"

"I have trouble sleeping. That's one of the reasons I need a female companion."

"I see." *James wasn't wrong when he suggested treating her like a child.*

Mrs Cuthbert continued to study her. "You seem a decent sort and there's no reason we shouldn't get along together. Report to me on Monday. There'll be a uniform ready for you and I'll tell Mr Jacobs I won't be needing him. As soon as he's gone, I'll have the maid clean the room and you can move straight in."

Nell smiled. "Yes, Mrs Cuthbert, thank you." With the distinct impression she was being dismissed, she put her cup and saucer on the tray. "May I ask how long Mr Jacobs has been here?"

Mrs Cuthbert shrugged. "Fifteen years or so. Since we arrived in Liverpool. Why?"

Nell took a deep breath. "Is he aware that you're looking to replace him?"

"He knows I find him incompetent, so it won't come as any surprise to him…"

"But you haven't told him he'll lose his job when I arrive on Monday? Not to mention his home."

Mrs Cuthbert flicked her hand. "I'm sure he'll be fine. He'll get a place in the workhouse easy enough."

"But that's not fair!" Nell stuttered as Mrs Cuthbert's cold eyes stared at her. "I mean … after all this time, shouldn't you give him more notice so he can find somewhere else to live?"

"What are you suggesting? That you share his room?"

"No, not at all, but I don't want to be responsible for him being homeless, especially if he's not had chance to find anywhere else to live."

"You speak as if you have a say in the matter, Mrs Riley."

"Perhaps I do … if I don't take the job, he can carry on as he is."

Mrs Cuthbert smirked. "I'm sure that's very noble of you, but it's only a matter of time. He knows he's too old for the job … and that I require a companion. If it's not you, it will be someone else."

Nell took a deep breath. "All right, but might I suggest that when I come to work on Monday, I won't live in? I'm not far away and could be here when you wake in the morning. That way Mr Jacobs can stay until he sorts himself out."

Mrs Cuthbert studied her. "Very well. Report for work at ten o'clock on Monday morning and we'll make a formal arrangement with Mr Jacobs about the exchange."

Nell gave a bow. "Thank you, madam. I'll see you then."

CHAPTER TWENTY-SIX

Sunday dinner was over, and the washing-up finished, when Nell and Maria pulled a couple of chairs from the dining table to join Alice and her brothers around the unlit fire.

"Are you all set for tomorrow, Aunty Nell?" Billy folded up the newspaper and sat back in his chair.

"As ready as I'll ever be."

"Why aren't you excited?" Alice studied her. "I'm sure I would be if I got a job."

"I suppose I am, but I don't think I like Mrs Cuthbert. The fact she considered throwing poor Mr Jacobs out of his room at a moment's notice suggests she's not very nice."

"I don't know why you're surprised. They're all like that, these toffs." Vernon looked to James for confirmation.

"I wouldn't say they're all bad. Some are worse than others. The advantage I've got on the ship is that they're only on board for a couple of weeks and once they get off, I rarely see them again."

"That won't be the case with Mrs Cuthbert, will it?"

Nell's bottom lip jutted out. "Once I start, I'll be stuck with her."

"Either that or she'll take a dislike to you and throw you out ... like she planned on throwing out the old butler." Vernon snarled as he spoke.

"That won't matter." Alice's innocence was such a contrast to her brother's bitterness. "She can come back here. She's not like Mr Jacobs who has nowhere to go."

"Hopefully, it won't come to that. I can come home each evening ... to start with at least."

Maria rolled her shoulders as she sat up straight. "I'm still not happy you took a live-in position. Didn't you think of me? And what about the girls?"

Nell turned her eyes towards the ceiling, above which her daughters were having their afternoon nap. "They'll be happy with you and Alice. I doubt they'll even notice I've gone." A lump formed in her throat, causing her to stand up. "I'll be back in a minute."

She hurried to the back yard and leaned against the wall of the outhouse. *By this time tomorrow, they'll have forgotten all about me.* She pursed her lips, determined not to cry, but opened them again on the count of five. *Pull yourself together. No they won't. As much as they like Alice, she's not their mam.*

She wiped a stray tear from her cheek and took several deep breaths. *If I don't like it, I can always come home.*

She nodded as if agreeing with herself. *I might even be back by this time next week.* With a sigh, she pushed herself away from the wall, but stopped as the back door opened and James stepped out to join her.

"Are you all right?"

"Oh, it's you." She gave him a brief smile. "I will be. I needed some air."

He stood between her and the door. "You don't have to take the job with Mrs Cuthbert if you don't want to."

"I do. I can't leave before I start ... and besides, if I do, I'd never get another job around there. I've no doubt Mrs Cuthbert will have a circle of friends who'd be only too pleased to hear about her unreliable new housekeeper."

James sighed. "You've got a point, but if you really don't like it, you needn't stay."

"I've already told myself that, although that won't look good either."

"Well, if you change your mind..."

Nell stood tall. "No, I've made my mind up. I've got to remember that I'm only doing it to give me enough experience to get a job on the ships. It won't be for long, whether I like it or not."

He placed a hand on her shoulder. "That's the spirit. See if you can manage two weeks. That's how long you'll have to put up with awkward passengers on the ship."

"I can do that."

"And..." James had a glint in his eye. "...you don't need to worry about Aunty Jane. I finally spoke to Uncle Tom in the alehouse last night. He was furious when he heard she was still planning to come home and said he'd write to her himself."

Nell grimaced. "I hope he's not too hard on your Aunty Sarah. I imagine he'll blame her."

James groaned. "I did get the impression he thought it was her fault, but she should have known better."

"She should, especially given how friendly she's been

with your mam. Anyway, at least it's sorted out now. That's one less thing for me to worry about."

The following morning, thankful she didn't need to report to Mrs Cuthbert until ten o'clock, Nell fussed her daughters with more enthusiasm than usual. When the time came to go, she gave Elenor a hug. "Mam will be back later. You be a good girl for Alice."

"She'll be fine. Which is more than I can say for me with all that washing as well as the cooking and cleaning to do." Maria stood with her arms folded as Nell leaned over to collect her handbag.

"I'm sure you'll manage. I'll see you later." Nell gave her a weak smile as she followed James down the hall. She waited for him to close the front door before taking his arm. "I do feel guilty leaving her to do everything by herself."

"Don't worry about her. Making you feel guilty was probably all part of the plan." He patted her hand. "Come on, cheer up. Old Mr Jacobs may have a cup of tea waiting for you when you get there."

The sun was warm as they walked to Upper Parliament Street, and at five minutes to ten, James knocked on the front door.

"I'll leave you to it. See you tonight."

He hadn't gone half a dozen paces when a young maid opened the door. "Yes?"

"G-good morning. I'm Mrs Riley, the new housekeeper. Mrs Cuthbert asked me to be here for ten o'clock."

The maid said nothing as she beckoned her in, but Nell

hesitated. *If looks could kill.* She led her to the bottom of the stairs. "She's in the sitting room."

"Shall I...?" Nell hadn't finished her sentence when the girl disappeared into the kitchen. *I'll show myself up then.* She hung her coat on the stand and made her way upstairs. Once she reached the landing, she wiped the palms of her hands on her skirt and knocked on the door.

"Come in."

Nell's stomach churned as she pushed on the door and stepped inside.

"You're late." Mrs Cuthbert was in her seat by the window and barely looked up from the magazine she was reading.

"Y-you said ten o'clock. I thought I was a minute early."

"Ten o'clock? What on earth would I say that for? I need you here at eight to bring me my breakfast tray."

Nell was paralysed. "Eight?" *She didn't say eight; I'm sure she didn't. I'd have remembered.*

"That dreadful domestic girl had to bring it up for me. It won't do."

For reasons she couldn't fathom, Nell curtsied. "I'm sorry. I must have been mistaken."

"Haven't you been upstairs to unpack your bag yet? I've left you a dress on the bed. I expect you to wear it at all times."

Nell's mouth opened and closed several times before anything came out. "My bag? We agreed I wouldn't be staying until after Mr Jacobs left."

Mrs Cuthbert flicked her hand. "Oh, he left yesterday."

"He's gone!" Nell instinctively looked over her shoulder.

"I didn't need both of you, although perhaps I should have kept him until after you'd arrived."

"But that was the arrangement ... that I wouldn't live in until he found somewhere else to go." Nell swayed and reached for the back of the settee to steady herself.

"I couldn't wait for that. He was too old for this sort of work and I wanted female company. I explained that to you."

"But ... but ... this was his home." The colour drained from Nell's face, but Mrs Cuthbert threw the magazine onto the chair opposite and stood up.

"What's the matter with you, woman? Do you want this job or not? If you do, go upstairs and change into your uniform and then go down to the kitchen and bring me up a pot of tea. I'll tell you what I need you to do when you get back."

After a non-stop day of checking stock, placing orders and running around after Mrs Cuthbert, Nell emerged from the kitchen to a darkening sky. She studied the back yard until she found an alleyway she hoped would lead onto Upper Parliament Street. As the back gate clanged shut behind her, she glanced up at the stars. *At least it's not raining.* She hurried towards the road and headed towards Windsor Street.

"Aunty Nell?"

The voice stopped her in her tracks, and she spun around to see a shape running up behind her.

"James?"

"It is you." James gasped as he offered her his arm. "I was beginning to think you'd never leave."

"You and me both. I swear she gave me more things to do just to keep me there."

James' brow furrowed as they started walking. "Why would she do that?"

"Because she wants me to live in. Despite what she'd promised, she told Mr Jacobs he had to leave and fully expected me to arrive this morning with my bag. When I didn't, I think she made it her mission to make me do two days' work in one."

"Will you move in tomorrow then?"

Tears pricked Nell's eyes. "I don't have much choice. It doesn't help though that Ethel, the maid, refuses to talk to me. According to the cook, Mr Jacobs was like a father to her and she thinks it's my fault he lost his job. She's probably right."

"No, she's not. Mrs Cuthbert made the decision to replace him." James patted her hand. "Do you want me to go and speak to her?"

"No, please, don't. It will only make things worse. Besides, I may as well move in. The girls will be asleep when we get home and I need to be back here for seven o'clock to give her breakfast, so I won't see them in the morning either. If the days are going to be that long, there's no point going home. She's said I can take every Sunday afternoon off, so that's something."

"I'll have to hope my shore leave includes Sundays then." He smiled as Nell looked up.

"Oh, I hope it does, although I could always ask to change days if you're only home during the week."

"Well, like you said this morning, it shouldn't be for long. In fact, it would be as well if you could finish ahead of winter setting in. You won't want to be walking home on your own in the dark. I won't be here to meet you every night."

"No." Nell's shoulders slumped. "You won't even be here to meet me tomorrow."

"No, I'll be on the ship by eight o'clock in the morning."

"Perhaps I could walk down Windsor Street with you then. We'll need to leave around the same time."

"Our last farewell." James laughed.

"Don't say that. You'll be back in a month and we can do it all again."

"I'm only teasing." His face grew stern. "Somehow it feels different going away this time."

"I hope it's not because you're worrying about me. Once I'm settled, I'm sure things will improve."

"I hope you're right."

Nell was grateful the light was fading. "Of course I am. I was probably slow today, too, with it being my first day, but it should be easier now I know what I'm doing."

"You're right. I remember how hard everything was when I first went to sea, but it's second nature now. You'll get used to it." James upped his pace. "We'd better get a move on if you've got to pack your bag for tomorrow."

CHAPTER TWENTY-SEVEN

For the fifth day in a row, Nell trudged up the second flight of stairs with a breakfast tray in her hand. Was it really less than a week since she'd started? She paused outside the bedroom and caught her breath before knocking on the door and letting herself in. The drapes were still closed, and she placed the tray on a table at the foot of the bed and drew them back.

"Good morning, Mrs Cuthbert."

Mrs Cuthbert stirred but remained where she was.

"It's lovely outside today. Might you like to take a walk to the park later?"

"A walk? Certainly not."

Ignoring Mrs Cuthbert's glare, Nell helped her sit up and straightened the bedcovers over her legs.

"Yes, why not? It might do you the world of good rather than sitting indoors all day." She placed the tray over her legs and lifted a lid that covered two softly boiled eggs and a slice of bread and butter. "I'll walk with you if you like."

"What nonsense. I have better things to do this

afternoon and I need you to polish the silver. I don't want Ethel getting her hands on it."

Nell groaned as she plumped up the cushions on the settee to the side of the bed. "No, I've not done it yet. I've been too busy sorting out those accounts. Do you realise there are grocers who haven't been paid for nearly two months?"

Mrs Cuthbert tapped the top of her egg. "Oh, they'll get their money."

When? Nell bit down on her lip. "I'm sure that will please them. I've had several this week asking when they can expect payment. I fear they'll struggle to make ends meet if they need to pay the farmers when they've not been paid themselves. It's very difficult."

Mrs Cuthbert said nothing, focussing instead on the sliver of bread she was dipping into her egg.

"Right, I'll go and start on the silver then." Nell strode towards the door, but Mrs Cuthbert called her back.

"What about our morning conversation?"

"Oh, I'm sorry, you seemed rather preoccupied with your breakfast. I didn't think you'd want to talk."

Seeing Mrs Cuthbert's scowl, Nell returned to the chair by the bed.

"I was telling you how many shopkeepers are struggling to pay the farmers..."

Mrs Cuthbert gave her familiar flick of the hand. "And I told you, they'll be paid, so enough of that. Tell me about your daughters."

Nell's heart fluttered as she sat down. "They're little angels, really. Elenor's the eldest, she'll be four next week, and Leah's the baby. She's eighteen months."

"That's very young to leave them."

"It is, but when my husband died..."

"How inconvenient. Do they remember him?"

"No." Nell's smile slipped, but it reappeared seconds later. "I had a letter from my sister yesterday, telling me how much they're looking forward to seeing me tomorrow."

"Tomorrow?" Mrs Cuthbert's head jerked up from her second egg. "They can't come here."

"No, I realise that, but it's Sunday ... my afternoon off..."

The skin beneath Mrs Cuthbert's chin wobbled as she shook her head. "You can't have time off tomorrow. I have visitors."

Nell stared at her. "But you promised. You said that if I moved in, I could go home each Sunday afternoon."

Mrs Cuthbert licked her fingers as she finished her breakfast. "Surely, you don't expect me to give you time off *every* week."

"Well ... yes. Especially after everything I've done this week."

"I'm afraid that's not possible. I need you tomorrow." Mrs Cuthbert moved the tray from her lap and pushed it towards Nell. "Here, take this if you're going ... and come back when you've finished. I've some mending that needs doing."

Nell grabbed the tray and blinked back her tears as she stood on the landing, fighting the temptation to throw it down the stairs. *What's the point? I'd only have to clean up the mess.* She took a deep breath and set off back to the kitchen. Cook looked up from her mixing bowl as Nell slammed the tray down near the sink.

"What's up with you?"

"She is." Nell pointed to the ceiling. "Who's she having around tomorrow afternoon?"

"Tomorrow?" Cook's forehead creased. "No one, I hope. She's said nothing to me."

"She's told me I can't have my afternoon off because she's having visitors."

Cook wiped her hands on a cloth and pushed open a door at the far side of the kitchen. "Do you know who's coming to visit tomorrow?"

Ethel jumped when she saw the cook. "Tomorrow. No, why would I? She doesn't tell me anything."

Cook left the door open as she strolled back to the table. "I'm not doing any extra cooking if she can't be bothered to tell me what's going on. She can do it herself."

The maid ambled to the sink as Nell took the cook to one side. "Since I started, I've noticed you've had no time off. Is that usual?"

"She's not fond of us leaving the house, but I usually get out about once a fortnight. On a Wednesday afternoon, if I'm lucky."

"Every two weeks? I need to go home more often than that."

"You're fortunate you've got somewhere to go to. She usually hires people who'll call this place their home, then they don't need to take time off. If I were you, I wouldn't make too much fuss about it."

Don't make a fuss? Nell wandered to the table and helped herself to a cup of tea. "What do I do if I want to see my daughters?"

Cook shrugged. "Sneak off when she's not looking."

"That's hardly ideal."

"It's better than nothing, and once you've been here for a while, she won't miss you so much."

Nell sighed as she stirred two spoonfuls of sugar into her tea. "May I ask another question? When do we get paid?"

Cook frowned at her. "That'll be up to you."

"Me?"

"You do the paperwork, don't you? Haven't you done anything about it? Mr Jacobs gave us our wages on a Saturday afternoon."

"That's today!" Nell placed her hands on her hips. "She didn't tell me that. And what about my money? Am I expected to do my own wages?"

"I couldn't tell you. Mr Jacobs didn't tell us about anything like that, but we never had any problem with him not paying us."

"I'm sorry. I swear she didn't tell me." Nell sat down and wrapped her hands around her cup. "I'd better go and speak to her."

Mrs Cuthbert had moved to the sitting room and was waiting for Nell when she arrived.

"About time, too. The dresses I was telling you about are in my dressing room. Both need the hems repairing. You'll see them when you go in. Come and fasten the back of my dress for me first. You should realise I can't do it myself."

Nell strolled to the middle of the room and undid the misaligned buttons more harshly than she intended. She worked in silence, pulling the material tightly until they were neatly fastened again.

"There you are." Nell watched Mrs Cuthbert take her seat. "May I speak with you?"

Mrs Cuthbert glared at her. "You want to apologise, do you?"

"Apologise? What for?"

"For storming out of the bedroom and leaving me with no help, that's what."

"I didn't storm out; you dismissed me. If you must know, I've come to ask about the staff wages. I wasn't aware it was part of my job to do them."

"If you'd done the job before, you wouldn't need telling."

Nell counted to three. *She's well aware I've not done the job.* "I don't believe all housekeepers manage the wages; nevertheless, it would have been helpful to know how much the staff earn and when they get paid. I'd also like to ask about my situation. Do you want me to do my own wages?"

Mrs Cuthbert studied her, confusion etched across her face. "Do your own?"

"If I don't do them, who does? Who did Mr Jacobs' wages?"

"Mr Jacobs?" It was as if she'd already forgotten her former butler. "I suppose my husband must have."

"But you don't know?"

Mrs Cuthbert focussed her attention on a speck on her skirt. "I'll speak to Mr Cuthbert tonight. Is that all?"

"Yes, thank you." *If she thinks I'm relying on her to get paid, she can think again.* Nell immediately made her way to a compact room off the kitchen, laughably called her office, and took several ledgers from one of the drawers. *I'm getting this sorted out instead of her stupid sewing.*

She flicked through the large leather-bound books until

she found details of the payments made to Cook and Ethel. On the assumption they received the same amount each week, she copied the figures onto some invoices and added them to the pile that already sat on her desk. *Now I need one for myself.*

Using the cook's wage as a guide, she assigned herself an amount. *That's not enough. There must be something here showing Mr Jacobs wage.* She found his original records. There were no errors. *I suppose we're getting free food and lodgings, but it's still not a lot.* She checked the papers again, reading each one thoroughly until she finally found what she was looking for. *There we are.* She scanned the page for his weekly wage. *Heavens, that's a lot more than Cook. In fact, it's more than Cook and Ethel added together. How could they justify that?* She'd already been told that the old butler only did half of what they did. *If he can earn that much, I don't see why I can't earn more than Cook.* She added an extra four shillings to her wage. *There, that looks better.*

It was almost five o'clock when she finished, and Nell hurried to tidy up. She needed to be upstairs to help Mrs Cuthbert change into her evening dress. She was about to knock on the bedroom door when Mr Cuthbert arrived home. *She can wait.* Nell raced down to the kitchen to collect her papers and followed Mr Cuthbert to his study. Straightening her dress, she took a deep breath and gave a short, sharp knock on the door. Mr Cuthbert opened it, a puzzled expression on his face.

"Mrs Riley. What may I do for you?"

Nell thrust the invoices towards him. "I've been sorting through the accounts, sir, and there are a number of bills that need paying. I've also prepared the ledger for the staff wages."

Mr Cuthbert stared at the invoices as he took them from her. "That's very efficient, I'm sure. I'll look at them next week."

"Forgive me for saying, sir, but I was led to believe the staff wages were due today."

He turned back to his desk. "Saturday, yes, my word, you're right."

"Shall I take them down to the kitchen with me?"

Mr Cuthbert dropped the papers onto the desk. "No, don't you worry yourself. I need to check through everything. I'll sort it out myself."

Nell gave a slight bow. "Very good, sir. I need to go and dress Mrs Cuthbert, but other than that, we'll all be in the kitchen for the next couple of hours."

By the time the clock struck seven, Nell was restless. She'd already paced the length of the kitchen several times and had no intention of stopping.

"Where on earth is he?"

"Did he say he'd bring the money down?" Cook had taken a seat at the table.

"Yes. I said we'd be here for a couple of hours, and the time must be up by now. If he's not quick, they'll be going to the dining room, then heaven knows when we'll see him."

"I don't like it." Ethel no longer pretended to work. "If they don't pay me, I'm not washing any more of those dishes."

"You'll do as you're told." Cook glared up at her.

"But why hadn't she been told to do the wages? Maybe the real reason Mrs Cuthbert wanted to get rid of Mr Jacobs was because he was as regular as clockwork with our money." Ethel folded her arms as she sat at the table. "I've heard of people like us not getting paid, and if the master of the house thinks he can get away with it, it will only get worse."

Nell's brow furrowed. "You mean they may stop paying the staff and expect them to work for nothing?"

"That's nothing but a rumour." Cook banged a hand on the table.

"No, it's not." Ethel glared at her. "I've a friend who worked for two months without getting paid. They wouldn't admit it was deliberate, of course, said it was a misunderstanding or something similar, but it wasn't."

"Two months!" Nell's mouth dropped open. "Why didn't she leave?"

"It was her home, wasn't it? If she gave up her job, she'd be out on the streets ... like the rest of us. The trouble is, they know it."

Nell shuddered. It had never occurred to her that she wouldn't get paid. She pushed herself up from the table. "Let me see if I can find him. We need to get this sorted out before we finish tonight."

Nell took the stairs to the first floor and paused outside the study to compose herself. She was about to knock on the door when she spun around. *Voices.* Her eyes darted around the landing. There was no one on the stairs and the doors to the rooms were closed. *Where are they coming from?* The sitting room? She stepped closer to the door and leaned forward.

"You had no right to spend so much money."

Mr Cuthbert.

"I specifically told you we had to watch what we were spending, and you've doubled what we spent last month ... and on what?"

"I *have* cut back. Why do you think I swapped Jacobs for this new woman? We can pay her half of what we paid him..."

Mrs Cuthbert.

"But you're not supposed to spend twice the saving on expensive dresses and new hats."

"I bought two hats. You can't deprive me of that."

"You'll be deprived of a lot more than that if the grocers cut off our credit."

Nell straightened up and scurried to the room next door. *Oh my goodness.*

"Stop fussing, it's done now. Pay the bills and we'll cut back next month."

Nell imagined the flick of Mrs Cuthbert's hand, but froze as the door flew open and Mr Cuthbert stormed out and down the stairs. *Where's he going?*

She stepped out onto the landing and was grateful to see Mrs Cuthbert staring out of the window. Holding her breath, she crept to the stairs and down to the kitchen.

"Ah, here you are, Mr Cuthbert. I was about to go looking for you."

"Yes, quite. I'm sorry I'm late." He reached into the inside pocket of his jacket. "Your wages." The coins in the envelopes jingled as he gave them out. "Have a good evening."

Without another word, he disappeared from the kitchen and stomped back up the stairs.

"What was that all about?" Cook asked.

"I'm sure I don't know." Nell scurried across to her office and shut the door. *Let's see what I've got here.*

She tipped out the coins onto her desk. A crown coin, a half-crown and sixpence. She peered into the envelope to check she hadn't missed anything. No. *Is that it? I gave myself two crowns and two shillings.*

She stared at the coins. I've been away from home all week for this? It's no more than Cook earns.

"Do you want a cup of tea, love?" Cook shouted through the door, causing Nell to tip the coins back into the envelope.

"Yes, please. I'll be out in a minute." *Once I've decided what to do.*

CHAPTER TWENTY-EIGHT

The following afternoon, Mrs Cuthbert's visitors arrived shortly after she'd left the dining table and retired to the sitting room. Nell was immediately dispatched to fetch a pot of tea and selection of cakes, and they'd settled down for an afternoon playing cards before she delivered the tray.

"Will that be all, madam?" She crossed her fingers behind her back as she edged towards the door.

"Yes. Tell Cook we'll take afternoon tea at four o'clock."

"Very good, madam."

Nell hurried back to the kitchen, and with the instructions passed along, she grabbed her cloak and slipped out of the back door and down the alleyway to Upper Parliament Street. She didn't slow down until she reached Windsor Street, but even then, her pace was brisk.

Maria was by the fire with Billy when she arrived home and immediately jumped to her feet. "You have remembered us."

Nell took off her cloak and rested it over the back of a chair. "Don't start. It's taken me a lot to get here."

"I'm not starting, we thought you weren't coming, that's all. What's the matter?"

"It's that woman. She thinks it's too much to give someone time off every week." Nell pulled a chair out from the dining table and poured some milk into a cup as she sat down. "Where are the girls?"

Billy buried his head in the newspaper while Maria disappeared into the kitchen.

"Well?"

"They'll be here shortly." She returned with the kettle. "Let me freshen up this pot of tea."

"What do you mean? Why aren't they here now?"

Maria poured the water into the teapot. "We were expecting you for dinner and when you didn't arrive, they were upset. Alice took them to the park to distract them. I'm sure they won't be long."

Nell's eyes stung. "I hope you're right. I've not got a lot of time."

Billy folded his newspaper and put it on the floor. "Let me go and see if I can find them. They won't have gone far."

"Thank you." Nell grabbed her nephew's wrist. "On your way out, would you tell Aunty Rebecca I'm here? I won't have time to go over there as well."

"How long can you stay?" Maria asked once Billy had gone.

"An hour, maybe an hour and a half. She doesn't know I've sneaked out, so I need to be back for teatime."

Maria's face paled. "I thought you'd be here all afternoon."

"So did I until yesterday. The woman has no consideration."

"You're not enjoying it then?"

Nell took a mouthful of tea. "The job's all right, but I don't like Mrs Cuthbert."

"Didn't I tell you to get a part-time cleaning job instead, then you wouldn't have any of this nonsense. Do you really need to live in?"

"There'd be no point doing anything else. By the time I finish in the evening, not to mention the time I'd have to leave in the morning, I wouldn't see the girls any more than I do now."

"You don't have to carry on, you know." For the first time in weeks, Maria's tone was calm.

"I do, for a little longer at least. To be honest, it's been quite an eye-opener. Have you any idea how much these people buy on account? They use almost every shop in the area and owe them all money."

"Who owes money?"

Nell looked around and smiled as Rebecca joined her at the table. "The Cuthberts. They're up to their eyes in debt. I haven't worked it out properly yet, but they owe pounds to various shopkeepers. The thing is, I overheard Mrs Cuthbert tell her husband she got rid of the butler and hired me so she could cut down on the costs."

Concern crossed Rebecca's face. "Will they be able to pay you?"

"They have this week, but not as much as I'd like."

"Why are you going back then?"

Maria straightened her back as she looked down at Nell. "I've already asked her that."

"Because I've only been there a week. Besides, I feel as if I want to help the shopkeepers. If I don't warn them, they could all lose a lot of money and I can't let that happen. We'll be getting some deliveries tomorrow and I'll mention the situation to everyone who calls. If I've got anything to do with it, the Cuthberts will have to pay up if they want anything else delivered."

"And then what?" Rebecca asked.

"I'll see how I get on this week. I need to make sure I'm going to be paid, and assuming I am, I want her to promise that I can have every Sunday afternoon off. If either of those things don't happen, I'll be back by bedtime on Saturday."

Rebecca reached for her sister's hands. "You will be careful? You don't want her to sack you."

"I don't think I'll mind if she does. I really don't like her. When I got the job, James told me to treat her like a child, but children are less trouble." Nell finished her tea. "Anyway, what's been going on here?"

Maria and Rebecca looked at each other as Maria spoke.

"Nothing much. James went back to sea on Monday, which you knew. I had a letter from George to say they were approaching Australia and then heading up to China."

"He won't be home anytime soon then."

Maria shook her head. "The girls have been fine with Alice, too, although she hasn't been able to do as much on her waistcoats as she usually does." Maria paused. "I wondered if you could give her a shilling to make up for it."

"Yes, I would, but I've not brought any money with me. I didn't think I'd need it. Mind you, I probably won't see her at this rate." Nell glanced at the clock.

"They won't be long." Maria stood up. "Let me make a

fresh pot of tea and put some cakes out for when they arrive."

"You don't look happy," Rebecca said as Maria disappeared into the kitchen.

"I'm not. I've not enjoyed this week and the only thing that's kept me going is seeing the girls ... and now they're not here." Nell looked at her sister. "Have they missed me?"

"I'm sure they have, but I've not seen much of them."

"What if they've not?" Nell's shoulders slumped. "They've always liked Alice. What if they've forgotten about me?"

"Don't be silly. You're their mam."

Nell looked up as Maria came back into the room.

"Have the girls missed me?"

"Have they ever! Elenor was very excited at dinner time when she thought you were coming home."

"I doubt Leah was."

"Now, stop this. The girls are safe and happy. You should be thankful."

Nell's shoulders slumped further. "You're right. Perhaps I shouldn't have come, not with it being so late. If I go now..."

"Sit down this minute. Billy's gone to find them, and if you're not here when they get back, that will be even worse."

Nell sat in silence while Maria brought the cakes through. She was about to sit down when the front door opened.

"Here they are." Maria went to the living room door. "Come and see who's here."

"Aunty Nell, you're back." Alice hurried to place Leah

on Nell's knee then crouched down beside the child. "There you are. Who's this, Leah? Mama's back."

Leah seemed not to notice and reached out to Alice.

"Not yet, let me help Elenor with her coat."

As Alice disappeared through the door, Leah struggled to follow her. Nell fought to hold onto her, but that only caused the child to cry.

"Ally."

She shuddered at the sound of her daughter's voice. She'd never heard her say that. She stood Leah on the floor and watched her waddle after Alice as a sheepish-looking Elenor came into the room.

"Come here." Nell held her arms wide. "Mam's missed you."

After a second's hesitation, Elenor ran into her embrace, but she felt stiff, not returning her hug as she struggled free.

Nell watched as her daughter returned to Alice. *I've lost my daughters for the sake of eight shillings.* She pushed her cup and saucer into the centre of the table and stood up.

"I'd better be going before Mrs Cuthbert misses me. I'll see you next week."

Billy had stayed outside and as soon as she closed the door, he offered her his arm. "Let me walk you back. You look as if you could do with the company."

Nell wiped her eyes. "Have you ever had the feeling you're not wanted?"

"Don't be daft. The girls were talking about you all through dinner."

"And I let them down..."

"Come on, cheer up. Alice will take care of them."

"I know she will." Nell wiped a tear from her eye as they walked. "Where was Vernon?"

"Probably in the alehouse."

"On a Sunday? Your mam won't like that."

"Mam doesn't like him doing a lot of things."

Nell's forehead creased as she stared at Billy. "What's been going on?"

Billy frowned. "Was it you who told her about the plan for the men to strike down their tools?"

"Oh goodness, yes. With everything that's been going on, I'd completely forgotten."

"As you can imagine, she didn't take it well ... and he blamed me. Except for mealtimes, we've not seen him all week."

"I'm sorry. I was angry with her and thought she needed to be told. Has she been to see Uncle Tom?"

Billy shrugged. "Not that I've heard, but I've not been to the alehouse since Monday. Not that one at any rate. It's now their unofficial headquarters, and anyone who doesn't agree with them isn't welcome."

Nell squeezed his arm. "I'm sorry. I thought I was helping..."

"It's not your fault. It was all bound to come out eventually. You should be glad you can go away and forget about it."

CHAPTER TWENTY-NINE

Cook was serving the tea when Nell arrived in the kitchen.

"You're just in time. She's been asking for you."

"I needed to go out." Nell unfastened her cloak as she walked, and hung it on a hook in her office. "What does she want?"

"Don't ask me. The bell was ringing so Ethel went up in the end."

Nell shook the teapot on the table. "Is this fresh?"

"No, it's been made half an hour or more. Aren't you going up to see her?"

"I'm sure Ethel can manage."

"What's the matter with you? You weren't like this earlier."

Nell sat down at the table. "Do you ever wonder why you bother?"

"What are you talking about?"

"You come into this kitchen, day after day, and get

nothing for your trouble. When was the last time you saw any of your family?"

"I only have a sister. I visit her once a month and it's enough."

"But what about Mrs Cuthbert? When did she last thank you for all you do?"

"I don't need any thanks. As long as I see clean plates when they come back down, that's enough for me."

"And you're happy with your lot?"

Cook raised an eyebrow. "Why wouldn't I be? I live in a nice house, Mrs Cuthbert doesn't give me any grief and they pay me. When Mr Jacobs was here, it was like me and Ethel were part of his family. I can't deny we don't miss him."

"But Mrs Cuthbert dismissed him without a second thought, even though I asked her not to. Don't you worry she could do the same to you?"

"She probably will one day, but I can always go to my sister's. Until then, I'm grateful for what she does for us."

Nell studied her. "How long have you been in service?"

"Since I was a girl. I started as a scullery maid and learned my trade over the years."

"So you've known nothing else? I suppose Ethel's the same."

"Didn't you?"

"No. Perhaps that's what I did wrong." Nell pushed herself up from the table. "I'll start taking this food upstairs."

Nell's feet and back ached as she crashed into bed that evening, but try as she might, sleep evaded her. *What a mess.* Images of Elenor and Leah crying for Alice filled her vision every time she closed her eyes, and when she opened them, all she could hear was Maria chastising everyone. *Maybe I am better off out of the way. The girls are happier without me disturbing them, and at least Maria can't criticise me here. That's Mrs Cuthbert's job.*

She tossed and turned for what felt like an age but must have fallen asleep because she was woken by a bell ringing in her room. *What on earth...?* She lay where she was, adjusting her eyes to the dark. *Did I dream that?* A minute later, the bell rang again, this time for longer. *For goodness' sake, what does she want?*

Taking the night light from the holder in the wall, Nell lit her candle and wrapped a gown around herself before she stepped from the room and headed downstairs. She knocked gently on Mrs Cuthbert's door and let herself in.

"Did you ring?"

"Come in quickly, I don't want Mr Cuthbert awake."

Nell closed the door and shuffled towards the bed. "What is it?"

"Take a seat. I'm struggling to sleep and want you to read to me."

"Read? At this time of night? I can barely open my eyes."

"Oh, you'll manage. Here, try this. There's the first instalment of a new story in this magazine."

Nell placed her candle on the bedside table and adjusted the magazine on her lap. She struggled to focus on the print and her words were stilted as she ran a finger along the page to keep her place. She hadn't read half a column when her head nodded over the page.

"Don't stop." Mrs Cuthbert rolled over to look at her, but Nell stood up.

"I'm sorry. I don't know why you asked me here, but I can't do this. I can hardly see the words in this light. Besides, I need my sleep as much as you do. If you'd like to read yourself, I'll light your candle, if not, I'll wish you goodnight." Nell waited a couple of seconds and when Mrs Cuthbert failed to respond she picked up her candle and left.

She climbed back into bed with a groan, and even images of the girls couldn't stop her falling into a deep sleep. She woke up with a start the next morning when the clock above the fireplace chimed for eight o'clock. She stared at the hands, willing it to be an hour earlier, but when she convinced herself it wasn't, she lay back down. *There's no point rushing. If Mrs Cuthbert didn't get to sleep until the same time as me, she won't be awake yet. And if she is, she can wait. It's her fault I overslept.*

Five minutes later, with a sense of guilt, she threw the bedcovers off and reached for her dress. *Cook will have made Mrs Cuthbert's breakfast by now, and I shouldn't waste it.*

"Where've you been?" Cook asked ten minutes later when she arrived in the kitchen.

"She had me up half the night and so she'll have to wait. Is there any tea in the pot?"

"What about this breakfast?"

Nell pulled it towards her. "I'll eat it. Can you do her a couple more eggs? She'll only moan that these are hard."

Cook bustled over to the range. "You're going to be a

right barrel of laughs today. I hope you've remembered we've got deliveries coming."

"Oh, yes, I won't forget that, but I need to see her ladyship first."

Mrs Cuthbert was sitting up in bed when Nell arrived.

"You're late."

"Yes." Nell plonked the tray on Mrs Cuthbert's lap. "I assumed you wouldn't want waking so early after last night's nonsense."

"I'd hardly call a bout of insomnia nonsense."

"No, neither would I. Waking your housekeeper and asking her to read to you, on the other hand, is."

"I'll have less of your insolence. My husband pays your wages and while you're in this house, you'll do as you're told."

Nell counted to three. "Very well, but if there are any more occasions like last night, please forgive me if you receive your breakfast late. I'm afraid I can't function without a good night's sleep."

"You'll be here at whatever time I need you."

With her hands behind her back, Nell rose up onto her toes and back down again. *You can think again, lady.* "Will that be all?"

"Yes, but I suggest you find your manners before you come to help me dress. I won't tolerate insubordination."

"Very well. I'll be back once we've had the deliveries."

. . .

Nell was in her office when she heard a loud knock on the back door. She opened it to find the butcher rummaging in the back of his carriage, and he joined her with the day's meat when he saw her.

"Good morning." She kept her voice light as she smiled.

"Morning, Mrs Riley. Straight onto the cold shelf?"

"Yes, please. On the left-hand side." She waited on the step until he came out again.

"Are you checking up on me?"

"No, not at all. I wondered if I might have a word with you."

The butcher pulled the door closed and they walked into the garden.

"What can I do for you?" There was a twinkle in his eye that caused Nell to falter.

"I hope you don't think I'm being forward, but I wanted to let you know I'm aware that Mr Cuthbert owes you rather a lot of money. I've given him your invoices and asked him to settle his account promptly, but..."

"But what?"

"I'm afraid I fear he may not be in a position to repay you. Not straight away, anyway."

The butcher took a step back. "You can't go around slandering a man like Mr Cuthbert."

"Oh no, forgive me. That wasn't my intention ... I wanted to warn you..."

"Of what?" A dark shadow passed over his eyes. "Mr Cuthbert's one of my best customers. I've a good mind to report you to him."

Nell stared at the man, who stood tall, his jet-black hair giving a sinister look to his angular face.

"I'm sorry. I thought I was being helpful. I didn't want to see you running up such large debts."

"It's all part of doing business. You'd be as well staying out of things you don't understand, Mrs Riley. Good day to you."

Nell watched the butcher storm back to his carriage, her mouth open. *That wasn't what I expected.* She was about to go back into the kitchen when the greengrocer arrived.

"Good morning, Mrs Riley." The elderly man with silver hair jumped down from the front seat of his cart and retrieved a box. "This should keep you going for a few days."

"Good morning." Nell smiled at the selection of vegetables he thrust towards her.

"Shall I take it in for you?"

"Yes, please, but may I ask a question first?" *Don't be so direct this time.*

"Certainly."

"I've been going through the invoices Mr Jacobs left, and I've noticed Mr Cuthbert owes you money."

"Oh, don't worry about it. I can't afford to lose a customer like Mr Cuthbert; he gives me credibility. I'm sure he'll pay me when he's ready."

Nell took a deep breath. "I'm sure he will but I wanted to check you weren't desperate for it."

"I must admit it will be nice when it comes, but we'll manage for now." He headed into the house and returned a minute later. "If you'll excuse me, I'd better get on."

Nell shook her head as she returned to the kitchen table. *I should mind my own business.*

CHAPTER THIRTY

She'd never been one for figures, so it had taken Nell the best part of the week to convince herself she was right about the debts building up in the housekeeping account. To owe five pounds to one store would be bad enough, but to owe that much to so many of them, she couldn't comprehend. It would take years to pay off the debt.

With a sigh, she collected up the papers she needed for Mr Cuthbert and closed the drawer. If he accepted her resignation, it wouldn't be her problem after tomorrow. And two weeks' work should be enough experience for the Steamship Bohemian Company, although whether she still wanted to go was another matter.

She heard Mr Cuthbert arrive home and she jumped up to follow him upstairs to his office. The door was open, and he looked up as she knocked.

"Come in, Mrs Riley. Is it that time of the week already?"

"Yes, sir. I've filled in the ledger for the staff wages and copied out the balances owed for the groceries." She handed them to him. "I'm afraid they're rather mounting up."

She'd expected to be dismissed, but he sat down and studied the papers.

"As bad as that? Does Mrs Cuthbert have any input into the orders?"

"She has a list of suppliers she insists I use, especially for the meat, and she's taken a liking to the highest-quality beef."

"Yes, I've noticed." He paused and looked up at Nell. "In future, can you run the orders by me? I'd like to make sure we're getting value for money."

"Yes ... of course, but..." Nell's cheeks coloured as she struggled for the right words. "I, erm, I was going to hand in my notice tomorrow, sir, once I've been paid. Mrs Cuthbert and I don't really see eye to eye, and my daughters are missing me."

Mr Cuthbert sat down at his desk. "She's upset you too?"

"I-I've found it hard, sir. And I had expected to get an afternoon off each week..."

"As you should." Mr Cuthbert rested his head on a hand. "I can't say I blame you. My wife can be difficult."

Nell flinched when he jerked his head to look at her. "If I increase your wages, will you stay for another week while we sort this out?"

"But ... don't you need to pay the suppliers? If I leave..."

"If you leave, what will I do with her? It's too late in the day to find anyone else and she won't have young Ethel or Cook taking care of her personal needs."

"Well..."

Mr Cuthbert's eyes pleaded with her. "I need time to decide what to do. Please."

"You're sure I'll be paid?"

Mr Cuthbert glanced at the list of unpaid bills. "You will. I'll also give you a respectable reference."

"Thank you, sir."

"It's the least I can do. Oh, and one more thing, once you've helped Mrs Cuthbert out of bed on Sunday morning, take the rest of the day off. Tell her I said you could."

At quarter past eleven on Sunday morning, Nell slipped out the back door and headed towards Upper Parliament Street with a smile on her face. She wasn't as free as she'd hoped, but with an extra three shillings in her pay packet, she wasn't as angry as she might have been either.

Maria was setting the table when she arrived home. "This is a better time. Have you handed in your notice?"

Nell flopped into a chair by the fire. "Sort of. If you pour me a cup of tea, I'll tell you my news."

Maria disappeared into the kitchen but was back moments later. "Here you are. It's not been made long."

Nell took it from her and placed it on the occasional table by the chair. "Where is everyone?"

"Church and Sunday school."

Nell looked at the clock. "Gosh, I didn't realise the time. Didn't you want to go?"

"And leave an empty house for you to come home to? I'm sure they won't miss me for one week."

Nell frowned at her sister. "That's not like you. I'm sure I could have let myself in."

"It's done now." She sat in the seat opposite. "What's your news? Have you finally seen sense?"

"If you mean, have I handed in my notice, then yes, I have. I don't finish until next Saturday, though."

"Why not?"

"Because..." Nell's answer was cut short when Alice came in with Elenor and Leah.

"You're nice and early. We weren't expecting you yet." She let go of Elenor's hand and put Leah on Nell's knee. "Say good morning to Mam."

"Mama." Leah pawed at Nell's face as Elenor hugged her.

"I'm here, too." Elenor snuggled into her as Alice watched.

"They're both in a good mood today. I'm afraid it was my fault they were tired last week. I should have let them have a nap rather than taking them out."

"Not to worry. I suppose this is all new to you."

Alice pulled up a seat beside them. "Have you had a good week?"

"No, not really. I've handed in my notice."

Concern crossed Alice's face. "But I thought you needed a job."

"I do, but not this one. Not with Mrs Cuthbert, anyway. I'd have left yesterday if I'd had my way, but Mr Cuthbert asked me to stay another week. He increased my wage to persuade me, so I leave next Saturday." She placed two shillings on the table. "This is for you. For looking after the girls."

Alice gasped. "For me! Thank you. They must think you're doing a good job."

Nell cocked her head to one side. "I wish they did, but I'd say Mr Cuthbert wants to keep me there until he finds a replacement. He won't want to look after Mrs Cuthbert himself."

"But he wouldn't have asked you to stay if you were doing a bad job."

Nell held Elenor tightly. "No, I don't suppose he would. Anyway, at least it'll be more money coming home next week. It should help a bit." She put two crown coins on the table for Maria.

"And you'll be here with us." Elenor wriggled free and pulled Leah off Nell's knee. "We don't like it when you're not here."

Nell blinked back a tear. "No. Mam doesn't like it either, but I'll have to get another job if we want new dresses."

Elenor pulled on her pinafore. "I like this one."

"But that's your Sunday best. You can't wear it all the time."

"Alice lets me."

Alice wagged a finger at her. "No I don't, now enough of this."

Elenor giggled but Maria stood up and scowled at her.

"Good girls don't tell lies. Now, Billy will be here in a minute, so go and wash your hands and sit at the table."

Nell put an arm around her daughter. "I'll take you. Come along." She stood up, and as soon as Maria disappeared into the kitchen she whispered to Alice, "What about Vernon?"

Alice put a finger to her lips. "Not now."

The dinner dishes had been washed and the girls were getting restless when Maria stood up and went into the back yard. The door had no sooner closed behind her than Nell leaned forward in her seat.

"What's going on? Where's Vernon?"

Billy's lips were thin. "Him and Mam had an almighty row on Friday, and he's moved out."

"Oh, gracious. Where's he gone?"

"Uncle Tom's."

Nell's stomach did a somersault. "He's not! And your mam knows?"

Tears collected in the rims of Alice's eyes. "She was really angry."

"I'm not surprised."

"Not a word to her, though." Billy peered down the side of the curtain on the back window. "We don't want to upset her again."

"No, we don't." Nell sat back in her chair as the back door opened. "Do we have time for a game of cards?"

Billy shrugged. "I don't see why not, if you're not in a rush to get back."

"No, I've an hour or two left yet. As long as you don't mind walking me back. I'll pop over to see Aunty Rebecca in about half an hour."

Billy smiled. "Of course I don't. It will give me chance to stretch my legs."

. . .

The girls were in bed when Nell fastened her cloak and took Billy's arm to walk back to the Cuthberts'. As they reached Upper Parliament Street, he stopped to admire the houses.

"How the other half live, eh?"

Nell followed his gaze. "They may have bigger houses, but I don't know that it makes them any happier. Mr and Mrs Cuthbert don't seem happy if you ask me."

"At least they don't have to worry about money. I think that's upsetting Mam as much as anything else. I'm the only wage earner now."

"Alice does her bit though, and I've given her some money, not that it will last long. At least James will be home soon. He may be able to sort things out."

"I hope so. He certainly earns more than the rest of us."

"I don't mean that. I'd say the main reason your mam's upset is because Vernon's gone to stay with Uncle Tom. Especially now they've fallen out. On top of that, she'll be missing him ... and his money. She can't exactly go round and tell him to come home."

"I hadn't thought of that." Billy put a hand on her shoulder. "Never mind. You enjoy your last week of freedom. I'm sure all our problems will still be around when you come home."

"I hope not." She squeezed his arm and, with a final farewell, walked down the alleyway leading to the back yard.

The kitchen was empty when she arrived at the house, and with a sigh of relief she went straight up the stairs. It might not be late, but she was ready for bed. The sun had been on the bedroom all afternoon and she opened a window to let in some air. She gazed out over the gardens below. *Am I doing the right thing?* If Vernon wasn't going to come home, Maria would need some money, and at least by having a job, she could give them that. But no, that wasn't the answer. If what James said was true, she could earn more on the steamships. It might be the excuse she needed to get Maria to agree to it.

Despite her tiredness, sleep was a long time coming and the following morning, the sound of a bell ringing in her room woke Nell from a vivid dream. *The stupid woman. What on earth does she want now?* She opened her eyes and blinked at the light coming in through the drapes. *Oh my goodness, what time is it?* She studied the clock on the mantelpiece. Eight o'clock! *Not again.*

She scrambled out of bed and tidied her hair without pausing to splash water on her face. She grabbed her dress and was downstairs within five minutes. With a loud tut, Cook pushed a breakfast tray towards her.

"You should thank me for putting them on a few minutes late."

"Thank you." Nell picked up the tray and hurried into the hall. *Slow down; you'll spill everything.* She paused for breath and took the stairs slowly. *Better late than never.*

Mrs Cuthbert was sitting up in bed when she arrived, and Nell hesitated at the look on her face.

"What time do you call this?"

"I-I'm sorry. One of the eggs split while it was being boiled and Cook had to start again." Nell placed the tray on Mrs Cuthbert's lap.

"I hope the other one hasn't gone to waste. We're not made of money, you know."

"No, it didn't." She started to leave the room, but Mrs Cuthbert called her back.

"Aren't you going to tell me your news?"

"News?" Nell had never been good at lies, and her cheeks flushed as Mrs Cuthbert glowered at her. "Oh, *that*. I was going to wait until you'd finished breakfast."

"How considerate of you." Mrs Cuthbert's sarcasm wasn't lost on Nell. "Would you care to explain why you told Mr Cuthbert and not me?"

"It was ... well, I didn't do it on purpose. I had some invoices for him and details of the wages, and it came up in conversation."

"I don't believe a word." Mrs Cuthbert smashed the top of her egg with a teaspoon. "My husband has no conversation, and certainly not with the likes of you."

Nell twisted her fingers together in front of her. "If you must know, he wanted me to do some work for him this week, so I had to explain that I wouldn't be here."

"Well, at least you could have had the common decency to come and tell me. I did you a huge favour by giving you this job, and this is how you repay me."

Nell released her hands and stared at the floor. "You did, and I'm very grateful, but it's not working out between us."

"I'm sure I don't know why. I've treated you with the utmost respect and you've been nothing but rude and insolent."

"I'm sorry. That was never my intention. I suppose I was disappointed not to get an afternoon a week off to see my daughters."

"Oh, that." Mrs Cuthbert flicked her hand. "You would have seen them soon enough."

Nell's heart pounded, but her face remained calm. "Did you ever have children, Mrs Cuthbert?"

"As you'll be well aware, the Lord decided that motherhood wasn't for me." She dipped a bread finger into her egg. "If you'll excuse me, I'd like to eat my breakfast in peace."

Nell almost ran from the room and released a deep sigh as she closed the door behind her. After a moment's pause, she walked down the landing, but as she reached the top of the stairs, Mr Cuthbert appeared from the room next to his wife's.

"Ah, Mrs Riley, I thought it might be you. Will you tell me when the deliveries arrive? I need to settle my accounts. I hadn't realised some of them were so long overdue."

"Yes, of course, Mr Cuthbert, although they won't be here until ten o'clock. Will you still be at home then?"

"I'll be here all day, in my office." His smile was warm. "There's no need to mention any of this to my wife. What she doesn't know can't upset her."

"Very good, sir." Once he'd dismissed her, Nell hurried back to the kitchen. "We'd better make sure everything runs smoothly today. Mr Cuthbert will be down here in an hour."

Cook's rolling pin stopped moving. "In my kitchen?"

"It sounds like it. He wants to speak to the delivery men." Nell picked up a cloth and started to wipe the table.

"What's he doing that for?"

"He wants to settle his accounts."

Cook's brow furrowed. "Mr Jacobs always used to do

that, but I suppose he wouldn't entrust you with the money."

"I was the wife of a sailor for ten years. I'm perfectly capable of handling money."

"Maybe you are, but they pay men more than us so they can deal with that sort of thing. They should never have got rid of Mr Jacobs. We need a man down here."

Nell paused as Ethel walked into the room. "Perhaps they'll get another one then. I've not had chance to tell you yet, but I'm leaving on Saturday."

"Leaving! But you've not been here five minutes." The rolling pin fell to the floor as Cook let go of it.

"You got rid of Mr Jacobs so you could come here for three weeks?" Tears filled Ethel's eyes. "I knew you were a wrong 'un."

"It was never my intention to leave so soon, and I didn't expect him to have left when I arrived. I specifically asked Mrs Cuthbert to let him stay until he found somewhere else to live..."

"But he wouldn't have gone anywhere if you hadn't turned up asking for a job. He'd still be here."

Nell took a deep breath. "We can't be sure of that. I only applied for the job because I'd been told they wanted a housekeeper. Mrs Cuthbert told me she was planning to let Mr Jacobs go, whether it was me who got the job or someone else."

"It's still not fair. He's been in the workhouse since you arrived. A proud man like Mr Jacobs..." Ethel buried her face in her hands.

"I'm sorry; truly I am."

. . .

On the stroke of ten there was a knock on the door and the butcher popped his head into the kitchen. "Morning, ladies. Shall I pop the meat onto the cold slab?"

Nell hurried over to him. "Yes, please, but once you're done, would you mind waiting for Mr Cuthbert? He'd like a word with you."

"Mr Cuthbert. With me?" The butcher's eyes widened. "What have you been saying?"

Nell took a step backwards. "I'm sure I've said nothing, but he asked me to tell him when you arrived. I'll only be a moment."

Mr Cuthbert was in his office when Nell found him, and she led him back down the stairs and introduced him to the butcher, who hovered nervously outside the pantry.

"Thank you, Mrs Riley, that will be all." Mr Cuthbert opened the back door, and as the two men went outside Nell took a seat at the table.

It was ten minutes later when Mr Cuthbert returned, and without a word, he strode across the kitchen towards the hall. As soon as he passed through the door to the hall, Nell followed him.

"Excuse me, sir. Might I have a word?"

He nodded. "Come up to my office. We won't be overheard in there."

He led the way, and once he was at his desk, he looked up. "What can I do for you?"

"It's Mr Jacobs, sir. I don't know if you've any mind to replace me with a butler, but I've learned that he's been in the workhouse since he left here. I wondered ... could you see your way to giving him back his old job?"

"That's most commendable of you, Mrs Riley." He gave

her a warm smile. "I'd already heard of his predicament, and in actual fact, I've been to the workhouse this morning. He'll be coming home on Saturday."

Nell let out a deep sigh. "Oh, I am glad, sir. Thank you. I feel so guilty that I've upset your usual routine. It was never my intention."

"Believe me, Mrs Riley, you've been like a breath of fresh air, and you may have helped Mr Jacobs in the long run. As you've found out, my wife isn't an easy woman, and she's had poor Mr Jacobs in her sights for months. When he comes back, things will be different."

Nell let out a deep sigh. "I'm glad it's not been for nothing. Thank you for telling me."

CHAPTER THIRTY-ONE

M r Jacobs was already at the kitchen table when Nell arrived for her final breakfast. Cook and Ethel both wore broad smiles as he sat between them.

"Welcome back, Mr Jacobs."

"Mrs Riley." He stood up and gave a slight bow. "I'm very grateful for you letting me have my job back. I don't know how to thank you."

Nell's face flushed. "I'm sure there's no need. It's Mrs Cuthbert you need to thank. If it wasn't for her, well, things may have been different."

"*Mrs* Cuthbert?" A frown crossed the butler's face. "Well I never. I didn't think she liked me."

"I really can't say, Mr Jacobs, but it didn't take me long to work out I couldn't work for her. Still, after all this, I've been led to believe she'll be nicer to you in future."

Mr Jacobs put a hand to his chest. "I'd like to think you're right, but as long as Mr Cuthbert values me, that will be enough."

"I'm sure he does. In fact, I suspect he needs you more than you realise." Nell joined them at the table and poured herself some tea. "If you give me five minutes to drink this, I'll show you what I've done with the accounts, and Ethel can clean out the bedroom."

Mr Jacobs was waiting with her cloak when she came back downstairs with her bag.

"That's everything done." She accepted his offer of help. "I've said goodbye to the Cuthberts and so I'll hand everything over to you. May I wish you the best of luck with Mrs Cuthbert?"

"You may indeed. Although I believe Mr Cuthbert will be keeping more of an eye on her in the future."

"I'm sure he will. "She took a final glance around the kitchen and settled her gaze on Cook. "It was nice to meet you, and you too, Ethel. I hope the three of you can get back to normal now."

Ethel grinned at Mr Jacobs. "I'm sure we will. It's like I've got my family back."

"It is, thank you, Mrs Riley." Cook patted Mr Jacobs' hand as she stood up. "As much as we're happy to have Mr Jacobs back, it was nice knowing you. It may even have been for the best in the long run. I hope you sort yourself out with something more suitable."

Nell reached for the door handle. "I hope so too."

. . .

Alice looked up from her sewing as Nell walked into the living room and knelt on the floor beside Elenor and Leah, kissing them both on the forehead.

"You're here!"

"About time, too." Maria plonked the teapot in the centre of the table. "Have you any idea how much we've had to do while you've been swanning off?"

"I'll be leaving again if you carry on like that." Nell got back to her feet. "What's up with you? Can't you at least put a smile on your face?"

"There's nothing to smile about."

Before Nell could ask any questions, Maria disappeared out the back door.

"What's going on?"

Alice lowered her waistcoat to the table. "She doesn't tell me much, but I think she's missed you."

"And I have." Elenor hugged her legs.

Nell bent down to wrap her arms around her daughter. "And I've missed you, but Aunty Ria's got a funny way of showing it. Has Vernon come home?"

Alice shook her head. "No. We've not heard from him."

"Not even through Billy?" Nell poured three cups of tea.

"He's not said anything if he has."

Nell sighed. "That must be upsetting her, then, or at least the fact she's not getting any money off him."

"You're right. I heard Billy telling her we'd manage the other day, but she didn't look happy. I think she's worried about James, too."

"James? Why?"

"Billy's been looking out for when he's due to dock and

there's no mention of his ship. We were expecting him home this coming Wednesday, but there's still no word."

Nell's stomach churned. "Has Billy been into the shipping line to ask after the ship?"

"I couldn't say. They don't tell me anything."

Nell patted her hand. "Hopefully, there's a perfectly simple explanation. I'll have a word with Billy later and let you know." She took a sip of tea but flinched as the back door opened and Maria burst in.

"Don't sit there all day. I've jobs for you."

"Why don't you come and sit down? You look as if you've got the weight of the world on your shoulders." Nell pulled out a chair for her. "What's the matter?"

Maria stood in the middle of the room, her hands to her head. "Everything."

"Well, sit here and tell me about it." Nell pulled a cup and saucer towards her and poured Maria a cup as she took a seat. "Alice, would you mind taking the girls into the yard for a few minutes? They're getting restless."

Alice threw the waistcoat onto the table. "Come on, you two, stop fighting." She prised the doll Elenor wanted from Leah's hands and picked her up. "Dolly can stay here."

Nell waited for the back door to close. "This can't go on. What's the matter?"

"Jane's here."

Nell's mouth dropped open. "Where? How do you know?"

"I saw her with my own eyes, yesterday, as bold as brass talking to the woman who lives next door to Sarah."

Nell stood up and rubbed a hand over her face. "What were you even doing around there?"

Tears ran down Maria's cheeks. "I wanted Vernon to come home."

"Did she see you?"

"I don't think so." She rummaged for her handkerchief. "She didn't let on, if she did. As soon as I'd got over the shock of seeing her, I came straight home."

Nell shook her head. "What's she playing at? She can't be staying with Tom and Sarah, surely. They won't have room."

"I don't know. I daren't go round there. I'm frightened to even go to the shops." She blew her nose as Nell returned to the table.

"Have you told anyone?"

"No. I'm too angry..."

"All right, leave it with me. I was planning to visit Rebecca this afternoon anyway. I'll see if she's heard anything about it."

After doing no cooking for three weeks, it was strange to be standing by the stove, but at least it was a quick dinner. Fried kidneys with onions and potatoes. Billy would be home soon, too. It was time to have a family chat, even if Maria didn't think so.

She was about to mash the potatoes when the front door closed and Billy appeared in the living room.

"Something smells good."

"It's nearly ready. Get your hands washed and it will be on the table."

Maria helped her carry the plates through, but Nell had no sooner sat down than the letter box rattled.

"I'll get it." She hurried to the hall and picked up the letter lying on the mat. After a quick glance at the envelope, she smiled and walked back to the living room.

"It's from James."

"James!" Maria snatched the envelope from her and handed it to Billy. "What does it say?"

Billy's shoulders sagged. "Can't I eat this first?"

"No, you can't. What does it say?" Maria passed him the letter opener, but Billy took his time and read it to himself before making a comment. "He'll be arriving late in Liverpool. There was a problem with the ship, and they needed to repair it."

"What sort of a problem?" Maria put her hands to her face. "Is he all right?"

Nell strained to read the letter as Billy put it down and picked up his knife and fork. "He's fine. They've repaired the ship and it was due to leave New York on Wednesday last, so he should be home the middle of the week after next."

"What a relief. Does he say what happened?"

"No."

"Is that why you've been so grumpy?" Alice's eyes were watery as she looked at her mam.

"No ... I wasn't to know he'd be late." Maria's shoulders sagged. "I worry when he's away."

"There's no need to take it out on us." Billy helped himself to a piece of bread. "We've got enough problems of our own without you making up new ones."

"He's my son. It's only natural to worry."

Billy didn't look up as he shovelled a forkful of mash

into his mouth. "What about Vernon? You should be more bothered about him."

"Do you think I'm not? I'd like nothing more than for him to come home and stop this nonsense."

"That's your problem." Billy pointed his knife at her. "He will come home if you stop going on about the strike. He's not a child; he can do what he wants."

"Not if he lives under my roof."

"Well, take your pick." Billy scraped the last of the gravy from his plate and lay down his knife and fork. "He either comes home on his terms or not at all." He stood up and put his chair back under the table. "I'm off to the alehouse. You can tell me later what you decide."

Maria pushed her untouched plate away and rested her head in her hands. "Why is everything so difficult? Is it wrong to want what's best for everyone?"

Nell stabbed a piece of kidney with her fork. "Perhaps it's time for you to accept that we all want different things. You can't control everyone."

"Why did they all have to grow up?"

"Because that's what happens. They become their own people. Wouldn't you rather have Vernon back here than at Tom's? From what Billy said, I'm sure he wouldn't take much persuading."

"But I don't want him striking down his tools. What if he loses his job?"

"Then he'll get another one. There are plenty of shipyards who'll have him."

"But we need the money…"

"You've lived without it for the last two weeks because

of this silliness, and it will go on longer if you don't stop criticising him."

Maria said nothing as she stared into her cup.

"Think about it." Nell stood up and collected the plates. "I'll wash these and then I'm going over to Rebecca's about the other matter." She smiled at Alice. "We'll talk later."

CHAPTER THIRTY-TWO

The decision to walk to the park after picking Isobel up from school had been an easy one. The air was still warm, and Nell walked alongside Rebecca as both pushed their prams.

"My, I've missed coming here." Nell squinted as the lake glistened with the sun's rays. "I tried to get Mrs Cuthbert to take a walk with me when I first started, but the thought horrified her. How people stay locked indoors doing nothing but receiving visitors, I'll never know."

"So you're not sorry you left?"

"Not really, although I was wishing I hadn't this morning when I got back. Maria was in a dreadful mood."

"I think she missed you."

Nell laughed. "Alice said the same thing, but I doubt it. She has other things to worry about." Nell indicated to a nearby bench as a couple stood up to leave. "Shall we sit down?"

"That would be nice. Did you find out what's troubling her?"

Nell put the brake on the pram and lifted Elenor from the seat on the top.

"She saw Jane outside Tom's house yesterday."

"Jane!" Rebecca nearly dropped Isobel as she placed her on the ground. "Why didn't anyone tell us?"

"I suspect it's because we're not talking to Sarah."

Rebecca sat down on the bench. "They should be speaking to me. I've done nothing wrong."

"It's probably because you're only over the road from us." Nell stared out across the lake, remembering the last time she'd sat there with James. "Do you remember the letter she wrote to Maria that I didn't pass on? I showed it to James when he was last home, and he opened it."

"He didn't! What did it say?"

"The main gist of it was that she wanted to come home and said Maria wasn't going to stop her. James spoke to Tom about it and he promised he'd deal with it, but it looks like he didn't."

Rebecca paused to stare out over the lake. "What happens now?"

"I've no idea. We really could do with finding out how long she plans on staying and where she's living. If she's here with the whole family, I can't believe they're staying with Tom and Sarah."

"Vernon would know."

"That's a point." Nell swivelled in her seat. "Billy said he wants to come home. Maybe if we encourage him, he could tell us what's going on."

"If he wants to come home, why doesn't he? He's never been shy."

Nell puffed out her cheeks. "It's Maria. She won't have

him back unless he gives up the idea of striking down his tools."

Rebecca shook her head. "She really is her own worst enemy. Can't you talk to her?"

"I did, and we're going to talk some more tonight. You should join us."

"I could try, but I'd have to leave the girls on their own. Hugh won't stay in on a Saturday night."

Nell watched Elenor and Isobel picking dandelions from the grass verge in front of them. "I'll tell you what, why don't I ask Alice to come and sit with them? Maria doesn't like talking in front of her, so it may help."

"Yes, all right then. Shall we say seven o'clock?"

Maria was setting the table when Nell arrived home.

"Where on earth have you been? I was expecting you over an hour ago."

"We picked Isobel up from school and carried on to the park. Did you want me for anything in particular?"

Maria waited while Alice took Elenor and Leah into the back yard. "I wondered if you'd mentioned anything to Rebecca ... about *her*."

"I did and she's coming over tonight after tea. We thought we should have a family discussion about it. After all, she is Rebecca's sister, too."

"Did she know anything about the visit?"

"No, she was shocked, but suggested that if we could get Vernon home, he could tell us what's going on. I thought Alice could go and sit with Isobel and Florrie."

Maria bit her lip. "Yes. We need to make sure Billy goes out, too. He's been home more than usual lately."

"No." Nell took a seat at the table. "He should be here too. If anyone can get Vernon to come home, it will be him, assuming you'll let him come home without constantly berating him. Can you do that?"

Maria twisted her fingers together as she perched on the edge of a chair. "Encouraging the men to strike down their tools goes against everything I believe in..."

"Would you rather not see your son again?" Nell raised an eyebrow.

"No." She stood up again as Alice rejoined them. "I don't suppose I would."

Nell kissed Elenor on the forehead and pulled the bedcovers over her before she crept from the room and pulled the door closed behind her. As she reached the bottom of the stairs the front door opened and Rebecca joined her.

"Are they asleep?"

Nell smiled. "Nearly."

"That's good. Alice is putting Isobel to bed for me. It makes a nice change."

"Come on in then. Maria's been very quiet since I got back this afternoon."

Maria and Billy were already at the table when they joined them, and Rebecca took the seat opposite her sister.

"Why didn't you say anything to me?"

Maria shrugged. "I was in shock, I suppose."

"Is anyone going to tell me what's going on?" Billy's gaze rested on Nell. "Aunty Nell?"

"All right." Nell took a deep breath. "Do you remember your Aunty Jane?"

Billy's forehead creased as he shook his head. "No."

Maria tutted. "He was only five when she left."

"I still should have heard of her if she's an aunty."

"Maybe you've forgotten. We never talk about her." Nell glanced at Maria for approval to continue. "She's a few years younger than your mam, but shortly after you were born, she married a man called Mr Read."

"Didn't you like him?"

"He was nice enough, until we found out he was Catholic."

"Ah. That explains it. So, what about her?"

"There were a lot of words said, as you can imagine, and eventually she moved to Ireland to be with her husband's family."

"Which is presumably why I've never met her."

"You did meet her." Maria's face was stern as they all stared at her. "She'd often look after you and James ... until she was married. That was when everything changed."

"That sounds a bit dramatic."

"No, it's not." Rebecca fanned out her fingers on the table. "Your Aunty Jane married Mr Read in a joint service with Uncle Tom and Aunty Sarah, but they didn't tell anyone."

"How could they keep it secret? They must have had the banns read."

"He's a Catholic and so they were married by special

licence." Rebecca's voice dropped. "They told no one except Tom and Sarah."

"And they were happy about it?"

"Aunty Sarah was Aunty Jane's best friend and so she turned a blind eye to it."

"But Uncle Tom…?"

"He and Mr Read were friends, too. Mother would have turned in her grave seeing them acting as each other's witnesses." Maria spoke through gritted teeth as Nell fidgeted in her chair.

"I was too young to know what was happening, but I remember arriving at the church for Uncle Tom's wedding, only to find Aunty Jane and Mr Read had just been married." Nell's brow creased as she studied Maria. "How come you weren't as angry with Sarah?"

"Oh, I was. I was furious with Tom, too, but well … over time we needed each other, and Tom and Sarah hadn't actually done anything wrong. It was *her*. *She* was the reason we didn't know anything. I'll never forgive her for what she did."

Nell's forehead remained creased. "But why not? It was a long time ago."

"I was expecting Fred at the time."

"Fred?" Billy scratched his head. "I remember him. The brother who died?"

Maria nodded. "Almost four years to the day after the wedding… She disgraced me that day and laughed in my face when I told her I'd never give her my blessing. She thought she knew better than the rest of us."

Rebecca fidgeted with her fingers. "Your mam was so upset

when we reached the church. She collapsed, and we ended up missing Tom's wedding because we had to bring her home." She gave Maria a weak smile. "We called the doctor, didn't we?"

"Not until the following day. I had a problem and he told me that for the sake of the baby I had to stay in bed." Maria shook her head as she spoke to Billy. "Can you imagine how impossible that was? I had you and James to look after, not to mention Aunty Nell and Rebecca. Your dad was here at the time, too. How could I run the house when I was in bed?"

"We tried to help," Rebecca said.

"You were still young. I couldn't leave you to do everything."

Billy's eyebrows were low over his eyes. "But you were all right? I remember him..."

"I may have looked it, but Fred was always a sickly child. He was half the size of you and James when he was born, and the midwife had to rub him hard to get him to cry." Maria caught her breath. "We had a private baptism the day after he was born because we didn't think he'd make it."

"But he did, and he got stronger." Rebecca's face brightened.

"He was still always small for his age though, and when the other boys caught measles, they recovered. He was the one who died."

Rebecca's expression slipped into a frown. "He had that nasty cough at the same time, though. That wouldn't have helped."

"Exactly." Maria took out a handkerchief. "Even the

doctor said he was weaker than the others and having the two complaints together was too much for him."

"You can't blame Jane though…" Nell shrank back in her chair as Maria glared at her.

"Why not? If she hadn't married that … that … *man*, I wouldn't have had the turn that caused the problems. That was what did it. That was why he was so frail."

Nell squeezed Maria's hand. "All right, calm down. I understand now."

"I'm glad someone does." A frown was fixed on Billy's face. "What's all this got to do with Vernon coming home?"

"Ah, yes." Nell took a deep breath. "The thing is, your mam saw Aunty Jane outside Uncle Tom's house the other day. We think she must be staying there."

Billy's eyes flicked around the group. "Are you sure? Uncle Tom must have known about the incident."

"Oh, he knew all right, but Jane and Aunty Sarah were always as thick as thieves." Maria shook her head. "I had nothing to say to Jane after Fred was born. I didn't even invite her to his christening a couple of years later or go to her daughter's the year after that."

Rebecca looked up. "She came to Fred's funeral, though."

"And I was furious." Maria's knuckles were white as she clenched her fists. "How could she upset me on a day like that? I told her his death was all her fault, but she denied it and made me out to be a liar."

"Is that why she left?" Nell's voice was quiet as she recalled Maria's anguish at the funeral.

"I presume so. I never asked."

"What do we do now?" Rebecca's voice was soft. "We can't run the risk of bumping into her."

Billy suddenly recoiled in his seat. "You don't want me to go to the alehouse and ask Uncle Tom, do you? I won't be welcome. They jeer anyone who doesn't support the strike action."

Maria banged her hand on the table, causing Nell to glance at Rebecca. "What on earth is Tom doing? You're his own flesh and blood."

"Quiet." Nell lifted her eyes to the ceiling, hoping the girls were still asleep. "We thought Vernon could help, but we can only find out what he knows if you agree to him coming home. He may be able to tell us more about Jane and how long she plans on staying."

Billy sighed. "If you want me to ask him, I'll have to catch him going in or out of work. By the time he leaves the alehouse, he's usually with Sam or Uncle Tom, or both."

Nell looked at Maria. "Can we ask Billy to do that? We'd all like Vernon home anyway, and from what Billy said this morning, he'd like to come home, too."

Maria rubbed her hands over her face. "I don't have much choice, do I?"

Billy nodded. "All right. It won't be until Monday now though, unless I bump into him on his own, which is unlikely."

"That will have to do." Nell sat back with a sigh. "Now we need to think about what to say if we happen to bump into her."

CHAPTER THIRTY-THREE

Nell placed the bread on the table but paused as the front door opened. She waited for the usual slam, but when it didn't come, she strolled to the hall. Billy and Vernon were hanging their caps on hooks.

"Good evening, stranger. Welcome home."

"Aunty Nell." Vernon rubbed the back of his neck. "I met Billy and he said you wanted me to come home."

"Yes, we do. Come on in. Tea's nearly ready."

He hesitated as Billy disappeared into the living room. "Mam *is* expecting me, isn't she?"

"She's hoping you'll be here, if that's what you mean. Come on. Let's go and cheer her up."

The girls were already at the table, and Alice beamed at Vernon as he approached the table. "You're home. Mam, he's here!"

Maria wiped her hands on a towel as she walked from the kitchen. "Sit yourself down then. There's a pan of scouse warming through."

Nell couldn't be sure she saw her smile, but the scowl

that had spoiled Maria's face since Saturday had finally disappeared.

"Have you been busy at work?"

"No more than usual." Vernon followed Billy's lead and took a slice of bread, but stopped to study Nell. "I thought you'd taken a job."

"I did, but I didn't like it. I left on Saturday."

"Just as well. Uncle Tom wasn't happy when I told him. He said you should be at home."

"It's all right for him; he can go out and earn his own money. I don't have a husband to do that for me."

"He thinks it's time you got one."

"Oh, does he?" Maria bustled into the living room with a large pan in her hands. "Perhaps you could tell him it's none of his business."

"Maria." Nell took the pan from her. "Why don't you let me serve this? You go and get the teapot."

"But he…"

"That's enough." Nell left no room for argument, and Maria hesitated but went back to the kitchen. "Right now, who's hungry?" She ladled several spoonfuls of the stew onto a plate and handed it to Vernon. "There you are, get that down you." She continued serving and watched as Vernon dug in with his fork. "I suppose it was busy at Uncle Tom's this last week or so."

Vernon shrugged. "No more than usual."

"Oh." She looked at Maria as she took her seat. "Didn't they have any visitors … besides you?"

"No." He didn't take his eyes from his food. "Should they have?"

Nell hesitated. "Your mam thought she saw someone

she knew standing outside the house. Someone who used to live around here but moved away."

"Don't know who you mean. There wasn't anyone new while I was there."

"Could you have imagined it?" Billy stared at Maria, but she shook her head.

"I'd recognise Jane anywhere. At least she's not at your Uncle Tom's."

"Jane?" Vernon swallowed a mouthful. "I heard them talking about someone called Jane."

"What did they say?" Nell's stomach fluttered as Vernon put another forkful of potato into his mouth.

"I wasn't really listening. Something about her looking for a house..."

"Around here?" Maria's shriek stalled everyone, but Vernon quickly returned to his food.

"I think so."

Maria's arms dropped to her sides. "I won't be able to avoid her, will I?"

"It's not happened yet. I got the impression it was only an idea."

"I hope you're right. Where is she now?"

"Couldn't tell you." Vernon wiped his plate with a piece of bread. "I'll ask Uncle Tom tonight if you like. I'm off to the alehouse."

Maria took a deep breath. "All right, but don't make a big thing about it. Say that Mam thought she saw Aunty Jane the other day..."

"*Aunty* Jane?" Vernon's eyes widened. "I didn't know I had an aunty called Jane."

"No, you wouldn't. We lost touch when she moved to

Ireland and I was surprised to see her. Could you ask Uncle Tom how long she's staying and where she is now?"

Nell choked on her food. "Why do you want to know?"

"So I know how to avoid her." Maria stood up and moved a cake from the sideboard to the table, but as she sat down again, Vernon jumped to his feet.

"Not for me, I need to be going. I'll see you in the morning." He walked to the door, but as he disappeared, Maria called him back.

"Welcome home, son. It's good to have you back."

Nell was woken the following morning by Vernon thundering down the stairs. With a quick glance at the girls to check they were still asleep, she grabbed her robe and followed him to the living room. Billy and Maria were already at the table.

"Running late again?" She took a seat beside him.

He laughed. "As usual."

"Do you have time to tell us what Uncle Tom said last night about Aunty Jane?"

"There's not much to tell." He reached for some bread. "I got the impression he didn't know what was happening."

"Sarah." Maria gave Nell a knowing look.

Vernon cleared his mouth. "Yes, she knows more. Aunty Jane was over here last week but stayed in a boarding house."

"Was she on her own?"

He shrugged. "He didn't mention anyone else."

Nell's brow creased. "Why would she be travelling alone?"

"I've no idea, but she's gone back to Ireland now. Like I told you, she wants Uncle Tom to keep an eye open for a house around here so she can come back, but he's no idea when that will be." Vernon grabbed another piece of bread and stood up. "I'll see you later."

"Wait for me."

Vernon was through the door before Billy got out from the table. "I'll see you tonight."

Nell waited for the door to slam then helped herself to a cup of tea. "What do you make of that?"

"I've no idea, although at least I can go to the shop without fear of bumping into her." Maria collected up the dirty plates and carried them to the kitchen. "It's strange she came on her own, though."

"Perhaps Mr Read couldn't afford to take time off work."

"Maybe, but whatever it is, she isn't here, so I suggest we forget about her and get this place cleaned up for James arriving home."

Nell couldn't help noticing that the house wasn't as clean and tidy as it used to be. *She must have missed my help.* A wave of guilt washed over her. At least they still had a few days to make it nice for James coming home.

Nell worked tirelessly, and by the time James was expected, the place looked spotless. She stepped outside to give the front step one more wipe.

"Aunty Nell."

Her face lit up as he walked towards her, and she hurried to meet him.

"You're nice and early. We're all waiting for you." She expected a smile or possibly a hug, but a frown clouded his face.

"I thought you'd be at work."

"Ah, yes. I'd forgotten about that."

"About what?"

"I left."

He rolled his eyes. "Was it that bad?"

"Worse." She grinned. "I'd rather look after a house full of children than Mrs Cuthbert."

"Never mind. How long did you last?"

"If I'm being honest only two weeks, but I stayed for three because Mr Cuthbert asked me to. I finished a week last Saturday."

"It could have been worse." He offered her his arm as they strolled towards the house. "Have I missed anything else?"

Nell groaned. "So much that I haven't time to tell you now, suffice to say, everything seems to be sorted out. For now, at least."

James puffed out his cheeks. "That sounds serious."

"It was. Probably the most important thing you should know is that Vernon's fallen under your Uncle Tom's spell and is planning on striking down his tools to get more money. Your mam wasn't happy, as you can imagine, and Vernon stormed off to live with Uncle Tom for a couple of weeks."

James' mouth dropped open. "Didn't anyone go after him?"

"Not with the way things are between everyone at the moment. Anyway, he came home last week, and they seem to be rubbing along all right, but don't ask him about work."

"No, I won't. Not while Mam's around anyway. I'll take him and Billy to the alehouse later and get their side of the story."

"Ah, that might be awkward. Billy won't go because the alehouse has been overrun by all those who want to strike."

"And he doesn't?"

"No."

Their pace slowed as they approached the front door. "Why do I get the feeling there's something else you're not telling me?"

"Because there is. We just don't have time now. You go in and see your mam and Alice. I need to do the ledge."

"Well, don't be long." The twinkle had returned to his eyes. "You're not the only one with a tale. I've something to tell you, too."

CHAPTER THIRTY-FOUR

Once Nell had wiped the window ledge and gone indoors, Alice was at the table entertaining the girls, while James was stretched out in his favourite chair by the fire.

"Are you going to tell us what happened?" Maria placed the teapot on the table.

James grimaced. "It's not that bad. One of the engineers dropped a rag onto the main driveshaft and it became so tangled that the shaft broke. Thankfully, we were off the coast of Canada, so we didn't have far to go to New York."

"What does the driveshaft do?" Alice looked up from her sewing.

"Turns the propeller, so without it, we had to rely on the sails."

"That was fortunate." Nell blew out her cheeks.

"It was, although not so much for the steerage passengers. They had to stay in their cramped conditions for longer than usual. We didn't though." James had a glint in his eyes as he looked at Nell. "Once we got to port and the passengers disembarked, the captain gave us the day off to go into New York!"

Nell clapped her hands. "You went ashore! How exciting. What was it like?"

James grinned. "Incredible. Not the dock area, that was full of building work, and it's nowhere near as extensive as our docks, but once we were in the city, it was amazing."

"New York hasn't been around for long enough to have docks like ours." Maria handed James and Nell their tea.

"You're right, but it wouldn't surprise me if the Americans haven't been to Liverpool to find out how ours work. Judging by what they're doing, I'd say they want a bigger port than ours."

"I doubt they'll do that." Maria took the seat opposite her son.

"What was it like once you left the port?" Nell bounced in her chair.

"It was much busier than here." James grinned at her. "Thousands of people are leaving Europe to go to America, but it's as if they are all getting off the ships and staying in New York. There's an area they call Downtown where they have the markets and offices, and there are hundreds of people who don't even speak English."

"I wouldn't like that." Maria shifted in her chair. "I find it hard enough understanding the Irish and Scots who come here, but at least they speak our language. You'd have no way of talking to them otherwise."

"They seem to manage. Those from the same countries tend to live together. There are a lot from Ireland and Germany, but the Italians seem to be following them now. The houses are small and cramped, and many are only made of wood or scrap metal, but they manage well enough. From what I gather, they don't bother with the Americans."

"Where do the Americans live?" Nell's eyes were still wide.

"Some of them live in Downtown, but not many. Once we were away from the river, the buildings changed." A smile crossed his lips. "I wish you could see them. The houses are made of stone and are so big and elegant that even those on Upper Parliament Street seem small in comparison. I tell you, anyone who lived there wasn't short of a bob or two."

"Were there many of them?"

"Yes, whole roads. But that's not all. Judging by the work that's going on, there are likely to be hundreds more."

"That's nothing unusual, they're building all around here, too; not that I agree with it." Maria rolled her shoulders as James took a mouthful of tea.

"The work they're doing over there makes our bricklayers look bone idle."

"It sounds wonderful." Nell's face shone. "I'd love to see it."

"Don't be so silly." Maria seemed determined to stay unimpressed. "How would you get over there? Besides, why do you want to travel so far to see a building site when you can walk down the dock road?"

Nell glowered at her sister. "I didn't say I *was* going, only that I'd *like* to. What's up with you? Can't we get excited about anything?"

"Getting excited about things you can't do only leads to disappointment."

"There's no reason why Aunty Nell couldn't go to New York. Women are allowed on ships."

Maria snorted. "Where would she get the money from?" She stood up and put her cup on the table. "I wish you'd stop giving her ideas. Alice, you bring the girls outside with me."

James leaned forward as they disappeared. "What's got into her?"

"She worries about you and your dad being on the ships. She doesn't want me to travel as well ... or Alice, by the looks of it."

"Hmm. That's unfortunate. Are you still keen to become a stewardess, or has Mrs Cuthbert put you off?"

Nell glanced towards the kitchen. "With everything that's going on around here at the moment, I'll be glad to get away."

He grimaced. "It's that bad, is it?"

"You've not even heard the latest about Aunty Jane, but there'll be time for that later. How long are you staying this time?"

"Only three days. I'm due back on the ship first thing Thursday morning."

Nell's shoulders sagged. "Is that all?"

James grinned. "Don't worry, the summer season's nearly over, and once we get to October, there'll be fewer sailings."

Nell checked Maria had gone outside. "Do you have anything planned while you're here?"

"Not especially. I'll probably go into town to catch up with some of the lads."

"May I walk with you tomorrow? We can't talk properly

with your mam here, and I want to hear more about New York. I'll tell her I'm going to the shops."

"That's fine with me, but won't she want to come with us?"

Nell shook her head. "I doubt it. She doesn't seem to want to do anything at the moment."

The following afternoon, as James pulled the door closed behind them, Nell let out a deep sigh.

"At least your mam's happy enough to sit with Alice most afternoons. I think she's about the only person she's not upset with."

"Is she still cross with you because of Aunty Jane?"

"Who knows?" Nell waved to a couple of neighbours who were standing over the road. "I thought she'd be better once we learned she'd gone back to Ireland, but she's clearly still angry about her coming over in the first place."

"It's to be hoped she mellows." James studied his aunt as they left the terraced houses and turned into Upper Parliament Street. "Which way do you want to go?"

"I thought you wanted to go into Liverpool?"

"I can hardly leave you to walk back by yourself."

"Oh, I'm sorry." Nell stopped. "I'll go back now if you like, so you can get on."

"No, I don't like. I'll tell you what, why don't we go down to the river? It's a nice afternoon for it."

Nell looked up at the three-storey houses on her left. "As long as we can walk on the other side. It's getting chilly in the shade."

James ushered her across the road, dodging the dung that hadn't been cleared.

"You still want a job on a steamship then?"

Nell grinned. "I'd love one, but I can't deny I worry about the girls."

"Why? Mam and Alice would take care of them."

"That's what your mam says, but while I was at the Cuthberts', it was Alice who did all the running around after them, and she got behind with her waistcoats. She didn't say anything, but I think she was quite anxious about it. If I'm honest, I like the idea of her having some money of her own, too. You never know when she might need it."

James sucked his teeth. "Have you any idea how much she earns for each of them once she takes out the cost of the material?"

Nell shrugged. "Not exactly, but sometimes the customer provides their own fabric, and she charges about two shillings to make it up."

"And how many does she make each week?"

"Now you're asking, I should pay more attention. One or two?"

"So you're saying that for all her hard work, she only makes four shillings a week?"

"At best. I reckon it's probably less than that."

The side of James' cheek creased. "All right, suppose you earn much more than that for every trip you make. How would you feel about giving her, say, fifteen shillings for each voyage so she could spend all her time looking after the girls and not have to worry about the waistcoats?"

"Fifteen shillings!" Nell's mouth dropped open. "I only

earned eleven when I was at the Cuthberts' house ... and that was after Mr Cuthbert gave me a pay rise."

"But that was for a week. I'm talking about paying Alice fifteen shillings every voyage. You'd be away for about four weeks at a time, so it would work out at about four shillings a week. The top end of what she might earn at the moment, for much less work."

Nell's eyes narrowed. "Would I earn enough to do that?"

James grinned. "You would. I spoke to our stewardess on the trip, and she said she earns between two pounds ten shillings and three pounds per voyage ... and that's not counting tips."

"Three pounds a voyage? That's sixty shillings." Nell's mouth dropped open.

"Exactly. I'm sure you could spare fifteen if you earned that much. You'd have enough to give Mam some keep, and you'd still have some left for yourself."

Nell stopped and put a hand to her mouth. "I could buy the girls some new clothes and shoes."

"You could get them anything you wanted."

She stared up at James. "And I'd get a week off between voyages?"

James winced. "Probably not a full week, but certainly a few days. More than you would if you'd stayed with the Cuthberts."

Nell's mind raced as they resumed their walk. "What if Alice prefers making waistcoats? Maybe those few weeks with the girls were too much for her."

"You can still ask."

"I suppose so, and if she doesn't want to do it, I'll take it as a sign that I'm not meant to go."

James squeezed her hand. "Stop worrying. Even if she's had enough of looking after children, Mam or Aunty Rebecca would have them, if it earned them extra money."

"Rebecca wouldn't say no to the extra money, although goodness knows what Mr Grayson would think of her earning her own money. I don't know how she'd feel about watching over four children either. I wouldn't want to do it."

"But that's why you're thinking of going to sea and she's not. You're different people."

They continued to walk in silence until the landing stage came into view. The memory of coming here to hear about Jack's fate still sent a shiver down Nell's spine.

"Are you all right?" James stopped, concern etched across his face.

"I'll be fine, but I always think of your Uncle Jack when I come down here."

"Are you comfortable enough to go back to the Bohemian office and tell them you have experience?"

"Now!"

"Why not? It will be September soon enough, and anytime now, they'll be getting the crews together for next season."

"Do you think so?"

James nodded. "They've already asked me if I want to sign up for next year."

She gazed down at her navy dress. "You could have warned me. I can't go for a job looking like this." She pulled her crocheted shawl more tightly around her shoulders, but James only rolled his eyes.

"You look fine, and even if you didn't, I'm sure nobody would notice. The thing is, if we don't go today, it will be another month."

Nell's stomach fluttered. "I suppose so."

James smiled down at her. "Good, that's settled. Let's go and make an appointment."

CHAPTER THIRTY-FIVE

Nell's heart thumped as they sauntered down the dock road towards the offices of the Steamship Bohemian Company. The mid-afternoon sun bounced off the small panes of glass in the windows that sat three abreast on each of the four floors, and Nell shielded her eyes as she studied the decorative gable set above them. She'd never paid attention to the detail, but then on previous visits she'd been rather preoccupied. *Did Jack feel this nervous when he first came here? No, he never worried about things like that.* She stopped as they approached the window on the ground floor.

"What are you waiting for?" James' brow creased.

"You don't need me to come in with you. I'll wait here."

James waved a hand at the crowds. "And leave you on your own in the middle of this lot? I don't think so. Come along, there's nothing to be worried about. I'll do the talking."

A knot twisted in her stomach as James held the door open and ushered her in.

A smartly dressed man in a dark-coloured business suit greeted him at the door. "Good afternoon, sir. May I help?"

"Good afternoon. I wonder if we might make an appointment for my aunt to speak to someone about the position of stewardess, Mr Hobson perhaps. She's the widow of one of your master mariners, and he suggested a few months ago that she'd be an ideal candidate."

The man looked Nell up and down then led James to a desk at the far side of the large rectangular entrance hall.

"May I take her name, sir?"

"Mrs Riley."

Nell watched as the man studied the diary on the desk. "We could do Thursday afternoon, if that's any good."

"Actually..." James ran a finger around his collar. "I know it's short notice, but I go back to sea myself on Thursday. Would it be possible to have an appointment tomorrow?"

The clerk sucked air through his teeth. "It won't be easy, but..." He stopped as a tall man with a balding head and dark beard arrived at the desk. "Mr Parry..."

"Tom!" Nell's voice squeaked as she grabbed James' arm.

"What are you doing here?" Tom's dark brown eyes flicked between James and Nell until they settled on Nell.

"I-I'm here with James..."

"And I..." James gulped. "I came to see if they had any stewarding jobs."

"You already have a steward's job."

"Yes ... right, but I ... I like to see what the competition are up to."

The clerk's head jerked up. "I hope you're not up to

anything untoward."

"Oh goodness, no, of course not. No. In fact, we'd better be going." James dropped his hat as he fidgeted with it and bent down to pick it up. "What brings you here, Uncle Tom?"

"A bit of business." He turned to looked down at the clerk. "I believe Mr Hobson is expecting me."

The clerk gestured towards the corridor to his right. "Yes, sir. I think you know the way."

Nell stood rooted to the spot as she watched Tom disappear through a door at the far end of the corridor. *What's he up to?*

"Mr Hobson couldn't see you tomorrow, but…"

"What's he doing here?" Nell didn't apologise for her interruption as she stared at the clerk. "Mr Parry. He seems very familiar with you and the office."

"Yes, madam."

Nell could have sworn the clerk snarled. "Does he come here often?"

"He calls at least once a week, but I'm afraid I can't say why. He always deals with Mr Hobson. If you'd like to wait. He's never usually long…"

"No, I'm sorry, I can't." Perspiration ran down the back of her neck. "We need to leave. I'd rather not be here when he comes out. Thank you, sir."

She pulled on James' arm and hurried back to the door. Once outside, they walked to the corner of the building and stopped in an area of shade.

"What was he doing there? Why is he never at work?" Nell dabbed her forehead with a handkerchief.

"This is his work … or to be more precise, the part

involved with bringing the men out on strike. From what I heard in the alehouse last night, he's one of a group trying to *encourage* companies to treat their staff more fairly. I presume that's what he's doing."

"But when does he make his barrels?"

James shrugged. "I'm not sure he does any more. He sees himself as a champion of the workers."

Nell shuddered. "I don't like the sound of that. I'm not even sure it's safe coming back here. He won't be pleased if he finds out what we're doing, and that's more than likely if he's on good terms with Mr Hobson."

"You'll have to tell him sooner or later, if you get a job."

"I'd rather it be later. As your Uncle Jack used to say, it's easier to ask for forgiveness than permission."

James chuckled. "I'm not sure he had Mam or Uncle Tom in mind when he said that. Come on, let's start walking in case he comes out again. Where would you like to go now? I presume you don't want to give up."

"Where would you suggest?"

They continued walking until James stopped and studied the buildings in front of him. After a moment, a smile crept over his lips. "Why don't we go to the Red Cross Line?"

"Your company?"

"Yes, why not? They may be the best place to try, given I've only one day until I leave. We may be able to see someone without an appointment."

"Now." Nell's stomach did another somersault as she glanced over both shoulders. "You don't think Uncle Tom will have followed us, do you?"

James peered in the direction they'd just walked. "I

don't see him. Come on, let's be quick so you've no time to change your mind."

The offices of the Red Cross Line were in one of the less intimidating buildings on the dock road, but it didn't stop Nell's heart from thumping as they stepped inside. James greeted the clerk on the front desk but didn't appear to know him.

"Would it be possible to speak with Mr Smith? I'm afraid I don't have an appointment, but I work for the company and wondered if he could spare me five minutes."

"Certainly sir, would you take a seat?"

The clerk escorted James to one of two chairs positioned along an adjacent wall, apparently oblivious to Nell following them, but she didn't mind. She'd rather be ignored than have people staring.

She leaned over to James. "Do you know this Mr Smith?" Despite whispering, her voice seemed to echo around the high-ceilinged hallway.

"I've met him once or twice, but I wouldn't say I know him. He probably doesn't remember me."

"Is he nice?"

"Nice enough." He squeezed her hand. "Don't look so worried."

Nell sat in silence, taking deep breaths as her heart raced. *You can do this.* She jumped when the clerk called James' name, and she wiped her hands on her skirt.

"Mr Smith is able to see you. Do you know the way to his office?"

"I do, thank you." James' stride was confident as he led

her up the central staircase to the first floor and followed the corridor into an impressive corner office overlooking the Albert Dock.

"Mr Smith, thank you for seeing us." James shook the man's outstretched hand then introduced Nell, who stood beside him.

"Madam." He gave a slight bow. "Would you care for a seat?"

Nell sat down in the chair James held out for her.

"What may I do for you?"

"You probably don't remember me, sir, but I'm a steward on one of your ships, the *Lisbonense*. You've obviously started employing women as stewardesses, and my aunt here, Mrs Riley, would be interested in a position."

Mr Smith gave the impression of trying to control a smirk. "Would she indeed? Unfortunately, so would half the women in Liverpool, but I'm afraid at the moment we've no vacancies."

"Really? I was led to believe that my aunt would be looked upon favourably. She's a widow, you see, and her husband was a master mariner who was lost at sea earlier in the year."

Mr Smith's attention increased. "I'm sorry to hear that. Which company was he with?"

"The Steamship Bohemian Company."

"And has your aunt approached them? They probably owe her the biggest debt of gratitude."

"No. For personal reasons she'd rather work for another company, and given my employment with you, we wondered..."

Mr Smith tapped his fingers on the desk as he studied

Nell. "I'm afraid I was speaking the truth when I said we've no positions available. In fact, I don't expect to be taking on any more women until well into next year."

Nell's shoulders slumped.

"I happen to know, however, that the Guion Line are recruiting. You may do well to call there." He picked up his pen and scribbled something on a piece of paper. "Here, take this with you. It's a letter of recommendation."

A smile brightened Nell's face. "Thank you, sir. That's most kind."

Appearing surprised that she could speak, Mr Smith nodded. "I hope they have something for you."

Nell's legs were like jelly as they walked from the offices and past the Albert Dock.

"I'm not sure I can go through that again. My heart's still pounding."

James raised an eyebrow at her. "Why?"

"It was such a smart office and then hearing that they had no vacancies..."

James studied her. "How did you feel when he said they wouldn't be taking on anyone else until next year?"

Nell paused. "It was as if he'd punched the stuffing out of me..."

"So you were disappointed?"

"I was." She put a hand to her mouth. "I really was. That means I want to go, doesn't it?"

He grinned at her. "I would say so. Come along, let's walk up to the offices of the Guion Line and see if we can get an appointment for tomorrow."

CHAPTER THIRTY-SIX

The rest of the family were at the table the following morning when Nell arrived downstairs with the girls, and as one, they looked up at her.

"What's the matter?" Her stomach flipped as the girls ran to Alice.

"That's what I'm itching to find out. We've been waiting for you." Maria crossed her arms over her chest.

"I'm sorry…"

"There's no need to apologise." James held out a chair for her. "We wanted to report that we were talking to Uncle Tom in the alehouse last night and he asked us to pass on some news."

"Get on with it then." Maria drummed her fingers on her arm.

"Yes, well, it seems that Mr Read, Aunty Jane's husband, died last week."

Maria put her hands to her face. "She's coming back, isn't she?"

"It's not that bad." Vernon rolled his eyes at Billy.

"Quiet." James glared at his brother. "Apparently, he'd been ill for a while, which is why she'd been planning her return. She can't stay in Ireland without him."

Nell gasped. "Do we know when?"

"I don't think she knows yet." James poured his mam a fresh cup of tea and put an extra spoon of sugar in it. "Here, drink this."

"I can't stop her, can I?" She wrapped her hands around the cup as Vernon stood up and pushed his chair under the table.

"I need to go, but I'm not sure why you're so upset. Shouldn't you want to see your sister again?"

Maria once again ignored him and spoke to Nell. "I need to call on Sarah. I can't have her coming back without knowing what's happening."

Nell's mouth dropped open. "Are you sure?"

"What else can I do?"

"From what I've heard, I doubt Aunty Sarah will have much more information." Vernon indicated for Billy to follow him out. "Maybe one day someone will tell me what's going on. We'll see you later."

James waited for the front door to close. "We can keep you updated. I'm sure Uncle Tom will tell us any news."

"I can't rely on him. He may not have the full story anyway. I'm sure Sarah doesn't tell him the half of it." She stared at Nell. "Will you come round to Sarah's with me this afternoon?"

"This afternoon?" Nell's voice squeaked and she coughed to clear her throat. "I ... I ... don't know."

"Why not?"

James winked at Nell and put a finger to his lips. "Why

don't I walk around there with you now? I'm sure Aunty Nell and Alice can tidy up here, and it's better to get it over and done with rather than spend all morning worrying."

"I suppose we could." Maria straightened her back. "She won't be expecting us so early, so we'll take her by surprise."

"We don't need to fall out. We're only going to talk and find out what's happening."

"It won't be me arguing. Sarah's the one..."

"That's enough." Nell pushed the unfinished teacup towards her sister. "Get that down you and then you can go and get changed."

Nell had cleared the table by the time Maria was ready to leave, and with Alice at the sink washing up, Nell peered through the front window to watch James escort Maria down the road. As soon as they disappeared around the corner, Nell hurried to the kitchen.

"I'm popping over the road. I won't be long." Without waiting for a reply, Nell dashed across the street and knocked on Rebecca's front door.

"You're early. I've not even finished the breakfast dishes yet." Rebecca stood at the sink as Nell joined her.

"I'm sorry, but I've got something to tell you that couldn't wait." Nell picked up the drying cloth and relayed the news as she stacked the plates on the dresser. "...so she's gone to see Sarah now to find out what's going on."

"Good gracious." Rebecca shook her head. "Didn't you want to go with her?"

"No, thank you. I don't want to argue with them, so I was relieved when James offered to escort her."

"You miss all the fun like that." Rebecca chuckled. "At

least he should be able to keep them apart. I wonder when they'll be back. I could do with hearing what she has to say myself."

Nell shrugged. "Who knows? We also don't know what sort of mood she'll be in. I'll tell you what, why don't I send Maria over here this afternoon and she can tell you herself?"

"Yes, all right. Will you come too?" Rebecca led Nell into the living room and took a seat.

"I can't. I, erm, have an appointment this afternoon."

"An appointment? Who with?"

Nell stared into the fire. "It's an interview. I've applied for another job."

"That's out of the blue. Is this all because of Maria?"

"Sort of, but I still need some money of my own."

"I suppose so. Does she know?"

Nell grimaced as she shook her head.

"Which is why you want her out of the way this afternoon." Rebecca smirked. "I know you too well."

"You don't mind, do you?"

"No, of course not. Are you hoping to be a housekeeper again?"

"Something like that." Nell stood up. "Right, I'd better be going. I need to get the fires cleaned before she gets back."

Nell was sitting at the table peeling potatoes when she heard the front door and immediately stopped what she was doing. Seconds later, James and Maria joined her.

"You've been gone a long time. How did you get on?"

"Mam and Aunty Sarah are speaking to each other

again, if that's what you mean." James grinned as he held out a chair for his mam.

"I'm glad about that, but what about Jane?"

Maria sighed. "It's all true. Mr Read's had consumption for the last six months. That's why Jane contacted you earlier in the year. She knew then that she wouldn't be able to stay in Ireland if anything happened to him. The guardians wouldn't support her, and according to Sarah, his family were no more keen on her than we were on him."

"Because she's not Catholic?"

Maria nodded. "And because they'd never had the boys baptised."

James sat with them at the table. "It shouldn't really come as a surprise."

"It doesn't make it any easier." Maria glared at him. "It's still happened very suddenly."

Nell leaned back in her chair. "So we'll have to get used to her being here?"

"Aunty Sarah said she was excited to be home the other week and that we shouldn't worry about seeing her."

"It's easy for her to say." Maria fanned her face with an envelope that was lying on the table. "What do we even say to her?"

"I'm sure you'll be fine once you get over that first meeting." James' eyes flicked between them. "Why don't you invite her here to meet the family? That should make things easier than if it was just the two of you."

"I'm not having her here." Maria jumped to her feet.

"But we could." Nell looked up at her. "We could ask Rebecca and Mr Grayson to join us with the girls. Children always help to soften these occasions. Talking of Rebecca..."

Nell turned her attention to Maria. "Will you go over this afternoon and tell her what's happening? She needs to know."

"I'm not making any of the arrangements. If you want to entertain her, you can do the inviting."

"And I will, but I can't call on Rebecca today. I've applied for another job and have an interview this afternoon..."

Maria's head jerked up. "Doing what? At a time like this, you're planning on disappearing again."

"It shouldn't be as bad as last time." Nell pursed her lips. "If all goes well, I'll be home for days at a time."

CHAPTER THIRTY-SEVEN

Nell needed to change into her Sunday clothes, and she urged Maria out of the house as soon as the dishes were washed. Once the door was shut, she ran up the stairs and five minutes later came down the stairs carrying a straw hat decorated with ribbon and stood in front of the mirror over the fire to fix it.

"Has Alice taken the girls outside?"

James stood up and reached for his hat. "Yes, I'm the only one here."

Nell grinned. "It worked out rather well with Maria disappearing over the road. I had a horrible feeling she'd be quizzing me about the job once I told her, but she's too preoccupied."

"I wasn't sure you were even going to mention it, but I notice you were selective with the truth."

"What do you expect? I wasn't lying, though. I will be home for days at a time."

"You forgot to mention it would only be once a month!" James laughed as Nell fixed her hat.

"It gives her a chance to get used to the idea of me getting another job first. There'll be time to give her the details later." Nell straightened her dress. "Don't forget, you go away again tomorrow. I've got to live with her."

"That's a fair point." He watched as she draped a shawl around her shoulders. "Very smart. Now, shall we go?"

The walk took half an hour, and as they arrived outside the double doors of the Guion Shipping Company, Nell was surprised at how calm she felt. It was as if all her nervous energy had been spent the previous day and she could finally relax.

James reached for the door handle. "Are you ready?"

"As ready as I'll ever be."

A short well-dressed man greeted them and showed them into another impressive office. It wasn't as grand as the Bohemian office, and the view of the side of the customs house was less dramatic than the Albert Dock, but Nell didn't mind. Perhaps this company was more on her level.

The man extended his hand, first to James and then to Nell. His grip was firm as they shook hands.

"I'm Mr Fisher."

James replied for them. "I'm Mr Atkin, and this is my aunt, Mrs Riley. Thank you for seeing us at such short notice."

"You must have called when I'd had a cancellation. What may I do for you?"

"My aunt here is interested in a job as a stewardess, and Mr Smith from the Red Cross Line suggested you may be recruiting. He gave me a letter of recommendation for her." He reached into his jacket pocket and handed Mr Fisher the letter. "Her husband was Master Mariner Riley from the

Steamship Bohemian Company, but unfortunately, he was lost at sea earlier this year."

Mr Fisher read the letter. "What made you go to the Red Cross Line first?"

"I work for them myself, as a steward, and decided it would be the best place to start."

"I see. So you know what the job entails?"

"Yes, sir."

"The job of a stewardess is slightly less onerous and obviously only involves tending to the ladies, but do you think your aunt would be suited to the role?"

"Yes, sir, I do."

Mr Fisher nodded. "Very well. Mrs Riley, have you done any work like this before?"

Nell froze. *He's asking me.* "Erm, no ... not on a ship, but I have been a housekeeper ... in one of the big houses on Upper Parliament Street. I've got a reference." She fumbled in her handbag and handed him an envelope.

With a series of deliberate moves, he opened the letter and studied it. "I see you're used to attending to ladies."

"Y-yes, sir."

"Excellent. Can you tell me why you want to go to sea?"

"Well ... it's something I'd talked about with my husband, but until recently, I didn't realise opportunities existed for women to be stewardesses. Once I found out, I knew it was something I wanted to do."

"Do you have any children, Mrs Riley?"

Nell's cheeks flushed. "I have two daughters ... but my sisters will take care of them." She gabbled the last few words.

James leaned forward in his chair. "Unfortunately, with being a widow, she needs to work to provide for them."

"I understand, but hasn't she been to the Bohemian office? I'm sure they'd be only too happy to help."

"No." James sat back again. "Because of what happened, she's not comfortable working for them. She'd like a clean break."

"Very well." Mr Fisher studied her. "I'm sure you look the part, and with a little training we could make a stewardess of you. The new positions start in January, and ideally we hope to recruit staff for the entire year."

"A full year?" Nell hoped the quiver in her voice wasn't obvious and was grateful that James interrupted.

"Mr Fisher, given that my aunt has never been to sea, would it be possible to use the first voyage to test her suitability for the role? Both from your perspective and hers."

"You mean to see if she's up to the job?"

"There's that, but also to make sure she's happy. As I said, I'm a steward myself and know that not everyone takes to a life at sea."

Mr Fisher eyed the two of them. "Yes, why not? She'll receive most of her training in that first month and so if she isn't suitable, either one of us can cancel the contract at the end of the first voyage. Beyond that, we'll expect her to work for the rest of the year. I can't say fairer than that."

"That's very generous of you, thank you, sir." James turned to Nell. "Are you happy with that?"

"Y-yes, thank you." Nell's heart was pounding again.

"Excellent." Mr Fisher pushed himself up from his

desk. "If you'll walk this way, I'll get my clerk to take down your details."

Nell and James spent a further half an hour with a clerk, who briefed her on reporting for work. Once they stepped outside, she breathed deeply. The breeze was cool after the warmth of the office, but she didn't mind. It was a refreshing change.

James watched her as she looked out to sea. "Are you sure you're happy?"

"More than I could have imagined. I've waited a long time for this." She studied the activity around the ships berthed in the docks and spotted a passenger liner further up the coast to her right. "Can you believe it? In a few months I'll be boarding one of those ships to travel across the ocean. It doesn't seem real."

"You'll get used to it soon enough. Come on, we'd better get home. Mam will be wondering where we've got to."

Nell pulled back on James' arm. "What do we tell her? I don't want to say anything about the job, not yet."

"You'll have to tell her sooner or later."

"Can't it be later? I'd at least like to wait until I've signed the contract."

"I might not be here when it arrives, and you can't hold off telling her for too long. She'll want to know what the delay is."

Nell bit down on her lip. "Perhaps I can hide it until you come back, if I tell her there were a number of applicants."

James cocked his head to one side. "Are you sure you can beat her to the post every day until the letter arrives?"

Already imagining Maria's reaction, Nell grimaced. "If I have to, I'll get up at dawn every morning. I can't imagine anything worse than her finding it when I'm not ready to tell her."

"Very well." He offered her his arm. "Come on, we'd better get a move on."

They cut through the backstreets around the customs house and headed towards Parliament Street. As they reached the corner, they spotted Billy heading towards them.

"Is that the time already?" James studied his pocket watch. "Mam will be on the lookout for us. What have you done with Vernon?"

"Good afternoon." Billy fell into step with them. "I've not seen him this evening. Where've you been?"

"Aunty Nell's had a job interview."

Billy grinned at her. "Are you going to last more than three weeks in this one?"

I would hope so. "I'm not certain I've got the job yet, but if I have then I'm sure I will. I needn't stay if I don't like it, though."

"When will you find out?"

Nell bit her lip. "I'm not sure. They're going to write."

Billy let out a low whistle. "That sounds official. Who's it with?"

"It's erm ... domestic work for the Guion shipping line."

"Making sure the offices are nice and clean? I imagine it will be better than being a housekeeper, although you'll have to get up early in the mornings. Still, you should be able to stay at home."

Nell caught James' eye and grimaced, but Billy didn't seem to notice.

"Have you told Mam?"

"I told her I had an interview, but that's about it. You won't say anything, will you, about where the job is? I'd rather tell her myself."

Billy laughed. "Are you worried she'll think you're going to sea?"

James indicated for them to cross the road. "You know what she's like. The less we tell her, the better."

"Promise I won't say a word."

Maria hurried into the hall as Nell went inside ahead of James and Billy.

"Where on earth have you been? I've been looking out for you for the last hour."

James joined them. "I'm sorry, we lost track of time. Have you had a nice afternoon with Aunty Rebecca?"

"Nice enough. We had a chat about Jane and she agrees with you that we should invite her round."

James raised his eyebrows. "Are you happy about that?"

"Not really, but I don't have much choice."

"Well, hopefully it will be when I'm home..."

"We'll make sure it is, but enough of her, I've a letter here from your dad. Will you read it to me?" She handed it to him along with the silver letter opener.

"I'm sure I can do that. Is there a cup of tea going?" He sat down by the fire.

"Nell, will you do that? The kettle's boiled but I've been staring at that envelope half the afternoon. I'm hoping George knows when he'll be back." An unfamiliar grin spread across Maria's lips as Nell retrieved the teapot from the table. She hadn't reached the kitchen when James stood up and ushered his mam towards the fire.

"You'd better sit down."

"Why? What's the matter?"

The fear in Maria's voice was unmistakable, and Nell stopped as James composed himself.

"There's been an accident."

The colour disappeared from Maria's face. "What sort of accident? Is he all right?"

"He doesn't give a lot of details, but it sounds as if there was a storm and he was thrown across the deck. He hit the main mast and broke his leg."

"Oh my goodness." Maria's eyes were wide. "Will he lose his leg?"

James shrugged. "It's hard to say without knowing how bad the break is. He says the ship's doctor bound it up as best he could, and once they reached port, the captain sent him to hospital to have it checked. They kept him in, which is when he wrote."

Nell had forgotten about the tea. "Where was the ship when it happened?"

James looked back at the letter. "Off the coast of Australia, but it doesn't say which bit. It's a rather large place."

Maria sobbed. "Will they have let him back on the ship?"

"I'm not certain. He's been told there's no infection, so

the captain's granted permission for him to travel back with them, but as I said, he was still in hospital when he wrote, so we don't know for sure if they have. We need to hope he sends another letter."

Billy shifted in his chair as Maria sobbed. "It should arrive in the next day or two if he did. In fact, either way he should have written..."

"This is unbearable. Until we get the next letter, we'll have no idea where he is and when we may see him again. Now do you see why I worry when you and Dad are away? Not to mention Uncle Jack's accident." She glared at James. "The sooner you give up the sea the better."

Nell's stomach churned and she backed away towards the kitchen. *She'll be furious with me.*

"Don't be silly. Stop and think how long Dad's been at sea." James' voice was firm. "It's well over ten years, and this is his first major accident. I'm on a passenger ship, and they're much safer, anyway, so stop worrying."

Maria wiped her eyes, but suddenly jerked her head to look at Nell. "He won't be getting paid if he can't work. Did you get the job you went for? We'll need the money at this rate."

Nell gulped. "Erm ... I don't know yet. They were seeing some other applicants. They said they'd write to me."

Maria laughed through her tears. "That'll be the two of us looking out for the postman then. Let's hope he brings good news."

Nell's heart sank. *Oh goodness. That's all I need.*

CHAPTER THIRTY-EIGHT

The mornings were once again getting darker and, as ever, Nell struggled to get out of bed early. She'd managed well enough for a week after James had left, but they must have a new postman because he was getting earlier.

Elenor nestled into her side as she lay in bed listening to the sounds downstairs. Maria was clearly up, but Nell couldn't hear any voices. The boys mustn't have arrived downstairs yet. She peered at the clock. Half past six. The postman could be here at any minute, and it was over a week since she'd been to the office. The letter must be due soon ... and so should George's. She really needed to get up.

Careful not to disturb Elenor, she swung her legs over the edge of the bed and reached for the dress hanging against the wall. She was about to fasten it up when she froze, a cold shiver running down her spine. *The postman!*

She fastened the button at the nape of her neck and hurried onto the landing, praying Maria hadn't heard the letter box but as she reached the top step, she stopped. She'd beaten her to it. Holding her breath in case Maria heard her, she stepped back, treading on Vernon's foot as she did.

"What are you up to, Aunty Nell? You're in the way there."

"Yes, sorry." Nell's step faltered as she tried to keep out of sight, but Maria peered up the stairs.

"Is that you, Nell? Your letter's here."

"Oh good." Her voice squeaked. "I'll be down shortly. I need to sort the girls out first." She waited for Maria and Vernon to go into the living room then knocked gently on the boys' bedroom door. "Billy. Are you in there?"

The door opened almost immediately, and he stood fastening the buttons of his shirt.

"What's the matter?"

Nell ran a hand over her forehead. "The letter I've been waiting for has just arrived, but your mam's picked it up. Would you mind going downstairs and bringing it up for me? I'd rather be on my own when I open it."

Billy's eyes narrowed. "Why?"

"Oh, I don't know, in case I don't get the job, I suppose."

Billy stepped back into the bedroom to reach for his jacket. "All right then. Wait here."

"If she asks where I am, tell her the girls are still asleep and I don't want to wake them."

Billy nodded. "Give me a minute."

He hadn't gone two steps down the stairs when there was crying from Nell's room. "For goodness' sake, it's Leah."

"What do we tell Mam now?"

"You tell me the truth." Maria glared up the stairs. "What's going on? What's up with Leah?"

Nell leaned over the bannister. "The noise woke her up.

Give me ten minutes and I'll be down. Would you pass the letter to Billy? I'll read it up here." She tried to sound as casual as possible.

"Why can't you open it downstairs?"

"Because I won't be down until the girls are dressed and I'd like to know what it is."

Maria disappeared into the living room and returned to make her way up the stairs. "Here you are. It looks very thick."

"Yes, it does." Nell took it from her and wandered into the bedroom where Leah had stood herself up in her cot. "Have you had a letter from George this morning?"

"No, not yet. Come on, are you going to open yours…?"

"In a minute." She slipped the letter under Leah's blanket as she bent down to pick her up. "You don't need to stay."

"The boys can look after themselves. There's a fresh pot of tea and plenty of bread on the table."

"Honestly, you go, I'll be a while yet." Nell stood with her back to Maria as she soothed Leah, but a second later Maria was pulling on the back of her dress.

"What are you thinking? You haven't fastened these buttons properly."

"No, I erm … I got distracted. Please don't fuss. You go and see to the boys before they go out."

"I'm sure they can manage perfectly well on their own for five minutes. Are you going to open that letter?" Maria's eyes sparkled in anticipation, but Nell breathed a sigh of relief as the tiny figure of Elenor emerged from the blankets on the other side of the room.

"No, let me sort the girls out first. I'll look at it later."

"Well, don't be long." With a snarl, Maria stormed from the room.

As soon as she disappeared, Nell closed the door and sat Leah on the bed beside Elenor. *What a start to the day.* With a deep breath, she retrieved the envelope from the cot and sat down next to the girls.

"What is it?"

Elenor tried to take it from her, but Nell pulled it away.

"Mam's going to get a job so we can have some new dresses. Would you like that?"

Elenor nodded. "I like dresses."

"I know, and if Mam goes to work, they'll give her some money and we can go to the shops."

Elenor clapped. "And Leah."

"Yes, Leah too." Nell prised open the top and pulled out three sheets of paper.

You are to report to the landing stage on the morning of Wednesday 4th January at seven o'clock where you'll be joining the SS Wisconsin *on the voyage from Liverpool to New York.*

Her stomach did a somersault as she read the words *New York,* and she put a hand to her mouth. *It's going to happen! But not for three months.* She flinched as Maria shouted to Vernon. *Will the time ever pass?*

She continued to read the list of things she'd need to take with her and then flicked to the contract that needed signing. All she had to do was put her name to it to confirm she was accepting the position and take it to the office. *A simple signature...* Her eyes flicked around the room, but she knew there were no pens upstairs. She'd have to wait until Maria went out to the yard.

"Are you coming down, Aunty Nell?" The sound of Billy's boots running up the stairs forced her to push the letter into a drawer.

"Yes, I'll be with you in a minute." She hurriedly pulled a dress over Elenor's head and opened the door. "Is everything all right?"

"Me and Vernon are about to go, and I wanted to check you'll be all right with Mam. She's still wondering about the letter."

Nell grinned. "I'll be fine. I got the job."

"Congratulations! Will you tell her now?"

Nell bit her lip. *What on earth will I say?* "I'm not sure yet. Don't mention anything, will you?"

"Not if you don't want me to." Billy waved as he disappeared down the stairs. "I'll see you later."

The front door had barely closed after the boys when Nell picked Leah up and ushered Elenor downstairs. Maria looked up from the table as they arrived.

"You're looking very cheerful. Did you get the job?"

Nell faltered under her gaze. "I'm not sure. They want to see me again this afternoon…" Nell sat the girls at the table with Alice.

"Why would they want to do that?"

"They didn't say. Perhaps they want to check whether they still like me."

Maria studied her as she buttered some bread for the girls. "Where is this job? I was so preoccupied with Jane I don't think you told me."

"It's … erm … with the Guion Line. Doing some domestic work for them."

"They're going to a lot of trouble if that's all it is."

Nell shrugged. "They seem to be a popular place to work. I think they pay more than your standard residence."

"I suppose so." Maria gazed out of the window. "It's a lovely day out there for the time of the year. You know what, I think I'll come with you."

"What!" Nell spilt her tea as she jerked her head to look at Maria.

"I'll walk to the offices with you and then we can nip up to the shops. I haven't been into town for an age, and it might take my mind off things for an hour or two."

"I'm sure there's no need for that. What about the girls? Somebody needs to watch them, and I can't ask Alice again."

"We can take them with us."

"No, we can't." Nell gasped for air. "It's likely to be another job interview."

"Did they say that in the letter?"

"Not exactly, but they want to speak to me about the job, so it could be..." Nell stood up and rushed into the kitchen for a cloth. "I'm sorry, but you can't come. Not today. I need to do this on my own and think about what I'll say."

Maria fixed her eyes on her as she sat back down at the table. "There's no need to be so jumpy. I only offered to walk with you."

"I know, but this is a big thing for me. It's not like a shopping trip. We can do that another day, but ... please, not today."

"Suit yourself." Maria snatched the cloth from her and wiped the table. "I'm going to start the washing. Come along, Alice."

Alice hurried from the room as Nell slumped into her chair.

"Aunty Ria's not happy."

"No, she's not." Nell stroked Elenor's hair. "Shall we do all the cleaning to cheer her up?"

"Me and Leah can dust."

Nell smiled. "Shall I help as well so we get it done quicker?"

"Yes, and then we can play."

Nell squeezed Elenor's hand. "And then we'll play."

Nell couldn't keep the grin from her face as she strolled back down Windsor Street later that afternoon. She'd signed the contract and delivered it to the office, all by herself. She wouldn't have dared do such a thing a month ago, but she had to start doing things for herself. She couldn't hope to be a stewardess if she was frightened of every man she spoke to.

Her stride faltered as she stepped into Merlin Street. *Maria's bound to question me about the interview. What do I say?* She gazed at Rebecca's front door. Maybe it's time I told her, see how she reacts.

Rebecca was still taking off her cloak after picking Isobel up from school when Nell walked in.

"You look warm. Where've you been?"

"Down to the Guion Line offices. They've offered me a job…"

"At the Guion offices?" A frown crossed Rebecca's face as she walked into the living room. "I thought you were going to be a housekeeper."

Nell pursed her lips. "Not exactly... but I had to sign a piece of paper to say I wanted the job and take it back."

"And you went by yourself?"

"I've got to get used to it." Nell took a deep breath. "I'm going to be a stewardess."

Rebecca's mouth opened and closed. "What do you mean? How can you...? In an office?"

"Why don't you sit down?" Nell perched on the edge of a seat near the fire. "I'm going to sea."

Rebecca's eyes carried a look of incomprehension. "On a ship?"

"Yes. Like James but working with the female passengers."

Rebecca shook her head. "What even gave you the idea? It was James, wasn't it? You've been spending too much time with him."

"You know I've wanted to go to sea ever since I was with Jack, and James suggested it as a way to make it possible. I'll only go on one trip ... to start with anyway. If I don't like it, I needn't stay." Nell shifted in her seat as Rebecca continued to study her. "Are you cross with me?"

"No ... well, I don't know. It's such a shock. Have you told Maria?"

"Not yet. I'd like James to be at home when I do, so he can calm her down."

Rebecca sat back in her chair. "Can you wait that long? He won't be home for another few weeks."

Nell bit her lip. "That's why I told you. I wanted to see what you think."

"I'm not sure, if I'm being honest. I'm pleased, if that's what you want to do, but I'll miss you. Especially with

Jane due to arrive. I'd imagined we'd all face her together."

"We might yet. I don't go until the beginning of January. I'm hoping George will be home first so he can stop Maria worrying."

"There is one benefit I can think of." A smile brightened Rebecca's face. "If George is unable to work because of his leg, Maria might not be so concerned about the type of job you do, as long as it pays well."

"That's a good point. I'll have to mention that when I tell her. I wonder how George will take it."

Rebecca blew out through her lips. "Who knows? If he's worried about his leg, he'll probably be pleased, although he may not think it's a job for a woman."

"Perhaps he should. Do you remember all those years ago when he was furious with James for wanting to be a steward? That was all because he said it was women's work. He can hardly object."

Rebecca's eyes widened. "You're not going to remind him, are you?"

"Probably not. Anyway, I'd better go. Maria will be wondering where I've got to."

"What will you tell her?"

Nell reached for her shawl. "That they haven't made their minds up yet. That should buy me a bit more time."

Nell strolled across the street and paused to take a deep breath as she pushed on the front door and let herself in. She hadn't reached the coat hooks when Maria raced into the hall to meet her.

"He's coming home!"

"Who?"

"George. We've had a letter and Alice read it to me. They let him out of hospital in time to be on the ship and he should be here by the end of the year."

Nell followed Maria into the living room. "That's good. Does he say how he is?"

"Not really. All he said is that he's confined to bed and isn't allowed to move."

"That won't be easy for him." Nell took a seat at the table. "Things could be different when he gets home, though. He's not likely to be going to the alehouse every night."

"You never know. I'm hoping his leg will heal on the way home and he'll be well on the mend by the time he arrives. If it isn't, well, it will be nice to have him at home." Maria beamed at her. "This could turn out to be a blessing. We never normally see enough of him, and he won't be going back to sea in a hurry."

"That will be nice." A lead weight settled in Nell's stomach.

"Anyway, how did you get on today? Did you get that job?"

Nell paused. *Do I tell her while she's in such a good mood ... and when she needs the money?* With a deep breath, she laid her hands on the table. "Yes. I did."

CHAPTER THIRTY-NINE

Nell's heart pounded as silence momentarily fell on the room. A second later, Maria threw her arms around her.

"Oh, Nell. That's wonderful. It's such a weight off my mind. When do you start?"

Nell pulled away and took a seat by the fire. "Not until January."

"January?" Maria took the chair opposite. "That's more than three months away. They'll need cleaners before then, surely."

Nell bit down on her lip. "I'm not going to be a cleaner. I've got a job as a stewardess. The money's so much better."

Maria spluttered and gasped for air. "You're going to sea? After everything that happened to Jack ... and now George. How could you?"

"I'm sorry, but you know it's something I've wanted to do for years ... I never thought it would be possible, but now it is."

"That's the most selfish thing I've ever heard. What about those two little girls?"

The heat rose in Nell's cheeks. "I was going to speak to you about them..."

"That's typical of you, expecting everyone else to pick up the pieces. You told me you'd be at home for days at a time."

"And I will ... in the same way that James is."

Maria stood up and paced to the table and back. "You can jolly well go back to the offices tomorrow and tell them you've changed your mind."

"What's got into you?" Nell got to her feet. "You were pleased not two minutes ago because you need the money. Just because it's a live-in job..."

"A live-in job! Is that what you call going halfway around the world?"

"Does it matter whether I'm living on a steamship or in one of the houses round the corner? The truth is, when George comes home, you'll need the space, and if I'm on a ship, I'll be out of the way but still paying you rent."

"I don't want your money ... I want you here, where you belong."

"Why don't you ever consider what *I* want? I'm grateful that you take care of me and the girls, but I need to fend for myself, preferably doing something I'll enjoy."

"People don't go to work to enjoy themselves."

"Well, they should. James likes his job, so when he mentioned they had stewardesses..."

"James put you up to this. I might have known." Maria stood with her hands on her hips. "Wait until I see him. Last time he was home, I told him it was about time he got a job in Liverpool. I didn't expect him to encourage you to go away with him."

"I won't be going with him..."

"Don't play clever with me. You may not be on the same ship, but you'll both be on the same sea. Who else have you told? Everyone except me, I suppose."

Nell fell silent, her cheeks burning. "No. I've only told Rebecca ... when I was on my way home."

Maria snorted. "And what did she say? Did she point out that the girls need their mam? Don't expect me to be running around after them."

Nell kept her voice level. "I wasn't going to ask you."

"Who'll have them then? Alice won't. She nearly lost all her customers last time."

Nell glowered at her sister. "I'm sure Alice would happily do it if I paid her more than she gets from all the sewing you make her do. Has it ever occurred to you that she may not like doing it?"

"It doesn't matter whether she likes it or not, as long as it earns some money."

Nell shook her head. "You don't even let her keep any for herself. Everything she earns, you take from her."

"Why does she need her own money? She's got George to provide for her while she's here, and once she's married, her husband will take care of her."

"That's not working out so well for us, is it? What if she ends up like me with no husband? Wouldn't you be happier to know she had a bit of money tucked away so she isn't forced from her home?"

"Stop being so dramatic."

"No, you stop. I'm only going on one voyage to start

with, to see if I'm suitable and if I like it. By the end of January, this might all be over."

"So you'd have Alice give up her customers again for the sake of one voyage?"

"I can't win." Nell threw her hands in the air. "The way you're carrying on, I'll be gone for the whole year … and you'll only have yourself to blame. The truth is, the man I spoke to said that if I really don't like it by the end of the first month, I can cancel the contract."

"And you better had. James can take you down to the Guion offices when he gets home and tell them you're not going."

"He'll do no such thing. This is my decision, not yours … and I'm going."

Maria's face was puce. "You stop and think about this, young lady."

"I've done nothing *but* think, and that's why I'm going. I'm never going to get an opportunity like this again." Nell reached for the door handle. "I'm going to Rebecca's."

"Trying to get her on your side…"

"She already is." Nell made to leave but stopped and turned back. "And a word of warning. If you've any plans to stop Alice looking after the girls, Rebecca said they can move in with her. I suggest you think on that and consider how much money you'll lose if you do anything stupid."

Nell stormed from the house, slamming the door behind her, and crossed the road to Rebecca's. Without bothering to knock, she barged through the front door, only pausing for breath when it closed behind her.

"What on earth...?" Rebecca appeared in the hall. "Oh gracious, you'd better come in. Did you tell her about the job?"

Nell's heart was pounding. "She was in a good mood when I got home, so I stupidly thought it would be all right to tell her."

"Maria was in a good mood?" Rebecca poured out two cups of tea. "Why?"

"She's had a letter from George to say he was on the ship and should be home by the end of the year."

Rebecca groaned. "As if that's anything to be happy about..."

"It didn't last long." Nell sat down and put her head in her hands. "As soon as I told her about the job, she was furious."

"You shouldn't be surprised."

"I know, but it was worse than I expected." Nell took the cup and saucer Rebecca handed to her. "I hope you don't mind, but I told her the girls can move in here if she won't let Alice look after them."

"You didn't..." Rebecca slumped down into the chair.

"I'd pay you and make it worth your while. I don't want Mr Grayson angry with me too." She took a sip of the tea.

"Did you tell her I knew about the job?"

"I had to, but I don't think she'll be cross with you. I said that I'd only told you this afternoon. It's James she's mad at. I accidentally mentioned it was his idea."

"Poor James, although I'm sure he'll be able to calm her down. When's he back?"

"Not for another couple of weeks. I hope she doesn't stay angry until then. It will be unbearable."

. . .

After finishing her tea, Nell stood up to leave.

"I can't put this off any longer, especially since I'm supposed to be making the tea."

Rebecca's face twisted. "You'll have to hope Alice is back. She's less likely to say anything if she's there."

"You're right." Nell took a deep breath. "Wish me luck."

Nell's heart was pounding as she crossed the road, and she pushed open the door, making as little noise as she could. The door to the living room was closed, and she wiped the palms of her hands on her skirt before clutching the handle and poking her head around the door. The room was empty. *Where is everyone?* She walked to the fire, but as she sat down, Alice walked through the back door.

"Ah, here you are." Nell turned to her niece. "Where is everyone?"

"Mam went out and took the girls with her. I don't know where they've gone."

Nell's heart sank. *Why would she do that?*

"Don't look so worried. She's probably gone into someone's house for a natter."

"Yes, probably." Nell took a seat. "Has she told you about my job?"

Alice grimaced. "She wasn't very pleased, but she said you're going to sea. Is it true?"

Nell nodded. "It is. For one voyage at least."

"Really?" Alice's face lit up. "You're so fortunate. I'd love to do that one day."

"Don't let your mam hear you say that. I've a feeling she won't be very pleased."

Alice's shoulders drooped as she sat down. "It doesn't make much difference. She wouldn't let me go, and then I'll have a husband and a baby, and the chance will be gone."

"Don't be too down. You're still young, and it may happen one day, you never know." Nell cocked her head to one side. "I've something I'd like to ask you."

Alice's face brightened again. "Would you like me to look after the girls while you're away?"

Nell chuckled. "How did you know?"

"Mam mentioned it. Not that she wants me to do it. She says I need to make my waistcoats..."

"What if you didn't need to?"

Alice studied her. "What do you mean? We need the money..."

"When James was telling me about the job, he gave me an idea of how much I could expect to earn. We worked out that if you look after the girls for me, I could pay you fifteen shillings for every voyage."

"Fifteen shillings!" Alice's mouth dropped open. "That's more than I make from the waistcoats."

Nell smiled. "That's what we thought, and what's more, I'll make sure your mam takes no more than ten shillings from you. I want you to save the rest, in case you need it one day."

"Why would I need so much money?"

"Hopefully, you won't, but if you ever end up like me or your mam, it could come in handy. Or..." There was a glint in Nell's eyes. "If you don't need it, perhaps you could use it to go on a ship yourself one day."

"Me!" Alice squealed, but Nell put a finger to her lips as the front door opened.

"Not a word for now. We'll tell your mam you're looking after the girls when she's in a better mood."

Alice nodded, but they both flinched as the front door slammed and footsteps marched down the hall. Nell instinctively jumped up.

"I'll be back in a minute."

CHAPTER FORTY

Nell darted to the kitchen but hadn't reached the tap before Maria glared at her through the door.

"There she is." She stood with an arm outstretched as Tom strolled past her and leaned against the kitchen door.

"What's going on, Nell? Is it true?"

Nell refused to acknowledge Maria's glare. "Is what true?"

"That you're going to sea."

Nell put the kettle on the range and stared at her brother. "Yes, it is."

Maria pushed past him. "Is that all you can say?"

"What else is there to say? Tom asked if I was going to sea and I said I was." Nell turned around to collect the cups and saucers and put them on a tray.

"You've got to stop her." Maria tugged on Tom's arm, but he stood firm and removed his arm from her grasp.

"Stop it. I'm perfectly capable of speaking to her myself." He stepped towards Nell. "What's brought this on?"

"I need a job, and ever since I married Jack I've wanted to go to sea. This is the chance to do both."

"I told you months ago that I didn't want you working..."

"And you also told me you'd get me some compensation, but that didn't happen."

"I'm working on it."

Nell snorted. "If I wait around for that, we'll be walking round in rags. Bohemian are hardly going to do you any favours if you're trying to get their workers to strike down their tools."

"That's why we're going on strike, so the likes of you get your money."

"Is that why you were on such good terms with them when I saw you in there?"

Maria's head whipped around as she glared at Tom. "You saw her in the Bohemian office? Why didn't you stop her?"

"I thought I had." Tom spoke through gritted teeth. "They promised they wouldn't employ her..."

"...without experience." Nell glared at him. "I knew I'd seen you that day we first went to the offices. Were you the reason I ended up working in Upper Parliament Street?"

"You shouldn't have been thinking of going to sea. It's no place for a woman."

"Why not? George spent years telling James he was doing women's work, but now I want to do it, that's wrong too. You don't want me to have any independence, that's what this is about."

"Women aren't meant to be independent."

"Are you going to give me an allowance every week so I can buy new clothes for the girls then?"

"You can earn some money without going halfway around the world," Maria snarled. "I want you on dry land. You've already lost Jack to the sea and George is likely to be an invalid. The last thing I want is to be panicking about you."

Nell shook her head. "There are hundreds of boats every day sailing the oceans, and most of them reach their destination without any problem. This way, I get paid a good wage, which I'll share with you, and the girls can stay here. It will also give you extra room for when George is home."

The sound of the kettle boiling distracted her, and she busied herself making the tea. "If you're not happy about it, I'll go and stay at Rebecca's instead. She'll have the girls for me, too."

Nell picked up the tray and pushed between them as she carried it to the table where Alice sat with Leah on her lap.

"You promised I could look after them." Alice's voice was faint.

"And so you can, as long as your mam stops this nonsense."

"It's not nonsense."

Tom stepped in front of Maria. "That's enough. Nell, you need to reconsider this." His voice trailed away as the front door opened and Billy joined them. His eyes flitted around the room.

"What's going on?"

Nell sidled over to him. "I told your mam about the job."

His brow furrowed. "Aren't you pleased?"

"You knew as well!" Maria rounded on him. "Why didn't you stop her ... or better still, why didn't you tell me?"

Billy put an arm around Nell's shoulders. "Why would I?"

"Why would you...?"

"I didn't tell him what the job was." Nell raised her voice as she fixed her glare on Maria. "He thought I had a domestic job."

Billy studied her. "You mean that's not what you're going to do?"

Nell gave him a sheepish grin. "I'm sorry I didn't tell you, but I'm going to be a stewardess..."

"Oh no you're not ... and you can wipe that silly grin from your face." Maria moved towards her, but Billy stepped between them.

"Leave her alone. What's wrong with her wanting to go to sea? It's something she's wanted to do for years, and this is her chance. Why should we stop her?"

"What a dreadful attitude. I thought you liked her..."

"Of course I like her. That's why I want her to be happy."

"By going to her death at sea..."

"Now you're being ridiculous." Nell rounded on her brother. "Tom, will you tell her to stop being so silly?"

"Only if you stop all this and tell the company you won't go."

"I can't do that. I've signed a contract. Besides, this is a once in a lifetime opportunity for me to leave Liverpool and see something of the world. Why should I turn that down because she's being unreasonable?"

Tom grunted and held up his hand to keep Maria quiet.

"Is it true that the contract only ties you in for a month and then you can walk away?"

Nell turned back to the table to pour the tea. "Yes."

"So you'll get out of it?"

"Perhaps. It depends whether I like the job or not. It also depends on how things are here. I'm not coming back to all this."

Maria flopped onto the nearest chair and put her head in her hands. "After all I've done for you…"

Billy rolled his eyes at Nell. "Mam, don't be so dramatic. Why can't you let Aunty Nell be happy? You know how she loves tales of the sea."

"Those two little girls…"

"I'll take care of them." Alice finally found her voice. "Aunty Nell told me how good I am with them and I won't let her down."

"And Rebecca will help out if Alice needs anything." Nell's comment had been matter-of-fact, but Maria sobbed.

"You've spoken to everyone and frozen me out."

"I've done no such thing. You know we're short of space, and we need the money to make up for George's lost wages. I'll be solving two problems at once. You should be thanking me."

"But this isn't how it should be done…" Tom walked towards Nell, but Billy stepped between them.

"All right, let's calm down. We're obviously not going to solve this tonight. Mam, you need to recognise how much Aunty Nell wants this job, and Aunty Nell, can you understand how much Mam worries about you?"

Maria huffed but said nothing.

"Mam, stop this. How about letting Aunty Nell go on

one voyage to satisfy her curiosity, and then once she's back, she can hand in her notice and you can stop worrying?"

"And have Alice give up her work for one month? No." Maria glared at her son. "She's only just caught up with her clients from when she last had the girls."

"Well, how about you spending more time with them so Alice can keep working?"

"And who cleans the house!"

"I'm sure they can help. Come on, Mam. It's only for four weeks and then we can get back to normal. Can't we at least let Aunty Nell have her adventure?"

Adventure. This is my future. Nell clenched her fists, fighting the urge to stamp her feet.

"Aunty Nell? Please."

She stared at Maria, who sat with her head in her hands. "Will she stop complaining?"

"Mam?"

Maria wiped her face with her handkerchief. "Only if she promises to do no more than one trip."

"Can you do that, Aunty Nell?"

Nell's shoulders slumped. "If I must."

Maria nodded. "All right then."

"Good." Billy patted Nell on the shoulder. "Can we have that cup of tea now? It will be cold at this rate."

CHAPTER FORTY-ONE

The room was still dark as Nell lay in bed staring at the ceiling. She must have dozed off shortly after going to bed, but her dreams had been filled with visions of steamships leaving Liverpool with her on board. Many had sailed into New York, but she woke up in a cold sweat when the ship she was on hit some rocks. At that point, she knew there was no more chance of sleep.

Elenor's small frame nestled against her, and a tear rolled from the corner of one eye. *Is it normal to want to leave her and go so far away?* She wiped it away. *It's not my fault I've got to work. Is it wrong to want to enjoy what I do?* She rolled onto her side and put her arm around her.

"I only want what's best for you." Her whispered voice sounded feeble, and she rested her lips in Elenor's hair. *I only want to give you what you would have had from your dada.*

Elenor didn't stir as Nell held her tightly, listening to Maria moving about downstairs. How could she face her? The atmosphere the previous evening hadn't improved, and she was thankful Billy had stayed in and kept the conversation polite. He wouldn't be here today, though. *Can we be civil to each other?*

The sound of Vernon stomping down the stairs roused her from her thoughts. Billy would follow him shortly, and she may as well go downstairs, too. Kissing Elenor on the head, she rolled over and reached for her dress as she checked on Leah. She was still asleep too. *I'll leave them be. It will be a good excuse to come back up if I need to.*

Billy looked up as she joined them at the table. "Morning, Aunty Nell."

"Morning." She glanced towards the kitchen. "Where is she?" No sound left her lips as she spoke.

"Outside. She'll be back in a minute."

"What are you whispering for?" Vernon took a bite of his bread.

Billy kept his voice low. "Mam and Aunty Nell had an argument last night and Mam's still mad with her."

"Why? What have I missed?"

"You'd know if you didn't spend so long in the alehouse." Billy rolled his eyes at Nell. "I'll tell you on the way to work..."

The three of them jumped as the back door slammed and Maria joined them.

"You've decided to grace us with your presence, have you?"

"Why wouldn't I?"

"Where are the girls?"

"Still asleep. I'll go and get them when I've had breakfast."

"Well, don't dilly-dally when you do. I want some help

with the drapes this morning. The weather's good enough to get them down and beat them out. We won't have many more chances before winter sets in."

Nell sighed. *Something to look forward to.* "I'd better go and wake them then. I don't want to keep you waiting."

Alice was leaning over the cot when Nell returned to the bedroom.

"Is she awake?"

Alice straightened up. "She is. Shall I get her out?"

Nell wandered over to the bed and sat beside Elenor. "Yes, please."

"Will you still go to sea after everything Mam's said?"

Nell held her back straight. "You try and stop me. I'll be there on the landing stage at seven o'clock on the fourth of January."

"You must be very excited."

"I was until your mam found out. Now I'm sad that she doesn't understand."

Alice picked Leah up and stood her on the floor. "I don't think she ever will. She's never been interested herself."

"But you have."

Alice nodded. "I love to hear James' stories as much as you do. I hope you can show her that it's acceptable for women to travel."

"I'll try my best, although I don't know how I'll convince her if I only go once."

"I'm sure you'll find a way and I'll support you if I need to. Not that she ever takes any notice of me."

Nell cocked her head to one side. "You're growing up now. It's about time she started listening to you. If you have a little money of your own, it will help." Nell clung to

Elenor as she crawled onto her knee. "If we stick together, we'll change her mind. You see if we don't."

By the time the drapes had been beaten and rehung and the dinner dishes washed, Nell was exhausted.

"I'm going to Rebecca's." She looked down on Maria, who'd taken a seat by the fire. "Elenor's going to help Alice with some stitching. I'll take Leah with me to give you a break."

"How can a three-year-old help with sewing?"

"You can do a lot of things if you put your mind to it. I'll see you later."

Rebecca was reading a magazine when Nell walked in, but she immediately threw it to one side. "I had a feeling you'd be over. How was everything last night?"

Nell sat Leah on the floor alongside Florrie and took a seat. "Terrible. While I was here, she went round to Sarah's and came home with Tom. To think I was pleased the two of them were talking again, but she wanted him to side with her and forbid me from taking the job."

"And did he?"

Nell grimaced. "He tried his best, but I won't let him bully me. In the end, Billy came up with a compromise."

Rebecca's forehead creased. "How?"

"She promised to stop moaning at me if I agreed to only go on the first voyage." Nell couldn't read the expression in Rebecca's eyes.

"And did you agree?"

"What else could I do? She was furious, and Billy was trying his best. I didn't want to let him down."

A smile flicked across Rebecca's lips. "Does that mean you'll walk away at the end of the first month?"

"I've not decided yet. There's a part of me that thinks once I get on the ship, she won't be able to stop me."

Rebecca gasped. "You'll keep working even though you've promised not to?"

"Don't you think I should?" Nell watched the girls playing by her feet.

"I don't think I would. She'll be even madder with you if you do."

"Maybe, but it'll be February when I'm home from the first voyage. By then, she'll realise I didn't drown and that I can earn a decent wage. The way she keeps going on about money, you'd think she'd be glad of it. Besides, George will be back. She won't have time to sit around worrying about me."

"Are you sure? You know what she's like when she gets a bee in her bonnet."

"She won't be pleased, but what she doesn't know can't hurt her. I've got Jack's voice in my head telling me it's easier to ask for forgiveness than permission. I used to hate it when he did something he knew I wouldn't like, but I understand now, and I don't want to let him down. He'd want me to go."

"But he's not the one you've got to live with."

Nell sighed. "I know, which is why I'll let her think I'm only doing the one trip. I'll deal with the others when the time comes. Besides, I might not even like it."

"Do you really think that?"

Nell grinned. "No ... but you won't tell her, will you?"

"I promise I won't say a word. You will speak to James about it though, won't you?"

"Oh, don't worry, I'll be speaking to him. The only problem is Maria's already gunning for him. The poor lad will wish he'd never come home."

"At least he can go away again."

"Which is exactly what I hope to be able to do in a few months' time."

CHAPTER FORTY-TWO

N̲ell picked up the teapot and gave it a shake. Empty. She glanced at Maria as she stacked the dirty dinner plates. *There's no point making any more now.* She pushed herself out of her seat.

"I'll take Leah up for her afternoon sleep and then I'll come and dry those for you."

"As you like." Maria carried the dishes to the kitchen.

"I'll take her for you if you like." Alice stood up and lifted Leah from the rug by the fireplace. "It will be good practice for me..."

Nell put a finger to her lips. "Not a word."

"Sorry!" Alice put a hand across her mouth to hide a giggle. "Come along, Elenor. Are you going to help me?"

Nell smiled as Elenor skipped to the living room door and held it open as the three of them disappeared upstairs. *They'll be in safe hands.*

She carried the teapot to the kitchen but paused when there was a knock on the front door. "Who's that? Are you expecting anyone?"

Maria shook her head. "No."

"They've not let themselves in. I'd better go."

She marched down the hall and opened the door with a flourish but froze as her eyes flicked between the two women on the doorstep.

"Good afternoon, Nell. It is Nell, isn't it?" The shorter of the two women grinned at her from under the rim of a black hat. A long black shawl covered her mourning dress.

"Y-yes ... Jane?"

Sarah put a foot on the doorstep. "Don't look so surprised. You knew she was coming. Aren't you going to invite us in?"

"I-I didn't know you were coming today. Is Maria expecting you?" Nell froze at the sound of the living room door opening.

"I told you, I'm not expecting anyone..." Maria strode to the door. "Jane!" She stared at Sarah. "You could have warned me."

"I did." Sarah looked up and down the street. "It would be easier to talk inside."

"Hardly...!"

Nell stepped back from the door and pushed Maria to the wall. "Come in. Maria, you go and put the kettle on. I'll be back in a minute."

As soon as Sarah ushered Jane inside, Nell darted out of the front door and hurried across to Rebecca's. Her sister was going up the stairs carrying Florrie.

"You've got to come quickly. Jane's here."

"Jane! Where? Have you seen her?"

"Yes, she's in our living room with Maria and Sarah. I'll have to go back to keep the peace, but follow me over when you've put Florrie down. Alice will watch her for you."

Sarah and Jane had taken seats next to each other at the dining table when Nell arrived home, and she peered into the kitchen to check on Maria.

"Sorry about that." She fidgeted with her fingers as she hovered in the middle of the room. "I thought Rebecca should join us. She'll be here in a minute."

"You're all very convenient for each other." Jane rolled her shoulders. "I feel quite left out."

"Why wouldn't we be?" Nell bit her top lip. "Excuse me a moment. Let me help Maria and I'll be back."

Maria stood at the sink, her hands resting on the rim as her shoulders rose and fell.

"Are you all right?" Nell kept her voice low.

"Do I look it?" Maria was white and she gulped before taking another deep breath. "How dare she bring her around here without a word of warning?"

"Let me get this tea made and we can go through. It may have been for the best to have no warning. You'd have been fretting about it if you'd known to expect her." Nell started at the sound of another voice in the living room. Alice.

"Good afternoon, Aunty Sarah."

Maria had obviously heard her, too, and stormed from the kitchen, grabbing hold of her daughter's arm. "Take Elenor out, will you...?"

"Wait a moment." Nell hurried after Alice. "Will you go to Aunty Rebecca's? She'd like you to look after Florrie." She escorted Alice to the hall, but Alice stopped by the door.

"Is that Aunty Jane?"

"It is, and trust me, you're better off over the road. I wish I could come with you."

Alice grinned as she reached for Elenor's hand and stepped outside. "I'll see you later."

Nell was about to close the door when Rebecca appeared and headed towards her. *Thank goodness for that.*

"How are things?"

Nell grimaced. "Maria's making a pot of tea, so you haven't missed anything. Come in."

Jane looked up as they walked in. "Good afternoon, Rebecca."

Rebecca gave a weak smile. "Good afternoon. May I offer my condolences?"

"Yes, you may. Thank you. At least *you* haven't lost your manners."

"I'm sorry, I'd like to offer mine, too." Nell's cheeks coloured. "It was such a shock seeing you. Let me see what's keeping Maria and then we can all sit down."

Nell dashed back to the kitchen. "What are you doing? That tea will be stewed."

"Do you honestly expect me to sit down at the table with her after everything that's happened...?"

"Yes, I do, so pick up that plate of cakes and follow me. The sooner we get this over and done with the better."

"Do you have the children with you?" Rebecca asked as Nell rejoined them.

"Naturally. I could hardly leave them over there."

"No, of course. Does this mean you're back in Liverpool for good?"

"We are."

Nell interrupted as she placed the tray on the table and

held out a chair for Maria. "There we are. Please help yourselves to cake. We've a lot to catch up on. When did you arrive back?" Nell ignored the pout on Maria's face as she focussed on Jane.

"Yesterday evening. We took the morning steamship from Belfast."

"And are you staying with Tom and Sarah?"

"Only for a night or two, until Tom sorts me out somewhere more permanent."

"They're starting to build around the Dingle area. You could try down there." Maria didn't hide her sneer.

"I'm not going that far away. Why should the rest of you be so close and not me?"

Sarah patted her hand. "There's no reason. Tom will find you somewhere closer."

"There's every reason." Maria's gaze was cold. "We don't want you around here, coming back as if nothing happened."

"Nothing did happen." The paleness of Jane's face was highlighted by the black outfit and the grey hair that framed it. "I met Pat and we were married. There's no sin in that."

"That's a lie." Maria's teeth were clenched. "Mother would have turned in her grave if she'd known you were marrying a Catholic. Not to mention the fact you didn't tell anyone, and we only found out when we arrived at the church. The shock ended up killing my son."

"Nonsense." Jane allowed her shawl to fall back onto the chair. "From what I remember, he died of measles like a great many other children."

"Only because he was too weak to fight it. James and Billy weren't so ill."

Jane reached for a slice of fruit cake but paused to stare at Maria. "Are you going to hold that against me for the rest of my life? At the time of our marriage, I didn't even know you were in the family way. I'm sorry, but the Lord obviously saw fit to take him from you. I hardly think you can blame me for that."

Maria wiped her eyes with the backs of her hands. "Will you excuse me? I need a minute."

The room remained silent until the back door slammed, and Nell got to her feet.

"I'd better go to her."

"I wouldn't." Rebecca reached for her hand. "She probably wants to be alone."

"I didn't think you were in her good books at the moment anyway." Sarah took a sip of her tea.

"I'm not, but it doesn't mean I don't care about her."

"Why, what have you done?" Jane asked.

"You've not heard?" Nell raised an eyebrow as she retook her seat. "I've got a job as a stewardess on a transatlantic ship. I start in January."

"No! I can imagine she wouldn't like that." Jane gasped at Sarah. "You didn't tell me."

"Tom isn't best pleased either, so I didn't want to upset him."

Jane's face finally broke into a smile. "I'm not the only one in the bad books then. That's a relief. What about you, Rebecca, have you done anything to upset her?"

Rebecca chuckled. "No, I keep out of the way as much as possible. The fact I have a husband probably helps."

"And I presume he's from the right side of the tracks."

Jane shuddered. "To be honest, I don't think I understood the implications of marrying a Catholic at the time…"

"Maybe you should have spoken to me about it first then, instead of doing everything in secret." Maria's tone was harsh as she rejoined them.

"Why? So you could explain everything to me and wish me well. Don't talk nonsense. You'd have tried to talk me out of it, which was something I wasn't prepared to do."

"Of course I'd have talked you out of it. About the only good thing to come out of all this is the fact you didn't turn and you resisted the pressure to have the boys baptised as Catholics."

"Which was no mean feat, I can tell you. I've lost count of the number of times Pat's family tried to pressure me into converting. Having a child should always bring joy to families, but not ours. Oh, no. There were always arguments about how to bring them up, so don't try to tell me you're the only one who's suffered."

"The difference is you brought it on yourself. I was an unwitting bystander."

"Well, thank you for your support." Jane glared at Maria.

"Don't blame me."

"Maria, please." Rebecca stood up and offered her a chair. "Whether you like it or not, we'll be seeing a lot more of each other from now on, so can we put it behind us?"

Maria sniffed as she sat down. "How can I?"

"There needs to be forgiveness on both sides." Rebecca's eyes flicked between her sisters. "Can you do that?"

"I don't know." Maria didn't look up from the tablecloth, but Jane grinned.

"I'm sure we can. I think we should let bygones be bygones. We are sisters after all."

Nell cleared her throat as the silence grew. "Have you found a house yet?"

"Nothing permanent. Pat left me some money, so Tom's arranged a room at a boarding house on Windsor Street for now."

"Not one three two?" Nell's heart skipped a beat.

"No, ninety-six, why?"

"I just wondered." Nell sighed. "Jack lived at one three two when we were married, and then I moved in with him for a few weeks. It brings back memories..."

"Ah. No, we're further down this way. Hopefully, we won't be there for long."

Nell glanced at Maria. "Do you remember James suggested we invite the family round when Jane came back? It might be a nice idea to do that."

Jane put a hand to her chest. "Oh, you don't need to go to any trouble on my part."

"It's no trouble, is it? James will be home next week, and George won't be long after that."

"George..." Jane put a hand to her chest. "I hadn't realised he was due home. How is he?"

"We don't know how he is, but he won't be joining any family gathering with you." Maria's face was stern. "He's had an accident."

"Oh, yes. Sarah mentioned it. I'll have to pay him a visit once he's back."

"I'm sure there's no need." Maria spoke through gritted teeth.

"All right." Nell stood up to refill the teapot. "Why

don't we wait until James gets home and we can arrange something then? Don't forget, we've two nephews we've not met yet. You've got to want to see them."

"I've an even better idea." Jane's face lit up. "I want to speak to the vicar on Sunday about having them christened. We can have a gathering for them afterwards."

"What a splendid idea." Sarah stared at Maria. "Surely even you can't object to that."

Maria glared at her sister-in-law. "What she chooses to do is up to her, but don't expect me to be happy about it."

CHAPTER FORTY-THREE

Nell hung up her cloak and hurried to the kitchen to peer into the pan of carrots that had been left boiling when they went to church. *They should be done.* She lifted the lid on the potatoes in the adjacent pan. *They won't take much mashing.* She pulled it to the edge of the hotplate and stepped into the living room where Maria was laying out the cutlery.

"These vegetables are ready. Shall I mash them and put them in the range to keep warm?"

Maria checked the clock on the mantelpiece. "You can do. Billy should be here with the meat any minute. Alice, take the girls upstairs and wash their hands."

Nell's stomach rumbled. "I hope he's not long. I'm famished." She'd no sooner disappeared back into the kitchen when she heard the front door open. "Ah, here he is. Let me get that meat." She hurried to the hall but bumped into Tom in the doorway. "Oh, I wasn't expecting you."

Maria stopped what she was doing and put her hands on her hips. "What are you doing here at this time of day?"

"I'll go again if that's the way you're going to be. I was only delivering a message." He turned to leave, but Nell called him back.

"Don't be daft. The boys aren't home yet. What's the message?"

"At least someone appreciates me." Tom glared at Maria. "After the service this morning, Jane confirmed the date of the christenings with the vicar. Six weeks today."

A frown settled on Nell's face. "That's a long time off."

"Jane has to be living in the parish for at least a month ahead of the service, and that was the first available week after that."

"Ah yes, I'd forgotten about that. Will you have the gathering at your house afterwards?"

Tom winked at her. "She'll have her own place by then, so I'm hoping she'll host it."

"Where?" Maria's voice was gruff.

"Down the road from us. Number sixteen."

Maria sank onto one of the dining chairs. "She's done that on purpose."

"What are you talking about? I found it for her because she said she wanted to be close. There was no point her getting a house on the other side of Toxteth when all the family are here."

"You'll get used to it." Nell cupped a hand on her sister's shoulder, but her posture was stiff. "It will be handy being able to call in so easily."

"I don't think so." Maria stood up and walked to the front door. "What on earth's keeping Billy? He should be here by now."

Tom raised an eyebrow at Nell as he turned to follow

Maria down the hall. "I'll tell him to get a move on if I see him."

The potatoes and carrots were mashed and the tea brewing when Billy arrived home.

"Where've you been? You were only supposed to be picking the meat up." Maria took it from him.

"I saw Vernon going into the alehouse, so I followed him to tell him to get himself here."

"Where is he then? I thought he was with you all along." Maria walked to the kitchen.

"He won't be long." Billy took a seat by the fire. "He was finishing his drink."

"What was he even doing in there on a Sunday?" Nell kept her voice low, but Billy put a finger to his lips and shook his head.

"Nell, are you coming to make this gravy?" Maria bustled back into the living room. "We're not waiting for Vernon. He can eat his cold if he's not here by the time we're ready."

"Yes, give me a minute. You can all sit down."

Nell was about to join them at the table when the front door opened.

"Here he is now. I'll go and fetch his plate."

"Where've you been?" Maria's voice was harsh.

"I needed to see some of the lads, and you can't go into an alehouse without having a drink."

"I'm sure you could have spoken to them after church."

"It was after church..." Vernon grinned at Billy.

"Less of your lip. What are you doing this afternoon?"

"Sitting in front of the fire, as usual. What else is there to do?"

"Good." Maria picked up her knife and fork. "Perhaps we'll have a game of cards later."

The following morning, Billy and Maria were at the table when Nell arrived downstairs.

"No Vernon?" She frowned at Billy. "He's going to be running even later than usual."

"He's been and gone already."

Nell checked the clock. "What on earth did he have to be out so early for?"

"He's going to strike down his tools." The anger in Maria's voice caused Nell to recoil.

"No...!"

"It's not just him," Billy explained. "Uncle Tom and his mates have persuaded half the workforce to strike until they get better pay. They need them all on the gate to the shipyard to stop the rest of us going in."

Nell's smile disappeared as she stared at Billy. "What about you?"

"That's what I'm about to find out." He stood up from the table. "I don't think many of our lads will be out, but I can't be certain. It's not the sort of thing you talk about when the bosses are around."

"You'll go to work though, won't you?"

"If I can, but not on my own. I'll wait and see what everyone else is doing. See you later."

Nell's stomach churned as the front door slammed. "They won't get paid, will they?"

"Vernon won't." Maria drummed her fingers on the table. "Wait 'til I see him. He'd gone out before I came down this morning."

"Well, watch what you say. You don't want him leaving home again."

"He might as well go if he's not bringing any money home, especially given the situation with George. We can only pray they don't stop Billy working." Maria dropped her head into her hands. "We're not going to be able to manage at this rate. Alice will be the only one earning any money and we can't live on that."

"Stop worrying. Hopefully, it'll only be for the day and the bosses will give them what they ask for. They won't want them not working."

Maria patted Nell's hand. "You're right. Come on, get some breakfast inside you while I start the washing."

Nell was standing at the range, giving the pan of scouse a final stir, when the front door slammed.

"Who's that?" She popped her head into the living room where Maria was slicing some bread, and a second later, Billy joined them.

"What are you doing here?" Maria straightened up and watched him take a seat by the fire.

"I couldn't walk past the lads on the gate. They were begging us to stay away, saying the strike would only work if we were all behind it."

"But what about your wages? You won't get paid now."

"No." Billy put his hands behind his head as he leaned back in the seat.

"Were the bosses there to see what was going on?"

Billy shrugged. "I didn't see them, but that doesn't mean they weren't there."

"Was there any trouble?"

"Not that I saw. I didn't walk up to Vernon's place though, so I've no idea what was going on up there."

Maria took a seat. "This could ruin the port. What if ships can't get in? They'll be forced to go somewhere else."

"They may have to wait, but I don't think it will be any worse than that. I believe they'll all be back at work tomorrow."

"You're sure?" Maria put a hand to her chest. "That's a relief. We can't afford for you two to lose your wages with your dad out of work too."

Billy stood up. "Stop worrying. Now, is there any dinner going?"

"What will you do this afternoon?" Nell asked as they took their seats at the table.

Billy blew out his cheeks. "Go down to the alehouse, I suppose. At least they're talking to me, seeing I didn't go into work on strike day."

"If you see Uncle Tom, tell him I want a word." Maria put a plate in front of Billy. "He's no right to cause families to go without food because of his own selfish cause."

"He's not being selfish. He's doing it for everyone in the hope we get a pay rise and have to work less hours."

Maria snorted. "As if you're going to get that. You'll miss your wages long before those bosses miss you. And even if you don't miss them, every wife or mam will."

"I'm sure it won't come to that." He picked up his knife and fork, but paused as the front door opened.

"Who's there?" Maria stood up and peered into the hall as Vernon joined them.

"What are you doing here at this time of day?"

He took a seat. "Is there any of that scouse going? I'm starving."

"Why haven't you eaten?" Maria didn't move as she stared down at him. "What have you been up to?"

"I'm trying to get myself a pay rise; that's what I'm doing."

"You should be ashamed of yourself. You won't get paid if you don't turn up for work, and we need the money."

"I'm sure you won't complain when I get more money." He leaned back in his seat as Nell put a plate down in front of him. "As we speak, Uncle Tom's having a meeting with some of the bosses to see what's on offer."

"Well, you'd better hope they're feeling generous, because there'll be trouble if you don't make up for your losing a day's wages."

CHAPTER FORTY-FOUR

The following morning, Billy and Vernon had left for work when Nell arrived downstairs, but by six o'clock that evening, there was still no sign of them.

"Where on earth are they? This food will be cold." Maria left Alice to brew the tea and burst into the front room to peer through the window. Nell followed her and leaned against the door frame.

"Maybe they had to work overtime to make up for what they didn't do yesterday?"

Maria stepped back from the window. "They can't fit two days' work into one. It was pure folly yesterday; I don't know what Tom's up to. If he did a proper day's work himself instead of messing about like this…"

"All right, calm down. We might as well eat and leave their tea in the range. There's no point spoiling ours as well."

"You're right." Maria followed Nell back to the living room. "It's times like this, I wish George was here to give them a good talking-to. He wouldn't take any nonsense from them."

No, he wouldn't. "At least James will be here on Thursday. I'm sure he'll have a word with them."

"I'm hoping there's nothing left to discuss by then, other than making sure they don't do it again."

"It was only Vernon." Alice placed the teapot on the table. "You can't blame Billy. He didn't want to be involved."

"He still was though, wasn't he?" Maria stormed to the kitchen to serve the sausages and mashed potatoes. "I hope they've not got into trouble today."

Nell waited for the plates to be put on the table and was about to sit down when the front door opened. "They're here now."

Maria jumped to her feet. "Where on earth have you been?"

Billy glanced at his brother. "We had a meeting…"

"A meeting? What sort of meeting?" Maria stormed to the kitchen and returned with their plates, slamming them onto the table.

"About yesterday. We wanted to know how the discussions had gone."

"And?" Maria sat down and pulled her seat under the table. "Will you get your pay rise on Saturday?"

"Erm … no." Billy focussed on his food. "It's likely to take a little longer than that."

"You mean you both lost a day's wages for nothing?"

"There was a reason … but it might not be as straightforward as we thought."

"Well, I hope you don't go trying again. We can't afford

for the two of you to be losing your wages. I still want the same amount of housekeeping from you on Saturday. We're not doing without for something that's not our fault."

As Maria paused for breath, Vernon reached for another piece of bread.

"You're very quiet." She glowered at him. "What have you got to say for yourself?"

"Nothing. You heard Billy."

"A guilty conscience more like. Let that be a lesson to you. It's the bosses around here who call the tune, and you need to fall into line and keep your head down. Do you hear me?"

Vernon pushed himself from the table. "I'm going to the alehouse. I expect I'll be late back. Don't wait up."

Vernon hadn't reached the door when Billy jumped up. "Wait for me." With a quick glance at Nell, he reached for his jacket. "See you in the morning."

"What was all that about?" Maria returned to her half-finished tea. "They were in a hurry to leave."

Nell's stomach churned. "Maybe they've a lot to talk about."

"I'm sure there's plenty of time for that." She picked up her knife and fork again. "No, you mark my words, they're up to something. It better not be striking down their tools again."

As ten o'clock on Thursday morning arrived, Nell placed her cup and saucer onto the occasional table and groaned as she settled into a seat by the fire. At least the floor was clean, and Alice and the girls were out of the way for half an hour. James could come home now. She checked the clock. *Anytime now.*

"What are you grinning at?" Maria took the chair opposite.

"James should be here any minute. It will be nice to see him."

"He can wait another ten minutes until this floor's dry."

Nell shook her head. "Can't you put a smile on your face? You should be glad to see him."

"Glad? He'll be getting a piece of my mind when he comes in for encouraging you to take that job."

"Oh, and that's really going to help. You've already got two sons not talking to you; why not go for the full set?"

"There's no need to be like that."

"And there's no need for you to be so angry with him. He's not forcing me to go. It was my choice."

"He gave you the idea..."

Maria stopped as the front door opened and James walked into the living room.

"Watch where you're walking." Maria held up a hand. "We've washed this floor and I don't want it dirty again."

James stopped and stared at his mam. "Shall I go out and come back in again?"

"No, of course not." Nell glared at Maria and jumped to her feet. "Come and sit down. I'll get you a cup of tea and a couple of drop scones."

Maria flinched as James strode across the room and sat in the empty chair.

"What's the matter with you then?" He gave his mam a smile, but it faded as she glared back at him.

"Where do you want me to start?"

Nell joined them and handed James his tea. "She's not happy about me being a stewardess."

"Ah!"

"I'll give you 'Ah.'" Maria's face darkened. "What on earth were you thinking, encouraging her to go to sea?"

James sat back. "Mam, I've only this second come home after four weeks on a ship and I don't want an argument. I didn't even know Aunty Nell had told you."

"Whether she told me or not doesn't matter. How could you even suggest she goes to sea when you're well aware of how much I worry about each one of you? It will be ten times worse with her."

"Passenger liners are perfectly safe. Have you seen the ones we're talking about? They're not cargo ships. They're enormous and well made, not to mention luxurious. How many times have I been away now...?"

"It's not only that. How will she manage amongst all those men?"

James shook his head. "She won't be on her own. The captain will look after her, as well as the ship's doctor and matron."

"They won't be with her the whole time. Who knows what could happen...?"

"I do." James gasped. "When did you last go on a passenger liner? You've no idea what it's like. For the most part, the passengers are segregated, so she's unlikely to have to deal with any of the men."

"There'll still be the stewards..."

"Mam, listen to me. She'll be perfectly safe, and she

needs the money. We all need the money after Dad's accident. Have you heard from him?"

"Don't change the subject…"

James stood up and put his cup on the table. "I'll get out of it easier than you think. I'm nipping into the yard, and if you haven't got a civil word to say when I get back, you'll be looking for another lodger to pay the bills. There are plenty of boarding houses around here." He pulled open the back door, slamming it closed after him.

"I hope you're pleased with yourself." Nell collected up the cups and saucers. "If you want my opinion, you'll get out there and apologise. With Billy and Vernon earning less this week, the last thing you need is for James to disappear and take his money with him."

"But it had to be said…"

"No it didn't, and not like that. James might have told me the shipping companies were taking on stewardesses, but I was the one who said I'd be interested. Giving me the help I asked for is no reason to drive him from his home." Nell glared down at Maria. "Now go out there and apologise."

Maria's eyes welled up as she turned towards the door.

"And put a smile on your face."

As soon as Maria was outside, Nell flopped onto the chair and took a deep breath. *Good grief. I'll be looking for a boarding house myself at this rate. There are still weeks to go before I can get away.*

She stood up to finish clearing the table but was disturbed by the back door opening.

"I'm sorry about that, Aunty Nell." James took the seat she'd just vacated.

"You've no need to apologise. Where's your mam?"

"She'll be back soon enough. Are you all right?"

Nell shrugged. "I've been better."

"What made you tell her? I thought we were going to talk to her together."

Nell sighed. "She was in a particularly good mood because she heard your dad was on the ship and expected home by the end of the year. It seemed like a good idea at the time."

James shook his head. "I'm guessing it didn't last long. When was this?"

"A couple of weeks ago."

"Good grief. And she's still this angry?"

Nell sat down again. "I'm sorry, but I think she's been saving it up for you. She brought your Uncle Tom into it and everything, and the only way I could pacify her was by agreeing to resign after the first voyage."

"You've agreed to that?" James puffed out his cheeks.

"Only on condition that she stopped having a go at me."

"Which she clearly hasn't done. There's no reason for you to resign ... unless you want to, of course."

"Not at the moment, but I won't know until I get on the ship. The way I feel at the moment, I'd happily go for the year."

"Well then, you should. She's hardly kept her side of the bargain." James rested his head on the back of the chair and gave her a weak smile. "Have I missed anything else?"

"Have you ever..." Nell stopped as the back door opened and Maria rejoined them. Without a word, she picked up the teapot and carried it to the kitchen.

Nell raised an eyebrow to James. "How was your trip?"

"Very good, thank you. They let a few of us get off the ship in New York, but it wasn't as good as last time. We only managed a walk around the docks and there's not much to see, other than the building work."

"It's still exciting, though." Nell was about to clap her hands but stopped when Alice and the girls arrived.

"You're home." Alice wrapped her arms around her brother's neck. "We've missed you."

"And I've missed you ... although nobody's filled me in on exactly what I have missed. Aunty Nell, were you about to tell me something?"

Maria walked back in with a pot of tea. "The only bit of good news we've had is that your dad should be home next month."

"Oh good." James couldn't conceal his sarcasm.

"Stop that. You should be grateful given the state of his leg." Maria stared down at him. "I've not got time to sit here doing nothing. I'm going to dust the bedrooms."

Alice pulled up a chair beside James' but waited for Maria to disappear. "How long are you here for?"

"Five days." He shuddered. "I was pleased about it, but now I'm not so sure. Have you been looking after Aunty Nell?"

Alice nodded. "Mam hasn't been very kind to her."

"So I hear. What do you think of her going to sea?"

Alice paused as Nell stood up to shut the living room door. "I wish I could go with her."

James threw his head back as he laughed. "Good for you."

"Aunty Nell said she'd pay me to look after the girls so I can save up and go on a ship myself one day."

James winked at Nell. "Did she now? That sounds exciting. You'd think Mam would be glad of the extra money."

"Especially with Billy and Vernon losing some of their wages." Alice looked close to tears. "Mam's not happy with them either."

"What?" James sat forward in his chair. "Why've they lost some money?"

Nell took a deep breath. "Half the men on the docks struck down their tools on Monday, including Vernon. Billy tried to go into work, but there were men on the gate who wouldn't let him in, and so neither of them will be paid for the day."

"And we've not seen much of them since," Alice added.

"I don't like the sound of that. Do you know any more?"

Nell shook her head. "They're being rather evasive."

James looked at the clock. "The alehouse should be open. Let me go and find out what's been going on. I'll report back over dinner." He strode to the door but stopped. "And not a word to Mam."

CHAPTER FORTY-FIVE

Nell stood in the front window waiting for James to return. As soon as she saw him, she went to open the door.

"Have you any news for us?"

He put a finger to his lips and shook his head. "Not now." He hadn't reached the living room door when Maria opened it.

"I thought I heard you. Come and sit down, the dinner's ready."

"That's good service. Something smells nice."

Nell hurried to the kitchen and came back with a steaming hot plate. "It's only liver and mash." She put the plate down in front of him. "Do you eat well on the ship?"

"Yes, we have decent cooks. Not that we ever get this."

"Well, you enjoy it." Nell stepped away from the table as Alice ushered the girls to their chairs.

They ate in silence until Maria stood up to collect the dishes. Nell waited until she disappeared into the kitchen.

"What are you doing this afternoon?"

"I thought we could take a walk, if you've no other arrangements."

"Would you take the girls with you?" Alice asked. "I have to get this waistcoat finished by tomorrow."

James smiled at her. "You won't need to make many more. I bet you won't miss it."

"No, I won't." Alice glanced over her shoulder. "Mam might miss the company, though. I don't plan on staying in every afternoon."

"Good for you."

The wind was cold as they stepped into the street and Nell hurried to sit the girls in the pram so she could pull her cloak tightly round her.

"It's amazing the difference a month makes." James adjusted his hat. "There was still sunshine last time I was here."

"We've not seen that for a while. I'm afraid winter's on its way. Where shall we walk?"

James glanced up and down the street. "Why don't we go to the park? It will be too windy down by the river."

"Lead the way." Nell turned the pram and they set off towards the end of the road. "How did you get on at the alehouse? Did you learn anything of interest?"

"I did." James grimaced. "I managed to speak to Vernon about what's been happening."

"Vernon? Why wasn't he at work?"

"That's the thing. He's not been in all week." James guided Nell across the junction at the end of the street and carried on walking straight ahead.

"They're not still striking down their tools, are they? Your mam will be livid."

"I wish that's all it was." James stared down the street. "He's lost his job."

She stopped and put a hand to her mouth. "No! Why?"

"Because of the strike action. Apparently, when those who laid down their tools arrived for work on Tuesday, the company bosses were waiting for them. They had the names of everyone who walked out and told them they'd replaced them with men who won't cause trouble."

"What about Billy?"

James carried on walking. "Thankfully, he's all right. They knew he'd been stopped from going into work by those on the gates."

"Thank goodness for that, although it won't be easy living on the money you and Billy bring home."

James patted her hand. "There's one consolation. At least Mam should be glad that you'll be earning something."

"I've tried telling her that, but she's not bothered."

"She might be now, though."

Nell's stomach churned. "Is there nothing Vernon can do ... or Uncle Tom? He was one of those who told them to walk out, so he should help them get something else."

"I take it you haven't heard that he's out of work now. Companies won't take on troublemakers, and there are none more troublesome than Uncle Tom as far as the dock authorities are concerned."

Nell shook her head. "No, we didn't know. Sarah will be beside herself with worry."

"If he's even told her yet. It's no accident you haven't seen much of Vernon. I think he's in hiding. What he'll do on Saturday when he can't pay Mam his keep is anyone's guess."

"Thank goodness you're here to keep the peace."

"I'm relieved I'm leaving again on Tuesday. I bet you wish you could come with me."

Nell fixed her eyes on the park gates ahead. "More than you know ... and not only because of Vernon. I haven't had chance to tell you yet that your Aunty Jane's moved back to Toxteth."

"Good grief. Is there no end to it? When did that happen?"

"A couple of weeks ago. You know Mr Read died? Well, his family wouldn't support her in Ireland, so she came back here."

"Where's she living?"

"In a boarding house at the moment, but she's moving in with another widow at the bottom of Elaine Street in the next week or so. That didn't go down well with your mam given she often walks that way."

"Handy for Aunty Sarah, though."

"I'll say. We got the shock of our lives a couple of weeks ago, though. They both came to visit. Unannounced. Aunty Jane basically put your mam right about Fred's passing and said it was God's will."

"Blimey. I'm glad I wasn't here."

"You may not be so fortunate soon. The boys are being christened on the second Sunday in November, and I get the impression she wants the whole family there."

James blew out his cheeks. "I should have asked to do an extra trip over Christmas."

The wind rustled in the trees as they entered the park,

causing the leaves to rain down on them. Nell pulled her cloak more tightly around herself as she gazed up at the clouds.

"I hope it stays dry until we get home."

James followed her gaze. "It should, although we won't want to sit by the lake today. Perhaps a quick walk round and then home."

"And to see the ducks." Elenor bounced on the pram as she looked around. "My get down?"

Nell lifted her from the pram. "All right then, but don't go running off." She sighed. "I do hate this weather, especially when your mam's in the mood she is."

"Don't worry, you've only a couple more months."

They followed Elenor to the water's edge, where they stopped to gaze out across the lake.

"Leah, look, the ducks." Elenor pointed out across the water as Nell positioned the pram so her younger daughter could see.

"At least they look happy." Nell grinned. "They can fly away, too, if they want to."

James chuckled. "Now there's a thought. Could you imagine...?"

A voice from behind interrupted him. "You look very happy."

Nell turned to see Jane and Sarah behind them. "Oh. G-good afternoon. I didn't expect to see you. I mean, there's no reason you shouldn't be here, but ... the weather..."

Jane rolled her eyes. "When you've lived in Ireland, you learn to live with far worse than this." She gave James a coy smile. "Aren't you going to introduce us?"

"Oh, yes. Jane, this is James, Maria's eldest. James, this

is Aunty Jane. And these are my daughters, Elenor and Leah."

Jane gazed at them. "Still only babies. How sweet."

James raised his hat. "I've heard a lot about you."

"And I of you, although nobody told me how like your dad you are. I always did like that distinctive ginger hair."

James' cheeks coloured as he replaced his hat. "Well…"

Sarah nudged her sister-in-law. "Leave him alone. Look, he's blushing."

"There's nothing wrong with that." Jane chuckled. "Do you know, it's nice to be myself again."

"I'm sorry." James regained his composure. "May I offer my condolences? It must be difficult for you."

"That's what family are for, but we'll be fine once we move to our new house."

Nell's stomach fluttered. "I'm sure that will make a difference. How have you found being back in Liverpool?"

"It's like I've never been away, except for all the building work. Neighbours I knew years ago are still here, and it's lovely to meet up with them all." She took a step closer to Nell. "I believe you didn't like being in mourning either. I'll give these clothes another month and then they're going. It's times like this you need to see people, rather than locking yourself away."

"I agree." Nell gave a deep sigh. "I feel so much better since I stopped wearing them. I imagine that's even more true when you move such a long way from home."

"Oh, Ireland was never my home. It was a place we settled for a while. That's why I had to get away. Pat's brothers and sisters never understood me." Jane looked up to James. "Will you be able to join us for the boys' christening? It's five weeks on Sunday."

"That's kind of you to ask, but I'm not certain. This is my last trip of the year, so I should be back, God willing."

"Will George be back by then?" Jane's eyes twinkled. "I'm so looking forward to seeing him again."

"He may be back, but he probably won't be going far, with his leg as it is."

Jane's smile didn't fade. "I'm sure he'll be as sweet as ever."

"Sweet?" James' mouth dropped open.

Jane giggled. "He always was a ladies' man. Or at least he was with me."

James' cheeks were scarlet. "Well, right ... it's been lovely to meet you, but we really must be going." He raised his hat. "Good day."

Nell raced to collect the pram and called to Elenor as James walked away.

"That was rather abrupt."

"I'm sorry, but I really didn't want a conversation about Dad. Especially not when she called him *sweet*. Can you imagine?"

Nell chuckled. "She was rather keen to ask after him. I don't remember them being particularly friendly when she left, though."

"Perish the thought she has a soft spot for him." He shook his head. "The last thing we need is for Mam to be upset because of that."

CHAPTER FORTY-SIX

The sound of the front door closing caused Nell to look up from her knitting, and she smiled at James as he strolled to the fire to smooth out his windswept hair.

"Where's Mam?"

Alice put down the waistcoat she was working on and reached for her cloak. "She took the girls outside to give them some fresh air. I'd better go and take over from her."

James took a seat. "What sort of mood's she in?"

Nell groaned. "What do you think? She's already mad with Vernon."

"This could get ugly." James grimaced. "I've left him and Billy in the alehouse, but they've been in there all afternoon. I don't think either of them will be in any fit state to deal with her having a go at them."

"They've not really got a choice, have they? Vernon especially."

"No..." James stopped as Maria joined them.

"Afternoon." She hovered over him. "Did you find out where your dad's ship's up to?"

"I did. The schedule says they're in Cape Town, so they should be back in about four weeks."

"What a relief." Maria put a hand to her chest. "It's going to be strange having him at home all the time, but he'll settle in soon enough."

"It will be a challenge for all of us." Nell put down her knitting and wandered to the kitchen. "I'll make a pot of tea. I imagine the other two will be home shortly."

James leaned forward in his chair and rubbed his hands in front of the fire. "That tea smells good."

"Have you seen Billy and Vernon?" Maria took the seat opposite him. "They'd better not have been in that alehouse spending my money."

"They may have had one... Actually, I need to pop outside."

A gale rushed through the house as James went out the back door at the same time as the front door opened.

"Oh goodness, shut those doors." Maria jumped up as the living room door blew open, but she hadn't reached it when a hand pulled it closed. "I didn't mean this door." She yanked on the handle to reveal her sons sniggering at the foot of the stairs.

"I'm glad you find it all so funny. Get in here. You'd better have some money for me."

"I have." Billy put a hand in his pocket and pulled out two shilling coins.

"Where's the rest?"

Billy smirked at Vernon. "I haven't got it. You knew that."

"I told you I still expected the housekeeping."

Billy put an arm around Maria's shoulders. "It wasn't my fault I couldn't work. I tried to go in."

"He did." Vernon hiccoughed. "It's not his fault."

"So where's your money?"

"Mine?" Vernon grabbed a chair as he staggered backwards. "I don't have any."

"None!" Maria's shriek caused Nell to recoil.

"They won't pay me."

"Who won't?"

"Work."

Maria rounded on James as he rejoined them. "What's he talking about?"

"No, no, no." Vernon wagged his fingers at James. "Quiet."

James put an arm around Vernon's shoulders and guided him to a seat at the table. "She needs to know."

"Nooo. Not yet. Is tea ready?"

"No, it's not. Where's my money?" Maria stood above him, her hands on her hips, but James ushered her back to the fire.

"Why don't you leave him for now? He's had a difficult week."

"*He's* had a difficult week. He's no idea..."

Nell grimaced as Vernon slumped over the table. "Is he asleep?"

Billy chuckled as he shook his shoulder. "Vernon, wake up."

"Leave him." James scowled at Billy. "The thing is, Mam, all those who struck down their tools haven't been allowed back into work this week."

"You mean he's lost his job?" Maria stared first at

Vernon and then Nell. "Did you know about this?"

"N-no. How could I?"

"From James, that's how. You've been as thick as thieves again this week."

"But he didn't say a word..."

"Mam, I only heard earlier today when I was in the alehouse. Leave Aunty Nell out of this."

Maria turned back to Vernon. "I'll kill him. I told him not to get involved. And your Uncle Tom." She paused. "What's happened to him?"

James raised an eyebrow. "He's not working at the moment either. Nor Sam."

"No!" Maria put her hands to her mouth. "What absolute fools. If it hadn't been for Tom, none of this would have happened."

"I suspect he knows that."

Maria shook her head. "What are we going to do? We can't live on two shillings a week."

"We don't have to. You've got the money I gave you, and Alice looks as if she's nearly finished another waistcoat. Dad should bring a bit home, too, when he arrives."

"That won't last long." Maria wandered to the table and shook Vernon's shoulder, but James stopped her.

"Mam, don't be angry. He was only doing what he thought was right. He didn't know this would happen..."

"But look at him. How much money has he wasted in the alehouse? He should have brought that home instead of drinking it."

"He was too scared to tell you. He knew you'd be angry."

"He should have thought of that..."

Nell looked up as the back door opened and Alice brought in the girls.

"What's the matter?" She stared across the room. "Is Vernon asleep?"

"He's lost his job and decided to drown his sorrows with ale rather than come home and tell us."

"Oh." Alice sat at the table opposite Billy. "It's a good job Aunty Nell has a job then."

Billy's snigger caused Maria to glare at him. "Do you think it's funny that Aunty Nell's been forced to be the breadwinner? You should both be ashamed of yourselves."

"I'll get my usual money next week."

"Well, you can give me extra to make up for the money missing this week. Wait until your dad hears about this. He'll knock the smiles off your faces."

"No, Mam, don't tell him." Billy's eyes widened. "There are loads of jobs on the docks. Vernon's bound to get something before Dad gets back. Please, don't say anything."

Maria stared at him. "We'll see how things are, but I don't want to hear of either of you doing anything like this again. Do you hear me?"

"Yes, Mam. We're sorry."

"We need to get this sorted out while I'm still here." James paced to the door and grabbed his hat. "I'll speak to Uncle Tom and find out what help these workers are going to get. They shouldn't be the ones who are punished, when they were talked into striking without any regard for the consequences."

"I'll come with you." Maria reached for her coat.

"No, you stay here. He's more likely to have a sensible conversation with me."

· · ·

It was over an hour later when James returned, his shoulders rounded.

"You don't look happy." Nell put down her knitting and offered him her chair.

"No." He glared at Billy. "What have you done with Vernon?"

"We managed to get him upstairs. He's sleeping off the ale."

"The fool boy that he is."

"All right, Mam. There's no need for that. I need to speak to him, but at the moment, things don't look promising. Uncle Tom's doing the best he can with the bosses, but they're adamant they won't hire any troublemakers."

"What's he going to do?"

James shrugged. "He doesn't know at the moment. He's in a bit of a fix himself, especially with Sam not working as well."

Nell gasped. "I've another thought. Who'll help Jane with her rent once Mr Read's money has gone? It won't last long, and they can't all live on the money Ada makes with her sewing."

"It looks like Cousin Mabel will have to finish school and find herself a job." James looked at Maria as she sighed.

"Is this going to be the new way of the world? Women needing to go out to work every time the men in their lives make a mess of things?"

Nell raised an eyebrow. "Perhaps I won't be so unusual after all."

CHAPTER FORTY-SEVEN

I t was still dark outside as Nell swung her legs over the edge of the bed. Elenor stirred as she moved, and rubbed her eyes.

"Is it morning?"

"Yes, it is. Shall we go down for breakfast?"

"Will Vernon be there?"

Nell put an arm around her daughter. "I think he was going out with Billy this morning. Shall we go and see?"

Nell fastened her robe over her nightdress and hurriedly dressed both daughters. "Come along."

Maria and Alice were at the table when they arrived.

"Have Billy and Vernon gone?"

"I sent them out early in the hope Vernon can find some casual work." Maria pulled out a chair for Elenor.

"At least that's something." Nell groaned as she sat down.

"What's up with you?"

"I can't believe it's been over three weeks since Vernon lost his job and he's not even been able to get day work since. If so many men struck down their tools, how are they managing without them all?"

"I don't think there were as many walked out as we've been led to believe." Maria pushed a cup of tea to Nell as her brow furrowed.

"Why do you say that?"

"Something Billy said last night. He said all the affected men were meeting in the alehouse on Windsor Street, but the place isn't big. There can't be that many of them if they all fit."

"Do you think they could keep punishing them for months?" Nell's forehead creased. "I wish James were here to find out more. I do miss him when he's not here."

"Perhaps you'll realise how I'll feel when you go on your trip then."

"Don't be like that. The way things are at the moment, you'll be glad of the money and don't pretend otherwise."

"I hope Vernon can get a job soon."

"Don't build up your hopes." Nell puffed out her cheeks. "I'm sure we'll all be thrilled if he does, but he may not, and he'll have George to deal with soon."

"I know." Maria sighed. "I should be looking forward to him coming home, but the way things are, I'm really not sure."

The telegram had arrived yesterday afternoon, and it sat in pride of place on the mantelpiece telling anyone who cared to read it that the company had arranged for a carriage to bring George home.

Maria picked it up and flicked the duster over it. "It was nice of them to write. It saved me worrying." Maria gave the tiles of the fireplace another polish.

"You've not got long to wait now." Nell checked the room. "Everything looks tidy, so I'll take the girls over to Rebecca's to give him chance to settle in."

"Yes, I think we're done. Alice will help me with George."

"Right, good." Nell bent down to pick up Leah. "I'll see you later. Come along, Elenor."

Rebecca was in the kitchen when Nell arrived, and with a final stir of the pan, she joined them in the living room.

"Is Maria all ready?"

"As ready as she'll ever be. I'm glad to be out of the way." Nell sat Leah on the floor with Florrie while Elenor took charge of the marbles Florrie had been playing with.

"Is Vernon at home?"

Nell shook her head. "No. He went out this morning to try and get some day work, and we've not seen him since. Hopefully, it's because he got something."

"Even if he didn't, I doubt he'll be home in a hurry. Do you know what time George is arriving?"

"No, it could be anytime."

Rebecca grinned. "Shall we sit in the front room and look out for him then? I've arranged the chairs for us."

"That sounds like a good idea." Nell chuckled. "Come along, Elenor. Will you help Leah and Florrie into the other room for me?"

Nell had already taken a seat by the window when Rebecca carried a pot of tea into the room. "I imagine George will have quite a limp."

"If he can walk at all." Nell shuffled in her chair.

"It should be mended though, shouldn't it? He broke it months ago."

"He did. That's why I want to be nosy and see how he is and whether there really is a reason for him not to go back to work."

"We'll find out soon enough."

Nell had finished two cups of tea and they were contemplating having something to eat when a carriage pulled up outside the house.

"Here he is."

Rebecca stood behind Nell's chair and the two of them peered through the window.

"The driver's taking a long time. What's he doing?" Nell sat forward. "He's giving him a lot of help. Can you see through the carriage windows?"

"Not really, but it doesn't look like George can stand up. Do you think he really could be an invalid?"

A cold shiver ran down Nell's spine. "I hope not. A proud man like him would find it intolerable to be dependent on Maria for the rest of his life."

"I'll come over with you after dinner to visit him."

"I'd like that. I'd rather not go back on my own. I've no idea what to expect."

Maria was at the table with Alice when they arrived, her eyes red.

"What's the matter?" Nell peered into the kitchen. "Where's George?"

"He's in the front room but he wants to be alone." Maria buried a sob in her handkerchief. "He might lose his leg."

Nell's mouth opened and closed as she stared at Rebecca. "Lose it?"

Maria nodded. "The fall shattered the bones beneath his knee and they're not healing as well as they thought they would. The ship's doctor thought they may need to amputate but didn't want to do it on the ship. We've a doctor calling tomorrow, but George is in so much pain, the doctor on the ship couldn't say if he'll ever walk again."

Nell took the seat next to her sister's and wrapped an arm around her shoulders. "Oh my, come here."

Rebecca hovered by the table before taking a seat. "How is he in himself?"

"Devastated. That's why he wants to be alone. He can't bear the thought of anyone seeing him as he is."

Alice reached out and patted her mam's hand. "He'll have to rely on us for everything."

Maria continued to sob. "I can already tell how frustrated he is, and he's only been home an hour."

"Can we see him?" Rebecca's brow creased, but Maria shook her head.

"He brought some laudanum home with him and took a large dose once we'd got him settled. He should sleep for most of the afternoon."

"Let me put the kettle on for you then." Rebecca went to the kitchen. "If you need any help, you must tell me."

The light outside was fading as Nell showed Rebecca out.

"I'll call and see you tomorrow to let you know how

things are." She was about to return to the living room when she heard her name being called. *George?* She knocked on the door to the front room and went in. "Did you call?"

He gave her a weak smile. "I did. Any chance of a cup of tea?"

"Yes, of course. How are you feeling?"

He shifted in his seat. "The pain's better for not being tossed about by the sea, but many's the time I wish they'd taken the leg off rather than leaving me like this."

"Don't you think it's healing?"

"I don't know what to think. I'll see what this doctor says tomorrow."

Nell sighed. "At least you can get comfortable in here."

George rested his head on the back of the settee and closed his eyes. "It's about all I can do." His fingers twitched as his hands rested on his legs.

"Let me get that tea."

She hadn't reached the door when he called her back.

"I hear you're going to sea." His eyes were still closed, and Nell hesitated as she took a seat beside him.

"Yes, in January. On the Liverpool to New York route, like James."

He lifted his head and studied her. "You be careful."

"I will."

"Those oceans change as quick as you like. One moment they're as calm as a millpond, and the next minute, the waves appear from nowhere."

"Is that what happened to you?"

His face paled. "A wave came right over the ship. It was so high it arched over the top of the mast, and then it crashed down on us..." Perspiration broke out over his forehead and cheeks.

"Try not to think about it. I'm sure that will be for the best."

It was as if he hadn't heard her. "Ten of us there were on the deck when it hit, but only eight once the water receded."

Nell gasped. "You lost two men overboard?"

"Two men lost, another five injured." His body trembled violently and he jolted forward and buried his face in his hands. "It was a miracle I held on."

"There, there." Nell crouched down by the side of the settee. "You're safe now. Nothing's going to happen to you here."

"But you ... and James. He should never have gone to sea..."

A shiver ran through Nell's body. "We'll be fine. We're on big steamships, not the sort of sailing ship you've been on. Please don't worry."

"We'll all be worrying." Maria bustled into the room, a glass of amber liquid in her hand, which she handed to George. "Here, drink this." She looked down at Nell. "Brandy. The doctor said to give him a measure whenever he gets the shakes. The problem is, this isn't the first he's had. It will end up costing me a fortune."

George emptied the glass with one gulp. "You'd better make sure we have another bottle. It may not be mending the leg, but between that and the laudanum, at least it dulls the pain and stops me remembering." He closed his eyes once more and Nell led Maria back into the living room.

"I'll make that pot of tea."

"I'll take it in to him." Maria followed her into the kitchen. "It was all that talk of going to sea that set off the tremors again."

"It wasn't me who brought it up, it was him."

"Only because he's worried about you. It won't help his recovery knowing you're going away, too."

"It will be different..." Nell played with the spoon in the tea caddy.

"Not different enough. Imagine those two little girls growing up without a mam or dad. They don't have an older sister to take care of them like you did."

"But they have you and Rebecca ... and Alice. You won't abandon them."

"You can't assume everything will be the same here. We'll have to make changes now George is like this."

"But you wouldn't kick them out?" Nell's head spun round to face her sister, but Maria walked back to the living room.

"Maybe not, but that doesn't make it right."

Nell took a deep breath. "Did George get any compensation?"

"A little, but it won't last long. It certainly won't be enough if he can't work again."

"All the more reason for me to go to sea then." Nell followed her to the living room. "I'll get nearly three pounds for each voyage, and I've promised to pay Alice to look after the girls. She'll be able to give you more money than she does currently, and I'll pay you on top of that. You've got to see it makes sense."

"You could earn money without going to sea."

Nell shook her head. "We've already been through this.

I wouldn't earn half that much if I stayed here, and with Vernon being out of work, we need as much as we can get. Does George know he's lost his job?"

"No, he doesn't." Maria glared at her. "And I'd like to keep it that way."

"I won't say a word, but he's bound to ask the boys how they're getting on."

Maria picked up the bottle of laudanum that stood on the dresser. "He's due another dose of this. That should make him sleep until the boys go out again tonight."

Nell eyed her sister. "You can't do that..."

"I can and I will, if it means he has one less thing to worry about. Now, do you want to make the tea and I'll take it through to him?"

CHAPTER FORTY-EIGHT

At the sound of a knock at the front door, Maria hurried into the hall.

"This will be the doctor."

Nell carried the last of the empty dinner plates through to the kitchen. "I'll get these washed and then go over to Rebecca's to get out of the way."

"I'll take the girls outside." Alice reached for her cloak. "I don't want to hear Dad screaming again if the doctor starts prodding his leg."

Nell grimaced. "Very sensible."

Maria and the doctor were in the front room with George when Nell crept down the hall and out into the street. The girls were playing ball and she waved as she passed, smiling as Elenor caught the ball Alice threw to her.

"There's a clever girl." The smile was still on her face when she let herself into Rebecca's.

"You look happy." Rebecca's fingers didn't stop as she looked up from her knitting.

"I'm not really." She sat down with a sigh. "George isn't himself."

"We knew he wouldn't be."

"I know, but it's more than the pain. He seems changed."

"In what way?"

Nell shrugged. "I can't put my finger on it. Maria's going through a lot of brandy though, to keep him quiet."

"That would explain it. He didn't use to touch the stuff."

"You could be right. He may have done me a favour, though."

"Really? How?" Rebecca raised an eyebrow.

"At first he sounded worried about me going to sea, but then he told me to be careful, as if he'd accepted I'd be going."

"Why don't you look pleased then?"

Nell held her sister's gaze. "I don't know."

Rebecca studied her. "You're not changing your mind, are you? Seeing George as he is may have given you second thoughts."

Nell bit down on her lip, tears stinging her eyes as she stared at Rebecca. "If anything happens to me, you will take care of the girls, won't you ... between you and Maria? You won't let them go to the workhouse?"

Rebecca scowled. "What sort of sisters do you think we are? Of course we won't. Is that what's bothering you?"

"Maria asked me if I'd thought of them. Obviously, I have, but only in so far as I'd be missing for a few weeks at a time, like James. The idea that the ship may not come back hadn't occurred to me."

"But seeing George made it real?"

"I suppose it did." Nell chewed on a knuckle. "I will be all right, won't I?"

Rebecca hesitated. "Yes … I'm sure you will. I've not read of any serious shipping accidents involving passenger liners, and there must be hundreds of sailings a year."

Nell's stomach churned. "No accidents on the transatlantic routes, anyway. What about further away though, around India or China, or even Australia? Do you think we'd find out if there were any shipwrecks there?"

"I wouldn't know. We should take more notice of the newspaper."

Nell groaned. "I can't wait for James to get home. He'll be able to tell us."

"You've not long to wait. Have you confirmed he'll be back tomorrow?"

Nell nodded but paused as the front door opened and Maria joined them. Rebecca stood up and got her a chair from the table.

"That was well timed. How are you doing?"

Maria flopped into a chair. "Not well. He's hardly sleeping and when he does, he's having nightmares and keeping everyone else awake."

"Is his leg getting any better?"

"The doctor seems to think it's healing, and George says he's not in as much pain as he was, so I suppose it is. The doctor's calling again in the morning."

"At least we've got James home tomorrow." Nell smiled as she sat back in her chair. "He should be able to help him."

Maria stifled a yawn. "That's what I'm banking on, although I'm not sure how he and George will get along."

"They were on reasonable terms last time they were together. Do you know if James has repaid the money for his apprenticeship yet?"

Maria shook her head. "I've no idea. I just take what he gives me. Not that it's going to be enough with the way things are. It will be Christmas soon, too."

Rebecca puffed out her cheeks. "What are we going to do for that? Will we come to your house as usual?"

"I doubt it. So much has changed since last year, I don't even want to think about it."

"We've got the christening first." Nell helped herself to a slice of cake. "Have you heard the plans for that?"

"No, not a word, although I've not called on Sarah since Jane arrived."

"I'm sure we'll hear soon enough. Assuming we're invited."

"Oh, we'll be invited; you mark my words."

A light drizzle was falling as Nell and Maria hurried back across the road, and as soon as they stepped into the hall, they shook out their shawls.

"What a horrible evening. The boys will be soaked when they get home." Maria popped her head into the front room. "Ah, you're awake."

Nell waited at the door as Maria went to straighten the pillows behind George's head.

"That laudanum isn't working as well as it was."

"Perhaps you didn't take as much."

"I took more and it still isn't working." George's eyes

flashed with anger before he spotted Nell. "Is there any brandy?"

"Yes, let me get you one."

Alice was on the floor playing with the girls when Nell went into the living room. "Did you get rained off?"

Elenor looked up at her. "We got wet."

"It's a good job you're by the fire then." She went into the kitchen for the brandy. "This has gone down a bit."

Alice glanced up at her. "I've not long since given him one."

"He wants another. I don't suppose we can stop him ... until we run out of money."

Alice grimaced. "I'm glad I won't be the one to tell him."

"I'll leave that to your mam." Nell picked up the glass and headed to the front room. George pushed himself up on the chair as she went in.

"I've had enough of being in here. I'm joining you all for tea tonight."

"But what about your leg? The doctor said to keep it as still as possible." Maria straightened the blanket over him, but he batted her hands out of the way.

"Will you stop it, woman? Give me that brandy." He reached for the glass Nell offered him and pointed to a crutch leaning against the wall. "There's no point having that if I can't move. Now, pass it here. I want to go outside."

"It's raining."

George's face reddened. "I've spent the last seven months getting soaking wet on a ship. A bit of rain won't hurt me."

"No, of course not. Nell, will you give me a hand?"

"How?"

"Come here." George beckoned her over. "Let me put an arm around your shoulders, both of you, and I'll pull myself up."

Nell copied Maria and crouched down, holding onto his arm as he sat forward in his seat.

"Right, after three, I'll stand up."

Nell waited for the count, but as they stood up, George's weight took them by surprise and the three of them toppled back onto the sofa.

"Argh!! You stupid women. What did you do that for?"

Maria clambered to her feet. "We didn't do it on purpose. You're too heavy for us."

"You could have put some effort into it."

"We did, and if you don't like it, you'll have to wait for the boys to come home." Without waiting for a reply, Maria stormed from the room, leaving Nell to make George comfortable.

"I'm sorry, did we hurt you?"

"Yes, you did as it happens. You'll have to fetch some more brandy. And be quick about it."

Billy and Vernon arrived home an hour later and joined Nell in the living room.

"Have you had a good day?"

Vernon kept his head down as Billy shrugged. "Same as usual."

"Your dad wants to see you both. Your mam's with him."

"What does he want?" Vernon's face paled.

"For one thing, he wants to join us for tea, so he needs

help getting in here. Besides, he's not seen you since he's been back."

"That's not our fault…"

"Nobody said it was, but I'd get yourselves in there if I were you. I'll start putting the tea on the table."

Nell bent down to the girls, who were still playing by the fire. "Go and wash your hands. Tea will be ready in a minute."

They hadn't moved when Maria barged through the living room and into the kitchen. "I'm leaving them to it. He hasn't got a civil tongue in his head at the moment. Drinking all that brandy won't help."

"If it makes the pain easier…" Nell stopped and winced as a shriek came from the front room. "It doesn't sound like they're doing much better than us."

"Well, I'm not going back to help." She rearranged the dishes Nell had placed on the table, but stopped as George joined them, one arm draped around Billy's shoulders while the other rested on the crutch.

"Ah, you made it. Good. Now, where would you like to sit?"

George grunted. "By the fire. I can't stretch my leg out anywhere else. The boys can sit with me."

"Yes, very well." Maria shooed the girls out of the way and hovered by the table while Vernon helped George onto a chair. "Nell, will you get a tray to put on his knee?"

By the time Nell returned from the kitchen and handed the tray to George, Maria was waiting with a large portion of meat and potato pie. "There you are. There's more if you want it."

He cut a large chunk of pastry while he waited for Billy and Vernon to join him. "How's work going?"

Billy had taken the chair opposite. "Fine. We're busy as usual."

"And what about you?" His eyes fixed on Vernon.

"Yes, fine..."

"Are you sure? That's not what I heard."

Vernon gasped then coughed to stop himself choking. "What's she said?" He glared at Maria.

"I've not said anything..."

"Then who has?"

"My leg may be broken, but my ears still work." George's eyes didn't leave his son. "Now, what haven't you told me?"

"Nothing ... it's just ... well, Uncle Tom had an idea..."

Billy nodded. "It was Uncle Tom's idea, and a few of the others."

"What idea?"

"They think we deserve more money and shouldn't work so many hours." Vernon gulped. "They decided the best thing to do was to strike down our tools."

"And you joined in?"

When Vernon stayed silent, George gaped at Billy. "What about you?"

"I didn't want to, but I couldn't go into work because they had men on the gate stopping us."

"How long did this last?"

"Only the day ... except when we went in the following day..." Billy glanced at Vernon "...they wouldn't let any of those involved back into work."

George's face was red as he looked to Billy. "They let you in?"

"Yes."

"But not you?" He glowered at Vernon.

"I tried." Vernon's voice squeaked. "I've been to the yard every day since..."

"But you've been earning no money?" George banged a hand on the arm of his chair, almost sending his plate crashing to the floor. "What on earth were you thinking? Didn't you realise I wouldn't be earning anything for a while?"

"We wanted a pay rise. We didn't know they'd stop us going back."

"There are hundreds of skilled men around here at the moment. They don't need to take on troublemakers. Of course they got rid of you."

Vernon wiped an eye with the back of his hand. "I didn't do it on purpose. Uncle Tom said..."

"I'll give you Uncle Tom. Wait 'til I see him. I bet he's not lost his job."

"Actually..." Billy cleared his throat as George stared at him "...he has ... and Sam. Neither have worked since the strike."

George's head spun around to Maria. "Why didn't you tell me? I imagine that's why he's not visited."

"I-I didn't want to upset you. You've enough to deal with."

"It's not going to make the problem go away though, is it? How are we supposed to eat if we have to spend all Billy's money on rent?"

Maria's face twisted. "James is home tomorrow. He'll give me some housekeeping."

"And how long's that supposed to last?" He rounded on Vernon again. "If I hear you've been near that alehouse wasting money, I'll take my belt to you, bad leg or not. You're a disgrace. What are you?"

"A disgrace." Vernon's words were barely a whisper as Nell stepped to his side.

"I'm hoping I can help. James says I'll be well paid as a stewardess."

George studied Nell before rounding again on Vernon. "Are you proud of yourself, relying on your aunty to provide for you?"

"She was already going when I lost my job."

"And it's as well she was." George shouted to Maria, "I want to see Tom here tomorrow. If he started this mess, he can damn well sort it out."

Maria flinched and looked at the girls. "Watch your…"

"Mam!" Billy raised an eyebrow as he popped the last piece of meat into his mouth. "If Dad wants to see Uncle Tom, why don't I go to the alehouse when I've finished here? I should catch him."

George nodded. "Yes, do that, but you can stay where you are." He glared at Vernon. "You're not going to that alehouse again until you have a job and you've paid your mam all the housekeeping you owe her."

Vernon groaned. "That will take months."

"You'd better try harder to get another job then."

CHAPTER FORTY-NINE

Nell stood at the bedroom window, praying James would walk into view before she went downstairs. *Please let him be here when Tom arrives.* George may want to see her brother, but she really didn't. Not with the mood George was in this morning.

"Nell, are you coming down?" Maria's voice sounded weary.

"Yes, I won't be a moment." She gave the window another polish as a huge grin spread across her face. *Here he is.*

James walked with his head bent into the wind, but as he approached the house, he looked up and waved. She waved back and raced down the stairs to open the door.

"You're here!" Nell beamed at him as he gave her a peck on the cheek. "Come on in."

"He can come in here first." George's voice boomed from the front room, causing James to freeze.

'Dad!' James mouthed the words as his eyes widened. "One minute, let me take my coat off."

Nell took the coat from him. "You go in. I'll bring you both a cup of tea."

Thankfully, the pot on the table was still fresh and Nell hurried back to the front room but stopped at the sound of raised voices.

"You knew about all this with Vernon?" George's voice was stern. "Why didn't you do something about it?"

"I only found out about it the day before I went back to the ship. Is he still out of work?"

"Yes, he is. You knew he was going to strike down his tools. Why didn't you stop him?"

Nell picked up the cups and gave a short cough as she entered the room. "I'm sorry to interrupt, but I don't think anyone could have stopped him. They were all encouraging each other. Billy was even barred from the alehouse because he wasn't supporting them."

"The alehouse on Windsor Street?"

"Yes. There were a number of evenings he didn't go out at all."

George sucked air through his teeth. "This is nonsense. Where's Tom? He's got a lot to answer for."

Nell looked at James. "Billy said he spoke to him last night and asked him to call. I expect he's out looking for work."

"He'll be out causing trouble more like... Here, James." George held out his arm. "Get me up from here and pass that crutch. I want to know what's going on."

"I'll take the tea back to the living room." As she bent to pick up the cups and saucers, Nell marvelled at how easily James got George to his feet. "My, it took a lot more effort than that last night."

James laughed. "You get used to it on the ship. There are more gents than you'd imagine who need a hand getting themselves to bed after too much brandy."

George draped his arm around James' shoulders. "You may be some use after all."

James waited for George and Maria to settle on either side of the fireplace, then reached for Nell's cloak and held it out for her.

"There won't be much we can do if Uncle Tom's not home."

George glared at James as he reached for his hat. "You can call into the alehouse and tell him to get here now. If he's got no work, I expect that's where he'll be."

"He'd better not be." Maria reached for her knitting. "He hasn't got the money to spend all afternoon in there."

"Whether he has or not, that's where you'll find him, and tell him there'll be trouble if I have to make my own way to see him."

"You can't go out!" Maria wailed.

"If that's what it takes to speak to your brother, then that's what I'll do. Right, be off with you. And don't dawdle."

Nell waved to Alice and Elenor as James pulled the front door closed and offered her his arm.

"So much for looking forward to coming home. I'd hoped to be here when he arrived."

"That would have been nice. I won't deny it's hard work with him back. How was the trip?"

James' shoulders drooped. "I've had better. The ship

wasn't full, but the passengers we did have were completely unreasonable. It was as if we were responsible for the bad weather. Really, if they choose to travel in November, they should expect it."

"I suppose they do it because it's cheaper."

James shook his head. "It's not the steerage passengers who are the problem. It's the toffs with all their money. Anyway, I'm back now for five weeks, so I can forget about them." He shivered and rubbed his hands together.

"Have you remembered we've got the christening a week on Sunday?"

James groaned. "I'd completely forgotten. What did Dad say about Aunty Jane turning up?"

"We've not told him yet. Your mam refuses to talk about her, and it's more than my life's worth to bring it up."

"It's as well you told me. I could easily have mentioned her over dinner. He doesn't mind you going to sea though?"

"He doesn't seem to. At least he realises we need the money, which is more than your mam does, but ... can I ask you a question?"

James studied her. "What is it?"

Nell slowed as they approached Tom's house. "It's nothing really, I'm probably being silly, but are there many ships that cross the ocean that don't come back?"

"That run aground or sink, you mean?"

Nell nodded.

"No, why?"

"I don't know. I think it was seeing your dad and, well, he said that when the wave hit his ship, two of the men on deck got washed overboard as well as five others being injured … and obviously there was your Uncle Jack. I don't want to leave the girls orphaned."

James patted her hand. "Have you been worrying about this ever since you saw Dad?"

Nell stared at her hands. "I've tried not to, but until he arrived home, it hadn't entered my head that I might not come back."

"And quite right, too, because you will. I've been sailing for nearly ten years, and in all that time, only two ships have been lost. One was because they didn't carry enough coal, and the other was a collision. Both happened shortly after I started, and neither would be allowed to happen nowadays."

"Don't you think I should worry?"

"Not at all. Do you think I'd go to sea if I was worried about having an accident?"

"I suppose not."

"You've seen the passenger ships; they're completely different to the sailing ship Dad was on when he had his accident. They're much bigger for a start, and not reliant on all those sails."

"I know, but … oh, it's all so confusing."

James smiled down at her. "I'd say you're getting the jitters because it's coming closer. Imagine, in two months' time you'll be halfway across the Atlantic and any nerves will be a distant memory."

Nell's stomach churned. "I hope you're right."

. . .

She shivered as she stood outside Sarah and Tom's house waiting for the door to be opened. When there was no answer, James knocked again.

"It looks like they've gone out." He peered through the front window.

"All of them? I doubt it." She stepped back to look up to the bedroom windows, but as she did, the door opened.

"What are you doing standing outside? Why didn't you come in?" Sarah held the door open with her youngest child on her hip.

"I'm sorry. We're looking for Uncle Tom and didn't want to barge in. Dad wants a word with him."

Sarah tutted and showed them into the living room where Jane sat by the fire crocheting.

"He'll have to join the queue. I think half the dockers in Liverpool want a word with him. You'll probably find him in the alehouse. Apparently, he's charging a pint of ale for every consultation. He'd better be, at any rate, the amount he'd drunk when he came home last night."

"You're not likely to get a civil word out of him by this time in the afternoon." Jane put down her crocheting and looked up at James. "How's your dad? I must pay him a visit."

"No, please ... I mean, he's not up to having visitors at the moment. He's still in a lot of pain."

Jane rolled her shoulders and tutted at Sarah. "There must be something up with him if he'd rather see Tom than me. Tell him I'll call soon, anyway."

"Actually, there may be no need." Nell flashed her best smile. "Have you made arrangements for the christening yet? I'm sure he'll make an extra effort to be there, especially if it's the only way he can speak to Tom."

Jane's face fell as she stared at Sarah. "Not yet. Have we?"

"Don't look at me. I'm getting everything on tick as it is at the moment. I can't be putting on a spread for half the neighbourhood with no money."

Nell put a hand to her head. "No, of course. I daren't offer our house, either, with things as they are with us. We've only got Billy's wage to last us until February."

Jane scowled. "What about Rebecca? Mr Grayson's still working, isn't he?"

"Well, yes, but..."

"Splendid!" Jane's face brightened. "We'll go there. It won't be far for George to walk either. Will you mention it to her? I'd be ever so grateful."

"I'm really not sure. Mr Grayson doesn't like entertaining."

"Nonsense. Who doesn't like a family gathering? Tell her I'll call to make arrangements." She stood up to adjust her hair in the mirror above the fireplace. "It will be my first day out of my mourning clothes. I'll look altogether more presentable." She looked Nell up and down. "Were there any tongues wagging when you abandoned yours?"

"Not that I know of, but I didn't care. Wearing black is nothing more than a reminder of why you're miserable, and I was tired of that."

"Precisely." A twinkle flashed in Jane's eyes. "And I've no intention of being miserable for the christening."

. . .

George was by the fire when they arrived home, an empty brandy glass on the table beside him.

"Where on earth have you been? I've still not seen that brother of yours."

"I'm sorry." Nell took the seat opposite. "Where are Maria and Alice?"

"Outside somewhere." George waved his glass at James. "Here, you're a steward. What's happened to Tom?"

Nell grimaced. "We didn't see him. Sarah said half the dockers in Liverpool are after him and he'll only speak to those who buy him a pint of ale. He's been in no fit state to speak to anyone for the last few days."

"Damn fool." George banged his hand on the chair. "I need to get to the alehouse..."

"I wouldn't go now." James handed him his brandy. "We can go tomorrow dinner time, before he's had too much to drink, if you like."

George gulped at the drink. "I do like. I'll give him what for."

"There might be another option, though. To save you struggling around there." Nell's voice squeaked.

"Go on."

"He's likely to be at the christening next week."

"Christening?" His brow furrowed. "Whose christening?"

Nell bit her lip and took the seat beside him. "Jane's sons. She's back."

"Jane?" George sat forward in his chair. "Your sister? Why hasn't anyone told me?"

"There was too much going on with Vernon and well ... Mam's not happy about it."

"No, she wouldn't be." George paused. "How long's she staying?"

"For good. Mr Read died, and it wasn't possible for her to stay in Ireland."

"She has the children with her?"

Nell nodded. "She does. She's living in a boarding house at the moment, but she moves into a house on Elaine Street next week."

George's hazel eyes flicked between Nell and his son. "How's she paying for that?"

James leaned forward in his seat. "We're not sure. She was hoping to get money from the guardians, and Uncle Tom was going to help her, but he can't now."

"Gracious."

"What's up with you?" Maria appeared with her hands on her hips.

"Why didn't you tell me about Jane?"

Maria's face coloured. "I didn't want to upset you any more. You've had enough on your plate since you came back."

"Why would it upset me? I always liked her."

"Well, you shouldn't. Don't you remember how ill she made me ... and Fred?"

"You can't blame her for that."

"I can and I will." Maria disappeared back into the kitchen.

"When were you going to tell me she was back? On the day of the christening?"

Maria let out a deep sigh as she stepped back into the living room. "I wasn't planning on going. You won't be able to get to church with your leg like that, so I thought I'd stay with you."

George straightened up in his chair. "I'm sure we could borrow a bath chair off someone." He turned to Nell. "Where are they having the get-together afterwards?"

"That's a bit of a problem." Nell beckoned Maria to sit with them. "They were hoping to have it at Tom's, but since he and Sam lost their jobs, Sarah says they've no money."

"They won't be having one then." Maria couldn't hide her grin. "It's probably no bad thing."

"But there might be. You know what Jane's like. She wants to do things properly and decided that as Mr Grayson has a job, we should have it at Rebecca's."

Maria's eyes widened. "I hope you put her right. There's not a chance he'll let us all go over there."

"We couldn't ... could we?" Nell appealed to James for support.

James shook his head. "Aunty Jane wouldn't take no for an answer and asked us to speak to Aunty Rebecca about it."

"She always was rather sure of herself." Maria rolled her shoulders. "And selfish. Someone needs to tell her..." Maria got to her feet, but George glared at her.

"Sit down. It's not her fault Tom's lost his job."

"But it's her who'll want a full spread put on."

"We'll do it here then."

"Here?" Maria was back on her feet. "After everything she's done."

"It was a long time ago, and I'd like to see her again. Besides, it solves the problem of how I'll get to the gathering."

"But we don't have any more money than they do."

"We have enough, and everyone can bring something with them for the table. It may not be as lavish as she'd like, but we can still make it nice. I imagine she's waited a long time for this."

Maria stormed to the hall. "Do as you like, but don't expect me to organise it. I'm going for a walk."

CHAPTER FIFTY

The sky was dark as Nell arrived at church, flanked on either side by the tall figures of James and Billy. She pushed the pram to the side of the building and lifted the girls down as she waited for Maria and Alice to join them.

"What have you done with Vernon?"

Maria looked over her shoulder. "He's coming. I suspect he wants to warn Tom about George."

Nell shook her head. "Today of all days. You'd think Tom would have called to see him beforehand so we can enjoy the day."

"I don't think there'll be many who enjoy it, if I'm being honest."

Nell followed Maria as she strutted into church, and immediately spotted Jane in the front pew looking more glamorous than she'd expected. She nudged Maria. "I wasn't expecting such a fetching royal-blue colour so soon after abandoning her mourning clothes.

"I hope she's brought a cloak as well. She'll be freezing with such a short cape."

Nell sniggered. "I'm sure she will have." She pointed to a young woman by Jane's side who wore her dark auburn hair under a fashionable navy hat. "There's no question who that is with her."

Maria studied the young woman. "She's the image of Jane at that age."

"Isn't she? But the boys look more like their father with that black hair." Nell sighed. "I often wish I had a son in the image of Jack. It would make him seem closer."

"It would only hold you back. You need to start thinking of the future, and a new husband."

"Not yet. It's too soon." Nell rolled her eyes at her friend Mrs Blackmore as she took the seat behind her. "Why does everyone want to marry me off?"

"To keep you in Liverpool, obviously." Mrs Blackmore smirked, but Nell's attention was distracted as Maria nudged her and gestured to Sarah, who arrived with her four younger children and settled into the pew behind Jane.

"Typical of Tom not to be with her." Maria turned in a full circle. "Rebecca's late, too."

"We should have knocked for her."

Maria snorted. "And disturb Mr Grayson's routine, I don't think so."

The guests hadn't finished filing in when the organ sounded to announce the arrival of the vicar at the front of the church.

"Here they are." Nell watched a flustered-looking Rebecca as she followed her husband down the aisle with the children in tow.

Maria rolled her shoulders. "That doesn't bode well for later."

"Nor does the look on Tom's face." Nell watched her brother as he strode past them. "Should we sneak off during the last hymn? We can always say we need to check on George."

"I'll be checking on him anyway. I wouldn't be here if it wasn't for him…"

"Shh!"

Nell gave the woman behind her an apologetic smile as the vicar continued his welcome. *Let's hope the service calms everyone down.*

The rain had started by the time the service was over, and Nell opened her umbrella and linked arms with Maria as they hurried from the building.

"They won't be hanging around in the churchyard with this weather, so we need to be quick."

"The floors will be filthy when we've finished, with everyone coming in with wet feet. That will be something else to deal with tomorrow, not to mention all the tidying up. George didn't think of *that* when he suggested this, did he?"

"Stop worrying. We'll have all day, and if the weather carries on like this, we'll have nothing better to do."

George was reading the newspaper when they arrived home. "Is it that time already?"

"Yes, we'll have everyone here in the next five minutes." Maria shook out her cloak. "It's horrible out there."

"Was Tom there?"

"Of course he was. Not looking best pleased, I might

add. Could you please be civil to him? I don't want an argument."

"Be civil, after everything he's done...?"

"All right, calm down. I'm sure he's already had more than enough lectures."

"It's no more than he deserves."

Nell peered into the hall as the front door opened.

"It's only me." Alice bounced the pram up the doorstep and led Elenor into the house. "I came as quickly as I could. Billy and James are behind me."

As if on cue, the two of them arrived and squeezed in behind the pram as Alice lifted Leah out.

"Let me take this into the back yard to get it out of the way." Billy grabbed hold of the handle and was about to push it into the living room when Maria blocked his way. "It's not coming through here dripping like that. You can take it round the outside."

"Good job I've not taken my coat off then." Billy smirked at Nell, but left the door open for Rebecca as he disappeared. She pushed the girls into the hall and stepped back.

"I'll go and fetch the sandwiches." She glanced up at the sky. "I knew I should have brought them earlier, but no, Hugh knew best..."

Nell raised an eyebrow at Maria, but she was too focussed on Alice.

"I presume Aunty Sarah's gone home for her contribution."

"I imagine so. I wasn't really paying attention."

"She will have done." Nell pushed on the door to the

front room. "Let's open this and we can send the men in here to keep them out the way while we arrange the table."

"Don't be sending all the men in there while I'm in here with the women," George's voice boomed from the living room. "James. Come and move me."

"Coming."

Nell walked into the front room and straightened the crocheted chair backs. "I think we've enough chairs in here. They'll have to stand up if we haven't."

"There'll be plenty." George hobbled into the room with the help of James' shoulders. "You can put me by the fire facing the window. That way I can see what's going on."

Nell and Maria made their way back to the living room, but as Nell filled the kettle, the front door opened again and Jane's voice filtered through to her.

"Oh, George. How lovely to see you!"

Maria wasted no time in going to the front room. "We're putting the food in the back room. If you've brought anything..."

"Oh, stop fussing. Here."

Nell arrived in time to see Jane hand two plated pies to Maria and pull up a chair beside George.

"It's been too long."

George's eyes sparkled. "It most certainly has. These are your boys, are they?"

"They are. Matthew and John. All legally christened now, and my daughter Betty."

"It's lovely to meet them ... and to see you again." He patted Jane's hand. "I don't know what possessed you to go running off over there."

"You most certainly do." Maria stared down at Jane but took a step backwards as George glowered at her. "Right, I'll put these on the table. Nell, will you shout Alice and she can take the boys upstairs to meet their cousins?"

Nell scurried to the bottom of the stairs as Mr Grayson opened the front door and Rebecca stepped inside with two large platters of sandwiches balancing on top of each other.

"Here, let me take those. Mr Grayson, the men are in the front room if you'd like to join them. Ah, Alice–" Nell spun around as her niece approached "–will you take Betty and the boys upstairs? It will be too busy for them down here."

James followed his mother into the living room. "Shall I serve some drinks for everyone? Unless you want to do it, Aunty Nell. To get in some practice."

"No, she doesn't." Maria straightened up after leaning over the table. "Don't encourage her."

Nell handed her the sandwiches. "Is Vernon not back yet?"

James grimaced. "I saw him sheltering under a tree with Uncle Tom and Sam. They won't be in a hurry to get here."

"I'd say now was a perfectly good time with your dad's attention elsewhere." Maria spoke through gritted teeth. "He might not even notice them."

"Don't be silly. I'm sure Jane will come in here as soon as Sarah arrives." Nell's brow creased. "I wonder why they didn't come together. They've been inseparable these last few weeks."

"I've got a good idea." Maria disappeared into the kitchen. "Nell, this kettle isn't even on!"

James blew through his lips. "I imagine Dad will want more than a cup of tea. Shall I give him a brandy?"

"You'd better, but go sparingly. We've only that one bottle. There's some ale in the pantry if anyone prefers that. They can't have much though, unless anyone else decides to bring anything."

Rebecca stamped her foot as James disappeared. "I told Hugh to bring something over, but oh, no. That would cost him money. As if we're not the most fortunate amongst you, but he couldn't spare a bottle of something."

"Don't worry. At least he's not got far to go if he changes his mind. Is, erm..." Nell checked behind her "... is everything all right. You didn't seem very happy when you came into church."

Rebecca shook her head. "It's nothing. You know what he's like around family gatherings."

"Don't let him spoil your day. It's not often we have a christening to celebrate."

"And this could be the last for many years."

"What do you mean?" Nell raised an eyebrow as Rebecca moved to a chair by the fire.

"You'd think he'd want a son, wouldn't you? But no. After all the delays having Isobel, which were entirely his fault, he says we're too old now."

Nell rested a hand on her sister's arm. "I'm sorry."

"So am I." Rebecca's shoulders sagged as she exhaled. "I know I should be grateful for Isobel and Florrie, but..." She paused. "Where are they?"

"We've cleared a space in the front bedroom, so Alice has them all up there. We thought it would be better to have them out of the way." Nell swept over to the pantry and came back holding a bottle of sherry. "Would you like one?"

The sparkle returned to Rebecca's eyes. "As long as you and Maria join me. I think we deserve it."

CHAPTER FIFTY-ONE

M aria walked from the kitchen and accepted the glass of sherry Nell offered her.

"Sit down for a minute and stop looking so worried."

"How can I not worry...? You've seen her."

Rebecca eyed Maria over the rim of her glass. "Did you know this might happen?"

Maria said nothing as she gulped her drink, but Nell noticed the stiffening of her shoulders.

"I met her in the park when I was with James last month. I thought at the time she seemed rather pleased that George was on his way home. Is there something you're not telling us?"

"No, there isn't, but she can keep her hands off him. He may not be perfect, but he's mine."

"I'm sure she wouldn't do anything improper." Rebecca placed her half-empty glass on the occasional table. "They've not seen each other for such a long time. There's a lot to catch up on."

Maria emptied her glass. "I don't want her here. Why did she have to come back?"

Nell stood up and refilled her glass. "Take a deep breath and calm down. Sarah will be here soon enough. She'll distract her."

Maria's shoulders rose and fell as she did as she was told. "They always got on well, but I always thought it was because she was like his daughter..." She stopped as the front door opened and Sarah popped her head into the living room.

"Sorry we're late. I lost Tom." She placed several bowls on the table and lowered her voice. "I think he was a bit bothered about coming. Vernon's warned him about George."

Nell's forehead creased. "Tom's not usually troubled by anyone."

"No, but this last couple of weeks have taken it out of him. He's not liking being out of work either."

"He was never there."

"Maria, calm down." Nell smiled at Sarah. "May I get you a sherry?"

"Nell!" Maria glared at her, but Sarah shook her head.

"I'd better not. I've got all the children with me. Where are yours?"

"Upstairs in the front bedroom. Alice is with them. You could send yours up there, too, if you like."

"Splendid. I'll have a sherry when I get back then." She relaxed back in her chair. "Where's Jane?"

A shriek from the front room gave them an answer. "Tom! What are you doing?"

Maria jumped to her feet and hurried next door. "What's going on?"

"Nothing." Tom cracked his knuckles and was staring down at George when Nell joined them.

"Tom, stop it this minute." Maria stood in front of him. "You can't hit a defenceless man."

"Well, he can stop the name-calling and the accusations then." Tom moved her out of the way. "We called the men out on strike to try and give them a better life. They all deserve more money for the hours they put in, especially given the profits the companies make. It wasn't our fault we underestimated how rotten the management was."

"You should have worked that out before you called them all out. Young boys like my Vernon look up to men like you; they're easily led. If it wasn't for you and your crowd, he'd still be in a job."

"I didn't force him into it. He was as keen as the next lad."

"Because you'd promised him more money."

"It wasn't like that." Vernon sounded timid next to Tom. "I was doing it for all of us. You've not seen Mam when she's worrying about money. I wanted to help. Sam was the same. Isn't that right?" He turned to his cousin.

"Yes. My mam can't cope on Dad's wage and with having Aunty Jane here as well…"

Jane had moved to the corner of the room, her arms drawn up across her chest. "I'm sure that's right, George. They were only trying to help."

"Whether they were or not, somebody should have realised there are enough men in Liverpool to take over from those who lost their jobs." He slammed his hand on the arm of the chair. "We wouldn't be in this mess if they had."

"We had to try." Tom's voice thundered around the room. "The men haven't had a pay rise for five years, and yet the companies expect more and more from them. Men are beginning to think the only way they can support their families is by going to sea."

"And what's wrong with that?"

"It's dangerous, that's what. Look at you, sitting there. You went chasing more money, but it looks like you'll never work again. Jack certainly won't."

Nell flinched at the sound of his name, but Tom continued, "Is that what you want for the women of Liverpool? To be sailors' widows?"

"Don't be daft."

"Well, you should support us then, not criticise everything we do. Now, if you'll excuse me..." Tom turned to leave the room but stopped when he bumped into Nell. He caught her by the arms and rounded on George.

"In fact, look at our Nell. She's got to work because the shipping companies put their profits ahead of their workers. By rights, she should have been paid compensation, but their idea of helping is to send her to work. Are you happy she'll be keeping a roof over your head? Because *I* wouldn't be."

George tried to make himself taller in his chair. "You're the one who's made it necessary for her to go to sea. If Vernon was still working, she wouldn't have to..."

Nell's heart was pounding as she stepped into the middle of the room. "Stop it, both of you. I'm going to sea because I've always wanted to. Not because I have to. Jack and I had talked about it for years, but just when I thought I was going with him ... well, I didn't."

"That's right." James put an arm around Nell's shoulders. "She may be a woman, but she wants to travel to see something of the world Uncle Jack told her about. Stop treating her as if she's abnormal and be thankful she'll be earning some money until Dad and Vernon can get themselves sorted out."

"It's still not right." Tom glared at Nell.

"Maybe not. But I'm going. Whether you like it or not." She glared at Maria. "Now, unless I'm mistaken the food's ready. This is supposed to be a joyful occasion, so I suggest we all put a smile on our faces."

For the fourth time that afternoon, Nell poured some boiling water into the teapot and carried it back to the table.

"At least there's no waste." She studied the empty plates on the table as she stacked them into piles.

"It was lovely, thank you." Jane sashayed into the room. "The whole afternoon's been nice ... once we got over our little disagreement."

Nell took a seat. "How are the boys? Have you been up to see them since they had something to eat?"

"Oh, they're having a lovely time with their new cousins. They're all getting on so well." She paused while Sarah joined them. "Ah, here you are. I was about to ask about Christmas. What do you usually do? Do you have a gathering for that, too?"

"No, we won't this year." Maria stiffened in her chair.

"It's George's first Christmas at home for years, so we've decided to have a quiet celebration this year."

Nell raised an eyebrow. *That's news to me.*

"Rebecca usually has the day with Mr Grayson anyway, but it will be Nell's first year without Jack…"

Nell's heart skipped a beat. *Will it be much different to all the other Christmases I've spent without him?*

Sarah sighed. "It's probably as well, given that none of us have any money. We'd better keep it simple, and at least we've had today."

"That's a shame." Jane's head dropped. "I suppose I'll have to make the most of things with my new landlady then."

Sarah rolled her eyes. "You can still call round for a sherry. We're not going to turn our backs on you."

Jane put a hand to her chest. "Thank goodness for that. Mrs O'Rourke might be nice enough, but not for the whole of Christmas Day."

Nell poured five cups of tea and handed them round, but stopped when she got to Sarah. "Do you remember, earlier in the year, I borrowed that travelling case from you?"

"That old brown one, you mean?"

She nodded. "May I borrow it again? If I can collect it one day this week, I'll start packing. I've not long to wait now."

"You've not gone off the idea then?"

Nell listened as Tom and George's voices continued to bellow from the other room. "No, not at all."

CHAPTER FIFTY-TWO

Nell knelt beside the bed and pulled out the travelling case she'd stowed there the previous day. Maria knew she'd been to Sarah's to collect it, but there was no point upsetting her by making it obvious. She lifted it onto the bed and flicked open the catches, gazing into the empty interior. Was it almost a year since she'd done the exact same thing? Back then she'd been full of excitement about travelling the oceans with Jack, but now ... well, she was still excited, but it wasn't the same. Last time she'd hoped to have a trunk to carry her dresses, but that wouldn't happen now. She'd probably have to wear the same dress for the duration of the trip. She studied the clothes hanging in her wardrobe. She didn't have much choice, but she'd better choose carefully.

She was about to close the wardrobe door when James came bounding up the stairs and knocked on the bedroom door.

"Are you in there, Aunty Nell?"

She closed the wardrobe door as he walked in. "I am. What's the hurry?"

"The postman brought this." He waved a letter in the air before handing it to her. "It's from the Guion Line, so I thought you'd rather read it without Mam being around."

She took it from him and moved to the chair by the window. "You're a good lad. Let's have a look." She took the letter opener he offered her and sliced the top of the envelope before scanning the text.

"It's telling me what to do when I report to the ship." She shuddered as she read it. "I've to go to the office first to pick up a card confirming I'm allowed on board and then go to the ship and find the matron on deck three." She gazed up at him. "How will I do that? The ships are enormous. I could walk around for hours looking for her."

James laughed. "You'll be fine. She'll be near the doctor's office and that's usually signposted."

"I'll be on my own, though."

"Don't worry. I'm not due to go away again until the week after you, so I'll walk you down to the office and sort you out. If you're fortunate, there'll be other newcomers looking lost and you can board with them. You won't be the only one worrying about this."

Nell fidgeted with a corner of the letter. "It's all right for you; you've done it a hundred times."

He took a seat on the edge of the bed. "There was a first time for me, too, remember? I was only seventeen and Mam was furious with me because Dad didn't want me to go."

"How could I forget?" She shuddered at the memories.

"Exactly. All the arguments didn't do much for my

confidence, I can tell you, and that first walk to the ship was hard … especially with no one to go with me."

Nell gazed at the wall above James' head. "I remember thinking how confident you looked when you left. It goes to show you can never tell what's going through people's minds."

James grimaced. "It was all bravado. I couldn't let Mam see how much they'd upset me."

"I think they knew, but it was their way of trying to stop you."

James snorted. "It was never going to work. Still, at least something good came out of Dad's accident."

"What do you mean?"

"Haven't you noticed? He's more than happy for me to wait on him now, especially when he wants a brandy."

"Or if he wants to move about."

James smiled. "I think he likes it. It's certainly the most I've ever spoken to him."

"He does seem to have mellowed." Nell reread the letter. "How long did it take you to settle in on the ship?"

"Not long. I was fortunate enough to meet another new steward as I was boarding the ship and we stuck together for the next six months."

"Why not for longer?"

"The company offered me a post on a different ship. It was a good move, because it had more first-class cabins, but it was a shame we were split up. I think about him from time to time and wonder what happened to him."

"I suppose it's difficult to keep in touch with someone when you're both at sea."

"It is. I often wanted to write, but I wouldn't have

known where to send the letter. I could have sent it to the office, I guess, but–" he shrugged "–it seemed more trouble than it was worth."

"I hope I can find someone to latch onto." Nell folded the letter and put it back in the envelope. "I'll study this later and write myself a list of what I need. I'm bound to forget something if I don't."

"Don't forget you'll only have a small cabin ... and you'll be sharing. You may be servicing the first-class cabins, but they won't house you in one. Stick to essentials."

Nell's eyes flicked to the wardrobe. "And there was me, worried about not being able to fit any dresses in my travelling case."

"Doesn't it say they'll give you a couple? They like everyone to wear a uniform of sorts, so you may have a dress waiting for you, or at least a skirt and some blouses."

The smile returned to Nell's lips. "I hadn't thought of that. That would be splendid."

James laughed. "Don't get too carried away. If they're anything like ours, they won't be terribly fetching."

"It will be better than nothing."

Nell rolled together the remnants of pastry that were strewn across the table and wrapped the resulting ball into some paper. It was cold enough outside that it would keep until she made some more tomorrow.

Maria popped her head around the door of the kitchen. "Are you all done?"

"I am for now. Another two dozen mince pies ready to join the others. One more batch should do it."

"Good. I'll get the kettle on. By the time they come out of the range, the tea should be brewed."

Nell rinsed a cloth in the sink and walked back to the table. "I'd better look at that list again and see what else we can do. I can't believe it's Christmas Day on Sunday."

"We're about done with most things. I just need to finish sewing those little dolls for the girls."

"And I need to wrap the sweets I made. I'll do that tonight when the girls are in bed." Nell wiped the used flour into her hand. "Are we making Alice a cake for her birthday?"

Maria filled up the kettle. "I wasn't going to. We've enough to eat on Christmas Day without making anything else."

"She will be sixteen, though. It's something of an event."

"I suppose, although I don't feel much like celebrating. Perhaps we could wait and mark her baptism date in January instead."

"But..." *I won't be here.* Nell stopped herself before she spoke.

"But what?"

"I was about to say it's not the same, but then having a birthday at Christmas isn't usual. Perhaps I'll wrap her a little something extra up instead."

Maria shook her head. "You spoil her."

"Somebody has to. Still, I'm glad we're only having a quiet day this year. I couldn't have managed much more either." Nell straightened up and gazed through the window. "To think it was only a year ago I was looking forward to Jack coming home again."

"I thought as much, although that's not why I said we weren't doing anything. I couldn't bear the thought of Jane being here again, especially after the way she was at the christening. If I'm being honest, I've seen enough of her for this year."

"Well, if you want my opinion, you did the right thing. Besides, I haven't heard anyone complaining. I think there are too many of us this year."

"And none of us have any money. I expect that helped."

Nell sighed. "I think you're right. You know, I won't be sorry to see the back of this year. I'm looking forward to 1882. Hopefully, it will bring better fortune for all of us."

CHAPTER FIFTY-THREE

Nell rolled over in bed and reached out an arm to where Elenor slept beside her. Her body was warm and delicate, and not for the first time a pang of guilt churned Nell's stomach. It was time to say goodbye ... but what if she didn't come home? She buried her face in Elenor's hair and wiped a stray tear onto the pillowcase. It had seemed like such a good idea back in the autumn when she'd accepted the job, but now it was here, she wasn't ready.

As her arm grew numb, she rolled onto her back. It was still dark, but there was no point staying in bed when she wouldn't sleep. She was about to swing her legs onto the floor when Maria knocked on the bedroom door and popped her head in.

"Are you awake?"

She pushed herself up. "I am. What time is it?"

The flicker from Maria's candle gave the room a gentle glow as she came in and closed the door. "Only five o'clock, but I had a feeling you'd be awake. Did you sleep much?"

"Not really." Nell shivered as she looked over to Alice in the other bed and at Leah's cot. "Shall we go downstairs and get the fire going? It's chilly in here."

Nell followed Maria down the stairs and filled the kettle while Maria knelt down by the hearth.

"It's not too late to change your mind." Maria shovelled coal onto the fire.

"It is. I can't let them down now, especially given I've signed a contract."

"Let's hope Vernon gets himself another job while you're away, so we don't need the money. I don't want you going away again."

"We'll see. I am looking forward to going; it's the leaving that's hard. It was bad enough saying goodbye to Mrs Blackmore on Sunday, not to mention Rebecca last night." She pushed herself up from the chair. "Let me go and get dressed and we can have breakfast. I'll need to leave soon after six."

The breakfast was as familiar as ever, but with little appetite, Nell could only force down a slice of bread and jam. Goodness knows what she'd be eating tomorrow. As the last piece of bread stuck in her throat, she pushed her plate away and reached for her tea.

"Morning, Aunty Nell. Are you ready for your big day?" Billy slid into the seat beside her.

"Why, what's she doing?" Vernon's brow creased as he helped himself to the bread.

"She's going to sea. How could you forget?" Billy rolled his eyes at Nell.

"I thought it was tomorrow."

"No." Nell played with the handle of her teacup. "I imagine I'll be sailing somewhere around Ireland by this time tomorrow."

"Are you nervous?" Vernon spoke through a mouthful of bread.

"Where are your table manners, Vernon Atkin? You're not at the docks now."

Nell gave him a weak smile. "He's all right. He's in a hurry."

"So, are you?" Billy asked. "Nervous, that is."

"I'm not looking forward to leaving, but I'm sure I'll be fine once I'm on the ship."

"You'll probably be too busy to remember us."

Nell gave a brief laugh. "I doubt it."

"For what it's worth, I'll miss you." Billy put a hand on hers. "You need to tell us the date you expect to be back so we can all be here. We can have a card night when you're back. Make it like old times."

Nell squeezed his hand. "That would be nice, once the girls are in bed."

"Ah good, you're still smiling." James grinned at her as he joined them at the table. "Are you excited?"

"I'm not sure excited is the word, is it?" Maria put a hand on Nell's shoulder as she stood up and poured a fresh cup of tea. "I'd better take this to George before he thinks I've forgotten about him. He'll be wanting to get out of bed soon."

Billy looked at Vernon as he took a final mouthful of tea. "We need to be off too if you want any chance of getting a day's work." He leaned forward to give Nell a peck on the cheek. "I hope it goes well, Aunty Nell. I'll see you when you get back."

Vernon leaned over the table and copied his brother. "Yep, see you when you're back."

"Thank you. And good luck with the job-hunting."

James watched Maria follow the boys from the room. "And then there were two. How are you really?"

Nell groaned. "My stomach's tied in knots, but I know it's the right thing to do. It will give your mam and dad time to sort themselves out, too. They don't need me getting in the way."

"You're not in the way. Mam couldn't have managed without you, even if she doesn't tell you, but I think it will do you good."

"I hope you're right." She pushed her chair back. "I need to go and get my bag and..." her voice choked "...and say goodbye to the girls. They should be awake."

Elenor was sitting on Alice's bed when Nell went into the room and lifted Leah from her cot. She hugged her tightly as she moved to the bed and ran a hand over Elenor's head.

"You know Mam's got to go away for a few weeks?"

Elenor clapped her hands. "To get some money for new dresses."

"That's right, but only if you're good girls for Alice. Can you do that for me?"

"They're always good, aren't you?" Alice stood up and took Leah from her. "Are you ready to leave?"

"I am. I've come for my luggage." She stared down at the brown case that sat on the floor at the end of the bed.

"It's strange to think I'll have to live with what's in there for the best part of a month. I hope James is right and they give me a dress or two."

Alice leaned forward and gave her a hug. "I'm sure they will. You take care."

"I will." She gave both girls a final kiss. "I'll see you soon."

Tears filled her eyes as she picked up the case, but she delayed wiping them until she was on the landing. *They can't see me upset.* Without a backwards glance, she went downstairs and found James in the living room holding her cloak.

"All done?"

"Almost. I need to say goodbye to your mam and dad and then we can go." She knocked on the door to the front room. "May I come in?"

"Is it time to go?" George looked up from his makeshift bed on the sofa.

"It is." Her shoulders rose and fell as she exhaled. "Hopefully, you'll be up and walking when I get back."

"I hope so..."

"I want you back in one piece." Maria flung her arms around Nell's shoulders. "You will be careful, won't you?"

Nell peeled herself away. "Of course I will."

"I'm going to miss you." Maria reached for her handkerchief.

"You'll be fine, especially with George here to keep you busy. Now, promise me you won't spend the whole time worrying. It won't bring me back any quicker."

Maria laughed through her tears. "I'll try not to."

"Right, well, we'd better be going if Aunty Nell's to be

on time." James squeezed his mam's shoulders. "I'll be back for dinner and give you a full report."

Maria walked them to the door, but Nell hadn't linked her arm through James' when Rebecca flew out of the house over the road.

"One last goodbye." She flung her arms around Nell's shoulders.

Nell prised her sister's arms from her shoulders. "I thought you said you'd be too busy to come out this morning."

Rebecca wiped a tear away. "How could I not see you off? You have a good trip."

"I'll try. You look after yourself, too." Nell returned her hug. "I'll see you in a month."

Rebecca stepped to Maria's side and they watched as Nell finally set off on James' arm.

She sighed as they turned into Windsor Street. "I don't know whether I want to enjoy this trip or not."

James tilted his head to one side. "Why on earth wouldn't you want to?"

"Because if I like it too much, I'll want to go again."

It was ten to seven by the time they reached the office and Nell gazed at the single-storey building in front of her.

"This is it. You will come in with me, won't you?" Her eyes widened, and he smirked as he held open the door.

"I've been with you every step of the way; I'm not going to leave you now. Besides, I still need to carry your travelling case to the ship."

"And then what do I do with it?"

"There'll be someone waiting to help you. Now, are you going inside?"

She stepped into the office and joined the queue of people already waiting. A tall, slim woman at the end of the queue gave her a cursory nod. Nell returned the gesture as she studied the feathers on her hat. After a moment, she moved to the side and peered down the length of the queue. "I hope they don't take too long. I need to be at the ship by half past."

"Don't worry, they know what they're doing." The woman gave her a crooked smile. "They're moving quickly enough. Is this your first time?"

Nell nodded. "It is. And you?"

"My second. I remember this time last year I was as nervous as you look."

Nell grimaced. "Is it obvious?"

"You'll get used to it soon enough. By Saturday you'll wonder what all the fuss was about."

"You mean I'll have three days where I don't?"

The woman laughed. "No, you'll be fine. Which ship are you on?"

"The SS *Wisconsin*."

"Oh, what good fortune. That's my ship, too." She offered Nell her hand. "Mrs Swift."

Nell grinned at James. "That is good news. I'm Mrs Riley."

The woman stepped forward as a couple of gents left the office. "When I'm done here, I'll wait for you outside and we can go aboard together."

"I'd like that, thank you."

Once Mrs Swift reached the front of the queue, James put a hand on Nell's shoulders. "You're going to be fine."

Nell put a hand to her chest. "I feel better already. It's always the goodbyes that are the hardest."

"You've only one more to go." He ushered her to the counter as Mrs Swift moved to one side.

"Ah, Mrs Riley." The clerk found her name on his list and handed her a card. "Welcome to the SS *Wisconsin*. If you'll make your way to the landing stage, there'll be an officer waiting to take you on board."

"Thank you." Nell bit her lip as she followed James from the office and found Mrs Swift. She looked up as they approached.

"Are you all official?"

"I am." Nell clung to James' arm as she gazed along the river to the large passenger ship standing at the end of a sloping pier.

"Is that it?"

James nodded. "It is. Shall we get you on board? You've waited a long time for this."

THE NEXT INSTALLMENT...

The Stewardess's Journey

In a man's world, can a woman survive?

Liverpool 1882: Nell's dream of travelling on a transatlantic steamship is about to come true. Although not in the way she expected.

Life is hard, and with only three women working amongst a crew of eighty, there are challenges Nell had not foreseen.

While she struggles to cope with the constant attention of her colleagues, not to mention their criticisms, there are some who will do whatever they can to support her.

Will their efforts be enough to settle her into life on board? Or will her first trip be her last?

To get your copy visit my website at:
https://valmcbeath.com/windsor-street/

If you're enjoying the series, why not sign up to my newsletter?

Visit: https://www.subscribepage.com/fsorganic

You'll receive details of new releases, special offers and information relating to *The Windsor Street Family Saga,* and my other series, The *Ambition & Destiny* Series. Occasionally, you'll also receive details of other offers relating to historical fiction.

AUTHOR'S NOTE AND ACKNOWLEDGEMENTS

As you may know, this is my second family saga series. Both are based on research into my family history and it's fascinating bringing my ancestors to life.

There are many documents that show a range of facts about our ancestors, but sometimes you come across something that makes you question why on earth they did what they did.

That was my immediate response when I stumbled across Nell's story. It roused my interest because of how unusual it was for Victorian-era women to work on transatlantic steamships, or indeed any form of ship. I was so intrigued, I was initially only going to write about that element of her life, but as I thought about it, the question of *why* she went kept troubling me.

It's true that Jack's ship ran aground off the coast of Ireland, leaving her a widow, but knowing Jack's fate, not to mention having two small daughters, must have made the decision to leave home and work on a ship incredibly difficult. While I was pondering this information, I realised that if I was to have a chance of working out why she did what she did, I had to explore her motives.

Like most things in life, I suspect money was a driving factor. She lived with Maria, and her brother-in-law and three nephews were working, so even though they'd lost Jack's wage, would they have been so badly off that she needed to work? I'm not sure.

Her eldest nephew, James, spent his life working as a steward, so I imagine he would have influenced her decision to go to sea. That was why I made them so close in the story, not that it explains *why* she went.

The storyline about her sister, Jane, was based on fact. It's true she married an Irish man, and they were living in Ireland at the start of the book. I suspect Mr Read was Catholic, as they were married by special licence, something that was common in couples of different religions or denominations. This contrasted with Tom and Sarah, who were married in the same church immediately after Jane and Mr Read, but who had the more usual banns of marriage read.

Whether there was a falling out in the family over this marriage, I don't know, although I wouldn't be surprised. The conflict between Protestants and Catholics in Ireland is well documented, but it is perhaps less well known that this sectarian divide was also very common in Liverpool. That being the case, I can imagine that the marriage didn't go down well with the family. Would Jane's home coming have been enough to drive Nell away, though? Somehow, I doubt it.

The only plausible reason I could come up with for her

leaving was money, but why might they have been so desperate?

The timing of the story was at the very start of country-wide tensions between workers and management, and the idea of men striking down their tools was in its infancy. Liverpool is known for its militant tendencies, and although I could find no reports of large-scale strikes at that time, it seemed feasible that there may have been some form of unrest stirring. I decided to use the strike and subsequent job losses as a way to cause money problems for the family and hence give Nell a reason to pursue a well-paid job.

Whatever her reasons, Nell left home at the beginning of January 1882, and in the next book, *The Stewardess's Journey*, she takes her first steps on board the SS *Wisconsin*.

If you'd like to join her on her voyage, you can preorder your copy of the book at:

https://books2read.com/TSJ

Finally, as ever, thanks must go to my husband Stuart and friend Rachel for reading an early draft of the book and providing feedback. I'd also like to thank my editor Susan Cunningham for her excellent work, as well as some members of my Advanced Review Team for providing additional comments.

Finally thank you to you for reading

Val

ABOUT THE AUTHOR

Val started researching her family tree back in 2008. At that time, she had no idea what she would find or where it would lead. By 2010, she had discovered a story so compelling she was inspired to turn it into a novel.

This first foray into writing turned into The *Ambition & Destiny* Series. A story of the trials, tragedies, and triumphs of some of her ancestors as they sought their fortune in Victorian-era England.

By the time the series was complete, Val had developed a taste for writing and turned her hand to writing Agatha Christie style mysteries. These novels form part of the *Eliza Thomson Investigates* series and currently consists of five standalone books and two novella's.

Although writing the mysteries was great fun, the pull of researching other branches of the family was strong and Val continued to look for other stories worth telling.

Back in 2018, she discovered a previously unknown fact about one of her great, great grandmothers, Nell. *The Windsor Street Family Saga* is a fictitious account of that discovery. I hope you enjoyed it.

Prior to writing, Val trained as a scientist and has worked in the pharmaceutical industry for many years. In 2012, she set up her own consultancy business, and currently splits her time between business and writing.

Born and raised in Liverpool (UK), Val now lives in Cheshire with her husband, Stuart. She has two daughters, the younger of which, Sarah, now helps with the publishing side of the business.

In addition to family history, her interests include rock music and Liverpool Football Club.

For further information about Val's books or the Victorian history that supports some of the storylines, visit her website at: www.vlmcbeath.com

ALSO BY VL MCBEATH

The *Windsor Street Family Saga*
The full series:

Part 1: *The Sailor's Promise*

(*an introductory novella*)

Part 2: *The Wife's Dilemma*

Part 3: *The Stewardess's Journey*

Part 4: *The Captain's Order*

Part 5: *The Companion's Secret*

Part 6: *The Mother's Confession*

Part 7: *The Daughter's Defiance*

The *Ambition & Destiny* Series
The full series:

Short Story Prequel: *Condemned by Fate*

Part 1: *Hooks & Eyes*

Part 2: *Less Than Equals*

Part 3: *When Time Runs Out*

Part 4: *Only One Winner*

Part 5: *Different World*

A standalone novel: *The Young Widow*

Eliza Thomson Investigates

A Deadly Tonic (A Novella)

Murder in Moreton

Death of an Honourable Gent

Dying for a Garden Party

A Scottish Fling

The Palace Murder

Death by the Sea

A Christmas Murder

To find out more about visit VL McBeath's website at:

https://www.valmcbeath.com/

FOLLOW ME

at:

Website:
https://valmcbeath.com

Facebook:
https://www.facebook.com/VLMcBeath

BookBub:
https://www.bookbub.com/authors/vl-mcbeath

Printed in Great Britain
by Amazon